"The rescue of Allied forces from Dunkirk in 1940 was a military disaster but a public-relations success. . . . Behind the drama lay a mixture of muddle, confusion, tragedy, resolve and individual courage, which Maureen Jennings has reflected in the novel she has written about the evacuation's aftermath. [Her] portrait of a society under threat . . . is engrossing."

– *Globe and Mail*

"[Jennings] gallops through her plot, doing justice to the remarkable drama of her scene and reminding that patriotic fervor was not an automatic reaction to the war when it was first declared in England in 1939. . . . [It will] appeal to the many readers who remain fascinated by the war that did indeed change the world."

– *Washington Times*

"Jennings' portrayal of a small English Midlands village on the cusp of war rings true. The dialogue is crisp, with believable local expressions and regional accents. . . . The first volume in a new series by Jennings, a welcome possibility."

– *Winnipeg Free Press*

"The acclaimed author of the Detective Murdoch mysteries scores with an exceptional new series set in wartime England. . . . [She] writes with a rare sense of familial reality, using daily tension that frame the grand event – war and murder. . . . Jennings' skill at plotting, description, dialogue and historical perspective . . . are evident through in *Season of Darkness*. A new hit series in the making."

– *Hamilton Spectator*

"A captivating puzzle tale, well told, with Jennings' trademark attention to historical detail, *Season of Darkness* will introduce many readers to a side of war too rarely revealed."

– Sherbrooke *Record*

Season of Darkness

ALSO BY MAUREEN JENNINGS

Except the Dying
Under the Dragon's Tail
Poor Tom is Cold
Let Loose the Dogs
Night's Child
Vices of My Blood
A Journeyman to Grief

Season of Darkness

A DETECTIVE INSPECTOR TOM TYLER MYSTERY

MAUREEN JENNINGS

McCLELLAND & STEWART

Library and Archives Canada Cataloguing in Publication

Jennings, Maureen
Season of darkness / Maureen Jennings.

Issued also in electronic format.

ISBN 978-0-7710-4328-4

I. Title.

PS8569.E62S43 2012   C813'.54   C2012-900949-0

We acknowledge the financial support of the Government of Canada through the Book Publishing Industry Development Program and that of the Government of Ontario through the Ontario Media Development Corporation's Ontario Book Initiative. We further acknowledge the support of the Canada Council for the Arts and the Ontario Arts Council for our publishing program.

Published simultaneously in the United States of America by McClelland & Stewart, a division of Random House of Canada Ltd., P.O. Box 1030, Plattsburgh, New York 12901

Library of Congress Control Number: 2012932237

Typeset in Caslon by M&S, Toronto
Printed and bound in the United States of America

This book was produced using paper with a minimum of 20% recycled content (20% post-consumer waste).

McClelland & Stewart,
a division of Random House of Canada Limited
One Toronto Street
Suite 300
Toronto, Ontario
M5C 2V6
www.mcclelland.com

1   2   3   4   5   16   15   14   13   12

For my wonderful husband and chief supporter, Iden Ford

And also for Thomas Craig, actor par excellence, who
inspired me to create Tom Tyler

"it was the season of light, it was the season of darkness"

Charles Dickens, *A Tale of Two Cities*

Prologue

Drawing the chair closer to the table, he sat down and shook a cigarette from the pack. He lit it and took a few deep draws, so that the tip glowed red. He'd already folded the handkerchief, and now he picked it up and stuffed it in his mouth. It wasn't that he doubted his own resolve, there was no question of that, but he'd learned to accept the body's instinctive weaknesses and to make allowances. The walls of this house were thin and he didn't want to risk being heard.

He raised his bare left arm and studied for a moment the small tattoo just below his armpit. Then, deliberately, he pressed the tip of the cigarette into his flesh and held it there. Sweat broke out on his forehead and he bit down on the handkerchief. When he thought he had accomplished what he needed to, he lifted the cigarette away. The stench of burning flesh was nauseating but he welcomed it. He'd smelled it before and it reminded him that he was a soldier. He spat out the handkerchief and leaned forward, hands on his knees, head bent until his breathing slowed. He allowed one soft moan to come from his lips. Then he took the tin of salve from the table beside him and applied it carefully to the wound.

He got up, went over to the tiny window, and looked down at the street below. A young woman was walking by pushing a pram. She was pretty in her red and white flowered frock, the early spring sun creating a halo of her fair hair. She bent over the pram, attending to a child he couldn't see.

He went to the table where he'd placed a bottle of brandy. He poured himself a tall glass full, picked up his cigarette, and took *another deep puff. He studied the glowing end. Ignoring the gag this time, he lifted his right arm and, with his left hand, pressed the tip of the cigarette against the soft flesh of his underarm.*

He held it there until he could stand it no longer.

1.

I<small>N SPITE OF THE FACT THAT SHE</small>'<small>D GOT ONLY A FEW</small>
hours sleep, Elsie Bates was in great spirits. Nothing like a
nice bit of dock to make a girl smile. When he'd told her this
was his first time, she'd expected him to be clumsy and done
too fast, but he wasn't. She'd helped him out here and there
but mostly he'd learned all by himself. Of course, like any man
born to Eve, he'd started to show a bit of possessiveness right
off the bat, and she'd had to make it clear that nobody owned
her. Elsie grinned at the memory, then impulsively pushed
down on the accelerator as far as she dared. The sun wasn't
yet up and the road, which was hemmed in on either side by
tall hedgerows, was pitch black. She had her headlights on,
inadequate as they were with the strips of blackout tape across
them, and she was driving as close to the middle of the road
as she could, the lorry rattling and shaking on the rough
surface.

She started to sing to the tune of the "Colonel Bogey
March."

Hitler has only got one ball,
Goering has two but they are small

Wait 'til she told Rose about last night. Rosie kept saying
she was saving herself, but as Elsie reminded her, "There's a
war on, my pet. Butter's rationed but that don't mean we have
to be."

Himmler has something sim'lar,
But poor old Goebbels has no balls at all.

Elsie fingered the strap of her dungarees and smiled at the feel of the two bank notes she'd sewn in there. Two quid would go a long way. When she'd told Rose the story, her friend had been nervous.

"Oo, Elsie, be careful. People don't like to be blackmailed."

"Who said anything about blackmail? I didn't say nothing. Nothing at all except to mention what I'd seen, and out it popped: 'Ow much to keep that to yourself? Didn't come from me first." She'd pinched Rose's thin cheek. "We won't be greedy. The occasional quid will do nicely. Stroke of luck, weren' it? Me being there at that moment. Next leave we get, we're going to Birmingham for a few larks. Nobody'll wonder where the dosh is coming from. If asked, we'll say it's our wages saved up, which is a joke."

"You're as cunning as an old cat," said Rose. "I just hope you've got as many lives."

Elsie had taken the remark as a compliment. She'd learned at too early an age to be that way. You had to if you were going to get out of that bleeding hellhole of a slum in any way intact. She made the sign of the cross over her chest. "May God see fit to drop a bomb on all of them."

Hitler has only got one ball,
The other is on the kitchen wall.
His mother, the dirty bugger,
Cut it off when he was small.

The lorry went over a bump, gave a short cough, a splutter or two, then went silent and began to roll to a stop.

"Sod it, not again."

It was the third time this month the bloody thing had acted up. Elsie managed to steer over to the side, as close to the hedgerow as possible, before the momentum died. The road was barely wide enough for two vehicles to pass, and she'd bring a lot of aggravation onto herself if she blocked the way completely. She tried turning the ignition key but the lorry was dead as a doornail. Sod, sod, and more sod. She was on a tight schedule. She had to pick up the girls at the hostel on time. Miss Stillwell, the warden, could be a bloody tartar. "Late again, Miss Bates? Do pull up your socks, or I shall have to put you on report." Toffee-nosed old cow. If ever a woman acted like a dried-up spinster, it was her.

Well, no sense in sitting here on her arse. Good thing she'd brought her bike. She climbed down from the lorry. Somewhere along the way her back light had been knocked out, but the front lamp was working. Not that it was a lot of use, with the obligatory taped strips across it.

The woods pressed in close here, narrowing the road even more. Elsie didn't like the country in the dark. She was used to paved streets and houses crammed together; a sense of the surrounding humanity. You could go for miles out here and not meet a soul. The rooks were putting up a God-awful clamour. Old Morgan had told them that sometimes birds can be as good as a watch dog, giving off warnings that there's danger near.

She almost wished she'd brought the gun with her.

As she pedalled, she began to sing again to the tune of "Land of Hope and Glory."

Land of soap and water
Hitler's having a bath
Churchill's looking through the keyhole
Having a jolly good laugh

Be . . . e . . . e . . . e . . . cause,
Hitler has only one small ball . . .

She was glad for her overcoat. The pre-dawn air was chill and damp, just a bit of a hint that summer was ending. Fresh though, very fresh; one good thing you could say for the country. Since she'd been here, she gained some weight and a good colour, which they had all admitted when she went home last time. After she'd signed up with the Land Army, her dad, the miserable bugger, had said she wouldn't last a week, which only made her determined to show him. It hadn't been easy. When she'd first arrived in Shropshire, she'd never even seen a live cow before, let alone the bloody huge bull with the ring in its wet nose and its enormous goolies hanging down. The work in the fields was backbreaking, the hours appallingly long, and at first many of the farmers had been contemptuous of the girls, not willing to take into account their inexperience. Now the Land girls had earned their grudging respect. They worked as hard as men and learned fast. Elsie, herself, had been promoted to forewoman after only two months. When she'd written to tell Ma and Dad and the others, nobody'd bothered to answer. Sod them anyway.

Dawn was starting to seep through the trees and the exercise was getting her blood flowing. She kicked her feet off the pedals and did a little swoop from side to side just for fun. *Whoopee!* There was something to be said about this war. She'd never have had this experience stuck in the filthy London back-to-back housing where she'd grown up. She kicked out again. *Whoopee!* There was a dance in the village tonight and she'd be there, new frock, new sweetheart.

Hold on, was that a car? Maybe she could cadge a lift. She glanced over her shoulder. She heard the roar of the car as it emerged out of the darkness, the slitted headlights gleaming like cat's eyes. It was travelling fast. Too fast. Elsie swerved out of the way.

"Hey, slow down," she yelled.

But in a moment the car was upon her.

2.

TOM TYLER, DETECTIVE INSPECTOR, SHROPSHIRE constabulary, was having another of his unpolicemanlike dreams. Ever since he'd run into Clare at the market a few days ago, he'd been dreaming about her. Sometimes, they were quarrelling and he was shouting at her, the way he had when she had told him all those years ago she was leaving. Sometimes the dream was unbearably sweet and he was lying with her in his arms. This time, he was trying to find her, running through the empty streets of Whitchurch, calling her name. He'd actually been crying. The pain of that loss was already bringing him to the surface of consciousness when he felt somebody shaking him on the shoulder.

"Dad. Dad. Wake up. You're wanted on the telephone."

He opened his eyes. His daughter, Janet, was standing beside the bed.

"Who is it?" he said, his tongue thick. Too much booze last night.

"Sir Percy Somerville. He says it's urgent."

Groaning, Tyler sat up, waiting until the room stopped spinning before he ventured to stand.

"Gosh, Dad, you smell of beer. That must have been a super party."

"It was a victory party and don't be cheeky." He yawned. "Did Sir P. say what he wanted?"

"Mom was the one who answered. All I know is he said it was urgent."

Vera's voice, shrill and irritated, came up from downstairs.

"What are you doing? Sir Percy's waiting."

Tyler winked at his daughter. "I need to go to the loo first. Tell your mom to say I'll call him right back."

Janet headed for the door, then turned. "Dad, I need to talk to you."

He regarded her. There were dark circles underneath her eyes and her normally sunny expression had disappeared.

"What's up, sweetheart?"

"I can't get into it now. Can we talk when you come home?"

"Of course. What is it, boy troubles?"

She flinched and answered sharply. "No. Nothing like that."

Oops. He'd trod on a sensitive topic, obviously. "You don't have to take my head off, Jan."

"Sorry, Dad . . . I . . ." She didn't finish and left.

He shuffled off to the toilet. His mouth was foul and his intestines felt as if somebody had had a go at them with a scrubbing brush. Relief from his bladder achieved, he pulled the chain, leaning for a moment over the toilet bowl, wondering if he was going to be sick. No, it seemed all right. He padded into the adjoining bathroom and stared into the mirror. He stuck out his tongue. Ugh. You could run a comb through that fur. His complexion was fair, the kind that goes with carrot red hair, and yesterday's sun had burned his nose and flamed his cheeks. He'd been in the open air all day, first visiting some of the local farmers to check their stock, and later playing football. His team had won the game and it was definitely worth a bit of peeling.

Moving as fast as his head would allow, he shaved, and rinsed out his mouth. Finally, he went slowly downstairs, still the worse for wear, not completely awake but at least alive.

He could see Vera wiping at something on the kitchen table. He had the feeling it was where he'd dribbled jam late last night when he'd tried to make himself a piece of toast. He'd hear about that one.

"Morning." Once he would have kissed her; now they didn't even exchange pecks.

"Take your time why don't you? Sir Percy is waiting." There was a tight knot between her eyebrows. "You were late coming home last night."

"I know, I know, but it's not every day the Wolverines win a championship. The lads had to celebrate." He poured himself a glass of water and gulped some down. "Did Percy say what he wanted at this ungodly hour?"

"No, but he was in a real tizzy. You'd better give him a ring right away." Vera was already dressed in her flowered house frock, her hair combed and pinned back. She must have been up at the crack of dawn. "Had a bad night, did you?"

She had turned away from him and he hardly heard the question.

"Why'd you say that?" he asked, startled.

"First, if you'll excuse the expression, you've got a face on you that would turn milk sour, and second, you were moaning and twitching in your sleep like the devil was after you."

He pushed away the feeling of guilt over his dream. Vera was very perceptive where he was concerned, but surely not even she could read his mind.

He shrugged. "One too many, I suppose."

Taking the glass of water with him, he walked into the minuscule hall and picked up the telephone. The operator's cheery voice came on the line first. "Number, please."

"Hello, Mavis. It's Tom here. Get me Beeton Manor, will you? I want to speak to Sir Percy."

"Tom? What were you lads up to last night? Charlie came home drunk as a lord and singing at the top of his voice. He woke up the whole neighbourhood."

Tyler groaned to himself, his memory of the final stages of the celebration lost in a beery haze.

"Good thing he's got a fine voice, Mavis. How is he this morning?"

"I haven't the foggiest idea. When I left he was dead to the world."

"Well, he did score the winning goal. He deserves to celebrate."

Mavis chuckled. "I suppose you're right. It has been a long time coming. Hold on, I'll connect you with Sir Percy. He sounds upset." There was a short pause and Tyler drank some more water. He felt as if he were trying to irrigate the Sahara.

Then Mavis was back.

"Go ahead please, Sir Percy."

The magistrate's rumbly, slightly neighing voice came over the line. "Tyler. We've got a nasty incident on our hands."

"What is it, sir?"

"There's been an accident. Very serious. I can't go into details over the phone, don't you know, but I need you to come at once."

"And where will you be, sir?" Tyler asked before the magistrate could hang up.

"Oh, yes. The incident seems to have occurred a mile or so above Ash Magna. On the Heath Road, not far from the crossroads. I'll meet you there."

Tyler hung up and went back into the kitchen.

Vera pushed a large cup of tea across the table. "What's up? Sins catching up with you?"

"For God's sake, Vera, put a sock in it. There's been an accident on the Heath Road. Bloody blackout again, probably."

She wasn't that contrite. "That'll probably take you all day to sort out. Just so you know, I'm at the Institute for the evening. It's bandage night. Dad gave me a nice pork chop for your tea. I'll leave it in the oven and you can warm it up when you get back."

Vera was nothing if not dutiful.

He reached for his hat and coat, which he vaguely remembered dropping on the floor when he came home but which were now on a hook by the door.

Vera wasn't done with carping. "I want you to have a word with your daughter. She's been late for work three times this past fortnight, and you know how Dad is such a stickler for punctuality. She'll get the sack if she's not careful, granddaughter or no granddaughter."

Janet had been adamant about leaving school and "doing her bit" for the war effort, and Vera had pushed for her to go into the family business. Tyler knew that his daughter hated her job at the butcher's shop his father-in-law owned. He wasn't surprised she was in no hurry to get there.

Vera shook her head. "What with her and our Jimmy acting so strange, I'm worried sick about the two of them. Jimmy doesn't come home until the wee hours. You don't even know, but I hear him. And he must have already gone out. No breakfast, no notice, nothing. He's not himself at all."

She looked so worried, he softened toward her. "I thought he was looking more chipper lately. I'll wager he's found himself a lassie."

Her expression changed abruptly. "Not everybody has that on their mind every minute of the day."

So much for softening.

He grabbed his hat and coat and picked up his cup of tea. "I'll take this with me."

When he stepped out of the house, he stood and gulped down some of the tea. Not quite the hair of the dog, but it would have to do. The intensity of his dream about Clare hadn't really faded, but there wasn't anything he could do about that. He wondered when he'd next see her.

He crossed the road to the tiny car park at the rear of the station where the sole police vehicle, an ancient Humber, was kept. As far as he was concerned, the wretched thing was more of a liability than an asset, but they had to make do with it. A lot of the time it refused to start, and he thought a trotting cow could move faster.

He forced himself to control his impatience and turn the crank steadily until the engine caught. Before it could change its mind, he jumped in and drove off.

The houses were bathed in the soft, golden light of early morning; cattle grazed on the green, lush hills behind the town. People bought postcards of places like this. England at its most beautiful. Whitchurch was too rural to be of interest to the Luftwaffe, and so far the bombers hadn't touched it. It was only when you saw the black wreaths on some of the doors; only when you noticed that the shop windows were displaying fewer and fewer wares; only at night, when the streets went dark in compliance with the blackout regulations; only then did you have to acknowledge the old life had gone forever.

Tyler was in no mood to dwell on those thoughts, although they weren't ever that far from his mind. Right now, he was concentrating on coaxing as much speed as he could out of the Humber. When he reached the turnoff, he was forced to slow down. The Heath Road was rough, dotted with potholes, and he couldn't risk breaking an axle. He'd driven no more than five minutes when he saw a Land Army lorry at the side of the road. There was no one in the driver's seat, and he felt a pang of alarm. Over the summer, he'd seen some of the Land girls who were billeted here. They seemed a grand bunch. He hoped one of them hadn't got into an accident.

He picked up as much speed as he dared and rounded another bend, stopping just short of Sir Percy's big white

Bentley. The magistrate was standing beside a lanky older man in soldier's uniform. It was Ron Ellwood, a man Tyler knew from town. He could see how relieved both men were to see him. What on earth had happened?

As Tyler parked the Humber and got out, Sir Percy hurried over to him, hand outstretched. Ellwood gave him a crisp salute, presented arms, then stood at attention with his rifle at his side.

"Ah, Tyler, thank goodness," said the magistrate. His hand was cold, the handshake the usual limp kind he always gave. "The, er . . . the victim is over there."

There was a tarpaulin a few feet away in a narrow pass-by. A swarm of flies hovered above the mound.

Tyler walked over, and pulled back the cover.

Underneath was the body of a young woman. She appeared to have been shot.

Her left temple was completely shattered. Pieces of white bone protruded from the blood and brain tissue.

"Oh, Lord. I know this girl," exclaimed Tyler. "Her name was Elsie Bates."

3.

TYLER LEANED OVER AND BRUSHED AWAY THE BUZZING flies. The congealing blood had sealed closed one of her eyes; the other, once blue, now already darkening, stared at him. The entire left side of her face and throat was caked with blood, as was the front of her tan coat. Gingerly, he pulled the tarpaulin farther down. Her snug dungarees were tucked into dusty gum boots and appeared to be undisturbed. Thank God for that.

The girl's arms were beside her, and a gun was lying underneath the fingers of her right hand.

"Look at that, will you," exclaimed Sir Percy. He couldn't keep the tremor out of his voice. "God forbid, have we got a suicide here?"

"I don't think so, sir. The wound is on the wrong side of her head for one thing. It would be on the right if she'd done it herself." Besides, Tyler couldn't believe this girl would kill herself. Not Elsie Bates with her palpable hunger for life. He'd last seen her on Saturday night as she walked down the street to the church hall where the dances were held. Her skirt swung around her tanned knees, her scarlet lipstick drew attention to her full lips.

He eased the gun free, holding it carefully by the tip of the barrel, then shook out his handkerchief, wrapped the gun, and examined it more closely. It was an older model German Luger P-08. The stock was blue and the letter *B* was carved on one side. He slipped off the safety catch, removed the magazine, and cracked it open. Only one bullet had been fired, and that recently.

He put it aside and turned his attention back to the body. Elsie had brown, straight hair, which she wore parted down the middle and swept up at the sides, where it was secured with two plain green combs. It was neat and tidy. Carefully, he lifted each limp hand. In life, they had been strong and capable, the palms showing signs of calluses and the fingernails cut short. What he'd expect from a Land Army girl. There was no smell of cordite on the hands, no sign of gun residue, no blood.

Curiously, there was a bunch of white flowers lying on her chest.

"Did you put these here?" he asked Ellwood.

"No, I didn't. Can't say I even noticed them. I just wanted to cover 'er up as fast as possible."

Tyler laid the flowers on the grass. They were white poppies.

Sir Percy inched closer and peered down. "Are they significant, Tom? I know all those conchies sell them. They're the emblem of the Peace Pledge Union. She's a Land Army girl. I can't imagine her being in with the Bolsheviks."

"I've no idea. They grow all around here and these are fresh."

He fished in the pockets of the dungarees. There was a shilling and a motor car key in one pocket, a packet of cigarettes and a handkerchief in the other. He put the key in his own pocket and placed the other items beside the flowers.

She was partly propped up against the hedge, and he slipped his arm around her shoulders, bringing her body forward. Her head tilted sickeningly to the side before he could stop it.

"The bullet exit wound is here, right at the base, but there's hardly any blood on the hedge where you'd expect it to be. Corporal, did you move her?"

"No, sir. She were exactly where she is now. All I did was cover her with a tarpaulin we had in the lorry."

At that moment, the sun winked through the trees and glinted red on a nearby sharp-edged rock. Tyler lowered the body gently and walked over to the spot. He dropped to his haunches.

"There's blood here." He saw the metal bullet casing lying about two feet away, and picked it up. "This is definitely where she was shot. I doubt she put a gun to her head over here, blew out her brains, then got up and sat down against the hedge."

The grass along the verge was slightly flattened and he could see scuff marks in the dust of the road. Here and there were more splotches of blood. "And then she was dragged over to the pass-by . . . We're looking at a homicide, all right."

"She's just a young lass," said Sir Percy. "What savage would do a thing like this?"

Tyler indicated the gun. "Whoever they are, they used a Luger."

"Gracious me, Tom, surely you're not suggesting we have a Jerry paratrooper prowling around?"

"Off hand, I'd say that's very unlikely. I don't know why Jerry would drop off a parachutist in rural Shropshire unless it was to subvert the cows. And if it was a Jerry, I'd think he'd take his gun with him. Besides which, it's an older model. The stamp says it was manufactured in 1917. It could belong to anybody. Guns like this aren't that difficult to obtain. A lot of soldiers brought them back from the Great War as souvenirs."

"Quite true," said Sir Percy. "I meself picked up a couple of cap badges."

"If it's a German gun you're after, sir," said Ellwood, "there are plenty of Krauts over in the internment camp."

"Surely they're all under guard?" Sir Percy wiped at his damp face. His white handkerchief would have been adequate as a flag of surrender.

"According to what I've heard," said Ellwood, "security at the camp is lax."

Tyler knew that was true. Nobody considered the enemy aliens a serious threat to national security anymore, and the fear of invasion was abating. His own son, who had sentry duty occasionally, had remarked that the internees were mostly soft-bellied, middle-aged eggheads. But it was also true the majority were German. Like most people who were imprisoned behind barbed wire, they probably were able to maintain a brisk business in barter. A Luger for a packet of cigarettes.

He straightened up. "Who found the body?"

"I did," answered Ellwood. "At least, that is to say, me and Private Walker did."

Sir Percy jumped in. "Walker arrived on my doorstep, and frankly I could hardly make sense of his story because he was as hysterical as a woman. According to the corporal here, he's suffering from shell shock, which is why he's been assigned to the camp and not to active service. Feather bed, really."

"He was at Dunkirk," said Tyler.

"Quite so. Didn't mean to imply . . . we have to give all those fellows some leeway then, don't we? Although as Mr. Churchill said, a retreat isn't going to win the war, and we mustn't fool ourselves, Dunkirk was a defeat."

Tyler tried not show his annoyance. It was so typical of Percy to make a tactless remark like that, the silly sod.

"Bobby Walker is a good lad," said Tyler, keeping his voice as neutral as he could. "I've known him since he was a nipper. He's a mate of my son's. They got off the beach together. By all accounts, it was a rough time."

Not that Jimmy had said much of anything. Neither one did, but Bobby Walker shook constantly and jumped at every sound. A door slamming, a car backfiring, would have him on the ceiling.

Sir Percy blew his nose. "Quite so."

"What did Private Walker say exactly?" Tyler asked.

"There's no exactly about it. All I could get out of him was that a girl was dead. I could hardly make tops nor tails of what he was saying. I suppose I should have packed him off to do his duty. Might have put a bit of steel in his backbone if he started acting more like a soldier."

He must have caught Tyler's expression because he added hastily, "Frankly, I took pity on the chap and I sent him home. Then I got hold of you, Tom, and got over here post-haste." His gaze flitted to the dead girl. "Should we cover her up, do you think?"

"I was just about to do that."

Ellwood helped him with the tarpaulin.

"What's our next step?" Sir Percy asked.

"We'll have to get the body out of here and have a post-mortem done as soon as possible. I suggest we bring in Dr. Murnaghan from Whitchurch. He's retired now but he was a highly competent coroner in his day."

"Shall I ring him for you? You've got a lot to take care of here."

"Thank you. That would speed things up considerably."

Sir Percy took off his tweed cap and mopped at his head again. He was a year younger than Tyler, but his hair was already greying and sparse. Right now, it was sprouting from his head in tufts as if he'd neglected to comb it when he got out of bed. He hadn't shaved and his stubble made him look grubby and down at heel. Tyler usually saw him in magistrate's court, all shiny chin and smooth hair. This current dishevelment made him more human. That and his obvious distress. Percy wasn't cut out to be a magistrate and lord of the manor.

All he wanted was to be left in peace to build up his prize herd of Ayrshires. Tyler felt the usual mixture of pity and exasperation towards him.

"I'd appreciate it if you'd also ring the station and have Sergeant Gough send me all available men," said Tyler. "I don't want people traipsing through the area until I've had a chance to look it over. Tell him we'll need the police van and to bring the camera."

"Should we notify the war office . . . in case there are parachutists?"

"Let's investigate a little further before we do that. We don't want to distract those blokes from fighting a war, do we?"

"Quite so. I'll hoof it back to the manor, then, and make those telephone calls. And I'll notify the camp that Corporal Ellwood is delayed."

"Thank you."

"Good, excellent. I will wait for your further report." He dithered. "I was planning to take a run up to Edinburgh on urgent business . . . a rather splendid bull I've been told about. I'm afraid I'll be incommunicado for a few days. That is, unless you need me here."

"That's all right. This is *my* job."

"Quite so." The magistrate's relief was palpable. He gave Tyler another hurried handshake and went back to his Bentley. With a hiss of tires, he backed up and drove away.

Tyler turned to the corporal. "Ron, give me your version, for God's sake."

4.

LIKE MANY LOCAL MEN WHO WERE TOO OLD FOR ACTIVE service but were still reservists, Ron Ellwood, a veteran of the Great War, had been enlisted as a guard at the camp on Prees Heath. There were over a thousand men incarcerated there, most of them classified as enemy aliens. As Jimmy had said, they were typically German intellectuals and professional men living in England who hadn't got their nationalization papers in order. They had been swept up in the fear of invasion that gripped the country after Dunkirk.

Tyler liked and respected Ellwood. He took a packet of cigarettes from his pocket and offered one. Ellwood leaned his rifle against a tree and accepted gratefully.

"I picked up Bobby Walker about six-thirty. He lives on Green Lane, and we always take the Alkington Road to the camp because it's faster. We'd just reached the crossroads where we turn when we encountered one of them Land Army girls. She was walking along the road, pushing a bicycle. She said her friend was their forewoman, and she was more than a half-hour late getting to the hostel where she's supposed to pick them up."

"They're the girls who've been billeted in Beeton Manor, aren't they?"

"That's it. I was surprised Sir P. didn't recognize the dead girl right off the bat. But then I didn't either, did I, although I must have seen her in town." Ellwood chewed on his lip. "It was the shock I suppose, and the mess the bullet had made of her face." He drew in a lungful of smoke. "Well, the girl said as how she thought the lorry might have broken down seeing as it had done that before, and she was on her way to find out. She'd started off on her bike but she had a flat tire. She asked if we could give her a lift up the road a ways to see. We had a bit of extra time, so I said as how we could do that." Another deep draw on the cigarette.

"What's the girl's name, by the way?"

"Rose, Rose Watkins. A little bit of a thing she is. You'd think she was no more than thirteen to look at her."

"That's not her bike, is it?" A maroon-coloured woman's bicycle was lying by the hedge a few feet away.

"No, it isn't. That one was there when we come up. We put Rose's in the back of the lorry."

Tyler went to have a look. "This one is certainly a good one. Not an official government issue like most of the girls have to ride. The back light is cracked, but other than that, it's in good shape." The cloud of flies was getting more dense and a few curious birds had hopped closer.

"Did Rose see the body?"

"She did. Me, I knew right off something serious had happened." He gave a little cough. "I seen action in the last war, as you know, Tom, and there's a stillness to a dead body that is unmistakable. I told Rose to stand back while Bobby and me checked, but she wouldn't. She came right up. Course, she turned white as a sheet when she saw all the blood. I was afraid she was going to faint on us. But she's tough for all she's small. She's a Londoner."

"Did she say anything?"

"She just sort of cried out, 'Oh no, Elsie. I warned you.'"

"Warned her about what?" Tyler asked.

"I don't know, Tom. She never said. Bobby had got into quite a state, shaking like a leaf. Like I said, this wasn't the first time I seen a dead body and I was thinking more clearly.

Not that it wasn't a shock, it certainly was, young girl like that. I thought at least we could get Sir Percy, seeing as he's a magistrate, and he'd be likely to be on the telephone. Somebody had to stay here and I thought it best be me, so I bundled Bobby into our lorry, telling him to take the lassie back to the billet. I ordered her not to talk to anybody. Just to say there'd been an accident. No sense in upsetting everybody until we know exactly what's happened here."

"Good thinking, Ron. You kept a cool head. What time was it when you found her?"

"It was about ten to seven. I'd say death had definitely occurred within the previous hour. She were still warm but the blood was no longer flowing."

Suddenly, there was a frantic flapping of wings and loud cawing as a flight of rooks flew out of the trees. Tyler jumped, aware his nerves were on edge. Ellwood tensed as well.

"That's probably Dr. Murnaghan coming, but I don't want anybody else driving through here. There's some police tape in my car. We can use that to create a barrier across the road. We'll stay here until reinforcements arrive."

He held out his hand to pull Ellwood to his feet.

"I don't remember anything like this happening here since Mrs. Evans clobbered her husband with a plank," said the corporal.

Tyler gave him a grim smile. "Rhys Evans was a miserable bastard who deserved what he got. It's hard to see Elsie Bates deserving this."

5

DR. MURNAGHAN ARRIVED SO QUICKLY THAT TYLER wondered if the coroner had been sitting by his telephone waiting for a call, any call. He examined the body, made the official declaration of death, and concurred with Tyler that Elsie had been moved and had not committed suicide. He promised an immediate post-mortem. "Corpses aren't exactly stacking up outside my door," he said.

Sergeant Gough had rounded up six constables, and they arrived a few minutes later. Three older men, three young fellows, all looking apprehensive. The body was transferred to the police van, and with orders to return, one of the older ones drove off. The coroner followed in his own car.

Tyler organized the remaining men.

"We're looking for anything and everything. Use your noggins but let me be the judge of what's important and what isn't. Maybe our killer dropped his identification card to make our life easier, but I wouldn't count on it. If you see any kind of tire tracks, put in a marker. Let's put tape around the pass-by and the spot where she was shot. I want one of you to concentrate on that area. We've got the casing, but there should be a bullet somewhere. It may have ricocheted off the rocks so look carefully."

One of the young constables was carrying the camera.

Tyler addressed him. "Collis, I want pictures of every inch of the surrounding area. If you're going to toss your biscuits, give the job to somebody else. If you're going to continue in the police force, do it yourself."

"Yes, sir. Right away."

"What would you like me to do, Tom?" asked Ellwood.

"Best thing is probably to get over to the camp. Make sure Percy delivered the news like he said. You can use one of the men's bicycles. I'll be there later."

He beckoned to one of the constables.

"Come with me."

Constable Eagleton was young, pink-cheeked, and enthusiastic. He had joined the police department when he'd been turned down by the war office because of his flat feet. He was smart and hard working and had soon earned the nickname of Eager. Tyler walked with him along the road to where the lorry that he'd passed on the way in was parked.

"Do you know anything about engines, Eager?"

"A bit, sir."

Tyler handed him the key he'd found in Elsie's pocket. Initially, the engine turned over feebly, but Eagleton managed to coax it into life.

"I think it was just flooded, sir."

Tyler walked around the lorry, examining it carefully. He could see nothing amiss. The same was true of the interior. Clumps of mud dotted the floor, but otherwise it was bare.

"We'll give it a more thorough going-over later," he said to Eagleton. "I don't think we're going to find much. I'm guessing it conked out on Elsie, she flooded the engine trying to get it restarted, decided to leave it, and took off from here on her bicycle. Unfortunately to her death. . . . All right, let's get back. Do you have a handkerchief with you, lad?"

"Yes, sir."

"Is it clean?"

"Yes, sir. Fresh today."

"Good. Don't blow your nose or wipe your face. There are some items at the crime scene that we will have to have examined. I've wrapped the gun. Whatever you do, don't touch it. Keep it in the handkerchief. The flowers and the items that were in Miss Bates's pocket should also be given to the sergeant. You can wrap them in your handkerchief in the same way."

Finally, everything was underway and Tyler left them to their tasks. He set off for Beeton Manor, not relishing his own task ahead.

At the beginning of the summer, the War Ministry had expropriated the dower house at Beeton Manor to billet Land Army girls. Lady Somerville, grumbling, had been forced to move in with her son. Percy was a confirmed bachelor, and although by most standards he was rattling around in such a large house, gossip had it that neither he nor his mother were too happy with this new, closer arrangement. He got away as frequently as he could.

Tyler was shown into the drawing room by an elderly maid dressed in the conventional garb of women in service: the three white *C*'s – cap, collar, and cuffs – and a severe black frock. She was stooped and looked as if she should have been pensioned off years ago. The room was now the girls' common room. The precious paintings had been removed, leaving patches on the walls where the wallpaper was brighter, and none of the furniture matched. Nonetheless, flooded with sunlight that poured through the tall windows, the room was cheery.

The warden, Miss Stillwell, was waiting for him. A thin woman, she was plainly dressed in a pale green linen frock. Her iron-grey hair was braided and pinned in a coil at the back of her neck. She was seated in a straight-backed chair near the fireplace, her knees pressed tightly together, her feet side by side in their sensible brogues. She was of the class and generation of women who had been taught proper posture, along with proper behaviour. In spite of all this severity, she had a pleasant face with well-defined laughter lines at the corners of her eyes.

"Inspector Tyler, please have a seat. Would you like some tea?"

"No, thank you, Miss Stillwell. But I would appreciate a glass of water."

"Certainly. It has been dreadfully hot. Violet, would you bring the inspector some cold water?"

The maid left on her errand, and Tyler took a chair facing. There was no way he could slouch in that hard chair even if he'd wanted to. He put his hat beside him on the floor, momentarily thrown back to school days and the lessons about good manners drummed into him by his teachers.

The warden gave him a wan smile. "I am so glad to see you, Inspector. As you can imagine, when I heard the news about Elsie Bates, I was appalled."

"What do you know so far, Warden?"

"Not much, to tell you the truth. Rose Watkins returned to the hostel about half past seven this morning. She had gone in search of Miss Bates, who was expected in the lorry about half six but who had not yet arrived. Rose was clearly dreadfully upset, but kept repeating she couldn't say what it was about except that Elsie had been in a bad accident, and that a police officer would be here soon."

"Where is Miss Watkins now?"

"She is resting in her room."

"I will need to speak to her."

"Of course."

"Are the other girls in the house?"

"No. I thought it better for all concerned if they went about their business until we had more information. They all have bicycles so I sent them off to work." She glanced at him. "I hope that was the correct thing to do."

"I'm sure it was, Warden."

She clasped her hands tightly in her lap. "Shortly after they had left, I received a telephone call from Sir Percy. He said that Elsie was dead and the police were treating it as a suspicious death. Is that the case, Inspector?"

"Yes, I regret to say, it is."

The maid returned carrying a jug of water and an empty glass on a tray. She placed them on the table beside Miss Stillwell, who waited until she withdrew before she poured water for Tyler. Her hand shook and she splashed some of it as she handed the glass to him.

"Please continue, Inspector."

He gulped back the water greedily. "Miss Bates was discovered lying at the side of the road. She had been shot in the head."

"Goodness gracious! . . . Do you know by whom?"

"It was not by her own hand, I can assure you of that."

She nodded, understanding, as he himself had, what a vital girl Elsie Bates had been.

"The Land Army lorry was some ways up the road and I believe she had been riding her bicycle. We found one close by. It's maroon with a wicker basket on the front. Would that have been hers?"

Miss Stillwell nodded. "The Land girls can have a regulation-issue bicycle if they wish, but some of them prefer to get better models of their own." She took a deep breath. "Elsie was proud of hers."

"It fits that description, I presume?"

She nodded again, lips held tightly together.

"She was lodging in Whitchurch, I believe," said Tyler.

"That is correct. She was a forewoman and living out was

considered a privilege of the position. Her job was to collect the girls here from the hostel and drive them to the different farms where their help had been requested." Again the wan smile. "Elsie fretted against rules, and she was often late . . . I was the one who had to deal with the complaints from our farmers, and I'm afraid she saw me as a hard task maker. But, as you are no doubt aware, we are still taken on sufferance here by many of the local people, and I was anxious that we establish a good reputation."

Tyler finished off the glass of water.

"You say Miss Bates was something of a rebel. Can you tell me more about her? Was she liked, for instance? Did she have any enemies that you know of?"

Miss Stillwell considered the question for a moment, and he could see she was selecting what she thought was appropriate to say and what wasn't.

"Initially, when she came here, I would say she had a chip on her shoulder. A rather large chip. She is . . . er, was, from one of the poorer sections of London, and some of the young women are from, shall we say, more privileged families. Elsie resented them and was only too keen to take them down a peg or two. She had quite a sharp tongue on her." She chuckled. "She could dredge up language that would embarrass a sailor. I had to have her on the carpet over that. She had not had an easy life. Occasionally she'd let slip something about her family. Quite dreadful really. Drunk and disorderly all the time. She settled down and lost some of her belligerence. She wanted to get on, to shake off those early influences." She took a handkerchief from her pocket and rubbed at her eyes. "Excuse me, Inspector. I know that Elsie and I had our disagreements and that she didn't much care for me, but I grew quite fond of her. I'm sorry she didn't know that."

"So, no enemies that you are aware of? No one who might want to do her harm?"

"Not here. She was very generous to the other girls, picking up extra chores if they were tired, for instance. As I say, the more they all worked together, the more they all learned respect and affection for each other."

"And outside of the hostel? Anybody who might hate Miss Bates enough to kill her?"

Miss Stillwell sighed. "I am not a young woman, Inspector, but contrary to what the girls sometimes think, I was once. I understand the power of love and what it can stir in a person. Elsie Bates was unusually attractive. She liked to flirt. I've seen how she was when we've had our male guests over. To put it rather crudely, she'd have the young men panting around her like dogs with a bitch in heat."

This was the first hint of acerbity that had leaked into the warden's speech. Tyler wondered if there was something personal in it.

Rather stiffly, she got to her feet and brought the jug of water over to him.

"It's a little early to offer you anything stronger, I suppose."

Tyler would have liked to accept, but he was on duty and, despite her good manners, he knew Miss Stillwell would be disappointed in him.

"Thank you, Warden. You have been most helpful. There is one more thing I'd like to ask you about. There was a gun beside Elsie's body. A German Luger, issued in 1917. We will have to have it tested, but there's little doubt it is the weapon that was used. Do you know if Miss Bates possessed such a gun?"

She stared at him in bewilderment. "Why no. No. I have no knowledge of such."

"Would any of the other girls in the hostel have owned a gun?"

"Not that I am aware of. It is against all regulations."

"Do you personally know anybody at all who might possess a German Luger? Anybody?"

"Not at all."

"No names you heard bruited about? No gossip?"

This time, she looked rather affronted. If she could have bristled in that straight chair, she would have.

"I was taught never to listen to gossip, Inspector. I cannot help you in this regard."

He closed his notebook. "Could I have the name and address of Miss Bates's next of kin? I will have to notify them. And I will need to talk to all of the women. How many are billeted here all together?"

"Seven."

"Do you have any kind of roll call in the mornings?"

"It's not necessary. The girls know that breakfast is served between six and a quarter past six. It is their responsibility to get up. They look out for each other. The early risers wake up the sleepy heads."

"Did you see who was at breakfast this morning?"

"Everyone except for Florence Hancocks, who is away on compassionate leave."

Tyler wrote that down. "What time will they return?"

"It's harvest time so they won't be back before dusk."

"Shall we say I'll come about nine o'clock, then?"

She hesitated. "They don't yet know what has happened. Fortunately, they are all working on a farm a little distance from town and it's not on the telephone. You know how rumour runs rampant. I'd hate for them to hear some garbled version of what has happened. Will you be the one to tell them?"

"Yes, I will. And, Miss Stillwell, please accept my sympathy. I know what I have had to tell you has been upsetting."

"Thank you. You have been most considerate." She bit down on her lip. "One thinks that one will never be touched by evil if all of one's life one has been surrounded by good people, but that is not necessarily the case, is it? Like so many others, I thought we had fought the war to end all wars, but look what has happened to us. And to Elsie Bates." She reached over and pressed an electric button on the wall. "I suggest you talk to Rose in the library. It is much more private than here, and the girls use it as their sanctuary. I shall sit for a moment or two, then I will get the information that you requested."

Tyler put his notebook in his pocket and stood up. There was something about Miss Stillwell that aroused in him an impulse to kiss her hand. He could see the young woman she had once been. Young and attractive. He wondered who had broken her heart.

The maid entered.

"Violet, show the inspector to the library, and fetch Miss Watkins down. Take them in some tea and see if Cook has any biscuits or cake to spare, will you?"

"Yes, ma'am. Is everything all right, ma'am?"

"Not right at all, Violet. But you will hear about it in good time."

"Yes, ma'am."

Tyler followed the maid out, leaving Miss Stillwell to her reveries. He suspected she had given him a rather idyllic picture of life at the manor, but he didn't think it was to deceive, so much as what she wanted to believe.

6.

Violet showed Tyler into the library. She didn't say a word, the good and faithful servant. Like the drawing room, the library was bright and airy with deep recessed windows that looked out onto the lawn. The walls were lined with glass-fronted bookcases and there were a couple of brown leather armchairs arranged near the fireplace. There was a sign on the wall, NO SMOKING! But the lingering smell of tobacco in the air made him suspect that some of the girls were sneaking a fag or two. He walked over to the window. A padded seat was built into the recess, a nice comfy spot to sit and daydream or read. There was a magazine on the seat. *The Land Girl*. He flipped through the pages. There were numerous articles for the girls, such things as how to take care of their gum boots. One letter caught his eye. The subject was pigs.

Store and fat pigs will sometimes suddenly turn on one of their mates and if not stopped in time will eventually kill the unfortunate ones.

He should send the piece to Winnie to use as a metaphor in one of his broadcasts.

He glanced out of the window. The dowager, Lady Somerville, was walking slowly across the lush lawn. She was accompanied by another elderly maid who could have been the twin to the one who opened the door to him. The maid was holding a white parasol over the dowager's head. The estate manager, Arthur Trimble, was trundling a wheelbarrow down the path. In spite of the warm day, he was well covered up in a corduroy jacket and breeches. He was wearing a brown cap, but when the dowager drew closer, he put down the wheelbarrow, removed his cap, and tucked it under his arm. Then he stepped forward, snipped off a rose, and handed it to the old lady.

Go ahead, you smarmy bastard, thought Tyler. *There's a war on and men are dying by the hundreds but she's probably asking you to pick the bleeding aphids off the roses. And you will. We must keep our priorities straight, mustn't we?*

Ever since he'd come to live in Shropshire, Trimble had acted as if he was superior to the local folk, and rarely associated with them.

There was a tap on the door and the maid entered. "Miss Watkins, sir."

She ushered in a young woman who was so tiny and scrawny, she hardly looked like an adult. Her dungarees hung on her.

"Thanks, Violet. Hello, Miss Watkins, I'm Inspector Tyler. I've come to ask you a few questions."

She nodded. "I know." Her tone was wary. He guessed that her previous experience of police officers hadn't been one of mutual friendliness.

"Where would you like to sit?"

"Over by the window."

She immediately went to the window recess. "Is there a chance of a cuppa? I'm parched."

"It's coming."

She tucked her feet underneath her. "Can you call me Rose? I'm not used to Miss Watkins."

"Of course. So, Rose, are you up to talking to me?"

"Glad to. It's been a long bleeding morning by myself. Just going over and over things in me mind."

"Didn't you have any company?"

"Naw. The girls had to go off to work and that just left the maids and Miss Stillwell. She's a good sort, really, but she and Elsie didn't get along, and I weren't in the mood to hear nobody running her down, if you know what I mean."

After a light tap, Violet entered the room, wheeling a tea trolley on which sat a silver tea service and, heavens above, a plate of biscuits. She put it next to Rose and retreated quickly.

Tyler waited until Rose had helped herself to a cup of tea and scarfed down three biscuits in a row. When she spoke, her mouth was still filled.

"What d'you want to know?" she asked.

"I think I've got most of the story from Corporal Ellwood. You were going to find Elsie but your bike got a flat . . ."

"That's right, bloody thing."

"The two soldiers drove you up the road a ways and you came across Elsie's body."

Rose was wearing a silver bangle on her arm and she began to twist it. "At first, I thought it was a joke. Elsie's a big joker and I thought, 'She's trying to put a scare into us, the little tosser.' We all got out of the lorry and went over. Then the corporal tried to keep me away so's I wouldn't see but it was too late . . ." Rose didn't cry although her voice became flat and low. "She was covered in blood, all down the side of her face. I knew right then that she was dead. The other soldier, Bobby's his name, he got a terrible case of the jitters. He was shaking like a leaf and I thought he might collapse any minute. The corp had to yell at him. Then he, the corp, told us that we couldn't help her now and we should get into the lorry and go and get Sir Percy, 'cos he's the magistrate. Bobby kept going on about the Germans were invading us, that a parachutist must have got her. I started to get the shakes myself when he said that." She shuddered. "Was it a Jerry who done her in?"

"I don't think so, Rose."

"Where'd you take her?"

"We have to do a post-mortem. She's at the mortuary."

"We'll be able to bury her, won't we?"

"Yes. As soon as the investigation is complete, we'll release her body to her family."

Rose shifted restlessly. "Them don't give a sod. But Elsie always wanted a fancy funeral. We talked about it once. 'I want black horses and plumes, Rose,' she says. 'And sad music.' 'Oo, listen to 'er,' says I. 'Only the good die young, Elsie. And that means you're going to live to be an old lady.'" Rose stretched out her arm and showed him the bangle. "Elsie gave me this for my birthday. I ain't had nothing like it before."

Tyler nodded. "She was your best mate, wasn't she?"

She looked at him. "What happened, mister?"

"I don't know yet."

Rose got out of the seat and started to walk around the room. She tugged at a couple of the cabinet doors, which were locked.

"Do they think we'd steal any of these books, for Christ's sake? Look at them, they're all old. Who the hell would want them?"

Tyler just murmured. There were probably some expensive first editions in those bookcases. Finally, Rose returned to the tea trolley and poured some more tea for herself.

"Do you have any idea who might want to harm your friend, Rose? Did she have any enemies?"

Rose shook her head immediately. "I wouldn't say enemies. Not enemies. 'Til you get to know her, she can . . . she could come across as a bit rough, but only 'til you got used to her." She turned the bangle. "She had a heart of gold."

"Everybody liked her then?"

"Yeah. She was very popular. She didn't get along too good

with the warden, but I think that was Elsie's fault more than anything. Miss Stillwell is a stickler for the rules and Elsie didn't like that. She was what you'd call a rebel. When we first moved in, the furniture in the bedrooms had been removed and the worst junk had been put in. Some of it was falling apart. God knows where they'd got it. Elsie complained to the county office and they came and made Lady Somerville get in better things. The rest of us would have put up with it, but not 'er." Rose smiled, enjoying the memory.

"Outside of the hostel, how did Elsie get along with people in general?"

"Good. She was a hard worker and the old codgers got to respect her." She helped herself to another biscuit. "Mr. Morgan didn't much care for her but that was his own bloody fault." She gave a bit of a grin. "We was working his farm last month and it was so bleeding hot we all decided to take off our shirts. It was our Elsie's idea, naturally, but we were out in the fields all by ourselves, so we thought, why bloody not. Then along comes Mr. Morgan. He had already been pestering some of the girls, making comments about their bottoms, getting in a sly touch now and again. He took a poke at one of Sylvia Sumner's knockers, saying how big it is. And they are, but she's only seventeen and she was upset by what he did. So anyway, his eyes got like bleeding saucers when he saw us half naked. I mean, we all covered up, but Elsie was fit to be tied. She just went over to him and said we were fed up with his behaviour. If he didn't stop, she was going to tell everybody what he was doing. His wife is a bit of a tartar so she wouldn't like that. He was gob struck and practically went down on his knees begging us not to. Elsie said as how we'd keep silent on the condition he treated us all to a round of shandies and a slap-up lunch at the Greyhound. He didn't want to, you could see that. But he had no choice so he handed over a pound, moaning that it was his last and what would he tell his wife." Rose giggled. "'Tell her you gave it to the Spitfire fund,'" said Elsie. He didn't try anything after that but I saw some of the looks he gave her. If looks could kill . . ." her voice trailed off.

That didn't surprise Tyler either. However, he didn't think Ewen Morgan, whom he'd known all his life, was capable of murder, miserable old geezer though he was sometimes.

Rose yawned and went back to the window seat. "I'm knackered."

"Just a couple more questions, Rose. Elsie was a pretty girl; did she have a sweetheart that you know of?"

"Not *a* sweetheart, dozens. The blokes swarmed her like bees on jam."

She glanced out of the window. Tyler saw that Trimble was crossing the lawn, a dejected hen underneath each arm. "'Im, for instance. She even got 'im panting after her and he's old enough to be her dad."

Tyler was momentarily taken aback. "Trimble?"

"That's him. Don't get me wrong. Elsie didn't give a fig for him, but she wangled some nice presents out of him. Silk stockings, some chocolates. He was fit to be tied when she told him not to come calling anymore. She could be like that. Generally, she let the young blokes down easy, but the slimy ones, she played them for what she could get."

"Was Arthur Trimble the most recent conquest?"

Tyler noticed Rose's hesitation.

"No. She'd started going with somebody else . . . she wouldn't tell me who it was except that he was a soldier. I mean, she would have eventually, we had no secrets from each other, but at first she liked to tease me a bit. This bloke was different. I could tell she was sweet on this one. She said he'd had a bad time over in France. She was always a softie for the lame ducks."

Tyler pushed away the frightening thought that flew into his mind. There were several young men in the area who'd had a hard time in France, including Bobby Walker and Jimmy. But it was Tyler himself who'd said maybe his son had found a sweetheart. *Oh God, let's hope he had nothing to do with this.*

Rose looked exhausted.

"We'll finish in a minute, Rose. Did you ever see Elsie with a gun, or did she ever mention knowing somebody who had a gun?"

The girl blinked rapidly. "She told me once her old man kept a pellet gun to kill crows and she was scared he might use it on her. That's why she left home as soon as she could and joined the Land Army."

"I found a bunch of white poppies that had been placed on her chest. Would you know anything about that?"

"No. I know the ones you mean, but I'm not fussy about them myself. They don't smell or anything. There's a lady that sells them. She's a bit of a queer fish, but she's good to us girls. Mrs. Thorne, her name is. She brings soap she makes herself and lotion for our hands." Rose held out her hands to show him. They were tanned and weather-beaten, the skin on the fingers cracked, and traces of dirt were still under her finger-nails. "The hedgerows tear them up fierce. Elsie was proud of her hands and she tried to keep them nice."

"White poppies are an emblem of the Peace Pledge Union. Did Elsie by any chance sign the peace pledge? I know Mrs. Thorne is always trying to persuade people to join."

"Naw, not Elsie," said Rose with a chuckle. "She said she liked having a war. It made men of the boys, was her expression. She said this had been the best time of her life." Rose's eyes watered but she bit back her tears.

"One more question. I promise it's the last," said Tyler. "The corporal reported that when you first saw Elsie, you said, 'I warned you.' What did you mean by that?"

He saw tension catch her shoulders, but she concentrated on the bangle. "I don't remember saying anything like that."

"Are you sure?"

"Course I'm sure. I mean, if I did say it I was referring to the lorry. I told her to be careful when she was driving the bloody thing."

"I tried it myself. It seems to be working all right."

Rose looked sulky. "Well, it might be now but it didn't always." She slid back into the recess. "I feel as if I could fall asleep right on the spot."

Tyler stood up. "Come on. You need a lie down."

Rose's eyes were actually drooping. "Can I stay here for a bit? It's sort of comfy." She brought up her knees and curled up like a cat. Within seconds, she was asleep. Tyler picked up a shawl that was draped across the other chair and covered her legs with it. The room was warm enough with the sun but it was he who needed the comfort of that gesture.

7.

Miss Stillwell had acted quickly and as Tyler came out of the library, she was ready with information regarding Elsie Bates's next of kin, and the names of all the girls in the hostel. She looked haggard, but she was calm and efficient. The kind of woman you were glad to have on your side. She showed him to her office, where the telephone was, and withdrew to check on Rose.

It took him a while to get through to London, but finally somebody answered and rerouted him to the police station in the East End nearest to where Elsie Bates had lived. Again, the telephone rang and rang before it was picked up.

"Sergeant Donaldson here."

Tyler identified himself and explained why he was calling.

"As soon as the post-mortem's done, we can have the body sent down. We just need some directions."

"Hmm. I'm afraid there was a bad incident yesterday, Inspector. Our RAF lads were engaged in a dogfight with Jerry and one of them was shot down. Unfortunately, he crashed right on the street you mention. He was killed and there were a couple of fatalities on the ground. Lots of houses were damaged. It's a tight, crowded street. But I'll do my best to get word to the family." The officer sighed. "Poor buggers. Bad news on top of bad news by the sound of it. Laid any charges yet?"

"Not yet. It's early days. I'd appreciate it if you'd ask the parents a few questions for me. Did Elsie have a boyfriend? You know, the usual drill."

"I'll do it if I can. I don't know the situation yet."

There was something about the sergeant's voice that threw Tyler onto the defensive.

"She didn't deserve to die like that. She wasn't even twenty years old."

Another sigh from the other end of the line. "Yes, well, you should have seen what my men had to dig out. We had an eight-year-old and a newborn. They didn't deserve it either."

Somehow the implication was that Elsie was not an innocent. Who knows, he may have been right.

The sergeant promised to call as soon as he had any information, and they hung up.

Tyler rang his station. Sergeant Gough answered.

"No news yet, sir. The lads are still out searching."

"Nothing here either. I'm going over to Prees Heath now. See if anybody knows anything."

He made one more call to Major Fordham, the commandant at the internment camp, who had to use a field telephone. The reception was poor, but Tyler gathered the major was expecting him, and the internees had been put on stand-by for his arrival. Sir Percy had done his job.

Miss Stillwell personally saw Tyler out. As he drove away, he glanced in his rear-view mirror to see her still standing in the doorway of the grand old house.

As he headed for the internment camp into the hot, sunny morning, he couldn't stop himself from wondering if Clare would be there. How old was he when they first met? Nine? That's right. He'd just had his ninth birthday and had been given a cricket bat by his parents. Clare was two months younger. She had come to spend the summer with her cousin Percy at the manor, and her aunt periodically invited the local children to afternoon tea.

"Mind your manners, Tom Tyler." His mother had sent him off in his Sunday best, shoes polished, hair slicked down. All of the children had looked forward to these afternoons and the chance to stuff themselves with cream buns. All except Clare, that is, who, with her knobby, pale, bare knees, skinny blond braids, and inexplicably shabby clothes, seemed more ill at ease than any of them. However, when she returned for each of the following three summers, she was gradually accepted into the little community of the country town. She learned to give back as good as she got, the children stopped teasing her about her posh way of speaking, and Tom discovered she didn't mind if he played horsey with her, both of them galloping about the lawn with him holding onto her long plaits as if they were reins.

Tyler slowed down to negotiate a blind corner. When they were twelve, Clare stopped coming to Whitchurch. He enquired at the manor and was told she had gone off to a finishing school in Switzerland. He pined for a while, then started to forget about her. When the Great War broke out, he enlisted as soon as he was old enough. The experiences he had there tended to wipe out any rosy memories of his childhood.

Tyler risked driving into the ditch and fished out and lit a cigarette. Memories of the war were still troubling to him. He preferred to think about Clare, although, to tell the truth, not all of those memories were sweet either.

When she finally returned to Whitchurch, he'd been demobbed for a year and had rejoined the constabulary. Funnily enough, they'd met in the same place where he'd run into her last week. He'd gone to the market to buy some vegetables for his mother. And there was Clare. No longer the shy little girl he'd known. She had blossomed into one of the most beautiful creatures he had ever seen. Plaits gone, blond hair in a fashionable chignon at her neck. There was even a hint of rouge on her shapely lips. She was wearing a loose-fitting, stylish cream suit of some lacy, gauzy material. Such a wide-brimmed hat had never been seen before in the streets of Whitchurch. Was it really a bright sunny day, or was that just his memory playing tricks? Clare, bathed in sunlight, standing at one of the stalls.

Rather to his surprise, Clare had seemed equally pleased to see him. As naturally as if she hadn't left, they started to spend all their free time together. He'd abandoned cricket and become adept at football. She came to all his games. He was both proud and jealous of the attention she drew from the men. If they'd set tongues wagging, they didn't care. His own parents nagged him constantly about stepping out of his class, but he wouldn't listen.

"She'll break your heart. Her kind always does," warned his mother.

And she had.

He hadn't seen her again until a week ago. She was standing at Alice Thorne's stall, breathing into a bunch of lavender. Her back was to him but he knew at once it was her, and he felt as if he'd taken a punch in the stomach. She was actually thinner than she'd been, and the white cotton frock hung loosely about her frame. She was hatless, her blond hair cut shorter than the prevailing fashion and touched with grey at the sides, but she was still Clare, and he didn't know what the hell he was going to do about that.

She'd turned and saw him. Was she as shocked? He couldn't tell. She'd smiled, but in his view it was a cool smile, the kind you'd give an old acquaintance, not a former lover.

"Hello, Tom. How nice to see you."

"And you, Clare. What brings you here after all these years?"

"I returned to England so I could do my bit for the war effort. I have a job over at the Prees Heath internment camp. I'm acting as an interpreter."

"Ah yes, you must be fluent in German. I'd read somewhere you were living in Switzerland."

The lie fell from his mouth cool as a cucumber. *He'd read somewhere. Ha!* For years he'd combed every newspaper gossip column he could find for information about her. Two years after she left him, she had married a much older man, a wealthy Swiss German industrialist. She appeared to have lived the typical life of a rich socialite, dividing her time between Switzerland and Austria, where her husband had large estates. They had no children.

She smiled. "You look well, Tom. How have you been?"

"I am well, thank you. Country air, you know."

He was aware that Alice Thorne was eyeing them curiously. She'd come to live in Whitchurch after Clare had left, but Alice was a shrewd judge of character, and as far as he was concerned his own consternation at this unexpected meeting was as loud as the air raid siren they'd installed in the square. *Danger, danger. Take cover.*

"How long have you been in the county?" he asked Clare.

"Not long. Less than a week." She added, quickly, "I knew I'd run into you sooner or later, Tom."

"Of course." But he couldn't stop the pang of disappointment.

She went on to say she was staying at Beeton Manor; yes, the summer had been wonderfully warm, hadn't it? But they could use some rain now, couldn't they? She hadn't asked him any personal questions – perhaps she knew the answers.

Surely no more than five minutes had elapsed when Clare had checked her watch and said she had to leave, that she was on duty. They must get together soon and catch up. She'd walked away and he turned to meet Alice's eyes.

"Ghosts from the past, eh Alice? They can shake you up when you're not expecting it."

8.

Jimmy Tyler and Alice Thorne were seated at her kitchen table, sorting out the herbs she needed for her sachets. Jimmy wasn't being very talkative but Alice had learned to give him time.

He picked up a bunch of greens that were in a basket. "Are these dandelion leaves?"

"Yes. I'm going to make some wine with them. The younger ones are good steamed as well. Very nourishing."

"I should tell my mom. She's always complaining about the dandelions in our front garden."

"I'm taking some over to the camp. The cooks there are always keen to try new things. I promised them some onions." She smiled. "Now, that really got them excited. I'm getting a good price."

They worked on in silence. Alice had known Jimmy since he was a child and a pupil in her class. As a young boy he had been beautiful, with his mother's dark eyes fringed with long, girlish eyelashes. When he first came to school, Alice had more than once been forced to intervene when other boys, considerably less beautiful, had picked on him. But she couldn't watch them all the time and even though she had lectured the culprits, the bullying continued. Finally, she had a word with Tom. "First, get his hair cut. Those curls incense the boys. Second, teach him how to fight back. He might get a few more bruises, but it will be better than the destruction of his spirit." Tom had looked grim, she recalled, but the next day, Jimmy had come to school, hair shorn as short as the other boys. When they'd started to tease him about that, he'd promptly hit the chief bully on the ear and sent him off howling. Things changed after that. She was grateful that, whatever it was Tom had taught him, Jimmy didn't misuse his own power. In fact, he became the rescuer of the downtrodden, and by the time she had left the school herself, he was securely in place as a class leader. And he kept his hair short. It was still close-cropped now, soldier style, but he couldn't do anything about those eyelashes.

Usually their times together were comfortable, but today Jimmy was fidgety and distracted. He began to twist a sprig of rosemary in his fingers.

"I ran into Wilf's mom, Mrs. Marshall, in town last week. She was bothered that I'd only been to see her once since I got moved up here."

"Don't you want to go?"

"Not really. She wants to talk about Wilf."

"People in a state of grief get comfort from sharing their memories with people who have known their loved one," said Alice quietly. "You and Wilf were such good pals."

"There really isn't anything I can say to her. I can't bring him back."

"What about your other friends, Bobby and Dennis? The four musketeers, you called yourselves. Have they gone to see Mrs. Marshall?"

"No, I don't think so." He grimaced. "Funny, isn't it? We've only been at war for a year, but already I can hardly remember what peacetime is like. It seems like years ago when the four of us were getting ready to sign up." He was quiet for a moment. "We all went for a last walk in the Acton Woods. 'What's on your minds about what's to come, lads?' asks Bobby. Well, we had a good time with that one. I said above all, I wanted to behave honourably." Jimmy ducked his head, embarrassed.

"I particularly didn't want to mess my trousers. Or pee down my leg or scream for my mom if I got shot. Bobby says he's worried that he might have to kill somebody. Me, I'd want to know who they were if I did kill a German. What sort of bloke the enemy was. Dennis thought that was ridiculous. 'They'll kill us first if they can without a second thought.'"

"Maybe, maybe not," interjected Alice.

Jimmy didn't seem to hear her. "Later, when we were in France, we found out the Jerry had shoved some prisoners into a hut and shot them like they were rats in a trap. I hated them then. Hated the Stukka pilots who fired on those French refugees on the road. They were all women and children and old people . . . We found a child's foot in the field."

Alice kept working.

"But back there in the Acton Woods, we hadn't experienced any of this yet, and the Krauts were still the unknown. Fellows just like us. 'I don't want to have no legs,' says Wilf. 'And I don't want to die no lingering death all by myself in some ditch. Bullet to the head for me, promise me lads?' 'I don't want to be blinded,' says Bobby. 'Same for me,' I said, 'blind or crippled, forget it.' Then Dennis pipes up. You know what he's like. 'For God's sake, I don't care if I don't have no legs nor arms and I'm stone blind, but promise me you'll do me in if I get my balls shot off.'"

Alice laughed and Jimmy looked at her in relief. "Sorry to be a bit vulgar."

"I've heard the words before, don't worry."

"'Well,' Wilf says, 'you'd better stop playing with your willy in that case or it will drop off. Then you won't have anything.' 'No, it won't,' scoffed Dennis. 'That's an old wives' tale. I'm keeping mine strong by exercising it.'" Jimmy glanced at Alice to see if she was all right with all this bawdy talk. "'That won't do you any good if you've got no legs nor arms and you can't see,' says Wilf. 'You'd be surprised. I'm very versatile,' says Dennis."

Alice laughed again, shaking her head.

"So we all promised each other," continued Jimmy. "We put our hands together. 'We'll watch out for each other. Shropshire lads. The four musketeers. All for one and one for all.'" He stretched his arms over his head. "Any chance of one of your teas, Mrs. Thorne?"

"I'll put the kettle on."

She got up from the table, and the dog who had been lying nearby looked up expectantly. He struggled to his feet. He was missing a front leg and getting up was difficult. He hopped over to the stove to see if anything would drop his way.

Jimmy watched him. "There are people who say it would have been kinder to Skip to put him down."

Alice turned around sharply. "By people I presume you mean Ewen Morgan whose trap it was that destroyed Skip's leg."

"Him and others."

The dog noticed Alice was opening the cupboard and was there in an instant, ears pricked, head up.

"He's seems to be functioning pretty well, wouldn't you say?" said Alice. "Dogs live in the present. He doesn't think of himself as crippled."

Jimmy clicked his tongue and patted his leg. Ever the opportunist, the collie hopped over to him. Jimmy scratched his head.

"He was hurt bad. How'd you know he'd recover?"

"I didn't, but I had to give it a try. Morgan owned him then and he magnanimously came over with his shotgun and offered to put the dog down, even though it was his bloody trap that had done the damage. I told him he could stick the bullet where the sun doesn't shine."

Jimmy grinned at her. She didn't usually talk like that.

She scooped up some herbs from a dish into two pottery mugs, added some hot water, and brought them back to the table.

"Let it steep."

Skip switched his attention to her, and she ruffled his ears affectionately. "I did the amputation myself and nursed him myself. It was touch and go but he's young. He pulled through. I wouldn't part with him for the world."

Jimmy grasped the mug, his hands encircling it as if he were cold. "You've always been a great help to me, Mrs. Thorne. I do appreciate it, but I don't know if I can talk to even you. It's hard to understand if you weren't there."

"I'll try. We were talking about the four musketeers and why you don't want to see Mrs. Marshall."

Jimmy drank some of the hot tea. "I need to tell you something else first."

"Go ahead."

Like a swimmer jumping into icy water, Jimmy plunged into his story.

"We were trapped on the beaches at Dunkirk for four days. There was just me and Bobby Walker by now. We'd got separated from our unit—"

"Wasn't Wilf Marshall with you? He died at Dunkirk, didn't he?"

"No," said Jimmy sharply. "No. We got to the beach, he didn't."

"Sorry, didn't mean to interrupt. Go on."

Jimmy leaned his head on his hands, and she thought he might stop talking, but after a minute he went on, speaking so softly she had trouble hearing him. "We had no food, almost no water, which was worse. Nobody knew what was happening. The Stukkas were dive-bombing us and there was nothing we could do except dig into the sand. Men were being blown to pieces all around. I don't know why I survived but I did. We both did, Bobby and me. There was one shell that landed a few feet away and I saw him thrown into the air like a rag doll. He landed on the sand and he was covered with blood. I thought he'd bought it, but he just had the wind knocked out of him. The blood was somebody else's, a bloke who'd been sharing a tin of water with us. He was a tough Scotsman who'd also got separated from his unit. He'd taken a direct hit. I ran over to Bobby and dragged him to a burned-out staff car and we huddled underneath it. Not that it would have done us much good, but it made us feel better. Like we were kids who cover their eyes and say, 'You can't see me . . .'"

His eyelid was twitching and he put up his finger to stop it.

"Drink your tea, Jimmy," said Alice. "We can go on talking at some other time if you'd rather."

"No, I've got started now. I'd like to continue."

"Why don't we work and talk? I'll start stripping down the herbs and we can stuff those little pockets with them."

Alice needed to keep her hands busy. She didn't want Jimmy to see that she was trembling.

He picked up one of the linen sachets but made no move to fill it. "The whole side of Bobby's face was pockmarked with blood, like he had the measles. The marks were caused by tiny slivers of Jock's bone. I had to pick them out for him. There must have been a dozen of them. We stayed under that blasted car for three or four hours. Maybe longer. A soldier came by, a sergeant. 'Come on, you sodding useless bits of shite. Get your arses out of there.' You wouldn't think somebody cussing you would sound like a love call, but it did. He told us this was the last day we could be taken off the beaches. The Jerry panzers were closing in fast."

Jimmy sniffed at a stalk of the fragrant lavender. "The destroyers weren't able to get in close enough so the Navy had commandeered dozens of small boats, which were coming in as near as they could to the shore. There were still thousands of men left to pick up and some of them were wading out up to their waists in the sea while they waited. The naval officers had managed to bring some order to the chaos, but it was precarious. One of them was a big burly bloke, a sergeant. He looked half mad to me and he kept repeating, 'Stay in line. Stay in line. I'll shoot any man that breaks rank.' He had quite a posh voice, which you didn't expect. Bobby and me got into a line that was heading for a makeshift pier some of the engineers had formed from abandoned cars and trucks, lined up nose to tail. We were all pressed close together but we were at least moving along. But we heard the Stukkas coming in . . . They have a sort of high-pitched whine like a saw that needs oiling. We were strafed again. Two men in front of me were killed instantly. They just gave a little leap forward from the impact and dropped to the ground.

"Then I saw a man break rank. He tried to shove the men in front of him out of the way. One of them, who was wounded, fell off the pier. The man didn't care. He was berserk, trying to get ahead to the waiting boat. That's when I recognized Fred Scobie from my unit. I hadn't even known he was on the beach. The sergeant yelled at him to get back in line but he couldn't listen. He was too panicked. So the sergeant took aim and shot him. In the back. Fred joined the other bloke in the sea, the one he'd knocked over. He was thrashing around and I could see the blood pouring out of him. I know blood is red, of course I know that, I'd already seen plenty of it, but the sea was blue that afternoon, it was broad daylight, and the blood looked so red as it flowed out of him. I kept thinking to myself, 'That is one hell of a lot of blood. We'd better staunch it before he bleeds to death.' But I didn't know what to do. I was afraid that if I went to pull him out of the water the sergeant might think I was breaking rank and shoot me too. The men behind continued to move forward. Scobie went on splashing frantically. He called out and he tried to lift his arm but a wave slapped him in the face and filled his mouth . . . he started to choke. . . . That's the last I saw of him. I was trapped by the men in front and the men behind me. I turned around best I could but I couldn't even see where he was anymore. Fred Scobie was one more carcass, face down, bobbing on the sea . . . And you know what? If you were to ask me to describe the man who shot him, I couldn't. I wouldn't recognize him if he passed me on the street. He was a naval officer, an Englishman, one of ours, doing his duty. He probably didn't even feel bad about it."

Carefully he lined up the little sachets one beside the other. "Fred Scobie died a coward's death. Those are the stories nobody wants to tell, but they happen. They happen all the time."

9.

EXCEPT FOR THE BARBED WIRE ENCLOSURE, THE CAMP could have been an army base. Over a thousand men were housed in row upon row of khaki tents. For safety and ease of administration, the camp was divided into three sections, each with a barbed wire fence but connected with each other by gates. There was a large mess tent at the north end of the camp where everybody ate in shifts. In non-meal times, it doubled as an assembly hall and entertainment centre. Behind the tent was a strip of grass set aside for recreation. It wasn't as wide as a regulation football field, but the young men used it anyway for games that were highly competitive. The occasional ball that was sent over the wire was willingly returned by one of the guards. The scrubby grass of the heath had been beaten down; was a good thing the summer had been unusually hot and dry, or else the camp would have been a sea of mud. There was a guard tower at each corner, and two wide walkways crossed the camp. This was a favourite meeting place for many of the older internees who strolled up and down, debating the Torah animatedly. Electric cables were strung across the enclosure. Except for running water, the internees had all the amenities.

Only on the east side were there any trees to speak of, a small copse just beyond the barbed wire. To the west were mostly high bramble bushes and a few solitary ash trees. Outside the barbed wire, the heath was as it had been for centuries: dun-coloured gorse dotted with purple heather, dainty blue butterflies flitting about.

Tyler turned onto the service road that ran down the western side and parked the Humber next to one of the army lorries. There was a dusty MG nearby and he guessed it belonged to Clare.

He tightened his tie, put his hat on, and headed for the commandant's tent, which was pitched underneath a stand of trees a few hundred feet outside of the main entrance to the camp. All of the flaps were up to get a little more air into the tent, and as he approached, Tyler could see the major was seated at a table talking to Clare. He'd told himself it would be better if she wasn't there, maybe the fire would die out naturally, but he couldn't suppress the rush of joy he felt when he saw her.

Major Fordham got to his feet at once. Clare turned and smiled. Today she was wearing a pale yellow frock with a scoop neck that showed off her tanned skin, but in spite of that, Tyler thought she looked tired and drawn.

The commandant was a jolly looking roly-poly sort of man whose flushed cheeks suggested a problem with blood pressure.

"Come in, Tyler. Dreadful business all this."

"It is that, sir."

"Allow me to introduce Mrs. Devereau, our translator and general liaison with the internees."

"We've met," said Tyler. "Many years ago." He tried to sound casual.

Fordham went back to the tent entrance and beckoned to the sentry standing nearby. "Nash, see if there's such a thing as a cold drink you can get us from the mess tent. I heard the cook made some lemonade. Bring us a jug, there's a good fellow."

The soldier strode off, happy at the task. "We've got some Eyeties in the camp," said the major. "Two of them were working at the Savoy in London when they were arrested. They do produce the most marvellous meals. I never thought salt herrings could taste so good. And the coffee is extraordinary. They say they put an egg in it, which is probably wickedly extravagant, but my oh my, it's divine."

He pulled over a folding camp seat for Tyler, and his manner became grave. "Sir Percy came in person to inform me about the young woman who was killed. I have told Mrs. Devereau. We are both dreadfully shocked. Dreadfully. I knew the girl, Tyler. She used to come over here regularly to help some of the internees write their letters and to teach them English. God forbid with her accent, but better that than nothing as far as I'm concerned." He grimaced. "She was actually teaching some of them a few good old Saxon cuss words, but I had to put a stop to that."

"Have you found out any more about what happened?" Clare asked Tyler.

"Not yet. The coroner promised to rush through the postmortem, so I'll know preliminary results later today."

Fordham picked up a piece of paper and began to fan himself. "Elsie Bates was a lively girl. Very attractive. A diamond in the rough. Who on earth would attack her?"

Tyler had no answer for him.

"Sir Percy told me about the gun being a German Luger P-08," said Fordham. "He wants me to question the internees and of course I will, but I tell you now it's not likely to have come from here. The place is guarded and I don't know how anybody could slip out and back again undetected. Besides, we hold regular surprise inspections just in case one of them is concealing something they shouldn't. But as I told Sir Percy, we are dealing with refugees for the most part, mostly professional men, teachers, musicians, students. We're even housing some priests. They're all in here because they were originally German citizens who emigrated to England

and for one reason or another hadn't got their British papers in order. You should see what they've set up. It's a veritable university. Talks and lectures take place all day long. We're not dealing with the criminal classes here, Inspector."

He spoke with undisguised pride, a school headmaster sort of pride, which he'd been before he was called up.

"We're going to have a roll call and you can come and address them. Mrs. Devereau will act as translator. A lot of them speak English, some of them better than I do, but there are others for whom it's still rudimentary. Mrs. Devereau's help is invaluable." He beamed at her. "She acts as a sort of ombudsman as well, fielding complaints or requests for them. She also handles the post." He frowned. "We haven't told them anything about what has happened but I'm sure they're speculating. They're probably getting frightened. Contrary to what our esteemed war cabinet might think, these men have no reason to want Herr Hitler to take over England. A few of them have already had terrible experiences under Nazi rule. They feel tied and trussed here, as one man put it. In the event of an invasion they are convinced Jerry will massacre them . . . Ah, thank you, Nash."

Private Nash had returned holding a tray with a jug of lemonade and some glasses. Fordham took the tray and put it on the table. "Nash, you know who the camp father is, don't you? Dr. Beck. Tell him to start the roll call. I'll be there momentarily."

"Yes, sir." He marched off, full of self-importance, to do his job.

The major poured three glasses of lemonade and handed them around. Tyler downed his at once. Somehow the cook had managed to cool the drink, and it was sweet and tart at the same time. Not as good as a long pint of bitter, but it would have to do.

He was so aware of Clare, but he wondered what she saw when she looked at him. He hadn't lost his hair, thank God, but he was heavier than when she first knew him, although the extra weight was mostly muscle. He wished he didn't have the sunburn on his nose and cheeks, then cursed himself for that little bit of vanity.

Fordham put down his glass. "I'll just go and keep an eye on things. Be right back."

He ducked out of the tent.

"Tommy . . ."

At the same time Tyler said "Clare," and they both laughed.

"Rock, scissors, paper," said Tyler. "You first."

"No, you."

If you had asked him a month ago if he would ever say what he said next, he would have scoffed.

"Clare, I have never forgotten you . . ." He stopped. "But then what bloke would ever forget the first beautiful lass that put out for him?"

It was a crude thing to say and he was glad to see she reacted with a flinching of her shoulders.

"I suppose it's a bit late to apologize?"

"What, for putting out? Not necessary."

"You know what I mean. I shouldn't have left so suddenly."

He shrugged. "At least you sent me a letter. I've still got it. It's in my 'life lessons' file."

She took a deep breath. "I suppose I deserved that. Now isn't the time, but I do hope that we will have a chance before long to talk properly."

"I won't hold my breath."

He was being a right pillock and he knew it, but the hurt and anger was as strong as if it were last week that she'd left, not twenty years ago.

10.

The internees were jamming into the mess tent. A half dozen irrepressible younger men were kicking around a football on the strip of grass outside. He would have loved to join in, to run and tackle, show off how good he was, but he dared not. A couple of months ago, he'd foolishly revealed some of his skills when a loose ball had come his way. They'd pestered him then to join in. But teams were demarcated, skins or shirts. His scars might be noticed and he couldn't risk that.

Fear had raced through the camp like a wind. First, a big white Bentley arrived and the driver, a typical tweedy Englishman, upper crust, had hurried over to the major's tent. Nobody'd seen him before, but one man said he was the local squire. One of the guards at the gate was summoned and he quick-marched to fetch the translator. The squire stayed about half an hour, then drove off fast. A while later, one of their regular sentries had bicycled into the grounds. There was usually two of them arriving in a lorry. The soldier, an older man, had also gone straight to the major's tent. This unusual activity had started to attract attention and rumours sprang out of nowhere that the second soldier was dead, shot by a Jerry parachutist. Something was up. More whispering. Another rumour. The Nazis had taken London. The beginning of the invasion. Churchill was dead.

The older sentry emerged and went to the guard towers where he had a confab with the sentries. Must be the invasion. All activities stopped. The men started to gather around the camp father, Dr. Bruno Beck. He had been a psychiatrist by profession and it stood him in good stead. He listened to the agitated comments and questions of the internees and reassured them that there was no invasion imminent, nor was Churchill dead. The commandant would tell them soon enough what was afoot.

Yet another car drove in. Not a toff but a man with authority. He too went into the commandant's tent.

He wondered what his next orders would be. Hold tight, look and listen. "Never show them your fear, they will turn on you like a pack. No matter what you feel, no matter how much pain you are experiencing, never ever show it." That had been drilled into him in the early days, and time after time in the training sessions, he had been put to the test. And never failed. Truth was he missed that. Longed to show his mettle again, to be commended and praised. It was all very well to say he'd been specially selected for this important task, but there was nothing exciting about being stuck behind barbed wire for months, with nothing to do but watch and wait.

One of the guards came with the message to gather in the tent. Roll call was going to be taken. He joined the others and squeezed himself into the back row. There weren't enough tables for everybody to sit in one shift, and getting all the internees together meant many of them had to stand. There was a lot of grumbling and, in spite of Dr. Beck's reassurance, the anxiety in the air was palpable. Dr. Beck set the roll call in motion, each section leader checking off his list.

Finally, they were done and the group fell silent. Three people from outside the wire, plus a guard, were coming through the gate: the commandant, the female translator, and the man who had been the last to arrive. The major, stick under his arm, led the way. He was soft and out of shape and he always looked worried.

He had only contempt for such transparency.

The woman was different, which was why he rather admired

her, although she wasn't really his type. Too long in the tooth and too thin. He liked his women young, coarse, and full-bodied. Nevertheless, he had to admit she had presence, a cool English elegance that he could see would be attractive. She had an erect carriage, head high, chin up. Her clothes were of good quality but not ostentatious. In her dealings with the internees, she was invariably pleasant and had quickly become popular in this woman-starved environment. However, he found her hard to read. He wasn't sure if her aloofness was a typical characteristic of the well-bred Englishwoman, or if it was from some other cause.

The third member of the trio was walking at her side. He was above medium height, with carrot red hair, and he looked as if he'd been in the sun too long. But he wasn't a milksop like Major Fordham. He seemed fit and strong. He was in civilian clothes but there was something about the way his eyes roved quickly around the assembled men that suggested invested authority.

As they entered, the red-haired man stood back to let the woman through first, and as she went by he touched her lightly on her back.

Most men would have missed that, would not have seen the feeling in the redhead's body, but he saw it. So that was the story, was it? He coveted her. Was the feeling returned? It wasn't possible to tell at this point, but he registered the impression. You never knew when such knowledge would come in handy.

The doctor called for silence, and the commandant made his announcement. The woman translated fluently. She spoke excellent German with a Swiss accent.

What the major said was very disturbing.

A Land Army girl had been found dead. He knew who she was. A tasty bit he'd often fantasized about. She had been shot with a German Luger.

For a moment he doubted himself, but he knew nobody could have stolen the gun he had hidden so carefully. It had still been there this morning. He checked daily.

The redhead was a policeman, as he'd suspected, and his speech was brief and to the point. "Please do not think you are betraying a comrade if you report to me any suspicion, however slight. I will assess any information. This is a vicious murder we are dealing with."

He'd got through to them, although the likelihood of any of this bunch telling on one of their fellows was slim. They had learned to be leery of any police authority. "See everything, say nothing." They were, after all, enemy aliens.

Dr. Beck raised his finger for attention. His English was impeccable. "I am sure I speak for all of my fellow internees when I say that I am deeply shocked to hear what Inspector Tyler has said. Miss Bates was a kind and generous young woman in the prime of her life. We will miss her. We will, of course, do everything we can to help you facilitate his investigation. However, I do want to point out that we here in this camp are at a disadvantage. Most of us are irrefutably German and it is possible one of us may be familiar with weaponry, as you say, particularly German weaponry, but we are here behind barbed wire and we are guarded. We hope there will not be what perhaps might be referred to as scapegoating if the real perpetrator of this crime is not found soon."

There were murmurs of agreement from those of the men who understood, and they translated for the others around them, not waiting for the Englishwoman to do it.

"Our relationship with the local people of Shropshire has improved over the summer," continued Dr. Beck. "Some of them even come to our entertainments. I would hate to see that friendly climate spoiled by the irresponsible spreading of rumour regarding this particular gun."

One of the internees, their captive poet and self-proclaimed genius, waved his clenched fist to emphasize his support.

"I agree with Dr. Beck," he yelled.

The commandant asked the section captains to start organizing the men for the search. All belongings were to be placed outside the tents in orderly rows. With everybody's co-operation the whole thing wouldn't take long and they could soon resume their regular activities.

He had to reassure himself of the security of the hiding place he'd created for his own gun. But he knew the search would be perfunctory. Nobody wanted to act like a Nazi toward their own countrymen.

The trio was leaving now. The redhead went through the gate and the woman was close as she passed. He was right. The policeman did desire her, and perhaps the feeling was returned; he couldn't quite tell. They were not strangers to each other, he was certain of that.

The internees started to move away, talking excitedly and nervously among each other. With this incident and the policeman, a door had opened. Suspicions could be discreetly voiced. He'd have to be very careful. This stupid girl's death could really upset everything.

11.

THE MAJOR WENT OFF TO SUPERVISE THE SEARCH.

"Why don't you take a break, Mrs. Devereau? It might be best for the internees to deal with this among themselves. We'll be all right for now."

"Thank you, Major." Clare turned to Tyler. "Shall we take a quick run into Whitchurch for a bite to eat? I'm famished."

"Sounds good to me."

"How about our old pub? They used to have the greatest cider."

"Are you referring to The Feathers?"

"Yes, the one on Main Street. We went there lots of times for their cider."

"I've become a beer man myself. But let's give it a try. I can recommend the pork pies."

"I'll follow you in my car."

"You'd better go first. The Humber isn't exactly speedy."

He soon lost sight of the MG and must have fallen behind by at least five minutes when he arrived at The Feathers. She was waiting for him at the entrance.

"Come on, slow poke. I've already ordered our ciders, and I've got us our favourite spot. The booth by the window. The place hasn't changed a bit."

Tyler had almost convinced himself that Clare had no interest in connecting with their shared past, but now he wasn't so sure. *Our old pub, we went there lots of times* . . . The strange thing was that instead of making him happy that he wasn't the only one obsessing about the past, the turnaround was confusing. Maybe he'd been a policeman too long. You developed a suspicious nature.

He followed her through the smoky lounge, aware of the curious glances thrown in their direction. Even at forty, Clare turned heads.

She slid into the booth and he sat opposite.

"They changed the upholstery," she said. "It was brown before."

"After twenty years, I think they should. That's a long time."

The publican, who was also one of his football mates, came over immediately with two glasses of cider.

"The pork pies'll be ready in a minute."

As he was leaving, he raised his eyebrows questioningly, but Tyler ignored him.

Clare lifted her glass. "Cheers, Tom."

"Cheers." They clicked glasses and their eyes met. Even in the low light of the pub, he could see how green her eyes were, how friendly they appeared.

He took out his cigarette case, snapped it open, and offered her a cigarette.

She shook her head. "No, thanks, I gave up smoking years ago." She noticed the silver case. "Didn't I give you that for your coming of age birthday?"

"One and the same."

He didn't tell her he had only begun carrying it again after they met in the market.

She grimaced. "Twenty-one. Were we ever that young, Tom?"

He lit his cigarette. "Young and foolish. But here we are in 1940. Why don't you bring me up to date on the last twenty years?"

"Do you want the short version or the long version?"

"I thought you only had an hour."

"Short version then." She started to run her finger around the rim of the glass. He could see she was choosing her words carefully. "Two years after I left here, I met a Swiss man, Valentin Devereau. I'd known him casually when I was at school in Lucerne. We married and I have lived in Switzerland ever since, really. Shortly before war broke out, I decided to return to England – I told you that already. I still consider this my home. I knew my fluency in German might come in useful and it has. I was hired as a translator with the War Office. Then the big sweep occurred and eventually I was sent up here to Shropshire. That's it. Life up to date."

He was keenly aware that she hadn't mentioned falling in love with her husband or how she felt about being separated from him.

"Any children?"

"No. All right. Your turn."

Frank returned with the pork pies and mash, both covered with steaming gravy.

"Tuck in."

Clare started on her meal, eating with gusto. He smiled at her.

"What? Why are you laughing at me?"

"You always liked your grub, didn't you? I don't know why you're so skinny."

She shrugged. "Never mind. It's your turn to talk."

"Short version. I got married to a local girl not long after you left. Vera Lambeth. Maybe you remember her?"

Clare dabbed at her lips with the serviette. "She was the butcher's daughter, wasn't she? She always had a pash for you."

So she noticed that. He was glad. "We have two children. A boy, Jimmy, who is with the King's Shropshire Light Infantry. He's twenty now. He managed to get out of Dunkirk and he's waiting to be reassigned."

"That was a rough go from what I've heard."

"He won't talk about it. My daughter, Janet, is sixteen. She's working in her grandfather's shop, also doing her bit for the war effort." He wanted her to be as curious about his marriage as he was about hers, but she didn't comment.

He balanced his cigarette on the edge of the ashtray and began his meal. He'd thought he was hungry, but his stomach was churning so much, it was hard getting the food down.

"And now you're an inspector. Acts of bravery, according to Percy."

"I don't know about that. I stopped a runaway horse, nothing to it. But I was already an inspector so it didn't count. I worked with the Birmingham force for a few years, but Vera missed her family here, and I thought with war looming on the horizon, sleepy Shropshire would be safer."

"You miss the challenge don't you?" Clare said sympathetically. "I can tell."

Tyler shrugged. "That's life. You make choices and you have to live with them."

He hadn't meant that statement to be fraught with hidden meaning but it lay on the table between them like a smelly piece of fish. Clare chose to ignore it.

"How is your family doing?" she asked.

"My dad died five years ago. My mom has gone to live with my sister in the Hebrides."

Clare toyed with the serviette. "They didn't like me very much, did they?"

He flicked the ash off the cigarette. "Dad thought I was betraying my class; Mom said you'd break my heart."

She sat back in the booth, her eyes lowered.

"I'm sorry, Tom. Can we lay the past to rest? I'd like to be friends."

He turned around so he could get Frank's attention. "Let's

drink to that. We can't spend the entire time apologizing to each other."

The silence was awkward between them and neither spoke until the publican brought more cider.

She sipped at it. "It's not quite as good as I remember, but then perhaps nothing is. We look at the past through rose-coloured glasses most of the time."

"Clare!"

"Tom. You could have got in touch with me. You never answered my letter."

"It seemed a waste of time. It was all over and done. As you say, we were young. What did we know?"

She put aside the glass, unfinished, and looked at her watch, a dainty silver one, no doubt Swiss.

"I have to get going soon. I just wanted to say that I was so sorry to hear about that young woman who was killed. It's dreadful."

"That it is. Did you ever meet her?"

Clare shook her head. "No, I didn't. Do you know what happened?"

"Not yet. It has the earmarks of a *crime passional*, but we'll have to see."

"You said she was found on a country road."

"Yes, she was. She was apparently heading for the manor."

"If there is anything I can do . . ."

Impulsively, he grasped her hand. "You can meet me again. I've been a right pillock. I would like to be friends."

Before she could answer, they heard a few *bravissimo* bars on the piano. There weren't many people in the pub, just a handful of men, all pensioners by the look of them, and only a couple of women, maybe their wives. One of the men, who had a natty cravat knotted around his throat, had gone over the piano.

"Any requests?"

A woman called out, "Play 'We'll Meet Again.'"

"Oh, no," muttered Clare. "Not that one, please."

Her eyes met Tyler's, and they both burst out laughing.

"You can ring me at the manor," said Clare. "I have my own telephone. I'm free most evenings."

He stubbed out his cigarette and began to stand up, but she stopped him. "Finish your cider." She leaned forward and her lips brushed his cheek. "Bye for now, Tom. I look forward to hearing from you soon."

She walked off and, in spite of himself, he watched her.

Then he took out another cigarette, lit it, and held the silver case in his hands. She'd had his initials engraved in the corner, and inside: *Love forever, C.*

The pianist's fingers were gnarled and stiff and his voice was slightly tremulous but he still had the technique.

We'll meet again,
Don't know where, don't know when
But we'll meet again some sunny day.

The others joined in, lost in the poignancy of the song.

We'll meet again, some sunny day.

Then a voice shouted from one of the corners.

"For Christ's sake, Gerald, sing something cheerful before we all give up the bleeding ghost. How about something lively like 'Pack Up Your Troubles in Your Old Kit Bag?'"

The singer didn't hesitate and switched immediately.

Tyler left them clapping their hands and singing loudly and off-key.

12.

HE CRANKED THE CAR, WHICH FOR ONCE STARTED nicely. He was about to drive off when a farm lorry drew up across the road. Arthur Trimble was driving. Tyler leaned out of the window. This was as good a time as any.

"Mr. Trimble, can I have a word?"

The manager favoured a long moustache that must have been a challenge when he was eating, and that added to his hangdog look. He wore tweeds and high leather boots. Natty clothes. Squire's clothes. The word muttered among the locals was that he was aping his betters, not a good opinion to have hung on yourself.

He squinted at Tyler through the sun. "What about? I'm just going for my dinner."

"Why don't I join you then? Save us both time."

Trimble didn't move. "I likes a bit of peace and quiet when I'm eating. What do you want to talk to me about?"

"If you prefer the whole neighbourhood knows your business that's all right with me, but I'm actually conducting a police investigation. You can talk to me out here in front of the door, or in a quiet place inside, or better yet, you can come down to the station."

"You can't make me do that."

"Oh yes I can. And I will. I was just giving you a bit of a break by suggesting we talk here. We can find a nice private spot at the back."

"I'll give you half an hour," said Trimble.

Tyler followed him inside and indicated the same nook

where he and Clare had been.

Frank came over looking surprised, but only said, "Another cider?"

"Nothing thanks. I'm just a spectator."

"The usual for you, Arthur?"

He got the nod and bustled off.

"This your office now, is it?" Trimble asked.

"Any place, anywhere, is our motto. Crime is no respecter of location."

Frank returned with a pint of bitter and a plate heaped with thick bacon strips, eggs, beans, and fried bread. Trimble dived into the food as if he hadn't eaten for days. Tyler watched fascinated to see what he'd do with his moustache, and sure enough it soon became smeared with egg yolk. He managed to avoid looking at the beer which had a nice head of foam. He took out a cigarette and lit it, not offering one to Trimble.

"You've heard about the death of this young Land Army girl, I assume?"

"I have. Sir Percy told me. Shame about that."

"You knew her, I understand."

Trimble shot him a glance. "She was one of the Land Army billets, if that's what you mean."

"What was your impression of her?"

Trimble sopped up some egg yolk with his fried bread. "Not much. Not that I'm going to speak ill of the dead 'cos I'm not, but she was a bit of a trollop in my opinion."

"I heard you were one of her conquests."

He'd hoped he'd get a rise out of him, but Trimble must have been expecting the question, and he showed no reaction.

"Who told you that?" He stuffed the last of the bacon strips into his mouth.

"Doesn't matter who told me. Was it true?"

Trimble shrugged, pushed back his plate, and started to pick his teeth. "I wouldn't say I was a conquest. Truth be told, she went after me. I felt sorry for her. Young girl like that from the city. Never seen a cow before. She said she missed all the excitement of London. She was homesick like. So I gave her a few things to cheer her up. Some chocolates once in a while, some fresh eggs when I could. That sort of thing. Nothing illegal. All on my own rations." He studied a piece of bacon that he'd rescued from his back teeth, then finished it off. "I soon saw she was using me and I moved on. Wounded her vanity, most like. She was quite nasty after that." He gulped down some of his bitter.

"Funny, that's not the story I heard," said Tyler, rather carelessly blowing smoke in Trimble's direction. "I heard you were smitten with the girl and you were furious when she broke off the relationship."

The manager frowned. "It was the exact opposite. It was me that ended it." He made a point of looking over at the grandfather clock near the corner of the bar. "Is that all you wanted to know?"

"Can you tell me where you were this morning between the hours of six and seven o'clock?"

"Where I usually am, working about the estate. We start early."

"Can anybody vouch for you?"

"Speak to Lady Somerville. I was clearing out a place to plant a victory garden. She knew about it."

"With you, was she? She keeps early hours."

"No, she wasn't with me as such, but she knew what I was doing."

Tyler knew that the talk was that Lady Somerville was starting to forget a lot of things and couldn't tell you what day it was unless it happened to be a Sunday, church day, or rent collection day on Friday.

"Did you see anybody else yourself?"

"I wasn't looking, was I? I had my jobs to do and I did them."

"Other than trying to determine how to avoid the rose beds, what else were you doing exactly?"

Trimble paused to fish for the last vestige of trapped bacon. "I was mostly tidying up the potting shed. Her ladyship likes to see it clean and neat when she does her own spot of gardening."

Trimble had dark brown eyes and heavy eyebrows. Where he was sitting was shadowy and it was hard to read his expression. Tyler sensed he wasn't going to get any further, not today anyway. The man had come well armoured.

"One more question. Have you ever owned a German Luger P-08 pistol?"

"Never."

"You didn't bring back a souvenir from the last war, for instance?"

"No. I wasn't in the front line. I was with the main quartermaster store down in London."

"Comfy crib, eh?"

Trimble scowled. "We can't all be heroes, can we? I was doing essential work. What about you? Doing the usual? Chasing down lost sheep, were you?"

"As a matter of fact I was with the Shropshires. We saw a lot of action."

"You'll have to tell me your war stories some time," Trimble said with a sneer.

Tyler drew on his cigarette. The bloody man had got the upper hand and he wasn't sure why. Perhaps because he'd scored a hit with the remark about lost sheep.

"Do you know of anybody who might have owned a Luger?"

"Sir Percy told me she'd been shot. Was that the weapon?"

Tyler wished Sir P. had been a bit more discreet, but it was too late now. "We'll have to run tests but we did find a Luger near the body."

"Well, I'm not the one who shot her. Personally, I'd think you should go to the camp. Crammed with Krauts that place." He upended his beer glass, leaving foam on his moustache.

Tyler got to his feet. "Thanks for your time, Trimble. Glad you got in your dinner. Try the apple pudding; I hear it's good."

He left him, nodded to Frank, and went out to his car.

He didn't like Trimble, never had. They'd first met at the local horticultural show where Trimble had been displaying Lady Somerville's roses. There was the usual hotly contested competition in the Best Bloom category. Trimble had actually accused the judge of undue bias and insisted that Tyler investigate. He had considered the issue utterly trivial, but had been forced to follow up. He'd found no instance of bias on the judge's part. "Better blooms, Inspector, much better blooms. Her ladyship needs to invest in some good sheep shit."

Tyler got into the Humber, took out his notebook, and wrote down some of the things Trimble had said. If it came to a choice of believing him or Rose Watkins, he'd take Rose anytime. Elsie wasn't a girl to elicit pity. Quite the opposite. However, the fact that the man was a fart catcher, and a shite bucket to boot, didn't mean he was guilty of murder.

Tyler stashed his notebook back in his pocket. A chat with Alice Thorne was in order and she was probably to be found at her regular stall in the square. He put the car in gear and backed out.

13.

AFTER THE STARTLING ANNOUNCEMENT BY THE police inspector, most of the internees had remained in the mess tent, talking amongst themselves. Worried, questioning talk. Several had clustered around Dr. Beck.

"We must present a petition to Major Fordham without delay," said Beck. "Kurt, will you help to draft it? Your English is good. We must emphasize our willingness to co-operate with the police if necessary, and our support of the British government. Lard it, as they say."

Kurt Bader was a young, round-faced lad, with straw-blond hair and clean-cut features. His mother was Jewish and he endured some teasing from the others about being the imperfect Aryan.

Bader grinned. "With a trowel, Doctor."

"What is 'lard it'?" asked Herr Gold.

Beck was about to explain when they heard somebody calling from the direction of the tents.

"Dr. Beck. Dr. Beck. Come quickly."

The seminarian, Hans Hoeniger, his black cassock flapping in the wind, was hurrying to the tent. Drawn by the urgency in his voice, Beck stood up.

"What's the matter?"

"It's Herr Hartmann," said Hoeniger, gasping. "He's in his tent. I was walking by and I heard him . . . he's distraught. I popped my head in and tried to talk to him, but it seemed to make him worse. You'd better come and see to him."

Gunther Hartmann was close to seventy, a violinist who

shouldn't have been in the camp at all, but had been brought there at his own request. He'd told the others it was the only place he felt safe. Earlier in the year, when the local police started to round up enemy aliens, he had chosen to go along with the other Jewish members of the orchestra he played with. The upheaval and the stress on an already fragile personality had brought him to the edge of a breakdown. Quietly and privately, Dr. Beck had been helping him.

The Jesuit priest, Father Glatz, looked at him anxiously. "Shall I come with you? I believe he trusts me."

Hoeniger led the way with Beck and the priest close behind.

As they approached one of the tents in Row A, they could indeed hear a loud wailing. Another voice was interjecting, but without effect, it seemed.

The seminarian lifted the tent flap and Beck stepped inside. Herr Hartmann was huddled in the far corner between his cot and the little cupboard the internees were given for their belongings. He was rocking back and forth, keening. A man was kneeling beside him, trying his best to soothe him. It was Howard Silber, in his previous life an actor of some prominence. Usually he was flamboyant and loud, but at the moment he was out of his depth. He turned to Beck in relief.

"What's the matter with him? I can't calm him down."

"Allow me," said Beck, and he went over to the distraught man and crouched down so he was on a level. He spoke in German.

"Dr. Beck here, Professor. Can you talk to me?"

Hartmann didn't seem to hear him. He was completely lost in his own terror. Beck glanced over his shoulder.

"Hans, will you run to my tent? In my cupboard you will find a leather case. Bring it here if you please. Quick as you can."

The seminarian hurried off. Beck's voice continued, calm and confident. "Father Glatz, would you open a few flaps so we can have more light and air? Mr. Silber, will you be so kind as to keep people out of here?"

Silber stood up, and suddenly Hartmann shrieked, pointed at him, and shouted something in German.

"What did he say?" asked the actor, startled.

More crying and words tumbled from the older man.

Silber had been born to German parents on English soil. He couldn't speak a word of German and considered himself English to the core. It was obvious he was the focus of the professor's fear.

"What's he saying?" he asked again.

Beck shook his head. "I can't quite understand him. He seems to think you are an enemy. A spy for the Gestapo."

"Me? Good grief. Why would he think that?"

Beck didn't answer, but reverted to German, and continued to talk to Hartmann, whose eyes were dilated with terror.

Hoeniger returned with the case and handed it to Beck, who took out a syringe and a vial.

"Hans, I'm afraid our friend will struggle, but I need to give him some sedation. Will you hold his arm steady for me?"

Hartmann fought like a man in fear of his life, and it took both Hoeniger and Father Glatz to hold him still so that Beck could administer the drug. It was normally fast-acting, but it was several minutes before the professor quieted down. Finally, he succumbed and his head fell back.

"Give me that pillow, if you please, Hans," said Beck. "We'll leave him where he is for the time being."

"What happened?" asked Hoeniger, as they made the old man as comfortable as they could.

"I'm afraid this noble man was arrested by the Nazis just before war broke out, and he was sent to the concentration camp at Dachau. He is as far from being a political person as is possible, but in his youth he wrote a critique of Wagner's music. He wasn't partial to our great German and made some derogatory remarks, as youth are apt to do. We can only think that the article resurfaced and that was why he was arrested, although the charge was never specified. He was severely mistreated in the camp, and when he was released, he discovered his wife of many years had died."

"Poor fellow," said Glatz. "He always seems so unassuming, except when he plays, when it is as if the angels visit."

"Will you please speak in English," interrupted Silber. "I have no idea what you're saying."

Beck translated what had just been said.

"I thought the relative tranquility of the camp life was helping him to heal, but what happened today has brought back all the injustice and trauma of his past incarceration. He believes we will all be killed. That the enemy is at the gates."

"Lordy, I hope that isn't true," exclaimed Silber. Even in the hot weather, he affected a long black cloak, the insignia of his profession, and he wrapped it around himself as if it could shield him.

"Should Herr Hartmann be sent to the hospital?" asked the priest.

"No. It would frighten him more," answered Beck. "If one of you gentlemen would be so kind as to relinquish your bed, I will remain here until he is himself again."

"Take mine gladly," said Silber. "People in that sort of state frighten me. By the way, Doctor, why did he pick on me?"

"He thought you were a Nazi spy. He says he's seen a man coming and going in the camp at night. He thinks it was you."

"Good Lord. It certainly was *not* me!"

This time it was Hans Hoeniger, the seminarian, who requested a translation. He looked at Silber, who guessed what he was thinking.

"For God's sake tell them I'm not a spy, Dr. Beck. They're both staring at me as if they believe it."

Beck admonished both of them, slipping from English to German with ease. "Let's be sensible, gentlemen. Professor Hartmann has suffered a psychotic episode. We cannot take seriously what he says. He also thinks the Italians are putting poison in the food, and that Major Fordham is in league with the Gestapo. When he is more himself, I shall question him, but I can assure you, he is quite delusional."

Hartmann moaned. Beck reached under the man's cot, and pulled out a worn leather violin case. He placed it in the professor's arms the way you might place a doll for a child.

"I fear he will never be completely stable. The trauma he suffered previously at the hands of the Nazis was too great. But as long as he can play his violin, he will survive."

"It's not just the announcement today that set him off, Doctor," said Hoeniger. "This morning I saw one of the guards aiming his rifle at us. He had us in his sights. We were playing chess outside your tent. I think Herr Hartmann must have seen him."

"That's unconscionable," said Beck. "I shall speak to Major Fordham about it. Which one was it?"

"Smallish fellow with a bit of a moustache."

Beck sighed. "I shall report him. Thank you for your help, gentlemen. I will sit here until the professor wakes up."

"Can I bring you something?" asked Hoeniger.

Beck smiled. "I do believe that I would thoroughly enjoy my chessboard. I like to play out games with myself."

"My dear doctor," said the priest, "I would be more than happy to give you a match."

"Thank you, Philipp, but you consistently beat me. When our friend comes to consciousness, I'd like him to wake into an atmosphere of tranquility and peace."

Father Glatz chuckled. "You are getting better all the time, Bruno. When we eventually leave here, I'll wager you will checkmate me."

Silber gasped. "God's socks. I should get going. The show must go on, no matter what happens. Hans, will you help me out?"

He mimed what he'd said.

The seminarian understood and he nodded. "Yah." He turned to the priest. "May I be excused, Father?"

"You may."

Beck said, "Will you reassure the others that Herr Hartmann is all right?"

"Yes, Doctor."

Silber gesticulated at the young man. "No say me spy. Understand? Not spy. Don't tell people."

Beck helped him out with a quick translation.

Hoeniger grinned. "Tell him I won't."

The two of them left.

"I'll fetch your chessboard," said the priest.

Beck moved to the cot and gazed down at the sleeping man.

"Beware children and mad men and those that have nothing whatsoever to lose," said his teacher, half ironically. *"They have a way of telling the truth, and usually that is the last thing you want."*

14.

THE MARKET WAS BUSY WITH HOUSEWIVES IN SEARCH of fresh produce and meat at a good price. Alice Thorne's stall was at the end of the row near a patch of grass where she'd tethered her goat. The locals added this to her long list of unacceptable eccentricities. A little pony was all right, even a donkey, but a goat pulling the cart was queer as far as they were concerned. Alice told all who asked that Nellie was very economical. She ate anything and everything and she provided milk. At the end of her days, she'd be food for the dogs.

Tyler parked the Humber and walked through the market. Ringed around the square were black-beamed Elizabethan houses with their narrow mullioned windows glittering in the sun. Pretty to look at, uncomfortable to live in, said the residents. For one fleeting moment, he enjoyed the illusion that everything was normal. That there wasn't a war burning up the world and that life was going along in the same way it had for a few hundred years on these old cobblestones.

Alice stood out among the farmer's wives at the other tables, with their flowered pinafore dresses. She was wearing a coolie-style straw hat tied underneath her chin with a white ribbon. Her khaki dungarees and green cotton shirt were practical, but certainly couldn't be considered feminine or proper. Two of her dogs were lying beside her. They both looked up as he approached. Tyler had visited Alice's cottage a few times over the past summer and the dogs remembered him. She saw him and smiled a welcome.

"Good afternoon, Tom. Don't tell me you've come to caution me again? My rabbit fence is escape-proof, I promise."

Several of the local farmers had complained that Alice was breeding rabbits that escaped and ate their crops. She claimed she was rescuing them from cruel traps and a nasty death from being gassed in the burrows. Tyler believed her, but periodically he was obliged to inspect her property to make sure.

"Afternoon, Alice. No, I'm here on a different mission today."

Nobody was buying at her stall and he could see the table was still loaded with her produce and herbs.

"The war news must have been particularly bad today," she said. "I've been practically boycotted." She gestured at the woman a few stalls down who seemed to be watching them. "Also, Mrs. Tanner scares away my customers. I have sold only three herbal bouquets and exactly one cluster of tomatoes to a visitor, an evacuee, I believe, who didn't notice my sign."

She indicated a large, neatly printed sign that was propped up against a pot of white poppies.

WEAR A WHITE POPPY FOR PEACE. Beside that was a larger framed notice.

I RENOUCE WAR FOR ITS CONSEQUENCES, FOR THE LIES IT LIVES ON AND PROPAGATES, FOR THE UNDYING HATRED IT AROUSES, FOR THE DICTATORSHIPS IT PUTS IN THE PLACE OF DEMOCRACY, FOR THE STARVATION THAT STRIKES AFTER IT. DR. FOSDICK. (FROM "THE UNKNOWN SOLDIER")

"These are nervous times," said Tyler. "Perhaps you could be a little more discreet. The sign is a bit blatant."

"I've never suggested you be more discreet about your sign that says 'Police Station,' have I?" she answered tartly.

"You know that's not that same thing. 'Police Station' isn't a political statement."

"To some people it is."

Tyler picked up one of the cards from a small stack by the poppies. The pledge was printed at the top. *I renounce war, and I will never support or sanction another.* Underneath was room for name and address.

"Did you have any takers today?"

Alice grimaced. "I respect you, Tom Tyler, but you are a detective after all. I won't burden you with knowledge you might feel compelled to act upon. These are nervous times, as you so rightly pointed out." She sighed. "I've had a dearth of visitors. Need often overcomes scruples, but today Mrs. Tanner's tomatoes, although nowhere near as plump and juicy as mine, were more palatable." She spoke with irony but Tyler thought there was a weariness in her voice he hadn't heard before. "I think she blames me for the fact that her husband is missing in action in France."

"That's not very rational, is it?"

Alice shrugged. "I'm surprised how attached she seems to have become to Alfred Tanner now that he's missing. It wasn't that obvious when he was at home. Perhaps absence does make the heart grow fonder."

The Tanners' tumultuous marriage was well known in the town. Tyler laughed, nodding his head. For some reason the movement caused a white hot stab of pain over his right eye. He winced and rubbed his temple. A fiendish drummer was playing a tune on his temples.

"You don't have something for a headache, do you, Alice?"

"As a matter of fact, I do." She picked up one of the small brown bottles that were on the table. "This is oil of lavender. Rub it on your temples . . . do you want me to do it?"

Without waiting for his reply, she took out her handkerchief and dabbed some of the oil on to it. "Bend forward a bit." Feeling all of six years old, Tyler did as she said. The oil was pungent. "Of course, you wouldn't get a headache like this if you drank less."

"I got too much sun," he said, trying to muster up some righteous indignation. *Crikey, Alice, a bit of tact goes a long way as the ambassador said.*

"Here." She handed him the vial. "Keep it. You'll probably need it again."

He slipped it into his pocket. Then he glanced around to make sure nobody was approaching them. Mrs. Tanner was as focused on them as a vixen on a hen. He leaned in a little closer to Alice.

"Have you heard about the death of this young Land Army girl?"

"It's the talk of the market. What happened? There are so many rumours flying around, it is hard to get to the truth."

Briefly, Tyler filled her in on the situation.

"I am very sorry to hear that."

"I found a bunch of white poppies lying on her body," continued Tyler. "I wonder if you know anything about that? Did you sell her some? Her name was Elsie Bates. Light brown hair, pretty girl."

Alice sighed. "Yes, I know who she was. She often came to the market. My political views didn't seem to bother her. She particularly liked my lemon verbena soap. She didn't buy any poppies. We had a laugh about her signing the Peace Pledge. She said she was enjoying the war and hoped it lasted a long time. I don't think she really meant it, but I think she liked to be outrageous. I liked her a lot. Two peas in a pod, you might say."

Ever since she had arrived in Whitchurch, Alice had scandalized the local residents. She wore men's clothes, was outspoken about her opinions, which were usually different from everybody else's, and lived by herself in an isolated spot in the country with only dogs and rabbits for company.

"So you're sure Elsie Bates didn't buy poppies?"

"Of course, I'm sure. It would have been a momentous occasion."

"And nobody else has bought any recently?"

"No, they haven't. But they do grow wild in the woods. Anybody can pick them."

"One more thing, Alice. Did you hear anything unusual early this morning? Bangs? Shouts? Anything like that?"

"No. Sound doesn't travel where I am. Too many trees." Alice got to her feet. "I think I'll start packing up. It looks hopeless for customers." She nudged the dogs. "Move Lucy, Skip, there's good dogs."

"Need any help?" Tyler asked.

"You can get those paintings down for me if you will."

Tyler hadn't noticed the paintings she had propped up high on a wooden shelf behind her. There were four medium-sized canvases; three were landscapes, the fourth was a reclining female nude, her back to the artist.

He stared at the painting. The lines of that shoulder and hip were achingly familiar. He'd studied them often enough, traced them with his fingertips. He felt as if his breath was taken away from him.

"Where did you get that painting, Alice?"

"I have a friend in London. He used to be an art dealer, but nowadays business is terrible for him. He asked if he could send me a few canvases to see if I could sell them up here. So far I've had no takers."

"Can I take a closer look?"

"It's good, isn't it? So evocative. The woman is naked and she seems quite at home in those rich furnishings. She's young and well nourished; look at the gold echoes: her hair, the sunlight, the satin pillow she's resting on. A contemporary princess. And yet at the same time, the artist has managed to suggest a certain vulnerability. Very skilful."

There was a signature and a date in the corner. Pamina Leiderer 1926. Nobody Tyler had heard of.

"You say you got it from an art dealer?"

Alice lowered her voice. "This is in confidence, Tom. Pamina is a German Jew. She was a most respected sculptor and painter living in Berlin, but like many others was forced to flee for her life in '36 with only a few of her art pieces. At the moment, she's interned with the other female enemy aliens in Holloway prison, of all places. I took the art in the hope of getting her a little extra money. But you've got to keep it under your hat. If word gets out that she's German, I won't sell a thing."

Clare had been in Berlin as a young woman; her path must have crossed with that of the artist then.

"I have another portrait of Pamina's if you're interested," continued Alice. "I didn't put it out because I've found it better to just show a few at a time. Besides, people seem to prefer landscapes. You're the first person to show any interest in the nude. It's the same model, I believe."

She unwrapped another canvas that was in a piece of clean sacking. This one was slightly smaller than the other and less finished. In this sketch, the woman was sitting in a chair, head slightly turned away. Her fair hair partially obscured her face, which was only sketched in. She was wearing a long sheer nightgown of some green gauzy material, and the light made it transparent, revealing the outline of small, exquisitely shaped breasts. He remembered them.

"How much do you want for the two of them?" he asked Alice.

"Three pounds."

"I don't have that much with me."

"You can owe me. I trust you. Here, I'll wrap them both together in this cloth. You don't particularly want folks gawking at them, I'm sure."

He'd have to keep them hidden in his office at the police station.

Alice handed over the canvases and Tyler tucked them both underneath his arm, said goodbye, and headed back to his car. He felt like Jack who'd stolen the golden goose.

As he went by the last stall, the woman called out loudly to him so that Alice could hear. "When are you going to charge that woman, Inspector? Our boys are dying for t'country and *that one's* preaching peace, as *she* calls it. She's a fifth columnist if you ask me."

15.

TYLER SUBSCRIBED TO THE THEORY THAT THE MORE you knew about the victim and their style of life, the more you'd get pointers as to who had committed the ultimate act of murder. He'd already gathered a lot from Rose. Now he wanted to see where Elsie had lodged for the last two months.

The Clarks lived at the end of a row of Victorian workers cottages, all of them now quite prettied up. The tiny patch of front garden was full of shrubs and flowers, the handkerchief-sized lawn was bowling green immaculate. Mrs. Clark was a widow with an attentive son.

Constable Collis was standing in front of the door.

"Afternoon, Collis. Anything to report?"

"No, sir. People came when they heard what had happened, but they all stayed in the living room talking to Mrs. Clark. She's in there now."

"Where's the girl's room?"

"Upstairs, sir, at the far end of the landing."

"I'll go straight up and take a gander. Tell Mrs. Clark I'll come and talk to her."

Tyler stepped into the dark hall. Both walls were lined with ornately framed oil paintings that were amateurish enough to be originals. There was a wooden hat stand, and a small table cluttered with china figurines. He could hear the sounds of a wireless from the living room.

He went up the stairs, which were carpeted but which creaked loudly.

Elsie's room was small, the bed narrow, and the dresser

minuscule. The largest piece of furniture was an old-fashioned mahogany wardrobe which took up most of the space. Mrs. Clark clearly liked flowers, and the coverlet and matching curtains were a riot of daisies and begonias.

Somehow, given Elsie's personality, Tyler had expected the room would be untidy, with pieces of her life scattered everywhere, but it wasn't. It was as neat as a sailor's.

He stood in the doorway, trying in some way to make contact with the life and personality of the dead girl. Even though it was tiny, the room was pretty, lots of light, nicely furnished, except for the monster wardrobe, which must have been a family heirloom by the look of it. He walked over there first. The front was mirrored, although there was a slight distortion in the glass which elongated his upper torso. He could imagine Elsie turning to see if her stocking seams were straight. Her presence felt very strong.

He opened the wardrobe door and a sweet flowery scent wafted out. There were four frocks hanging there, all summery, three of them flowered prints, the fourth more elegant in blue and grey striped silk. On the upper shelf sat four wide-brimmed straw hats with ribbons to match the dresses; on the bottom of the wardrobe were her shoes: two white leather slingbacks and one pair of black patent high heels, clearly meant for dancing.

Next, he turned his attention to the dresser. There was a dainty ceramic tray on top of a crocheted runner; a little bag of sweets stood next to a large bottle of scent; beside it, a jar of cream, the label hand-printed with the initials *A.T.* He unscrewed the lid and took a sniff. The ubiquitous lavender, or maybe that was all he could smell at the moment. Alice's oil was potent.

In a matching china dish was Elsie's makeup. Two lipsticks, both bright red; a silver powder compact; an eyebrow pencil and a little pot of rouge. Her war paint. He opened the wooden jewellery box. An ivory hair comb; silver and pearl drop earrings; a pair of plain gold hoops that looked expensive. She also had a silver charm bracelet which clinked when he picked it up to look at it. The usual assembly of charms. Janet had been collecting hers since she was fourteen. Teapot, shoe, horse, cat, her initial. Charms were a popular and easy gift to give a girl. Over the years, she could collect as many as would fit on the bracelet. None of these looked particularly new. No heart with a fake diamond in the centre that might be a special gift from a boyfriend.

He pulled open the top drawer. Here Elsie kept her working clothes, all Land Army issue. Sturdy cotton knickers, wool socks, an extra cream-coloured shirt, green wool pullover, and tie, tossed around as if she dressed in a hurry or didn't care. The second drawer was very different indeed. An after-hours drawer this one, with everything neatly folded. Silk underwear, lace brassiere; three pair of silk stockings, two still in the package; a pair of cami-knickers in black taffeta. Carefully, he lifted out all of the items and placed them on the bed. Tucked away at the back of the drawer, he discovered an unopened package of prophylactics, stamped with the British Army insignia. Also shoved to the back of the drawer was a box of Cadbury's chocolates. Two pieces had been eaten already. He wondered why Elsie had hidden the chocolates. In this house she had privacy so she didn't have to keep them secret, unlike the French letters, which would have shocked Mrs. Clark if she'd even recognized what they were.

He returned everything to the drawer except the condoms, which he put in his pocket. He'd save Mrs. Clark or Elsie's mother the embarrassment of finding them.

On the bedside table was a pile of magazines. He took a quick check: *Woman's Weekly, The Land Girl.* No letters, no diary. Nothing personal. There was one cup with congealing milk in the bottom.

He looked underneath the bed, but there was nothing, not even dust.

There was a soft tap-tapping at the window. A branch from a tree outside was scratching on the window pane. He pushed up the sash and almost laughed out loud. Growing outside was a chestnut tree with wide, big branches, which partially obscured a ladder leaning against the wall. He could have climbed out himself if need be, and he'd bet any money that Elsie, young and agile, would have used this as a special exit if she didn't want Mrs. Clark to know what she was doing. By the same token, she could have entertained a lover in secret.

He closed the window. That seemed to be that. He collected the cup and went onto the landing. Constable Collis was waiting at the bottom of the stairs, half leaning against the wall, not knowing what to do with himself.

"I've seen all I need to for now, Constable. You can go back to the station."

Collis headed off, and Tyler went to the kitchen where Mrs. Clark was waiting for him.

"I made a pot of tea, Inspector. Would you like some?"

"Thank you kindly, Mrs. Clark. Here's a cup that was in the room."

Mrs. Clark's eyes filled with tears. "She loved her Horlicks. She'd never had it before . . . I don't think her family was very well off. There were lots of things that were new to her. Matching china for one. She particularly remarked about that." Mrs. Clark pulled a handkerchief out of her apron pocket and wiped at her eyes. "I'm sorry, Inspector. I think it's just really hitting me what has happened. There were some as didn't like Miss Bates. They thought she was on the common side, if you know what I mean. But she was very good to me.

Always giving me a hand when she could. She even bought me a pair of silk stockings. Can you imagine me in silk stockings? But it was a nice thought."

Tyler made sympathetic noises and sat quietly until she had poured his tea and he had doctored it up to his liking.

"I'll be in touch with her family to see about her possessions, but that will take a little while. I hope it won't be inconvenient for you if we leave he room as it is for now."

"Not at all. That is the spare room and I never use it except at Christmas when my sister visits." She wiped her eyes again. "It will be so strange without Elsie. She worked long hours and, being a young woman, she was often out in the evenings, but she was good company when she was here. We'd listen to the wireless together."

"Did Miss Bates ever bring anybody home with her?"

Mrs. Clark blinked. "A boyfriend you mean? Oh no. Not that I would have minded as long as they sat in the living room, but no, she never did. She could have anybody she wanted, she was that pretty, but she always met them out at the dances."

"Did she mention anybody in particular? Any names that you recall?"

"Now that you mention it, a couple of weeks ago she did say she thought she had met somebody special. She gave a little laugh, like a schoolgirl, and whispered in my ear. 'Mrs. C–' that's what she called me. 'Mrs. C., I might bring him home one of these days and you can tell me what you think.' She treated me more like a mother than a landlady. Her own parents and her didn't get along. They never wrote to her and she never wrote to them, so I were a substitute I suppose you'd say." She hesitated and put her hand to her mouth. "Do you think it was a jealous boyfriend that killed her?"

"I don't know. It's a possibility."

"She did have a best friend who came with her from London. She lives at the manor with the other girls. She probably knows a lot more than me. She came here a few times on the weekend to meet Elsie if they were going to a dance. Little scrap of a girl. A proper cockney that I could hardly understand sometimes, but very polite. She was in Elsie's shadow and hardly said boo when she was here, but they seemed like really good friends. Rose is her name."

"When did you last see Miss Bates?" Tyler asked.

"Last evening, it was. She brought in some fish and chips for our tea. She was always good like that. I went to bed early, oh about eight o'clock. I was feeling a bit poorly with my rheumatics. I left her sitting right there in front of the fire. She was listening to the wireless."

Tyler waited while Mrs. Clark wiped at her eyes.

"Did she go out again?"

"Not that I'm aware of." Mrs. Clark fiddled at her ear. "I wear hearing aids and I take them out at night. They're so uncomfortable if you don't."

"So you didn't hear anything?"

"No."

"What about this morning?"

"We have an arrangement because she has to get up so early. I leave her tea ready and the bread for toast. She makes her own breakfast."

"Did she do that this morning?"

"No, she didn't. Everything was where I'd left it. It wasn't that unusual if she was late, though. She would just rush out and get something to eat at the hostel."

In fact, Elsie Bates could have been out all night, thought Tyler.

He got to this feet. "Thank you so much for your help, Mrs. Clark. I'll probably have to come and talk to you again, but I will certainly let you know when we have any news."

"I would appreciate that, Inspector. I know she was only here for two months but I did grow very fond of her."

16.

Rose had slept for less than an hour when Violet came into the library and woke her up. For one blissful moment, Rose didn't know where she was, then the dreadful reality of what had happened crashed in on her. She lifted the silver bangle to her lips and kissed it.

The maid looked at her with sympathy. "How are 'ee feeling, miss?"

"I'm so knackered, Violet. I could sleep for a week."

"It's the shock, miss. I was the same way when we had the news that my youngest brother had been killed at Somme. It be like walking in sludge all the time."

Rose stared into the maid's lined face. She felt like putting her head on Violet's shoulder and crying her eyes out, but she was afraid that once she started she wouldn't be able to stop.

"Miss Stillwell said to tell you she had to go out, but she said to make sure you was taken care of."

Rose swallowed hard. "Thank you."

Violet reached into her apron pocket. "Here. My doctor gave them to I for my nerves. They'll make 'ee sleep." She held out two white pills. "Swallow 'em down. I'll bring you up a nice cuppa and biscuits later on. Go on. Go and have a bit more rest."

Rose hesitated, but the prospect of temporary oblivion was too tempting. She took the pills and swallowed them as best she could. Violet nodded approvingly. "Good lass. They'll do 'ee the world of good, 'ee'll see."

Impulsively, Rose caught her by the hand. "Who would kill our Elsie like that? I simply can't believe it."

The maid's voice was soothing. "I'm sure Inspector will sort things out. Those carrot tops are a determined lot. Now off with 'ee."

Obediently Rose crept off to her room. It was strange being in the hostel alone. She was used to the chatter, the calling back and forth and open doors as girls visited each other. Her room, formerly a servant's room, was on the third floor. At first she and Elsie had shared it, but her friend had leaped at the chance to get out of the hostel and take a billet in town. After a couple of days, Rose had come to enjoy having her own room, tucked out of the way.

She plopped down on the hard bed and closed her eyes. Immediately, the image of Elsie's shattered face sprang into her mind and she shuddered. What was she going to do without Elsie? They had grown up together, and ever since she could remember, Elsie had been her protector. She'd loved her, chivvied her, taken her into wild adventures that Rose would never have done on her own. And now she was dead. The copper who'd come seemed decent. She supposed she should tell him what Elsie had been up to. Probably, she should've told him right away, but it was almost second nature not to talk to the police about anything.

She yawned. The pills were already taking effect.

She was awakened by a knock on the door, and Violet came in with a tea tray.

"Here 'ee go, miss. A nice hot cuppa."

Rose sat up. The light coming through the window was softer. "What time is it, Violet? How long did I sleep?"

"It be going on for six o'clock. I told 'ee them's good pills."

Rose's tongue felt thick and her mouth was dry, and she

didn't feel better, her head was so heavy. She didn't feel rested and her grief seemed as close as ever.

The maid poured her some tea. "I thought 'ee might be hungry so I brought up a bit of cold savoury pie."

"Ta, Violet. You've been . . . er . . ." Rose searched for an appropriate word. "You've been a brick." She'd heard some of the girls using the word but it sat awkwardly on her tongue. She could almost hear Elsie laughing at her. "Oo, listen to Rosie putting on airs. Good as a duchess she is."

"Thank 'ee, miss."

"There's something I must do, Violet. Is Miss Stillwell back yet?"

"No, she's not, miss. But she did ring and ask after 'ee."

"Do you think it would be all right if I made a telephone call?"

"I'm sure it would. Now why don't 'ee tidy yourself up a bit. 'Ee'll feel better for a wash. I'd better get I downstairs and help Cook with tea for her ladyship."

After she left, Rose polished off the pie, cramming pieces into her mouth as she had when she was growing up and nobody knew what good manners were. She got up and went to the washstand. There was enough water left from morning in the urn to wash her face and neck. The bedroom felt hot and stuffy. She pushed the window sash up as far as it would go and leaned out. Her room looked out onto the yard, which right now was deserted. The cows were still in the fields and wouldn't be brought in for another hour. It had been because of the cows that she and Elsie had had one of their rare barneys. Rose wanted them both to volunteer for milking duty, but at their first attempt Elsie had been kicked by a cow, impatient with her clumsy tugging on the udder. She wouldn't go back but Rose continued. She started to love the big placid beasts and the shed that smelled of grass and manure, a smell that Rose found pleasant, much to Elsie's scorn. "How can you like that pong?" she'd asked angrily. Rose sighed. She'd milked the cows this morning in the pre-dawn hours, never knowing the tragedy that was ahead of her. She'd enjoyed the morning. Old one-horned Dolly had been particularly good. Rose had discovered that if she sang to the cows, they gave up more milk. Mr. Trimble thought she was barmy, but she could point to her full frothing pails, almost a quarter more than he got. What had she been singing this morning? Oh, now she remembered. She'd sung that Vera Lynn song, "We'll Meet Again."

At the memory, Rose almost burst out crying. While she was singing, her cheek pressed against Dolly's warm hide, the milk hissing rhythmically into the pail as accompaniment, her best friend was probably already dead or close to it. Maybe she'd had a psychic message? Maybe the song had come into her head from Elsie? To comfort her . . . we'll meet again, don't know where, don't know when. For a minute, Rose was afraid. She didn't know how she'd feel if Elsie's ghost did drop in on her. She'd better ask the Father about that. She'd been raised as a Roman Catholic but she was a bit hazy about the church's position on departed spirits.

A little while ago, one of the girls had passed on a pretty frock with a matching hat. Rose loved the outfit, although Elsie had been a bit jealous. She was possessive of her Rose's affections. It was this frock that Rose reached for. She was almost out of the door when she remembered her rosary. She snatched it out of its box, put it in her pocket, and went downstairs to Miss Stillwell's office. At the door, she hesitated, not only because she was entering the warden's territory but because she wanted to run from her own decision. She could hear a bluebottle fly buzzing at the window. Outside, a dog barked in the distance. Rose shivered. She felt more alone than she had in her entire life. But the copper had promised he would find Elsie's killer.

Go on, she muttered to herself. Get it over with.

She walked to the telephone and picked up the receiver. The operator's cheery voice came over the wire.

"Number please."

"I'd like the police station." Rose could hear her own heart thumping. "I want to speak to Inspector Tyler."

"Shall I say who is calling?"

"Tell him it's Rose Watkins. Will you say that it's important?"

"One moment, please. I'll connect you."

The phone rang and rang at the other end. Rose waited until finally the operator came on again.

"Nobody is answering. Shall I take a message, caller?"

"Er . . . no, I'll ring back later. Thank you."

She replaced the receiver. That was done, then. She wished she could have finished there and then, but at least she had taken the first step. No going back now.

Like Rose, Elsie was Roman Catholic, but she had rebelled against the church as she'd rebelled against any authority she didn't respect. Rose remained devout. Initially, she'd attended Mass at the Catholic church in Whitchurch, but it was a long way to go and she'd found another closer sanctuary. Not sure if it was something she should be doing, she hadn't told anybody. Elsie liked to sleep in on Sunday mornings so even she didn't know.

This evening, Rose desperately wanted the solace that her religion gave her. She would ask the priest to say a prayer for Elsie's soul. Once again, that thought almost caused her to break down into sobs, but she knew if she was going to get there in time for evening Mass, she had better hurry. Elsie had always said there was time for tears later. "When's later?"

Rose had asked her. "Later never comes, silly. By then you've forgotten what you were crying about."

Rose went outside. It was turning into a lovely evening, cooler now but soft; a slight mist was creeping in over the fields. Rose wished she'd thought to fix her flat tire but it was too late now. She would have to take the shortcut through the woods. She straightened her hat, took her rosary out of her pocket, and set off.

17.

TYLER HAD SPENT A COUPLE OF HOURS AT THE
station. He supposed that closing doors and cancelling out
possibilities was progress, but he was impatient. Nothing
significant had emerged yet. Major Fordham had rung earlier
and said the search of the camp had yielded nothing.

"I walked around the enclosure myself and I could see no
evidence of the wire being tampered with. The two sentries
on duty swear that nobody can get out without them being
alerted. I doubt you're going to find your criminal here,
Inspector."

Tyler thanked him, but just as he was about to hang up,
Fordham said, "Lordy, I almost forgot. One of the internees
offered his services to you."

"What is he, a chimney sweep? We have been having
troubles with the flue."

The major chuckled. "Nothing like that. He's a psychiatrist.
Apparently, he's a specialist in the criminal mind. Written all
sorts of papers. He's highly respected in his own country."

"Has he been a police officer?"

"Not as far as I know."

"But he's read a lot of books and is now an expert?"

The major coughed. "I know what you're getting at, Tyler,
but it would be very good for camp morale if they saw that
one of their leaders was conferring with the police. Besides,
you never know, the chap might prove useful."

Tyler thought that highly unlikely. When he was in the
army, as well as during his time as a police officer, he'd had

sufficient experience with some of the top brass to distrust the ones who'd learned everything from a book. In his opinion, they were dangerous.

"Perhaps you could come over to the camp tomorrow and meet him. His name is Beck. Dr. Bruno Beck. He was the one speaking for the internees when you addressed them this morning. He's their elected representative."

"I remember. He has a beard. He looks like George V."

Fordham chuckled. "I don't know about the late king but he does resemble the big cheese, Sigmund Freud."

Whoever that is, thought Tyler.

Reluctantly he agreed.

He sat for a moment at his desk, tempted to take out the paintings that he had stowed at the back of one of the drawers. *My God, Tyler, you might as well be a silly girl mooning over a film star. Take hold of yourself.*

Admonishment received, he grabbed his hat and coat. Sergeant Gough had gone home for his tea. Tyler locked the door behind him.

He didn't hear the telephone ringing.

The hospital where Dr. Murnaghan had conducted the postmortem was on the edge of town. Not willing to wrestle with the Humber, Tyler decided to walk there. He was hoping the coroner would have something helpful to tell him. He had many reasons to want this investigation to be concluded quickly, not the least of which was his desire to be seen as an officer capable of dealing with serious crime, not just a kind of headmaster slapping the knuckles of petty thieves and rule breakers. Not for the first time he regretted moving back to the quiet backwater of Whitchurch. The work in Birmingham had been much more dangerous and challenging. *And I wonder who you're trying to impress, mate?*

At the turn of the century, the hospital had been a poorhouse. The plaque was on the wall. *This house is intended for the Relief and Comfort of the Poor of this Parish.* In spite of the soothing words *relief* and *comfort*, there was nothing welcoming about the place. In fact, in the deepening dusk, the square, severe building appeared grim and cheerless. *Can't make the poor too comfortable or they'll want handouts all the time.*

There was a masked light over the entrance, but all the windows were blacked out.

Tyler went into what was now the lobby, deserted except for a young woman in a white, starched nurse's uniform who was sitting behind the reception desk. When she saw him she broke into a wide smile.

"Inspector, what a lovely surprise! What brings you here? You not be ill I hope."

Tyler knew they'd met before but for the life of him he couldn't remember where. "No, I'm quite healthy, thank you Miss . . . er . . . ?"

"Parsons, Winifred Parsons."

"I'm here to see Dr. Murnaghan."

"He'll be downstairs. I'll let him know."

She switched on the intercom. Tyler thought she seemed disappointed that he hadn't known who she was. She was a pretty girl, nicely round with smooth skin and light brown hair tucked under her stiff cap. Why was he thinking Christmas? More to the point, why did he feel vaguely guilty?

The coroner's voice crackled over the line. "Yes?"

"Inspector Tyler to see you, Doctor."

Murnaghan's answer was unintelligible to Tyler, but Miss Parsons replied, "I'll send him down." She looked up. "He be in the morgue. Go through that door at the end of the hall and follow the stairs down."

"Thank you. . . . Excuse me, I have a pounding headache. Do you have any aspirin?"

"Of course."

She reached into a drawer and took out a bottle. "You can have the whole thing if you like, we've got lots."

"Thank you. How much?"

She gave him a wink. "Ten shillings."

"What!" For that price he'd expect an entire box of pills.

Her face fell. He'd disappointed her again.

"Never mind. I was joking. There's no charge."

He popped three pills into his mouth and swallowed them down.

"I would have fetched you some water," said the nurse.

"Thanks. I couldn't wait."

He put the bottle in his pocket, tipped his hat, and headed for the morgue. Where the heck had he met her before? As he shoved open the heavy wooden door, he suddenly remembered. Last Christmas there had been an auction at the church hall to raise money for the Spitfire fund. Some of the local girls were sitting at a row of booths, a sprig of mistletoe over their heads, selling kisses. Ten shillings a kiss was steep, Tyler thought, but all for a good cause. Most of the men gave perfunctory pecks on the girls' cheeks or a hasty press on the lips while their wives watched. The coroner's nurse was in one of the booths. She looked appealing with her wavy hair down about her shoulders, her lips rouged and her eyes bright.

She'd called him over. "All in a good cause, Inspector." She reached up and grabbed his face between her hands, giving him a smacker on the lips.

The vicar was standing nearby supervising. "I think that was worth at least a pound," he said disapprovingly.

Tyler had paid up, but he saw the look in the girl's eyes and suspected she'd be more than happy to give him a kiss for free next time. He was almost ready to hand over another ten shillings for a repeat performance, but Vera had come along at that moment.

"Sins catching up with you, are they?" she'd asked. Perhaps they were.

The morgue was the same one that had been used for the poorhouse when it probably had plenty of business. Long and narrow with a low ceiling, the walls were thick whitewashed brick, the floor grey slate. High windows on one side let in a meagre light and a huge stone fireplace took up a large section of the rear wall, although its presence seemed to contravene the necessity for low temperatures. A portrait of Queen Victoria in her regal, plump prime was hung over the hearth. She stared at a round railway clock on the opposite wall. Several storage rooms led off from the far end, used for maintaining samples and, on rare occasions these days, a body. The place was so cool even on a warm day that refrigeration for short stays wasn't always necessary. One single bright electric light dangled from the ceiling over the antique porcelain gurney where Murnaghan conducted the post-mortems, but the original gas sconces had been retained and they hissed softly, casting out a yellowish light.

As Tyler entered the hall, Murnaghan was just removing his surgical gloves. He was a short, trim man with a neat sandy moustache and springy, greying hair. Underneath his rubber apron he was dressed in a brown corduroy jacket and high-necked jersey. Tyler could understand the need for all the clothes. He could almost see his own breath.

The coroner greeted him. "Good timing, Tyler. I've just finished. I should probably have sent her over to Shrewsbury or Birmingham where they have more equipment, but I know you wanted a result as soon as possible."

"I rather thought you were glad of the opportunity to work again, sir."

The coroner chuckled. "True enough. When I got the call I was in the middle of cleaning out my mother's attic. Mostly old books, lots of filth."

Tyler assumed he was referring to the state of the library, not the contents.

Murnaghan rubbed his hands together. Tyler couldn't tell if he was cold or excited. Perhaps both.

"Basically the girl was in excellent health. I have taken the usual organ and blood samples, but I don't think we'll find anything remarkable there. Liver and kidneys look to be in excellent condition. There was some indication of early malnutrition in the bones, but she was well nourished as an adult." He walked over to one of the specimen jars standing on an antique marble-topped table. "There were partially digested fish and chips in her stomach. That was the last thing she consumed, probably last evening. She smoked and there is some residue in her lungs, which would indicate she has been a heavy consumer for some time." He glanced over at Tyler. "She had sexual relations not long before she was killed."

"Rape?"

"No, I don't think so. She was not a virgin, but as you saw, her clothes were intact and there was no sign of forcing in the vagina." He went over to one of the wall shelves and took down a cardboard box. "She had money concealed in her dungarees. Two pound notes in the straps. I might not have found it, but I cut off the clothes for easier access. Of course, she might have put it there for safekeeping. Strange girls at the hostel and all that, but it's a lot of money for a Land Army girl to have."

"Are you saying she was on the game?"

Murnaghan raised his eyebrows. "Not necessarily. Ordinary young women are, shall we say, giving favours for as little as a pair of silk stockings. Sad really. It's yet another of the consequences of war. There was absolutely no sign of venereal disease, but she may have been paid for the sex. There's no way to tell really. . . . Here you go, I put the bills in here with the rest of her effects, the hair combs and so forth. I'll have everything sent over to you, shall I?"

"Thanks."

Murnaghan returned to the gurney and removed the sheet. "Look at this. I found something quite unexpected. This is the *pièce de résistance*." He had sewn up an incision he'd made in the upper thigh, but surrounding it was a livid bruise extending all the way from knee to hip. "I thought there was something wrong with the way the body was lying when I put her on the gurney, so I opened up the hip and the thigh. Her femur was broken in two places."

"Did she fall off her bike?" asked Tyler.

"Most unlikely. The bruising goes very deep."

"What then? Don't tell me somebody put the boots to the poor lassie?"

"No. There is no sign of imprints. I'd say she was struck by a vehicle of some sort."

He gave Tyler a moment to digest this information.

"I've looked for any evidence of paint chips on her clothes, but so far I haven't found any. Besides, when it comes to a collision of machine and human flesh, there is no contest. The vehicle might be completely unmarked."

Tyler stared down at the dead girl. The coroner had wiped away the blood and fluid from her face, and if you didn't look at the gaping hole at her temple, she looked normal. Death had smoothed away all expression, leaving the face as white and cold as the porcelain she was lying on.

"Let me get this straight, Doctor. You're saying that somebody knocked her down, then shot her?"

Murnaghan shook his head. "Don't jump to conclusions, Tyler. It's more correct to say she was struck by a vehicle, shortly after which she was shot at short range with a pistol. There was powder residue on the cheek, and as you ascertained earlier, the bullet entered at a sharp angle. The assailant was standing over her, quite close."

"Was she knocked unconscious? Is that why there are no signs of defensive wounds?"

"She didn't defend herself because she couldn't," said Murnaghan. "She couldn't have lifted her hands to fend off an attacker even if she'd wanted to. She was paralyzed."

"What!"

"I cleaned away the blood and bone fragments and cut off her hair so you can see more clearly. Help me turn her over." The coroner indicated a wound at the base of the skull. "That wasn't caused by the bullet exiting. This injury happened first. The second and third thoracic vertebrae are shattered and they in turn severed the spinal cord. In common parlance, she suffered a broken neck. She would have been completely paralyzed from the neck down."

"My God!"

"It is most likely she remained conscious. I didn't see any signs of concussion. And even with that sort of injury, she wouldn't necessarily have died immediately. I've known a similar case. Remember Squire Otley from Bitterley?"

"Dimly."

"His horse threw him when he was riding to hounds and he landed smack on top of his head. He was a big man and his neck was broken in three places. He couldn't move a muscle, poor chap, but he could still talk. He was quite *compos mentis*. The servants carried him into the hall and he was able to tell everybody what sort of funeral arrangements he wanted. Made them promise they wouldn't blame the horse.

He said goodbye to his wife and kiddies who were all gathered around him. Terribly sad the whole thing. He lasted for seven or eight hours." The coroner paused, lost in thought.

"You're saying Elsie could have lived after this injury?"

"Yes, quite likely. But minutes, hours, there's no way to know."

Tyler ran his hand over his hair. "In other words, she was lying there helplessly when her killer shot her? She would have seen him, probably understood what he intended to do, but been unable to move or defend herself."

"Yes. Precisely."

"And after he shot her, he moved her over to the hedge, and propped her up."

"Yes."

"Why? Why didn't he just leave her where she was?"

"That's your province, Inspector, not mine. Maybe he intended to bury her in the woods but got interrupted or frightened and ran away."

Tyler didn't think so. The careful arrangement of Elsie's body was too deliberate. Too complete.

"Anything else?"

Murnaghan shook his head. "Nothing directly pertinent to her death, but I thought you might find this interesting." He pulled away the sheet and pointed to a tattoo in the middle of Elsie's left buttock. It was a heart shape around the word *LOVE*.

"She couldn't have drawn that on her rear end by herself. But it's not a permanent tattoo. It was done with an indelible pencil. My wife uses one to mark the laundry, but that's the first time I've seen it for tattooing."

"How long has it been there?"

"Impossible to tell. On the laundry, it would last forever, but on human flesh, I can't say. Maybe a week, maybe less.

I've taken a photograph. I've got a dark room here; I'll develop it for you. Let's turn her back, shall we?" He covered Elsie with the sheet. "When can I release the body?"

"We're trying to contact her next of kin now," answered Tyler.

"Very good. I'll have my report typed up and sent over to you with the effects."

"Thank you, Doctor."

"Not all. I'm glad I could be of help." For a moment, the coroner looked grim. "It's easy to detach oneself in this line of work. You have to, really. A body ceases to be a person. But I think this death is particularly tragic. She had so much to live for. I hope you catch the blighter who did it."

They shook hands and Tyler went back upstairs. The nurse had left.

The previous raucous evening that had followed the football game was taking its toll, and Tyler felt bone tired. However, he was propelled by a sense of urgency. The image of Elsie lying conscious while she saw her own death approaching had profoundly disturbed him. But it happened. It happened to soldiers on the battle field. He'd killed, himself. Fast, to be sure, but he'd bayonetted a German soldier who had fallen in the mud. As the man struggled to get to his feet, he'd looked into Tyler's eyes. He'd known what was going to happen.

Tyler shook himself like a dog coming out of the water, trying to shake the memory. It was war. The Jerry would have just as quickly and mercilessly killed him if he'd had the chance.

18.

SERGEANT BASIL GOUGH WAS BACK AND WAS SEATED behind the high counter in the front hall. He was working on one of his endless crossword puzzles. Gough's passion for crosswords was legendary in the station. As Tyler entered, he put the paper aside.

"Good evening, sir."

The aspirin was helping Tyler's headache but he would have shaken hands with the devil for a beer.

"Anything to report, Guffie?"

"Yes, sir. We had a call from a Sergeant Donaldson in London. He said he was able to get hold of Mr. and Mrs. Bates, but they cannot do anything about their daughter just now. Might be several more days."

"Ring Dr. Murnaghan for me. The body will have to stay in the morgue until we get further instructions. Got any better news?"

"The constables put what they collected into the gas mask boxes as you suggested. They are all there in the duty room."

"Anything interesting?"

"No, really. The bullet hasn't shown up yet. The rest of the stuff is mostly sweet wrappers, fag ends, and bits of newspapers. We haven't had any luck with footprints or tire marks. Everywhere is so dry and dusty, Sherlock himself wouldn't be able to make out anything. Constables Pearse and Eagleton are still out there. I told them to call it quits by seven and we could continue in the morning if we need to. Did you get anything from Mrs. Clark?"

"She gave Elsie Bates a very good report. Mrs. Clark didn't actually see her leave this morning and she takes off her hearing aids for the night so she didn't hear her either. There is a most convenient tree outside the girl's room and, even more convenient, a ladder. I'm betting she left the house that way. She could have been anywhere and with anyone after eight o'clock last night until this morning. However, there's something you should know. Dr. Murnaghan has done a post-mortem." He filled the sergeant in on what the coroner had discovered.

Gough whistled between his teeth. "Are we looking for one killer or two people working together?"

"At this stage, it's impossible to tell. All Dr. Murnaghan could say was that she was hit first and then shot. He couldn't determine how much time elapsed. But we've got to get onto the vehicle right away. Start with registered vehicles in the vicinity. The car that knocked her over could have been coming from Edinburgh for all we know, but let's not complicate our lives unless we have to. I want all available officers checking up on the owners. There can't be that many people cruising around the countryside at six in the morning. Get alibis, as they say in the flicks."

"Will do. I'll start on it myself." Gough reached into the cubbyhole behind him. "Mustn't forget. There are two messages for you, sir. A reporter named Madox from the *Gazette* rang and wants a statement."

"Like hell he does. He's a prurient son of a bitch. Crass as a monkey. Give him a call. I don't want to talk to him. Tell him it's a suspicious death, but for God's sake downplay it. He'll have some mad killer running around the countryside raping and killing Land Army girls if he gets half a chance. Make murmurs about national security and so on. Also let him know I'll kill him personally if he exploits this situation."

"Very good, sir. Would that be with your bare hands?"

"Yes. What else?"

"Do you want the other message, sir?"

"Is it from Mrs. Fuller down the road offering to read our tea leaves? What would she tell us, Guff? 'I see . . . I see a newspaper . . . white and black squares.'"

"Sorry, sir," said Gough, ducking his head in embarrassment. "I thought I'd keep myself busy . . ."

"Of course. Don't worry. I'm just pulling your leg."

Gough blinked. "Tease. That's it. A five-letter word meaning to make fun of, to humiliate, to embarrass . . . Thank you, sir."

Tyler laughed. "I'll make sure all these extra hours are compensated for. Days off when we've finished the case. You and the constables. I'm going to get a cup of tea before they arrive. We don't have anything like coffee, do we?"

"Just the Camp Coffee Essence, which you loathe."

"Forget it." Tyler opened the door to his office.

"Don't you want to know what the second message was?" the Sergeant asked.

"Almost forgot. Read it to me."

"A Mrs. Devereau telephoned. She asked if you would ring her when you got in. She can be reached at the manor."

That was a better jolt than coffee. "When did she call?"

"About twenty minutes ago."

"Get me the number, will you? I'll try her right now."

He went back to his office, taking off his jacket as he did so and closing the door behind him. The intercom buzzed almost immediately.

"Mrs. Devereau is on the line, sir."

Tyler grabbed the receiver. "Clare?"

"Hello, Tom. Do you have a minute?"

"Certainly."

"Look, I was reflecting on our luncheon this afternoon and I realized I must have sounded a tad ungracious."

"How so?"

"Well, I was very touched by what you said to me in Fordham's tent and I . . . well . . . I don't know if I conveyed that to you."

He tried to make a joke to ease the tension, mostly his own. "You didn't say you'd elope with me if that's what you mean. But blimey, it's been twenty years."

She chuckled. "Time flies, doesn't it?"

He felt like saying he doubted she'd called merely to pass along a cliché, but he bit his tongue. She'd get to the point sooner or later.

She did. "If you do have to question any of the internees, I would be most willing to act as your translator. Some of them speak English quite well but most do not. Have you got any further with the case? Do you suspect someone in the camp?"

"I suppose the answer is, no and no. The major has assured me that is completely out of the question, but I'm not ruling out anybody."

"Did the post-mortem reveal anything?"

Tyler could feel himself quailing. This was Clare he was talking to, but he also wasn't prepared to discuss Murnaghan's findings with a non-officer, even though the sound of her voice was creating a stir in his nether regions. He was saved by the buzz of the intercom.

"Excuse me a tick, Clare."

He covered the receiver and pressed the intercom button.

"Constables Pearse and Eagleton are here, sir."

"I'll be right out." He returned to his call. "Clare, I'm afraid I've got to go. I'll take you up on your offer, though. I'm coming to the camp tomorrow to meet a Dr. Bruno Beck. He's a psychoanalyst, whatever that is, and he has insight into the way a criminal mind works. He's offered to share this knowledge with me."

"I've met him. He speaks excellent English but I'll ask to sit in on the interview." She paused. "It will give me an excuse to see you."

"Crikey, Clare. No excuse needed."

"Good. Because I was going to invite you for dinner tomorrow evening. My treat. Is the Acton Lodge still in existence? As I remember they had a wonderful wine cellar."

Another little prod to his nerves. They had gone to the Lodge a few times when they were together. It was a hotel as well as a restaurant, and Clare had finagled them a room with much covert giggling. She'd booked it, and he had snuck upstairs later.

"It's still there. I haven't tried the food or the wine for a long time, though, so you'll have to take your chances."

"All right. Shall we say seven o'clock?"

"Done."

"Tom?"

"Yes?"

"Oh, nothing. It's just . . . well . . . it's been quite marvellous seeing you again."

"I can second that."

He hung up. He felt as if he'd stepped into a rushing river that could quite easily sweep him off his feet. He'd better damn well keep in touch with the bottom.

19.

Tyler went out to the front hall where the constables were waiting for him.

"All right, lads, what've you got?"

Eagleton unfolded the handkerchief he was holding, and rather like little Jack Horner pulling out a plum, he held up a flattened bullet.

"It was lying in a clump of grass, three feet and four inches from the place where the lady was shot." He beamed. "We measured exactly, sir. As you thought, it must have ricocheted off the rock."

"Good lad. Hand it over to Sergeant Gough, who can put it in an evidence bag. Next."

"Something very interesting, sir. Show him, Pearse."

Obediently, the other constable reached into his gas mask box, and using the tips of his fingers took out a long, grubby piece of white rubber tubing. "It's a French safe, sir. It's bin used."

"I can see that, lad. Where was it?"

"There's a little clearing about a mile in from road, directly west from where lorry was. We come across this shelter. A big tree's been uprooted and the roots make a bit of a cave. Somebody put branches all around, made a roof from a piece of tin and everything. Real snug t'was, sir. There's moss laid on the ground and there's an old blanket on top. The safe was tucked away in the corner. The place must've been used for a lover's meeting."

"Good deduction, Constable. I doubt a man would go to

the trouble of walking into the woods so he could wank off into a rubber. Anyway, I know the place you mean. It's at the bottom of a slope."

"That's it, that's the one."

"We used to play cowboys and Indians there when I was a nipper. That was our fort. I do believe it's been a popular spot for courting couples for a long time."

He didn't add that he and his pals liked to creep up on the couples whenever they could and spy on them. Early sex education. He also didn't add that he himself had used the tree cave when he got older. He'd even taken Clare there once, but she wasn't fussy about it. She said there were too many creepy crawlies for her liking. She was a clean sheets and firm mattress sort of girl.

"Sir?"

"What?"

Eagleton gave him a cheeky grin. "Just curious, sir. Were you a cowboy or an Indian?"

"An Indian of course, you twerp. The cowboys had to stay in the Fort to keep watch. Very boring. Us Indians could creep through the forest and then swoop in on them making blood curdling, whooping noises. Then we got to scalp them. I liked that part. Gave me a chance to pull Percy Somerville's hair. He played with us sometimes in the summer."

Eagleton and Pearse both gaped at him. "Sir Percy?"

"He wasn't *sir* then, just a pimply, fat little nipper who we all picked on. Poor bugger. He could have told on us but he never did. I think he saw it as his duty to allow the peasants to vent their centuries' old anger. He knew he could get revenge when he inherited the manor and took over as magistrate."

"Do you think the, er, the safe is relevant?" asked Pearse.

"If we had any way to know who used it, maybe. But we don't and it might have been there since Roman times."

The constable looked doubtful. "Roman times, sir?"

"Never mind. Did you find anything else? A monogrammed hankie, a cigar paper?"

"No, sir, but this is rather odd."

Pearse dived into his box again and took out a small pencil.

It was an indelible pencil. The same kind that somebody had used to draw a heart and the word "love" on Elsie's round young buttock.

"It was on the blanket."

Dr. Murnaghan said Elsie'd had sex recently, but if he could detect semen, it meant she and her lover hadn't been the ones to use the rubber. What if she'd spent the night in the Fort? She could have parked the lorry, then left early in the morning, intending to drive it to the manor. The lorry had broken down, and she'd set off on her bicycle.

Where had her lover got to, and who was he?

Eagleton was clearly eager to show him more finds.

"All right, Constable. What've you got?"

"These cigarette butts were strewn around the area." He handed Tyler an envelope.

"Woodbines. Great. Too bad most of the country smokes Woodbines."

Tyler sent the constables home, then together with Gough he went through the litter and debris that the other officers had brought in. There was nothing that stood out that seemed related to the case. He packed it all back into the gas mask boxes. He was glad to have finally found a use for the things.

"That's it for tonight, Guff. Go home. We'll get onto that vehicle registration list first thing."

They closed up the station and Tyler was about to cross the street to his house, but almost on their own accord, his feet turned left. Home was the last place he wanted to be. He was officially off duty now and he could go for a beer. His head was quieter and the warmth of the day still lingered on the night air. There was a fragrance to it, but that could have been the lavender scent that surrounded him like a miasma. A dog barked from its kennel. With no streetlights and the houses all blacked out, it would have been dark indeed without the moonlight.

Alice was right; the news from the front was bad. According to Churchill the RAF was winning this particular fight – the Battle of Britain, as he called it – but Tyler had his doubts. The Luftwaffe was still sending over a lot of planes. He looked up at the moon, serene and indifferent in the star-dotted sky. It was possible that in one of the cities there was a raid going on at this very moment, people dying, getting injured, frightened, possessions gone forever. Here in this little country town it was quiet, only a soft rustle from the trees and shrubs in the front gardens of the houses he was walking past.

Initially, after the declaration of war, when nothing much happened, a lot of Brits had moaned about what a phony war it was and all, a political ploy to scare people into compliance. The country had needed work and this was one way to create it. However, since May, Hitler had put paid to that theory. Ever since the occupation of Belgium, the collapse of France and Holland, and then the shocking disaster at Dunkirk, the country now knew the Germans were in deadly earnest. This sceptred isle was in real danger of being invaded. As for the silver sea, the U-boats appeared to be invincible, and it seemed a random chance that any shipping got through at all. *Shite. If England collapsed, what then?*

Suddenly, there was a flash of light, sharp and brilliant, that vanished as quickly as it had appeared. Somebody had lifted a parlour curtain. He realized he was walking past the Walker house. He might as well see how Bobby was faring.

"Psst. Tom. Over here."

A man was standing at the side of the house in the entry between the Walker house and the neighbour's. In the dim light, Tyler could just make out Fred Walker, Bobby's dad. He was holding a pigeon, which cooed softly.

"Evening, Fred. How's your lad doing?"

Walker shook his head. "Not grand. He's not good at all. We had to have the doctor in and he's ordered him off to the hospital in Shrewsbury. To the loony ward."

"What?"

"Oh, they try to pretty it up by saying Bobby's suffering from battle fatigue and he needs a good rest, but what they mean is he's gone crackers. I seen it lots in t'other war."

"I'm sorry about that, Fred, but it's probably true, he does need a good rest. He had a bad shock this morning. He must have told you about the poor gal who was killed on Heath Road?"

"Ay, he told us." Fred stroked the pigeon gently. "Why don't you walk back to the coop with me. I've got to put this one to bed. She's tired. She's flown more than three hundred miles to get back home. She's one of my champions. Look at these wing feathers." He spread out the bird's wing. "I used to release the birds in France, but we can't do that anymore so I have them shipped up to Scotland. One of the chaps in the club liberates her from there. She's going to have a special supper tonight to celebrate." He opened the door of the pigeon coop. The other birds gave their liquid coos of welcome. Fred removed a band from the bird's leg and slipped out a tiny piece of thin paper. "This records the date and time when she was released. I do the same when I have birds to send off from here. The army used these birds all through the last war to carry messages. Most of them survived. Gunfire, hawks, storms, they got through it all. And look, I can hold her in the palm of my hand."

Fred was a small man who had gone bald at an early age. Tyler could hardly remember seeing him without his cloth cap. Tonight he was bare headed, and it made him seem naked and vulnerable.

"When you say pigeon," Fred continued, "most people think of the fat, slow birds that waddle around the churchyards, but racing pigeons are athletes. I have to train them at least three times a week so they can build up their stamina. They're just like any other competitive creature, they've got to stay fit." He placed the bird inside the cage. "Our Bobby has always been athletic. He must have got it from his mum, not me. I'm useless but he was a good little football player, wasn't he, Tom?"

"He was that. The best."

Fred was watching to make sure the pigeon was eating. "Do you remember that day they held the trials for the under-sixteen football club in Whitchurch?"

"I do indeed. It was bloody cold and miserable. Your Bobby was the best by far. He played his heart out. He got in easily."

Fred still didn't turn from the coop. "He's always been the kind of lad that if you knocked him down, he'd get right up again."

Tyler thought Fred was weeping but in the darkness he couldn't see him properly.

"He will again, Fred. You'll see. You've got to give it time."

"They were like the four musketeers, weren't they? Your lad, ours, Dennis, the scamp, and Wilf Marshall."

"It's a rotten shame about Wilf."

"Bobby hasn't said much about Wilf. Hasn't said much about anything is truth of the matter."

"Mine neither."

"Funny how life goes, in't it, Tom? My old man was a tough bloke who spoke with his hands first and asked questions later. I remember thinking when he was whaling the tar out of me or one of my brothers that I'd do it differently if ever I had a son. So when Bobby came along I stepped back, left him more to his mother. I never laid a hand on him. . . . Perhaps that were a mistake. It made him too soft. It didn't do him no good when he went in the army. They don't want soft lads there. They take ordinary decent fellows that have been raised to respect them that are not as strong, like the elderly and the unfortunate, that sort of thing. The army takes these lads and wants them to become killers. It's not surprising some of them crack, is it?"

He started to cry, the dry, hard, shattering tears of a man who had never expressed any sort of feelings since he was a child. Awkwardly, Tyler patted him, then finally put his arm around his shoulders and comforted him.

20.

TYLER DECIDED TO FORGO THE PUB AND CHECK IN at home.

Janet was listening to the wireless, tapping her foot to the lively music. She smiled with delight when she saw him.

"Dad. I was wondering when you'd be home." She screwed up her face at him. "Gosh, Dad, you look beat. Can I get you some tea? Have you had your supper?"

"Mom said she'd leave something in the oven for me."

"Sit down. I'll get it for you."

"You know what, pet? I don't have much time. I've got to go out again. If you can make me a fried egg on toast, I'll double your allowance."

"I'll keep you to that."

"I'll come and keep you company while you slave."

He followed her into the kitchen, happy it was just the two of them.

Janet peered into the pantry. "You're in luck. We've got one egg left. And there's a sausage. Do you want that as well?"

"Just the egg, thanks."

She put some lard into the frying pan and broke the egg into it. She was obviously enjoying making the food for him and he was touched.

"Where's the bread? I'll cut it myself."

She pointed at the loaf of bread in the larder and he brought it out, slicing off two thick pieces.

"You can fry these in the fat."

He sat down at the kitchen table, loosening his tie.

"Where were you?" Janet asked.

He paused, unsure how to tell her what had happened, but she forestalled him.

"Granddad told me about the girl being killed. It's the talk of the village."

"Is it, indeed?" No wonder the Ministry of Defence was putting on such a campaign about keeping information close to the chest. He supposed one of the constables must have said something.

"Is that what you were called out about?" Janet asked.

"It was."

"It's so horrible to think about, Daddy. I've seen the Land girls in town and they're such a jolly lot. Do you know who did it?"

"Not yet."

Janet looked at him, her expression fearful. "Granddad said she had been raped and then shot."

"She was shot but there was no rape."

"He says it was probably an escaped Jerry from the camp. He thinks we should send all those internees back to London and put them in jail, or better still, hang them. He says they're all dangerous criminals."

"Your grandfather is wrong about that." He bit back what he'd been about to add: "the stupid old coot." He didn't want his daughter to be caught between two loyalties. As far as Tyler was concerned, Walter Lambeth was an ignorant, hard-headed cuss who wouldn't recognize an independent thought if it bit him on his backside.

"The men at the camp are mostly Jewish refugees who escaped from the Nazis. Good blokes who got caught in the squeeze. Oi, I like my eggs soft." Janet had been splashing hot fat over the egg.

"Sorry."

There was something in her voice that made him gaze at her more closely.

"Don't worry about it, pet. I didn't mean to sound sharp with you. I know this news is very upsetting."

She gulped. "It's not only that Dad. It's something else. Something I have to talk to you about."

Crikey. Both of his children were acting as if they had the troubles of the world on their shoulders. He stood up and gently removed the frying pan from the stove. His bread was in danger of burning.

"I'll finish this. You sit down and tell me what's the matter."

She did as he said, and he slid the hardening egg onto his fried bread and slipped it onto a plate. He sat down opposite her and chomped on his sandwich. Egg ran out of the sides and down his chin. He licked it off with his fingers.

"You've dripped egg on your shirt," said Janet.

"Shite." He rubbed at it with his handkerchief.

"It's Granddad . . ." She swallowed hard.

"Has he been giving you a hard time? You weren't late again, were you?"

"No. It's not that . . ."

"Spit it out, Jan. I'm all ears."

She answered quickly. "I think he's into the black market."

Tyler mopped up the remains of the egg with his bread. "What makes you say that?"

"You know part of my job is to keep inventory of the eggs and chickens that the farmers bring in. For the past month, I keep coming up short. The numbers don't balance from what I know we've taken in and what we've sold. It's not just a little difference. It's as much as two dozen eggs a week and two or three chickens . . . I told him about it and he said I must be mistaken. He said I never was good at arithmetic. He was really ticked off with me. So all last week, I double-checked and triple-checked but it was the same. There's also a side of beef gone. We're short of chops and we ought to have a lot more mince than we do."

"So you think he's selling the produce on the black market?"

"Lady Somerville's cook comes by on a regular basis. She always waits until the shop is empty, then Granddad takes her into the back pantry." Suddenly she gave an impish grin. "If Mrs. Sharpe wasn't as ugly as the side of a barn, I'd think they were up to some hanky panky. She always comes out looking like a cat that swallowed the canary . . . She's not the only one. Mr. Morgan dropped by on Monday. He had a sack of new potatoes and I know for sure he left them with Granddad, who gave him a couple of pork chops. And sometimes he takes people's ration coupons and sometimes he doesn't. They pay cash across the counter instead. It's not fair to the other people who are playing by the rules, is it?"

"Not only is it not fair, it's illegal."

They heard the front door open and both involuntarily jumped. Vera was home.

"Let's talk about this later," said Tyler quietly.

"I don't know what to do, Dad."

He patted her hand. "Don't worry. We'll figure something out." He looked at his watch. "I've got to get over to the hostel."

Vera came into the kitchen in time to hear these words.

"Did you get the tea I left?"

"I didn't have time. Our Jan made me an egg instead."

"What about the chop? What am I going to do with that?"

"I'll have it tomorrow," said Tyler, trying to keep the impatience out of his voice. He kissed his daughter on the cheek, went to do the same for Vera, but practically bounced off the angry cloud surrounding her.

He left and went back to the police station to pick up the Humber.

And what the hell was he going to do if Lambeth was into profiteering? The penalties for black marketing were severe. Vera would be devastated if Tyler had to bring charges against her own father. She wouldn't see it as him having to do his job. She would expect Tyler to be loyal to the family first and foremost. But he had little doubt Janet was right in her suspicions. Lambeth as long as he'd known him had been a cheat. Tyler had received several complaints that he was short weighting his customers, or that he bought inferior meat and sold it as prime. The trouble was he had a virtual monopoly in the village, and unless people wanted to travel all the way to Market Drayton or to Shrewsbury for their meat, he was it.

When he got to the Humber, he channelled all his frustrations into cranking the old car.

21.

MISS STILLWELL HAD WISELY ASSEMBLED THE SIX Land Army girls in the common room as soon as they returned so as to quell the exchange of anxiety and speculation. They were still wearing their work clothes: khaki dungarees and cream-coloured shirts. As Elsie had, they all looked fit and healthy with fresh tanned skin, but even those who were showing a lot of control seemed young and vulnerable. Only one girl was dressed in civilian clothes, a smart navy suit. Her hair was drawn up to a fashionable roll. This must be the girl who had been away on compassionate leave. What was her name? Francis? No, Florence. Rose Watkins was not present.

Tyler told them as simply and directly as possible what had happened, but mentioned only the shooting. He decided to keep the details he'd got from Dr. Murnaghan to himself for a while.

Shock ran through the group. Two or three of the girls wept and were comforted. Finally, they quieted down and he was able to continue.

"I can assure you, we are doing everything in our power to find the culprit. I will need to ask a few questions." He took his notebook out of his pocket. "I would also appreciate it if you would state your name first."

One of the girls seated on the couch raised her hand. "My name is Molly Cooper and *I* have a question." Her voice had the rather nasal pitch typical of the upper class.

Tyler jotted down in his book: *Molly. Brown hair and eyes. Good breeding.*

"Do you think that the rest of us are in danger? You are telling us that Elsie was shot. Can we rule out a Jerry parachutist?"

Tyler hesitated. "There has been absolutely no sign of an enemy in the vicinity. No planes have flown over for several weeks. And in the absolute unlikelihood that there was such a man, I can see no reason for him to have attacked Miss Bates."

Another girl, whose hair was as carrot red as his own, blurted out, "Yes, there is. If Elsie saw him, he would have killed her to avoid discovery."

"That is Pam Reynolds, better known as Freckles for obvious reasons," said Molly, who had naturally taken on the role of spokeswoman.

Tyler made a note.

"We are, of course, investigating every possibility, but until we do find the person involved, I want you to use common sense." He smiled at them. "I know you Land Army girls have lots of that. Stay with each other at all times and go out only in daylight. Report any strange activity to the police at once."

"Frankly, I'm scared silly," jumped in another girl. "My name's Jessie Bailey . . . better known as Titch. Why weren't we told earlier? What if some Nazi is on the loose? We were out in the fields. We could easily have been attacked."

One of the younger-looking girls dropped her head onto her neighbour's shoulder.

"I want to go home," she said in a muffled voice.

She had a smooth, rosy-cheeked face. Tyler couldn't help but notice the rather extraordinary swell of her bosom underneath her close fitting dungarees. This must be Sylvia, the recipient of Morgan's unwelcome attentions. Her neighbour, a dark-haired, rather dour-looking girl, patted her. The others started to shift and talk to each other. The red-haired girl was sniffling.

Tyler held up his hands. "Wait a minute, ladies. This isn't the attitude of the Land Army I know."

Miss Stillwell spoke up. "Girls, please. I have every faith that Inspector Tyler will not expose us to danger. If we go galloping off on the trail of non-existent Jerrys, we might miss the obvious."

That got through to them. All eyes focused on him.

He continued. "Right. Your warden makes a very good point. Can I go on?"

"Please do," Molly answered for them.

"Did Miss Bates have any enemies that you know of? Did she quarrel with anybody? Is there anyone she might have angered?"

More uneasy silence, then Molly spoke again.

"She was very well liked here. She was generous and kind-hearted, and if we were down at all, you could count on Elsie to cheer us up with a singsong. Isn't that right, girls?"

The others were nodding except for the dark-haired girl seated beside Sylvia.

"Believe me, none of you are under suspicion," said Tyler. "Miss Bates was killed while you were all having breakfast."

He noticed that Freckles glanced quickly over at Florence.

"I know you said it's not likely it was a Jerry," said Titch. "But what if it was a fifth columnist? Somebody local. What if Elsie found out and they killed her?"

"Anybody you have in mind?" Tyler asked.

Titch shook her head.

He went on. "Did Miss Bates have any boyfriends?"

The dark-haired girl was the one who answered first. Her tone was flat and unemotional. "I think that would depend on what you mean by boyfriend, and what day of the week it was.

Elsie was a flirt. There always seemed to be some bloke or other coming to the hostel to call for her. She never let on she was living in town. Gave her an escape hatch."

"And you are?"

"Muriel Fellows. I'm usually referred to as Lanky."

She didn't look particularly tall to Tyler but her accent was Lancashire. He wrote in his book: *Muriel. Heavy eyebrows. Plain. Jealous of Elsie?*

"I spoke to Mrs. Clark and Miss Watkins earlier," said Tyler. "They both thought that Miss Bates might have had somebody more special recently. Did anybody else think that?"

Again the girls shook their heads.

"Speaking of Rose," said Molly. "How is she? She must be devastated. She and Elsie were inseparable."

"She is resting," answered Miss Stillwell. "I thought it better that she not have to go through all this questioning again."

"Can we talk to her?" asked Freckles.

"Of course. She will probably join us for supper."

Tyler drew their attention back to the matter in hand.

"As I have told you, Miss Bates was shot. The gun was a Luger. A 1917 model. It would certainly help us to trace the owner. Does anybody know of, or has anybody seen such a gun?"

Florence Hancocks's hand flew to her mouth. "Good Lord! I have a Luger. My brother gave it to me. It's in my room."

Clearly not everybody had heard of this, and there was a gasp and twitter in the ranks.

"Oh dear," said Miss Stillwell. So much for regulations.

"Did this gun have any particular distinguishing marks on it?" Tyler asked.

"There is a letter *B* engraved on the stock, which is blue. It must have been put there by the previous owner."

"Will you check to see if it's still there?"

Florence hurried out of the room. The rest of the girls sat in an uneasy silence. Tyler didn't try to break it.

The girl soon returned. She was carrying a worn leather holster.

"The gun has gone!"

"Can I see the holster?" Tyler asked.

She handed it to him. The leather was scuffed in places, but in good shape otherwise, the brass studs intact. There was a long shoulder strap. It was German all right. He'd seen enough of them to know.

"You say you got this from your brother?"

Florence was pale and she looked frightened. The others were staring at her.

"My older brother, Simon Hancocks, purchased a German Luger in London after the war. It was quite above board and legal and all that. The registration paper is in the holster."

Tyler verified that was true.

"He decided to lend it to me when I joined the Land Army because he thought I might need to control vermin, or rabbits, or such. I wasn't sure I would be allowed to keep it and I certainly didn't want it to be confiscated, so I put it in my drawer and frankly forgot all about it." She had a pleasant county accent that reflected diligent teachers but was not necessarily one she had been born to.

"When was the last time you saw the gun?"

"It was certainly there the day I left for Bath. I was considering returning it to my brother, but in all the rush, it slipped my mind."

"When was that, Miss Hancocks?"

"I heard that my mother was taken ill on Tuesday. I left that afternoon."

Abruptly, she reached into her handbag and took out a gold cigarette case. "Miss Stillwell, I'm sorry, but do you mind if I have a cigarette? My nerves are all to pieces."

Tyler noticed she was wearing an engagement ring that sported a sparkling diamond.

The warden nodded. "Very well. Just this once."

"Me too," said Titch, and without asking for permission, she held out her hand to Florence, who gave her a cigarette. Molly took one as well. Tyler made notes while he waited for them all to light up. The cigarettes were Players.

"You were not present at breakfast, Miss Hancocks?"

"No, I only returned a half hour ago."

"Everything all right at home, I hope."

She sucked in smoke. "Yes, thank you. My mother suffers from rheumatism. I was the tonic she needed, so she's right as rain now."

Tyler flipped to a fresh page in his notebook. "And she lives in Bath?"

"Yes."

"I will need the address if you don't mind."

Muriel Fellows burst out. "I had no knowledge of that gun, I want you to know." She turned to Tyler. "Florrie and I share a room."

Florence jumped in. "I didn't tell anybody it was there, not even Muriel. As I say, I actually forgot about it."

"You should have said. I don't like the idea that there was a gun a few feet away from me all the time."

"It was quite safe, Muriel," replied Florence. "It's hardly going to go off on its own."

There was a dead silence. Tyler could tell that this presented the girls with an alarming image.

Molly Cooper stubbed out her cigarette. "Does this mean that the gun which killed Elsie belonged to Florence here?"

"I'll have to check the serial number," said Tyler. "It very well might be."

"The gun must have been stolen from Miss Hancocks's room while she was away," said Miss Stillwell.

"What are you implying, Warden? Nobody here killed Elsie Bates," said Molly.

Miss Stillwell spoke softly. "I'm not implying anything, Molly. But the gun didn't just walk out on its own."

Suddenly, Sylvia began to cry again, deep childlike sobs. "I want to go home. I'm so scared." She was joined by Freckles, who dived into Titch's shoulders.

"Me too. This is horrible."

Molly stood up and went to comfort them. Florence Hancocks didn't move, but to Tyler's eyes, she looked wretched.

Titch eased herself away from Freckles. "Excuse me, Inspector . . . I wasn't going to say anything at first because it seemed sort of mean-spirited now that Elsie's dead, but perhaps I should."

"You must try to let me be the judge of what's important, Miss Bailey, and it certainly isn't mean-spirited if it means we get the murderer."

Titch gulped. "It's my belief that Elsie Bates herself could have took that there gun . . . Tuesday last, I had to come home from the fields because I had a bit of sun stroke . . . you remember don't you?" she appealed to the others.

"That's right. You came back to the hostel about three o'clock. We were at Morgan's," said Molly.

"Well, I almost bumped into Elsie in the hall right outside of Muriel and Florence's room. I knew Florrie was planning to leave by two, and I didn't think anybody was in the house. 'How come you're not out in the fields?' I asks Elsie. She looked a bit miffed. 'I have a headache,' says she. 'I thought I'd have a lie-down before I collect you lot.'" Titch hesitated. "She was carrying a jersey over her arm. I did wonder why, considering it was a warm day, but never thought more about it until now . . . She could have been hiding the gun."

"How would she know it was there?" Tyler asked her. "Miss Hancocks has said she told no one."

The redhead, Freckles, put up her hand. "Some of us have found things gone missing over the past two months. Just little things, almost too silly to mention really . . ." Some nods from the others.

"What sort of things?" Tyler asked. "Tell me exactly."

"Why is it the first I've heard of this?" exclaimed Miss Stillwell.

Freckles continued to address Tyler. "I had a bag of sweets that my mum sent me and I put them on my chest of drawers. When I came home I thought several were gone . . ." She was blushing. "You know how it is, you start wondering, did I eat more than I thought? Did somebody –"

"You thought I'd been into them," said Sylvia. "But I hadn't. I don't like barley sugars."

"The same sort of thing happened to me the following week," said Titch. "I was missing one of my favourite ivory hair combs. It's so easy to lose things like that without realizing it, so I didn't fuss. Then I mentioned it to you, Molly, and you said you'd had something gone too. You were sure you had a half-dozen *Woman's Weekly* in your drawer but you couldn't find one of them."

"True," said Molly, "but then Freckles admitted she'd been helping herself."

"Only one. I only borrowed one," said Freckles. "I read it and put it straight back."

"I had a pair of new gloves," said Lanky. "I have to admit I'm not the tidiest of people but when I went to look for them, I couldn't find them. That was about two weeks ago." She looked shamefaced. "I didn't report it because I wasn't sure."

"But now you think Miss Bates may have taken them?"

"Possibly."

Miss Stillwell interjected. "I regret to say, Elsie would have had lots of opportunity. The house was usually deserted during the day, and she could come and go without anybody thinking anything of it. I would absolutely vouch for the honesty of the maids."

The girls fell silent watching Tyler. It was not implausible that Elsie had stolen Florence's gun. But then what? How did it get into the possession of her killer? It still didn't explain who had shot her with it or why.

Before they could go any further, the door opened and Violet burst in.

"Miss Watkins be gone, ma'am. I went to see on 'er and she ain't in 'er room. I've looked all over. She be gone."

22.

THE FEAR THIS NEWS CREATED RACED THROUGH THE six young women.

Violet kept repeating, "Is she dead, ma'am? Is she be dead?"

Tyler tried to ignore a terrible sinking feeling.

Miss Stillwell stood up. "Ladies, ladies. Please. Let's maintain some order. There is probably a perfectly simple explanation. Violet, did you check the bathroom? Perhaps she is taking a bath."

"No, ma'am," answered the maid. "I checked bathrooms and lavatories before coming here. I swear she ain't in the house."

"Maybe she's gone home," said Molly, ever sensible. "There's a late train to London, I know."

"She would need her ration book," said Miss Stillwell. "They're all kept locked in my desk."

Tyler turned to the elderly servant whose face was awash with tears. He spoke gently. "Violet, when did you last see Miss Watkins?"

"It must have been going on for seven o'clock. I did happen to look out of the window when I was coming back from 'er ladyship's suite, and I saw the little mite crossing the yard. She were all dressed up, hat and everything. She was moving quick. I says to myself, I says, good, she is going out for a bit, see a pal or something of that sort. It will do 'er the world of good." She wiped at her eyes with the edge of her sleeve. "I'd took 'er up a pot of tea and a piece of savoury early on. She liked savoury, poor little thing. But I had to make 'er ladyship's tea. So I left 'er, Rose that is. She did say there was something important she had to do but she didn't say what. But she wanted to use the telephone."

"Warden, will you check to see if Rose's ration book is still in your desk," said Tyler.

She left immediately.

He addressed the girls, keeping his voice matter-of-fact. "When you came in from work, did anybody see Rose or speak to her?"

Nobody had.

"When we got back from work," said Molly, "Warden was waiting for us and asked us to gather here. You arrived shortly afterward. I assumed Rose was in her room."

"Me too!" came a chorus of agreement.

"Maybe she's gone to visit friends in the area," said Tyler. "Anyone come to mind?"

"None," answered Molly. "She was usually with Elsie. I don't know if she ever went out on her own."

Miss Stillwell returned carrying a ration book. "This is Rose's. She can't have gone far without it."

Tyler put it in his pocket. "I'll hang onto this for now. Miss Stillwell, I need to use your telephone." He addressed the young women again. "I recommend you have your supper. You must all be famished. Let's not get the wind up until we know for sure Rose is missing."

The warden nodded at Violet, who had been following the proceedings anxiously. Tyler heard her mutter, "I can feel it in my water. Something bad has happened."

Molly spoke up. "If Violet saw Rose heading for the barn, she might have been going to get her bicycle. That's where we keep our bikes. Shall I go and see if hers is still there?"

"Yes, please. Good thinking."

Freckles jumped to her feet. "I'll do it. You stay here, Molly." She practically ran from the room and Tyler thought two or three of the other girls would have liked to follow her. They were huddled together, like deer sniffing the scent of an approaching fox.

He turned to Violet. "Now then. A Shropshire lass is made of sterner stuff than this. Rose probably needed to get out a bit. I do that myself when I need to think about things."

"And so do I," said Miss Stillwell briskly. "Violet, I want you to go and bring in our supper. Pamela and Muriel, perhaps you could help?"

There was a flurry of activity as they obeyed.

"I'll show you where the telephone is," said the warden to Tyler.

He wished he could offer them some more honest reassurance, but in truth, he couldn't. Rose going missing at this juncture didn't feel good at all.

Tyler got through to Sergeant Gough and filled him in about the latest development.

"I'm hoping she's going to turn up all apologetic about worrying people. You know how young people can be thoughtless. But it would be better for the others if we located her soon. Roust one of the lads; Collis, if possible. Send him over to Mrs. Clark's again. See if by any chance Rose went there. Ring me back if there's any news."

He returned to the common room. Violet and the other two girls had brought in a tureen of hot soup and a large basket of bread. With the resilience of youth, in spite of their upset, the girls were already tucking in.

Freckles was seated at the table and she waved at him, wiping at her mouth.

"Inspector, Rose's bike is still in the barn. It has a flat."

Tyler turned to the warden. "I'd like to have a look at Miss Watkins's room."

"Of course."

"I'll show you," said Molly. "Save my soup," she said to the other girls. "If we're not back in an hour, call out the army." Even that remark couldn't conjure up a smile.

Tyler followed Molly across the grand foyer and up the curving staircase to the second floor.

"This floor is where most of us sleep. That's mine. I share with Freckles. The end one is Muriel's and Florence's. We have to go down the hall and up the back stairs," said Molly. "Rose's room is in what were previously the servants' quarters. There's just maids now, and they've moved over to the manor. The other girls didn't want these upper rooms because they're small and they get hot in the summer. Rose and Elsie shared one of them until Elsie moved into Whitchurch two months ago. We all thought Rose would mope but she didn't. She really liked it. She said she'd never had a room all to herself before. "

As they had probably been for decades, the narrow stairs were carpeted with sisal, worn in places, and the walls looked as if they could do with a coat of paint. There was a tiny landing at the top with two closed doors leading off it.

"The second room is used as a box room . . . this is Rose's."

There was a sign hanging on the door knob that said DO NOT DISTURB.

"Elsie got that from a posh hotel in Birmingham," said Molly.

The room was spartan: white walls, a bed, one dresser, a washstand, and a small wardrobe. The coverlet on the bed was slightly rumpled as if Rose had been lying there, but nothing else seemed out of place. He touched the cover for warmth. There was none.

There was a gilt crucifix hung above the bed. The top of the dresser was completely bare except for a framed print of a blue-robed Virgin Mary, eyes lifted to heaven; beside it was a round china box about three inches across with a picture of Jesus on top, His arms outstretched. There was a clasp on one side and Tyler flipped it open. There was nothing inside. He sniffed at it, but there was no discernible smell.

"It's a rosary box," said Molly. "Rose showed it to me once. It was her confirmation gift, I believe. She was proud of it."

"Miss Watkins is a Catholic, I gather?"

"Quite staunch."

"Where does she go to church?"

Molly looked disconcerted as if she should know the answer. "I'm not sure actually. Nobody else here is Catholic. Elsie was, but she said she was lapsed. She would use Sunday to sleep in. The rest of us go off to the Anglican church in Whitchurch or Ash Magna, except for Jessie Bailey, who's Methodist. She goes to Market Drayton. Rose did come with us to Whitchurch at first, but she hasn't done that for the past while. I never thought to ask her about it." Molly suddenly looked upset. "I almost used the past tense. Isn't that awful?"

"Not awful. It's easy to do. Anyway, this is useful to know. If she did decide to go to church this evening, it would make sense given what has happened. The Catholic church in Whitchurch is a bit of a haul knowing you'll have to come home in the dark, but that might be what she's done."

There were no notes or letters on the dresser or the night table, no indication of Rose's intentions.

He pulled open the top drawer. Like Elsie's, it contained Land Army–issue underwear and socks. The second drawer had even less. He moved a few undergarments aside but there was nothing else. The entire room was even more impersonal than Elsie's except for the Catholic mementos.

Molly had been watching him. "I don't think she has many clothes other than the ones the Army issued her. Both she and Elsie seemed to be quite hard up when they arrived. Not that Elsie stayed that way for long. She was always decked out in some new outfit. Every penny of her wages went on clothes. Rose sends most of her money home."

Tyler opened the tiny wardrobe. Like the dresser drawers, there wasn't much in it. A pair of dungarees, corduroy trousers, a mackintosh, two shirts; all of them Land Army uniform. There was one plain green dress forlornly shoved to the far end.

"She must've changed into a frock," said Molly over his shoulder. "She only has two. That one there, and one I gave her."

"What does it look like?"

"White with pink and yellow flowers, with a V-neck and short sleeves. Rose is a little sprat of a thing and my frock shrunk in the laundry. What with that and me putting on some muscle, it didn't fit anymore so I gave it to her. There was a straw hat with yellow daisies around the brim that went with it. That's gone too. Oh, and a handbag. Muriel gave her one. White straw."

Tyler wrote that down. He might be called upon to send out a description of the missing girl. He hoped it wouldn't come to that.

He bent down to look underneath the bed. Bits of dust fluff and a pair of heavy regulation-issue shoes.

He went over to the window and cautiously lifted the blackout curtain. The room overlooked the yard, but it was too dark to see much.

They heard somebody coming up the stairs, and for a second the hope flashed through Tyler's mind that it was Rose returning. It wasn't. Freckles looked nervously around the door.

"I just wondered if you needed any help."

"I think we've finished here, but I would like to take a look at the barn where you keep your bikes. I'd appreciate it if you'd come too, Miss Cooper."

"For goodness sake, call me Molly. Only the servants address us so formally."

"And call me Freckles," said the redhead. "Everybody does."

The three of them trooped down the stairs. There was a rear exit on the ground floor, which opened onto the cobble stone yard. The barn was directly across. Freckles had a torch and she flicked it on, pointing it dutifully to the ground. Tyler walked behind her and she led the way inside the barn, closing the door behind them.

"I lit the lamp. The blackout curtains are all pulled."

The barn was large and obviously now used as a garage and storage for farm implements. Tyler unhooked the lantern and held it high. The light shone on Sir Percy's Bentley in one corner. Next to it was the silver-grey Rolls-Royce that belonged to Lady Somerville. The new restrictions on petrol didn't seem to have curtailed her trips. Tyler had seen her sailing past on her way to church. He supposed her chauffeur was claiming to be in a reserved occupation.

Parked beside the Rolls was the farm lorry, and against the wall, an ancient black Ford. One other car, a solid-looking brown Riley, was next to the Bentley. The Land girls' bicycles were all in a rack to the right of the door.

"That green one belongs to Rose," said Freckles. "The nice red Raleigh is Molly's and the blue is mine."

Suddenly, the barn door banged open and Arthur Trimble came in. His anger was palpable and Tyler even thought the man's moustache was vibrating.

"What the bloody hell's going on in here? You're showing a light."

"One of the girls is unaccounted for," said Tyler. "Her name is Rose Watkins. I was just checking to see if she had taken her bike."

Trimble gave a contemptuous snort. "Them girls are always taking off with some excuse or another." He glared at Molly and Freckles. "One of you two, go and close the blackout curtains properly up in the loft. There's a gap can be seen from here to Germany."

"Yes, Mr. Trimble," said Freckles, and she scrambled off up the ladder.

Molly glared right back at him. "It's absolutely not true what you just said about us being irresponsible. The opposite is true."

Her posh accent was cutting, but Trimble didn't seem dashed.

"Naturally enough, these young women are worried about Rose, given what happened to Elsie Bates," put in Tyler.

Arthur shrugged. "She'll be back when she's good and ready."

Tyler could hardly contradict him, seeing as how he'd said more or less the same thing not too long ago, but as usual the man rubbed him the wrong way.

"We think she left the hostel about seven o'clock. Did you happen to see her?"

Trimble scowled. "I don't have time to sit around idle. I was working in the rose garden 'til it got dark, then I went in to get my supper. I haven't seen nobody."

Freckles came climbing back down the ladder.

"There's a little tear in the curtain, Mr. Trimble. I fixed it as best I could but it will have to be sewn."

"You'd better bloody well get on it, then. Jerry can see a pinprick of light and use it for a guide."

Trimble's voice had been harsh and contemptuous. Freckles looked as though she would burst into tears.

"We're not supposed to do domestic duty," said Molly.

Trimble's moustache really was quivering now. Tyler intervened before the man could explode.

"Let's not get into that, Molly," he said. "I'll leave you to sort out the curtain. It should be repaired right away."

She looked as if she was going to protest, but thought better of it.

"Ladies, you've been most helpful. Why don't you get back and finish your supper? I'll come over in a minute."

Molly, somewhat reluctantly, nodded her agreement, and the two girls walked past Trimble, the redhead shrinking against her friend.

"Have you done?" Trimble asked Tyler. "I'm going to lock the door. I don't want nobody else coming in here until we fix that curtain."

"In a minute. I just want to have a look around."

"What for?"

"Police business."

He walked over to Sir Percy's Bentley. To give the car a thorough examination he'd need daylight, but he wanted to aggravate Trimble a little more on principle. He couldn't see any dents or scratches on the Bentley, and he moved over to the Rolls, Trimble behind him.

"I don't like you being in here with a light on. What are you looking for?"

Tyler ignored him. The Rolls was also immaculate and looked as if it had been polished recently.

"Who looks after Lady Somerville's car?"

"Me, now. Jack of all trades, me. Her regular chauffeur got seconded or whatever you call it. He's driving some nob from the Ministry around."

"Did you clean it today?"

"I did. You never know when she wants to go out. What of it?"

Tyler turned on him. "Look Trimble. I'm conducting a murder enquiry. I've got authority to arrest anybody, man, woman or child, who hinders my investigation. And I'm starting to consider you a hindrance."

The manager looked at him, his jaw clenched stubbornly. "It's all very well for you to throw your weight around, but I'm responsible for these cars. Anything happens to them, it'll be my job on the line."

"What the bloody hell do you think I'm going to do, piss up the wheels?"

"I wouldn't put it past you," muttered Trimble, but he backed off and sat down on a wooden box by the door.

Tyler examined the Ford, which, in contrast to the other cars, was dusty and battered. He ran his fingers lightly over the bonnet and they left traces.

"When did you use this last?" he called out to Trimble.

"It's dead as a doornail. Hasn't been out for a fortnight. I can't get the right part for it."

"Who owns the Riley?"

"One of the girls in the hostel. Name's Hancocks. What a girl her age needs with a Riley is beyond me, but she's spoiled rotten. Father making a fortune turning out airplane parts. There's always some sod who gets rich during a war, ain't there?" He spat on the floor.

The Riley wasn't new but the chassis looked in good shape. No dents or scratches there either. Tyler went over to the lorry. More to irritate Trimble than anything else, he opened the door on the passenger side and peered inside. It reeked of tobacco but there was nothing he could see of importance. A few feathers drifted around the interior, otherwise it was empty.

He turned back to the manager. "All right. I'm done here. Let's go."

"Bleeding waste of my time, this is," growled Trimble.

He followed Tyler out and locked the door carefully behind

him. Tyler walked back across the yard to the house, leaving Trimble to shuffle himself off to his quarters.

The thought was going round and round in Tyler's head: *Rose, Rose, please come back to us unharmed.*

The common room was deserted except for Florence Hancocks. She was sitting on the couch with her feet up, smoking yet another cigarette. Tyler thought she still looked nervous and too haggard for a young girl.

"The others have gone off to have their baths, Inspector. Miss Stillwell is in her office. I gather from Molly there are no indications as to where Rose has gone."

"No. Any ideas?"

"None. I wish I did."

"By the way, Miss Hancocks, I believe you own the Riley that's in the barn?"

"Yes, I do."

She was gazing at him and she seemed tense and wary.

"You were with your mother in Bath and returned to the hostel shortly before nine tonight?"

"Yes, that's correct."

"Which route did you take?"

That question caused a stiffening of her body. "I came straight down the canal road. It's better surfaced than some of the others."

"Take you about two hours, did it?"

"Yes, about that."

"Good for you. Last time I did that drive, it was in daylight. I would have thought driving in the blackout would take twice as long."

She stubbed out her cigarette.

"Are you stringing me a line, Miss Hancocks?"

She opened her case and removed a fresh cigarette but didn't light it. "I apologize, Inspector. I was being slightly devious. In fact, I left Bath at about eleven in the morning. I stopped off at Shrewsbury. Frankly, I seized the opportunity to do some shopping and have a good meal."

"That's not such a sin. Why'd you lie about it?"

"I didn't want to upset Miss Stillwell. She's big on loyalty and hard work. If she knew I could have been back earlier, she would be disappointed in me. Please don't tell her."

"I had no intention of doing that, Miss Hancocks. Well, I'll wish you good night. Try to get some sleep. And if you do need to reach me, you can ring at any time."

"Thank you."

At the door, he paused. "What did you buy in Shrewsbury?"

"I beg your pardon?"

"You said you did some shopping."

"Not quite. I said I was going to do some shopping but I didn't find anything I liked. The shops are quite bare these days."

Tyler nodded, and closed the door behind him.

23.

The rendezvous was to be used only in cases of utter necessity and he'd received the sign requesting a meeting tonight, usual time, early hours when it was the safest. He'd gone to sleep right after lights out, knowing he was always able to wake himself at the appointed time. Tonight, however, he woke well before two. The men in his tent were restless, the usual relentless cacophony of snuffles, grunts and snores. Their straw palliasses were covered with canvas which creaked when they moved. The sound reminded him of the sailing ship he worked on as a boy when the sails stirred and snapped in the wind. A ship is never silent, and sometimes the tent felt the same way. He'd loved those few years, the toughness of it, the comradeship, the rare peace he'd found when he was on the night watch, the boat moving like a live creature under his hands. If he allowed himself such a feeling, he would have said he was lonely now, an alien in more ways than these mumbling, dreaming fools knew.

He lay on his back, his hands folded across his chest, as he tried to ascertain from the level of breathing if the other men were all asleep. He heard somebody moving outside, the sound of the tent flap as the man returned to his bed. He held his watch close to his eyes, the moonlight sufficient for him to read the time. He had to wait another twenty minutes. He heard a faint distant barking, not a dog, more likely a fox.

His overseer was not much given to poetics, but shortly before he was to leave, he'd said, "Think of yourself as a fox. You must operate by cunning and stealth. You must be as ruthless and . . ." here he'd actually chuckled ". . . you must have teeth that are just as sharp."

He sat up, waited to make sure he'd disturbed nobody, then slipped out of bed. He picked up a black fedora. He didn't need it; the nights were still warm. However, sometimes it was better to be slightly conspicuous if afterward you wanted to be inconspicuous. As expected, he saw the faint glow of a cigarette as the guard walked the perimeter of the camp, his fag cupped in his hand. He paused, timing his move so that the soldier would be at the farthest northern side, then he walked swiftly and confidently, simply another man in a hurry to get to the latrine. Sensibly, the authorities had situated the row of latrines in the southeast corner of the camp where the prevailing Welsh wind would blow the odours away from the tents. The rear wall was a mere inches from the barbed wire, underneath a stand of trees, the idea being that the shade would also keep the place from getting too noisome. The outer design was reminiscent of an English park, the entrance by way of a canvas-covered walk; discreet, private. Ah, the foolish English. A fence post stood a couple of feet from the latrine and the wire was fastened to one of its walls. It had been so simple to loosen the screws. The gap between the fence and the wall was just wide enough for him to slip through. The adjacent copse was still lush and thick with summer growth and provided a perfect cover.

First, he made sure there was nobody inside any of the stalls, and then, waiting for a cloud to cross the moon, he slipped out. The guard would complete his circuit in about ten minutes but he would never notice the wire was not secure at the latrine. He smiled to himself. He could stay out until dawn if he wanted to.

The rendezvous spot was close by, and for once, his contact was waiting. They didn't greet each other; words had to be as few as possible.

"Get down," he ordered, and crouched low on the soft moss. In order to hear each other, their heads were as close together as if they were lovers; for him, unpleasantly intimate. A sour smell came from the other man. The stink of fear.

"Well?"

"A girl saw me. She saw what I was doing. I had to silence her. There was no other way. I couldn't take a chance."

"Tell me exactly what happened."

He listened to the story, forcing himself to be patient.

"You did the right thing. Did you hide the body?"

"Temporarily."

"Hmm. We need to do better than that. Is there somewhere you can put her that will, shall we say, mislead the police?"

"I don't know . . ."

"Think. Can you tie it to the death of the other girl?"

"Maybe. No, I can. I'll think of something."

"Good."

"I've got to get away. The police are combing the woods."

"Where do you intend to go?"

"Fuck that. You know bloody well where I'm going. And I want more money."

"Very well. But it will take a while to get it."

"Sooner the better."

The other man sounded less frightened now, more belligerent. His usefulness would soon be over.

"You must be careful. Don't do anything to get yourself noticed. I have no desire to be hanged and I'm sure you don't either."

Initially, he'd regretted accepting this particular task. He considered himself a man of action. A warrior. But he was ripe pickings when the others had approached him. He was still seething at being virtually cast out in spite of his protestations that his old wound didn't impede him. But the others flattered and soothed him. His excellent English was such an asset; the job required a man of intelligence and subtlety, as well as the mindset of a soldier. However, time seemed to pass slowly and he fretted at the inaction. He'd done everything that was required of him, *including working with this useless piece of English shit. Worse, in spite of the assurances he'd been given as to the value of the information he was after, sometimes it seemed as if it would merely add one more small piece of flotsam to one more useless pile.*

"Be patient. When you must strike, do so quickly and ruthlessly."

These were the words that kept him going.

24.

FOR THE SECOND MORNING IN A ROW, TYLER WAS awakened by somebody shaking his shoulder.

"The warden from the hostel rang. She wants you to ring her back right away." It was Vera.

"What time is it?"

"Half past six."

He swung his legs out of bed. He'd been so tired when he went to bed he'd slept soundly, no dreams to torment him. His head was clear, his stomach quiescent, for which he was most grateful.

"Damn. I should be up. I thought I'd set the alarm for six."

"I turned it off. You know how I hate the bloody thing. It sends my nerves through the ceiling."

Vera was in her dressing gown, her hair in the inevitable curlers.

She went over to the dressing table. She was still a good-looking woman, but time had worn away at the lush beauty he'd first found attractive. She was pinched where she had been full. Even though Tyler knew he'd been on the rebound from Clare, at first he thought he and Vera might be happy together. She was caring, accommodating, and for one or two years, they had lived in the glow of youth and sex. It didn't last, though; couldn't really. She knew he wouldn't have married her if he hadn't put her in the family way, and that knowledge lay buried deep in her heart like a sliver beneath the skin. Invisible but constantly festering. He wished he could have given her the love she wanted, but had long ago lost even the desire to try.

He sighed. Vera glanced over at him sharply.

"What's wrong?"

"Nothing. Just work. Why don't you catch a few more winks?"

He tried to put some civility into his voice, but Vera must have picked up on his thoughts or seen them in his eyes because her voice became hurried.

"Now I'm up, I may as well stay up. Dad asked me to come over and help add up ration coupons. He likes to do it before he opens." Her dark hair was sitting in sausages all over her head and she started to brush them out. Thick and wavy, her hair was one of her best features. It was still dark; she plucked out the grey strands immediately.

He took his dressing gown off the hook on the door. "I'd better get on to that phone call. God knows, it would be nice if it was good news, but somehow I doubt it."

Vera began applying her makeup.

"You look nice, Vee."

"Good Grief! A compliment. I wonder what I did to deserve that?" She wet her finger and smoothed her eyebrows. "Celia Clark was at the Institute last night. She told us about that Land Army girl getting herself killed."

"Yes, I was going to tell you myself."

"I should hope so. Some of the women think it's a Jerry on the loose. Somebody escaped from that alien camp. Is it?"

"We haven't found the culprit yet, but it's not likely it's anyone from the camp. They're all behind barbed wire."

"That's what I said to her. It's somebody closer to home if you ask me. I saw that girl around town and she was clearly no better than she should be. If you ask me, she probably got what was coming to her."

"I didn't."

"What?"

"I didn't ask you, Vera. This girl didn't deserve what happened to her."

"Well, pardon me for breathing."

This was Vera at her worst, lips a straight line, the lipstick a slash of crimson.

She went over to the wardrobe for her clothes, and Tyler headed downstairs.

I'm going to leave her, he thought. *I can't stand this, I'm going to leave her. As soon as this case is finished, I'm moving out.*

It wasn't the first time he'd had these thoughts, but it was the first time he'd felt such resolve. He'd been tied to Vera for years; guilt, responsibility, shame, all of them obdurate as forged steel. But now Clare had walked back into his life and he remembered what love was like. It was so utterly unfair to Vera to live with a man whose heart belonged to another woman. And always had. It was strange, but as he voiced these feelings to himself, the anger abruptly left him. It was going to be hard telling the kids, but he suspected they wouldn't be surprised. He'd start looking for a place to live as soon as he could.

He put the kettle on for his tea and cut off a couple of jagged pieces of bread. While the water was boiling, he walked into the hall and picked up the telephone. Mavis answered.

"Number please?"

"Hello, Mavis, it's Tom. Will you connect me to the dower house? I want to speak to Miss Stillwell."

"Oo, Tom, I've heard about that poor soul who died. One of them Land Army girls, I hear. I hope you catch the killer soon. We none of us women feel safe now. I had to have our Charlie come and get me last night."

"Good. I want you to tell all the women you know to be careful. This is most likely an isolated incident but you never know. If anybody sees anybody acting suspiciously, tell them to get in touch with me right away."

Mavis sniffed. "These days you can see somebody acting suspiciously on every corner. They're ARP men . . . Carol Haycroft says she heard that the dead girl were mixed up with some of the enemy aliens. She weren't a spy, were she?"

"My God, Mavis. I can't believe how rumours get around. No, of course she wasn't a spy."

"Just wondering. It's my skin I have to protect. . . . That other girl sounded right urgent last night when she called. Put the chills into me."

"What other girl?"

"One of the Land Army girls. She were ringing from the hostel. She wanted to speak to you. I put a call through to the station but nobody answered. I offered to take a message but she said she'd call again."

"What time did this happen?"

"About a quarter to seven. I was getting ready to leave."

"Did she give her name?"

"Rose Watson or something like that."

"Watkins?"

"That's it. Rose Watkins. She said as how she wanted to speak to you, and to say it was important."

"And that's it? No mention of what it was about?"

"Not at all. I already told you what she said and what I said. That's it."

"Damn it, Mavis, you should have insisted on taking down a message. Why didn't you try me at home?"

She snorted. "I'm not a mind reader, Tom. If she had wanted to leave a message with me she could have, but she didn't, so there. And as for ringing you at home, she was off the line in a flash."

"All right, all right. I'm sorry."

"And so you should be."

The kettle began its shrill whistle from the kitchen. "Mavis, kettle's boiling. Ring me right back when you get Miss Stillwell for me."

He replaced his receiver and went into the kitchen to silence the kettle. Dear God, he hoped the delay in talking to Rose wasn't going to turn out to be a crucial one. *Something important.* When he had talked to her in the library, he'd had the feeling she was withholding something, something to do with Elsie. Why hadn't she called him back? Had something made her change her mind? Or was it worse than that?

The phone rang. He hurried to answer it.

"Inspector?" Miss Stillwell's voice was tight. "I do apologize for the early hour, but Rose Watkins has not returned. I was anxious to know if you had any news."

"Not yet, I'm afraid."

"First Elsie, now Rose missing. What is happening?"

"I thought it might be worth pursuing her connection to the Catholic churches in the area. I understand that she attended Mass in Whitchurch."

"Yes. Yes, she did. As soon as she arrived here, she sought out a church she could go to . . . but . . ." The warden's voice became animated. "Usually, all the girls who are going to church pool together. I've given them permission to use the lorry. Sometimes, they bicycle but most of them are wearing their Sunday best and don't want to get their clothes dirty. But Inspector –"

"What is it, Miss Stillwell?"

"I just realized that I saw Rose once or twice walking out of the gate on Sunday mornings. She wasn't going in the direction of Whitchurch."

"Where would she be going?"

"I believe she was going over the camp at Prees Heath."

"The camp?"

"I'm sure of it. I have a friend who is Roman Catholic, and she told me recently that she has been attending the service at the camp. They aren't all Jewish there; a small group of them are Christian. She said that the priest regularly says Mass twice a day, and in the past month, outsiders have been allowed to attend. It is easier for Mrs. Dwyer to go to Prees Heath than to go to St. Paul's in Whitchurch. She quite likes it, she says. In spite of being German, the priest is very friendly. In fact, Inspector, I'd wager that when Violet saw Rose last night, that's where she was going."

The information didn't explain why Rose hadn't returned, but it was something.

"I have to go to the camp today. I'll make enquiries."

He heard Miss Stillwell clearing her throat and he wondered if she was crying.

"I've let the girls have a little sleep-in this morning. I don't know whether to send them off to work. There's such a lot to do at this time of year, but with this troubling turn of events about Elsie Bates, I don't know if they would be better staying home. What do you think, Inspector?"

"Unless they are dead set against it, I recommend they continue as usual," said Tyler. "Take their minds off everything. I promise I will contact you immediately if any news comes in."

"Thank you, Inspector."

"Try not to worry, Miss Stillwell."

Empty words. He had a bad feeling about the whole situation. Rose Watkins was no wild child, no rebel. If she could have, he was sure she would have let the warden know where she was.

They hung up and he headed back to the kitchen.

Miss Stillwell rang again a few minutes later. Her voice was shaking.

"Inspector, I'm afraid I have quite dreadful news. I just received a call from Mr. Watkins, Rose's father. Apparently, there was a terrible accident on the street involving two fighter planes. They collided with each other and one dropped onto the house. Their house is quite destroyed and Rose's mother has been injured. He wanted me to give the news to Rose and he wants her to get leave and return to London." The warden's voice cracked. "Inspector, I did not know what to say to him. I'm afraid I was a coward. I simply said Rose was not available just now, but I would have her get in touch as soon as I could. Was that the right thing to do?"

Tyler's heart sank. This was what the London constable had told him. Elsie's family too. How could you tell a man his daughter was missing, maybe even dead like her friend, when the poor sod was already in the midst of tragedy?

"You did absolutely the right thing, Miss Stillwell. We don't know where Rose is as yet. Better not to alarm her father at a time like this."

They hung up and Tyler returned to the last of his tea.

Outside the thunder rumbled threateningly. Vera came into the kitchen.

"Did you have a talk with Janet last night?"

"I did. She's got some things she needs to sort out."

"I see. I'm to be excluded as usual? I am her mother. I'd like to know what's on her mind."

"You're not being excluded, Vee. It's just that—"

"She's Daddy's girl," interrupted Vera.

Some time ago it seemed as if he and Vera had come to an unspoken agreement. A girl for him, a boy for her. Nevertheless, Vera resented her daughter's closeness to her father. For his part, he would liked to have much more communication with his only son, but Vera got in the way.

She began to tug on pristine white gloves. "Jimmy's already

gone. No breakfast again, I might add. He said he was going to help Mrs. Thorne with her garden. She sees more of him than his own mother." At the door, she turned. "You'd better make sure Janet is up. It takes her an age to get going. She shouldn't be late."

She had expressed no curiosity about his early call from Miss Stillwell.

The door snipped shut behind her and Tyler went to the bottom of the stairs. "Janet. Time to get up."

A rumpled girl appeared on the landing. "I am up, Dad."

"Tea's on."

He returned to the kitchen. Ominous black clouds were roiling in the sky. A thunderstorm was coming.

Janet came down the stairs in her dressing gown.

"I've got to go, pet," said Tyler. "I should have been at the station ten minutes ago. It's going to rain by the look of it; take your umbrella."

She gave him an exasperated grin. "I could have figured that out myself, Dad."

He wagged his finger at her. "Don't be cheeky. I'll see you tonight."

He folded up the bread and jam and crammed it into his mouth. Janet poured herself some tea.

"Look, Jan. I want you to be careful."

She turned around. "Careful in what way?"

"Use common sense. Don't go into deserted places by yourself."

"Dad! I'm working today. You can hardly call Granddad's shop a deserted place."

"Nevertheless. All I'm saying is be sensible. I can rely on you for that, can't I?"

She concentrated on drinking her tea. "Of course you can. See you tonight then."

25.

THE STORM OPENED UP JUST AS TYLER STEPPED OUT of his door. He made a dash for the police station but even in that short distance, he got drenched.

Sergeant Gough was behind the desk. The clock on the wall showed a quarter past seven.

"What time did you get in?" Tyler asked.

"About half an hour ago. Shall I get you a towel, sir? You resemble a drowned rat, if I may put it that way."

"You may not. And I can get my own towel."

The wc was off Tyler's office. Not quite his own private toilet but close enough. There was another one for general use. He was thinking he might hang his pictures of Clare in here but he hadn't yet got up the nerve.

He returned to the front desk. "I had a phone call from Miss Stillwell, the warden at the hostel. Rose Watkins has not returned. She thinks she may have been heading for the Prees Heath camp when the maid saw her. They have a priest there who says Mass. Apparently locals have been attending."

"Yes, I heard about that."

"What! How come you know of it, and I didn't?"

"From Constable Collis, as a matter of fact. He's RC and found out he could attend Mass there. It's closer than his own regular church. He was worried, in case it would look bad. An officer of the Shropshire constabulary cavorting with enemy aliens."

"You said it was fine, I presume?"

"I did. The super apparently attended a concert at the camp not so long ago." Gough did an imitation of the posh, marble-mouthed superintendent. "Quite superior music, I'd say. As good as Albert Hall."

Tyler laughed. "I'll speak to the priest when I go over there today. In the meantime, Guff, let's go over what we have so far?"

Gough handed him a piece of paper. "Here's a list of all vehicles that have been registered since the outbreak of war. It's by no means complete, but it's a place to start."

Tyler glanced over it. The local ones he was familiar with. Sir Percy had three registered: his Bentley, the Rolls, and the farm lorry. Arthur Trimble had a Ford; Dr. Murnaghan and the vicar both had Austins; the headmaster of the private school in Market Drayton drove a Rover. See how long he'd get to drive *that* with petrol rationing.

He drew a line through the vicar's name. "Reverend Pound's Austin has been up on blocks for the past six months. He goes everywhere on his bike."

To his surprise, there was a 1933 Morris registered to Alice Thorne. He'd never seen her drive it, but she'd renewed the licence just last year.

"There are two temporary registrations," said Gough. "They're both garaged at the manor. A Mrs. Devereau, who owns an MG, and a Miss Hancocks, who has a Riley. Isn't she the same girl who claims her brother gave her a gun?"

Tyler had rung Gough the previous night to tell him what had occurred at the hostel.

"One and the same. She says she was at home in 'Barth', with her mummy and daddy until eleven in the morning. Have the local plod go to the house and confirm that. He should also get a sworn affidavit from the brother. From the description, the Luger that killed Elsie is no doubt the same as the one he purchased. The holster I put in the drawer of my desk, with a piece of paper with the serial number of the gun on it. Compare the two, will you Guff?"

"Will do. You said it seems like the Bates girl stole the gun herself. Was she carrying it with her, do you think?"

"Might have been. Maybe she aimed it at her killer and he grabbed it." He rubbed his head vigorously, and turned his attention back to the list of registered vehicles, checking off each name. Seven vehicles belonging to local farmers, all men he knew well. Two motorcycles; one of them registered to Jimmy, and the other to Bobby Walker. He remembered they had bought them at the same time, shortly before they signed up for the army. Come to think of it, he'd lent Jimmy the money and he hadn't paid it back yet.

"Good work, Guff. Let's get our lads for this job. They should talk to everybody on this list who I haven't crossed off. We need to ask the owners for their whereabouts yesterday morning between six and seven, no, make that five-thirty and seven. I want to talk personally to anybody who can't account for themselves."

"Yes, sir. Does that include Jimmy?"

"Of course. Why not? Complete impartiality is our middle name." Tyler tried to make a joke of it.

"Yes, sir. I just thought that if you could vouch for Jimmy's whereabouts, it would save us some time."

"We're talking about six o'clock in the morning, Guff. I don't sleep with the lad. I didn't see him when I was hauled out of bed by Sir P.'s phone call, which was at seven. He's the original Scarlet Pimpernel, that boy. Speak to Bobby Walker, too, if you can get permission from the hospital."

Tyler realized how peculiar his words must sound, and he touched his finger to the side of his nose.

"Here's a clue for you, Guff. Seven-letter word for a major cock-up of this war."

"I'd say that was Dunkirk."

"And you'd be right. Perhaps one of these days my son will tell me what went on."

A thunder clap sounded close, and they stopped for a moment to listen to the rain drumming on the roof.

"I've a cousin as lives in Dover," continued the sergeant. "His fishing boat got commandeered by the navy. He could have left it to them blokes, but he dotes on that boat of his and he insisted on, skippering it himself. Nobody would tell him what was going on, but he was ordered to cross the channel. They says he'd get his instructions when they got there." The sergeant paused. "He's not what you'd call a fanciful man, is my cousin, but he wrote to me after. He said it was like sailing into hell itself. The smoke from the burning tankers was making everything dark, like it was night, even though the sun was shining. The sea was thick with the dead, bobbing like apples on a pond . . . his words, not mine, sir. There were hundreds and hundreds of men waiting to get off the beaches. The little boats like his were used to ferry the soldiers to the destroyers, which couldn't get in close enough. But Jerry was strafing them as they waited. My cousin was told to get out and return to Dover, so he did. He was overloaded and could have hit a mine at any time, but he made it. He says he has nightmares."

This lengthy speech by the normally taciturn sergeant was unprecedented and took Tyler aback. Then he nodded. "So does Jimmy. But he won't talk about it. I don't know how to help him."

"Maybe it's just a matter of time, sir."

"I don't know how much of that we've got. He'll be sent back to join his unit soon and then to the front. I'm not happy knowing he'll be fighting in the state he's in now."

"I saw him in the market a couple of weeks ago," said

Gough. "He bought one of Mrs. Thorne's concoctions, I noticed. I got some soap for the wife myself. Perhaps your lad has a lass he's courting on the sly."

Tyler registered this information but said nothing.

"What about the car belonging to Mrs. Devereau?" asked the sergeant. "The MG? Do you want us to speak to her as well?"

Tyler drummed his fingers on the desk. "Let's put it this way, Guff. Mrs. Devereau is living on the Somerville estate and she works at the Prees Heath camp. She had no reason to be on the Heath Road. I think we can assume she's not involved."

"If you say so, sir. Shouldn't we follow up anyway? Then we can cross her off the list."

Tyler handed the list back.

"I'll look after it, Guffie. I will also speak to my son. Happy now?"

"Yes, sir."

"Have Eagleton and Collis come in yet?"

"I told them to be here by seven-thirty."

"Ah, speaking of the devils."

The door banged open and the two constables burst in. They too had got soaked and were laughing together at their mutual state.

"Well look at the sweet little duckies," said Tyler. "Don't you lads have enough sense to carry brollies?"

"Morning, sir," said the two constables in unison.

"You're dripping all over the floor. Here." He threw them the towel. "There's another one in the kitchen. Eager, go and get it. I don't want you lads catching your death. I don't have any replacements." The constable scurried off.

"And while you're doing that, make us all a cuppa. Extra sugar for me. Use your own ration if you have to. I'll owe you."

—

When the two young men had dried off as best they could, and the tea was made, the three police officers gathered around Tyler's desk.

"All right. Do I now have your complete attention?" They nodded. "Collis, when will the photographs of the body be ready?"

"Mr. Henry promised to have them developed early this afternoon."

"Good. Dr. Murnaghan has completed his post-mortem and is sending those photos over as well. We'll pin them up in the duty room so we can have a good study. If either of you faints, you'll have to lie there; I'm not picking you up and rubbing your cold little hands. Understood?"

"Excuse me, sir," said Collis. "I don't think any photograph could be as bad as the actual thing."

"Quite right, lad. You lads did good. Now then." Tyler tapped on the piece of paper. "Guff here has made three copies of this list. I'm giving you one. Don't lose it. You've got to track down everybody. Get alibis. While you're at it, see if anybody heard anything, saw anything, smelled anything . . . I don't care which. We know somebody was driving on the Heath Road around six o'clock, and that shortly afterward a girl was shot. Ask if anybody heard the gun shot."

"Yes, sir." Eagleton especially was having difficulty containing his enthusiasm.

"While you're asking these questions you are also what, Eagleton? What are you also doing?"

"Keeping our eyes and ears open for anything that seems suspicious."

"Good. Now it's very possible, given the precarious times we are living in, that the person you are talking to may be evidencing signs of guilt. It doesn't mean they know eff all about Elsie

Bates. They may be into profiteering or messing with the neighbour's wife while the poor sod's on the front line. Don't arrest them. Just make a mental note and tell me about it later."

He looked at his watch. "Sergeant, get hold of the Barth chappies, will you? Tell them it's urgent. You know how lackadaisical they are. Too much sulphur in the water. Collis, go and fetch that blackboard. The one we used to teach the infant school kiddies how to put on their gas masks. There's one more thing I want to think about before we all scatter. Then I've got to get over to the camp to meet a German professor who thinks he can help us. He's an expert on the criminal mind, apparently. As far as I am concerned he can stuff his theories up his jacksie but he's an enemy alien. He might be able to tell me more than he realizes."

Tyler stood the blackboard in the centre of his office. "All right, lads, put on your thinking caps. I want you to say anything that comes to mind, don't worry if it sounds right stupid. We'll sort out the gold from the dross as we go. Now then, Collis, you can be teacher. Draw a line down the middle; on the left, write 'certain', on the right, 'possible'. You'd better write small; there are more variables in this case than there are pieces in Guffie's dog's sick up."

The constables allowed themselves little disloyal grins. Sergeant Gough owned a racing greyhound that he was very proud of. It had a sensitive stomach.

Tyler drank some of his tea. "Ready? Question number one. Where was the vehicle going at that hour of the morning? Was it driving *south* from the direction of Whitchurch or north *toward* Whitchurch? The Heath Road is joined further down by the number four road, which comes from Shrewsbury or from Market Drayton. And of course anywhere beyond that. Any ideas?"

Both constables were quiet, then Eagleton said tentatively, "There aren't many people out driving in the dark these days, sir, unless their journey is urgent or . . ."

"Or what, Eager? Spit it out."

"Or they are doing something nefarious, sir."

"Good word, nefarious. I like it. Makes me feel educated. Or in common parlance, they are doing something against the law. Which could be a variety of things, such as?"

"B and E. The driver was coming from a robbery."

"A well-heeled crook if he has his own car, but that's all right. Besides, nobody has reported a robbery. Go on."

"Black marketeering," chipped in Collis. "The driver had either made a delivery or was on his way to do so."

"Or was collecting something himself on the black market," said Eagleton.

Collis scrambled to write all this on the board.

"Now for convenience sake we are referring to our crook as male, but the driver could have been female," remarked Tyler.

"Or more than one person," said Eagleton.

"Exactly, could be a whole bloody gang for all we know."

"In which case we should particularly take a look at lorries," said Eagleton, dead serious.

"Good point. If there was more than one person in the vehicle, it possibly makes our case a bit easier. Why is that, Eager?" Tyler pointed at him.

"Because there is no honour among thieves and somebody could snitch."

"Exactly. All right, let's continue. We still don't have much on the certain side. I think we can safely assume Elsie Bates was heading south toward the hostel, although we can't totally rule out that she had left her lorry, biked off, met somebody for a bit of a shag, then was returning to the lorry in a northerly direction."

"That would put her having sex about five o'clock in the morning, or sooner, sir," blurted out Collis. "It's a bit early, isn't it?"

"Lad, are you a virgin?"

The constable blushed. "Well yes, sir, I am. I live at home and . . ."

"I thought you must be with a comment like that. You'll find out. Mornings are the best time to do it. For a man, anyway. So where were we? The lorry worked quite all right when we tried to start it, and we were able to drive it to the station. However, according to Elsie's friend, Rose, it had been giving her trouble. Anyway, let's go for the simplest explanation. The lorry conked out and Elsie left it and set off to bike to the hostel. The coroner said Elsie was hit hard on the left thigh. What does that tell you, Eager?"

"Not a lot, I'm afraid, sir. The road isn't wide, so we can't assume the vehicle was keeping to the left-hand side. They rarely do. In fact they'd be foolish to do so in the dark."

"Continue then."

"Sir," said Collis, "if I were biking on the road in the near dark and I heard a car coming, I would move over to one side or the other to get out of the way."

"Right. So we're betting even odds that the vehicle was coming from the north, but we won't close our minds to the possibility that it was the opposite. Write that down, Collis. But dammit. I feel like I'm trying to do a crossword puzzle without any clues."

"You should speak to the sergeant about that, sir," said Eager. "He's an expert."

Tyler drummed his fingers on the paper in front of him. "What else do we know? Just give me the certainties."

"She was killed approximately one hour before a quarter to seven, when her body was discovered. It wasn't light yet and it can be really dark in the lanes. The car was probably driving quite fast, which would suggest the driver was familiar with the roads."

"Not necessarily. Because he hit her, it might mean he was *not* familiar with the roads. We can't even assume the vehicle was travelling at a high speed. Even a tractor colliding with a human frame can inflict a lot of damage."

"Maybe it was even pursuing her."

"You certainly do have a good imagination, Eager. Why would the car be pursuing her?"

"I don't know, sir. Perhaps she'd had a quarrel with somebody."

"Hmm, you have a point. Her boyfriend couldn't get it up and things turned ugly. Nothing like disappointment in sex to kindle unpleasantness." Tyler bit his lip. "So far we have got piss all that's definite. And that brings us to the really big question. Did whoever who knocked her down get out of the car, go over to her, and shoot her? With a German Luger no less; a gun that Elsie probably stole from a girl at the hostel. If so, why?"

Eagleton answered. "To keep her quiet. So she couldn't tell on them."

"Right. And what if, as you so cleverly say, she was trying to get away? They catch up with her, boom. Deliberately knock her down then finish off the job with a gun."

"I think that's the best bet yet, sir."

"But the *why* of it is hanging out there like an old pisser's shirt. Unless we go for the furious lover angle."

"There is another possibility, sir."

"Spit it out, Eager."

"What if the vehicle hit her by accident? The road's treacherous, they're driving too fast. All of a sudden, there's a girl in the road. They can't stop in time, boom. They knock her over. They don't know they've hit somebody so they drive on . . ."

"Maybe."

"What if they did know then, but they panicked and just continued on driving? Then along comes the Luger man and he shoots Miss Bates as she lies there helplessly."

"Two people involved then?"

"Yes, sir. But they don't necessarily know each other."

Collis stopped scribbling and said timidly, "What if there were three people, sir? One who hit her, one who shot her, and one who put her up against the tree?"

"Do these three people know each other, by any chance?"

"Not necessarily," said Collis primly.

Tyler looked at him. "I did tell you to say anything, didn't I? Even if it is right stupid."

"Yes, sir. Sorry, sir."

"No no, lad, I don't want to shut you up. We do have to introduce some common sense, however. The likelihood of three different people wandering around in the wee hours before dawn in exactly the same place is really stretching it. If there was more than one person involved, they must have been accomplices." He pressed his thumbs into the corners of his eyes. "This is bringing my bloody headache back. Let's leave all the speculation for a minute. Can we add to our 'certain' column? . . . We do know the girl had sexual relations shortly before she died, and even that could be a range of four to five hours. The sex was most likely consensual according to the doctor. Another thing for the 'certain' side; she had money hidden in her dungarees, two pounds to be exact. Why'd she see the need to hide it? In addition, she also had a heart drawn on her behind in indelible pencil. Not necessarily having anything to do with her being killed, *or* everything to do with it. Where are we so far, Eager?"

"I think we're still in the dark, sir."

"And that is the only sure thing to date. The problem is that at the moment we don't have the foggiest as to *why* she was shot in the first place, never mind why she was moved and laid out like that."

Both constables stared blankly back at him. He sighed. "Thank you, lads. Now before you swim off, there's something else I should tell you. Elsie's best friend seems to have disappeared."

He filled them in on what had occurred.

"Do you think she's befallen the same fate?" asked Collis.

Tyler's eyebrows shot up. "What on earth have you been reading? Your mother's weekly magazine? Never mind, I know what you mean. If she doesn't show up soon, we're going to treat her as a missing person. Now off with you. The storm seems to be passing but don't stand under any trees. Remember what I said. We don't have any replacements."

The two constables trotted off and Tyler swallowed down his now tepid tea. For a minute, he studied the blackboard. Bloody hell, trying to sift through all this was like trying to read a foreign language. It might make sense to somebody, but it certainly didn't to him.

26.

Otto Schreyer ushered his last patient out the back door of his office, trying to conceal his irritation that Frau Katz had once again contrived to linger past her hour. She always managed to introduce an important dream five minutes before her time was up. He knew he had to confront her with this behaviour, which was unconsciously intended to make him annoyed with her, but he knew she'd be wounded and then he'd have to deal with that. He sighed. He probably had a counter-transference toward the lonely widow that he ought to bring up at his next supervisory session.

"Gute nacht."

"Gute nacht, Herr Doktor."

He locked the door behind her, picked up his jacket and hat from the coat tree, and walked over to the other door. All analysts' offices were set up so that a patient could enter by one door and exit by another and not run the risk of being seen by the other patients. He opened the entry door and was almost nose to nose with a man in a long leather coat.

"Ah, thank goodness I caught you, Doctor. My name is Bosen. I am from the Security police, and I would like to ask you a few questions if you don't mind."

Otto did mind. He had been looking forward to going to his bowling club for a game and a beer. However, there was something about the man that was intimidating. Otto made a show of consulting his watch.

"I am on my way to another appointment."

"I won't keep you."

Bosen extended his arm for all the world as if it were his office and he was ushering Otto into it. Otto had no choice but to return to his desk. He sat down again and the visitor took the other chair.

"I'll come straight to the point, Doctor, as you are in a hurry. It has come to our attention that this institute, against regulations, has been accepting patients who are non-Aryan, and that some of the analysts themselves are non-Aryan. As you must know, this is against the law."

Otto stiffened. "That has nothing to do with me. You must take it up with the director."

"Yes, of course, I intend to do so, but it has come to our attention that you yourself are in violation of these laws."

"I don't know to what you are referring," said Otto, swallowing hard but determined not to be cowed. "I am a pure German. I can show you my papers to prove it."

"Ah yes. We have checked that, but you are a junior analyst at the institute, are you not? You are still required to be under supervision."

Otto's heart sank. He had a feeling he knew what was coming next.

"I am. It is a regulation."

"Who is your supervisor?"

If he'd checked on Otto's ethnic status, he probably already knew the answer.

"Dr. Reitman." He dared a little. "He is also a German, from a well-established family here in Berlin."

"But he has only been your supervisor for a short time. Before that it was Dr. Bruno Beck? Who is a Jew."

"That's correct, but Dr. Beck is no longer here. He has emigrated to England."

Bosen made a show of fishing out a notebook from his pocket and flipping it open.

"Ah yes. The Jew was here at the institute until August of 1939. Before that, contrary to the law, he was accepting patients and was a fully functioning member of the institute."

"I believe that Dr. Beck was here strictly as a consultant, which was permitted. If he did have patients, they were Jewish only."

"I am glad to hear it. However, given this irregularity, I am authorized to examine your papers for the period from January to August of last year."

Otto gaped at him. "My papers? What do you mean?"

"It's quite simple," said Bosen with a touch of ice in his voice. "You take notes on your patients, do you not? I want to see them for the period I just mentioned."

"But they are confidential. They have nothing to do with what you are investigating."

"I am the best judge of that."

Otto could feel his heart beating faster. They were alone in the office, the secretaries had left. It was a lovely summer evening and he could hear the sound of children playing outside. He was a young man, naïve and inexperienced in many ways, yet he could sense that he was facing something more malevolent than anything he had yet known. He put his hands palms down on the desk.

"I'm afraid you will have to speak to the director. I have no authority to show you confidential material."

Bosen didn't reply but glanced around the room. In one corner was a filing cabinet.

"I quite understand your scruples, Doctor, and I admire you for them. However, the safety of the fatherland supersedes all such petty concerns. Besides, what would I be looking at? The trivial meanderings of neurotic, self-indulgent intellectuals who should be fighting for their country."

Stung, Otto replied with more spirit than he'd yet shown.

"You're quite wrong about that. The majority of our patients are women, unhappy women for the most part, and surely they have a right to get to the bottom of their unhappiness? After all, if you had a cancer, you would go for treatment would you not? It is not any different."

The other man didn't answer, but the look he gave Otto was full of contempt. "In fact, it is one such woman that I am particularly interested in." He glanced at his notebook. "Frau Mueller is her name. She was one of your patients. Do you remember her?"

Otto felt himself go cold. Of course, he remembered Frau Mueller. She was his first case, and from the beginning there was something about her that had troubled him.

"Why are you interested in this woman in particular? She was not Jewish. There was nothing illegal in her coming here for analysis."

"As I said previously, Doctor, allow me to be the judge of that." Bosen got to his feet so abruptly that Otto jumped. "You said you had an appointment. Let's not waste time. Give me the notes. I will give you a receipt, all quite above board, and I will let you go."

Otto shook his head. "No, I'm sorry. If my director says it is all right to hand them over I shall do so, but I'm afraid without his authorization I cannot do it."

The other man walked over to the window. "You are making things so much more complicated than they need to be, Doctor." He turned and studied Otto for a few moments. "By the way, as we are talking about confidentiality and you seem to be prepared to defend the principle to the death, were these notes confidential? No little seminar group pored over them, I assume? Just you and Dr. Beck."

"That's right."

"Does he have copies of your notes?"

"Yes, he does."

Bosen began to pull on his gloves as if he were leaving. Almost *abstractly, Otto noted this. A warm summer evening and the man was wearing leather gloves. "One more thing. According to my sources, Frau Mueller sent you some photographs, did she not?"*

"I must object to your question, sir. Whether she did or did not is still within the bounds of confidentiality."

"Ah yes. That word again. You weren't raised a Catholic by any chance, were you Doktor?"

"No . . . I don't see . . ."

"I was, and you sound like some of the priests I have known."

He reached into his pocket, took out a thin narrow case, and opened it. He removed a syringe, and before Otto could move, before he could comprehend what was happening, Bosen stepped forward and plunged the syringe deep into the artery in the side of his neck.

27.

IT WASN'T JUST THE STORM THAT HAD DRIVEN MOST of the internees into the mess tent. The nervousness was palpable. Groups of men huddled together or wandered around the various tables, seeking reassurance, questioning, fearful.

Dr. Beck had gone to meet with Fordham early that morning and now the men were waiting eagerly for him to return. They went quiet as he entered and walked briskly to the podium. He cleared his throat. "The commandant himself will address us all later this evening, but he assures me that there will be no more searches. He is content that we are not criminals and we are hiding nothing. I reported the incident of a guard pointing his rifle into the compound and he has promised to deal with the young man in question. He also says we will be transferred to better quarters soon. That is to the Isle of Man, for some of us. He will do his best to speed up the tribunal process so that we will not be held longer than is necessary."

Some men let out a cheer. The slowness of the tribunals – the only chance they had to plead their cases – was a source of great aggravation.

"Now I suggest we return to our regular activities," continued Beck. "I do believe the chess championship will soon be decided, not to mention the football cup."

The men began to gradually disperse. Father Glatz and the seminarian approached Beck.

"How is Herr Hartmann?" asked the priest.

Howard Silber was nearby and jumped in. "I hope he's not

going to accuse me of being a spy again?"

"I don't think so," answered Beck. "He's back in the real world today. But his lucidity is tenuous. I wondered if I could leave him your care, Father, while I have my meeting with the policeman."

"So that's why you're all dressed up," chuckled Silber. "I thought it had to be for more than just the major."

Beck was wearing a neat navy blazer, white duck trousers, and a straw panama.

"Obviously an important meeting," said the actor. He brushed some hairs off Beck's lapel. "You have trimmed your beard for the occasion, I see."

"As a matter of fact, I'm going to present the inspector with an article I wrote."

Silber threw up his hands in mock horror. "Let me guess. The game of chess as a manifestation of the Oedipal conflict. The entire aim is the capture of the king, the queen is all powerful, and the pawns are like children, weak and disposable."

"That is not the subject of my article," said Beck. "However, you make a good point. I have noticed that it is particularly men who are drawn to the game. What does it say of our own Oedipal complex, that Father Glatz and I are both compulsive players? Are we resolved or unresolved?" He smiled a rather professorial smile intended to disarm.

The priest smiled back good-naturedly. "I was always of the opinion I had grown up with respect and admiration for my father and a normal healthy affection for my mother. Shouldn't that make me rather bad at chess?"

"I cannot tell from what you are saying whether or not it is a good thing that I am mediocre at the game," said Hans Hoeniger. "Do I therefore have a well-balanced personality?" His eyes danced with mischief. Beck came in for a lot of teasing in the camp. Although he was highly respected, many of

the internees considered the practice of psychoanalysis peril-
ously close to the art of telling fortunes through the cards or
tea leaves.

Beck wagged his finger at them. "You are both being far
too simplistic. Unless I analyze you, I cannot determine all
the complexities of your respective personalities."

"Remind me not to start," laughed Hoeniger. "But I am all
ears. What is the article you are presenting to the inspector?"

Beck tapped at his pocket. "I presented this to the London
Psychoanalytic Society in thirty-eight. It is entitled 'The Urge
to Confess: an Analysis of the Criminal Mind.' Given the
recent circumstances, I hope it will be helpful to him."

"A provocative title. I would like to read it. Do you have
another copy?"

The professor looked pleased. "I'm afraid this is the only
one and it's an English edition. But I would be happy to
present the gist of my argument at the psychology club meeting, if you wish. However, you will have to be content with
something a little less polished than I would like. I have not
yet been able to obtain my complete files." He shook his head.
"I was arrested quite abruptly and had hardly time to pack
anything."

"As were so many of us, Herr Doktor," said Silber.
"Fortunately, a dear friend sent me a few books, so I am not
totally bereft. Surely there is somebody who would do that
for you?"

"I have sent word to my landlady, but so far she has not
replied."

"I think everybody would be delighted to hear what you
have to say, polished or no," said Glatz. "Don't you agree, Herr
Silber? Hans?"

"No good asking me," said Silber. "I don't have time for
anything except the drama club. I've promised to do a version

of *Henry V* before we disband." He shrugged at their expressions. "If you want to understand the English soul, you have to be familiar with *Henry V.*" He thrust his fist into the air. *"God for Harry, England and St. George.'"* With a theatrical swirl he strode off, shouting out, *"Gentlemen in England now abed, Shall think themselves accursed they were not here . . ."*

Father Glatz looked at Beck. "Is the man a genius, do you think?"

"He thinks he is," said Hoeniger.

A football suddenly bounced toward them, almost hitting the professor on the head. A tanned and lithe young man in a singlet and shorts came darting between the tents.

"Oops, sorry gentlemen." He grabbed the ball and dashed off again.

"Bader, you shouldn't be playing so close to the tents," Father Glatz shouted after him.

"There's another subject worthy of your analysis, Dr. Beck," said Hoeniger. "The obsession mankind has with trying to get round objects of various sizes into some kind of crevice, also of variable size."

Beck chuckled. "Very good, Hans. Very good. You've been paying attention to my talks I see." He touched the brim of his hat. "Excuse me, gentlemen, I must get to my appointment. Good luck with the championship. Father, if Herr Hartmann gets restless, see if you can persuade him to do some violin practice. That usually soothes him."

Beck headed off toward the gate.

"You can use my chess set for the game," said Father Glatz to the seminarian.

Hoeniger beamed in delight. "How generous of you, Father."

The chess set was the Jesuit's prized possession, brought out only under special circumstances. The pieces were polished rosewood and exquisitely carved; each one, including the pawns, had different features. Philipp Glatz obeyed his vow of poverty, but had never been able to relinquish this set, which was a gift from his father.

Hoeniger nodded in the direction of the guard tower. "They don't seem to be interested in us today, thank goodness."

"Keep your eye out. Any further infraction and we'll report it again. Come on, I'll give you the chess set and collect Professor Hartmann, poor fellow."

28

CLARE CLOSED THE DOOR OF THE HUT AND PULLED the curtain across the window. Not that it was likely anybody in the camp could see her, but she didn't want to be disturbed. She unlocked the desk drawer and took out an envelope marked *Top Secret*. She opened the seal and removed the piece of paper inside. Written on it were six names.

Herr Kurt Bader
Dr. Bruno Beck
Father Philipp Glatz
Herr Rudolph Gold
Professor Gunther Hartmann
Herr Oscar Schmidt

In a few minutes, she had committed the list to memory. She then reached for the cigarette lighter that was on the desk. She set fire to the sheet of paper, letting the ashes fall into the tray.

When Tyler arrived at the camp, he was aware that he seemed to elicit much more curiosity from the internees than before. He was sorry he had been the one to bring such fear to the camp. He gave a friendly wave to the group that was closest, but the response was perfunctory.

Major Fordham emerged from his tent and greeted Tyler with a hearty handshake.

"Morning, Inspector. Any news?"

"I'm afraid not, sir. Nothing concrete."

"Well, perhaps Dr. Beck can throw some light on the subject. Very clever man by all accounts."

"So I understand."

"Quite. In the interest of public relations, Mrs. Devereau has asked to sit in on your meeting. I saw no reason why not. I'm off to have a word with the cooks to see if we can organize a strawberry social. Our relations with the local people have vastly improved, but this terrible tragedy could be a setback."

"Before we start, I wonder if I might have a word with the Catholic priest in the camp? It's to do with another matter. Elsie Bates's friend appears to be missing."

"Good Lord."

"According to the warden at the hostel, she probably attended the service of Mass here in the camp at least a couple of times. She may have been heading here last evening. She hasn't been seen since."

Fordham clicked his tongue. "I have allowed some people from the area to celebrate Mass with our internees. Catholics are in the minority here and it seemed like a nice bridge between us." His gaze shifted toward the gate. "I see Dr. Beck approaching. He and Father Glatz are good friends. He'll know where he is."

Fordham ordered the sentry to open the gate. Tyler didn't recognize the man walking towards them dressed as if he were a cricket umpire until the major called out to Dr. Beck.

"The inspector wants to have a word with Father Glatz. Could you locate him for us?"

"Of course. He was about to engage in a chess match in the mess tent."

"The father's English is a bit rudimentary," added Fordham. "Things might move faster if Dr. Beck translated for you,

Inspector." Beck had only the slightest of accents.

"Seeing as my German is non-existent, that sounds like a good idea." said Tyler.

"I'll fetch him," said Beck. He stepped back with a little bow. "Come this way." He pointed to a group of chairs that had been placed under a tarpaulin a few feet away. "We can meet over there if you like, Inspector. We call it our reading room. During the day, the sun blazes into the camp. I hoped we would have a reprieve today but it doesn't look likely."

The rain had stopped and the dark storm clouds were moving away. A patch of blue the size of a sailor's trousers was showing to the west.

"I'll leave you to it" said the major, and he headed off. He was immediately accosted by a handful of internees who wanted to speak to him. They walked off together, Fordham leaning his head intently as he listened.

Tyler went over to the "reading room." He could understand why it had been set up. There was no shade at all in the camp, except that provided by the tents. He sat down in a canvas field chair. One of the ubiquitous blue butterflies danced around his head for a moment, then fluttered off to better sustenance.

Dr. Beck soon reappeared with a tall, distinguished-looking man in the black robe of a Catholic priest.

"Inspector Tyler, allow me to present Father Glatz." He continued in English, speaking more slowly. "The inspector would like to speak to you about a young lady."

Glatz had thick, dark hair combed back from his face, a ruddy complexion, and keen blue eyes. Tyler didn't know why he should be a little surprised at such a masculine appearance, but the clergymen he'd met in the Church of England had all tended to be rather delicate and high-voiced. The priest gave him a firm handshake.

Beck helped out with the language, but it didn't take long to elicit from the priest that, yes, a young woman such as he described had been a regular celebrant for the past three weeks or so. There was a handful of people from round and about who came to Mass. He set up his altar on one side of the gate, and they stood outside and received the consecrated bread through the wire. "I sometimes found it hard to distinguish who was a prisoner and who wasn't," said the priest. "Nevertheless, I am most happy to demonstrate the unity of the Catholic community, no matter whether German or English."

"Did this young woman attend Mass yesterday evening?" asked Tyler.

"She did not. There were only two outside celebrants. An older woman and a young man from a nearby farm."

"What time was this, Reverend?"

"Seven o'clock. It is always at seven. The meal is over by then."

There was nothing more the priest could offer, so Beck and Tyler proceeded to the major's tent.

Tyler thought Glatz looked wistful as they parted. Nobody found being behind barbed wire an easy thing.

Once outside the gate, Beck stopped and took a deep breath.

"I realize this is fanciful, but the air on this side of the wire smells sweeter to me."

Clare was waiting in the tent and she smiled a warm greeting at Tyler. Pleasure ran through his body, suffusing him with energy. He wanted to rush over and kiss her, but had to content himself with smiling back and touching her arm lightly as he sat down.

Dr. Beck gave a little bow, took her hand, and brushed his lips across her fingers. "Good morning, Frau Devereau. May I say that, as always, you look completely ravishing."

Clare laughed. "You yourself look very smart today."

He patted his stomach. "I have not worn these clothes all summer and I find the trousers to sit quite tightly on me. The result of camp cooking, I suppose, and not enough exercise."

It was hard to say how old the doctor was. His hair and beard were streaked with grey, but his body was trim and fit for all his self-deprecation. His brown eyes were shrewd. For absolutely no rational reason, the man was irritating Tyler, and this made him jump in abruptly.

"Perhaps we could get down to business. As I understand it, you have done some study into the minds of criminals, and you thought you had some insights that could help me with my case."

Both the professor and Clare glanced at him with surprise. His tone must have been sharper than he realized.

"I do hope you don't consider me an arrogant ivory-tower dweller who thinks I can tell you how to do your job," said Beck. "I assure you that is not the case. I have the utmost respect for the British police force. However, I have made a particular study of crime, and I thought the only responsible thing to do was to pass along some of the things I have learned. It is up to you to use these insights or not as you see fit."

"I shall endeavour to keep an open mind."

Beck nodded. "That is all anybody can ask, Inspector."

Clare smiled at Beck, which only aggravated Tyler more. He looked at his watch. "I'm afraid I do have a rather limited amount of time."

Beck was unruffled. "Would it be simpler if I gave you a copy of my article and you can peruse it at your leisure?"

"Oh dear, what a pity," said Clare. "I was looking forward to hearing what you had to say, Dr. Beck."

"And I to imparting it. A professor with no classroom is like a solider without a regiment." He took a slim, cloth-bound book from his inner pocket and handed it to Tyler. "I do ask you to return it when you are finished. It is my only copy. The others were confiscated by the Nazis and burned."

"What a shame you didn't get Herr Hitler to lie on your couch," said Tyler. "I bet he would be an interesting case."

Beck shrugged, a gesture more Gallic than Germanic. "On the contrary, Inspector. The closed mind such as exists in most Nazis is dull and ultimately untreatable. I prefer to take on the lowly station clerk who has an open mind."

"If he could afford analysis," said Tyler. "I believe it is an expensive process."

"It is. But I myself subsidize the therapy if I find the patient worthwhile."

There was an uncomfortable silence. The doctor began to pat his pockets, a man searching for his tobacco. Tyler took out his own case and offered him a cigarette. Beck accepted and they both lit up, relaxing with the ritual.

"I used to smoke only cigars," said the doctor, "but alas my dear friend and mentor, Dr. Freud, was quite addicted to his cigars and suffered dreadfully before he died from a cancer of the jaw. I thought there might be a connection between the two things, so I have now switched to cigarettes." He chuckled. "You've no doubt heard the story about Dr. Freud and his little weakness? No? Somebody once asked Freud if he had ever analyzed his predilection for cigars, as they might be considered phallic symbols and all that. The good doctor replied, 'Sometimes, my dear sir, a cigar is only a cigar.'"

Tyler gaped at him. He didn't have a clue what he was blathering on about. He personally didn't like cigars, or pipes. Clare had laughed as if she understood.

She turned to Tyler. "Do let's hear what Dr. Beck has to say, Tom. I'm sure it won't take long and it may prove invaluable."

Tyler threw up his hands. "How can I refuse two such persuasive people?" He unfastened his wristwatch and placed it on the table. "You have ten minutes. Go."

Beck made a tent of his fingers and pressed them against his lips. "How shall I start? . . . Let us say that in this area, the base proposition of psychoanalytic theory is that we all carry with us a primeval, profound, but not conscious sense of guilt. I won't go into the explanation for this guilt at the moment; suffice to say it is universal and unavoidable to the human condition. This buried guilt creates its own pressure."

Tyler shifted in his chair and sneaked a glance at the watch.

Beck held up his hand. "Allow me to use an analogy which is rather unpleasant but vivid. You might have had the experience of eating something that does not agree with you. At first you are not aware of this, but as time goes on, you realize there is a great deal of discomfort in your stomach, much rumbling and belching, perhaps your head begins to ache. All indicating there is an internal war going on. Your stomach both wishes to repel the offending food and use it for fuel. Finally you face the fact that the only way to settle the conflict is to vomit . . ." He paused. "Are you with me so far?"

"Ugh," said Clare. Tyler merely nodded.

"It is the same with guilt," continued Beck. "The material that we refer to as repressed causes us great inner discomfort. To obtain relief, we will seek a place to let go, to bring equilibrium to our troubled self, to vomit up the offending incident or incidents that have brought about our distress. For the fortunate, that place might be undergoing psychoanalysis or some other kind of therapy. For the criminal it is not as simple. He does not consciously seek to reveal his crime. If you ask him, he will tell you he wants to get away with it. Nevertheless our criminal has a compulsion to confess."

He paused and looked at his audience. Tyler raised his eyebrows.

"Strangely enough, Dr. Beck, in all my experience as a police officer, there hasn't been a long queue of riff raff waiting to pour out the stories of their crimes on our broad shoulders."

Beck nodded acceptingly. "I don't mean quite the same as what the common usage means by that remark. The murderer who enters the police station and says, 'I done it, arrest me,' is not that to which I am referring. What I mean is the unobtrusive little clue, or clues, that the criminal has unconsciously given which betray his identity and point the finger in his direction . . ."

Tyler interrupted him. "In the case of Elsie Bates, the murderer left behind the weapon, which is hardly unobtrusive. We're checking it for fingerprints. It appeared to have been carefully placed beside the body."

"Really, how interesting. Such a gesture suggests a reverence of some kind. I would say the killer felt remorse for his action, pity for his victim."

"I'm glad you think so, Doctor. In fact, he shot an unarmed and helpless girl in cold blood. He should have had some pity before he acted, don't you think?"

Beck eyed him curiously. "Are you referring to something in particular?"

Tyler shook his head. He'd already said more than he should have. "Can't reveal any details, Doctor. But please continue. I'm taking it all in. Open as the air, that's me."

Beck tented his fingers again. "In my opinion, the criminal has the urge to be discovered as powerfully as the detective needs, for his own unconscious reasons, to discover him."

"Explain that, will you?" Tyler asked, trying not to let his aggravation seep through in his voice. Clare's warning glance showed he wasn't altogether successful.

Dr. Beck gave his Gallic shrug. "Why men take up the profession of police officers is another book unto itself. A sublimation of their own anti-social tendencies perhaps . . ."

"Let me get this straight, Doctor. You are saying that instead of most criminals being stupid, useless pieces of shite, they are in fact afflicted with a conscience that make them do stupid, obvious things that even stupid, obvious detectives like me, who are barely on the side of the law, can understand?"

"Tom! Of course he doesn't mean that."

Dr. Beck, for the first time, looked disconcerted. "I do apologize if I have inadvertently offended you, Inspector Tyler. Perhaps it is a language problem . . ."

"Come off it, Doctor. Your command of English is superior to mine. And no, you haven't offended me, I'm just trying to understand exactly what you're saying so us thick plods can use it in pursuit of B and ES with bodily harm; the conscience-stricken rapists, murderers, and thugs. It's good to know these scum secretly want us to find them. And punish them. Which of course, we are, as you say, most eager to do. In non-analytic circles, that's called seeking justice."

Beck sighed and built the tent again, a little habitual gesture of his that Tyler thought he should analyze. He looked as if he were praying. Perhaps Tyler should suggest that to him.

"I was wrong to think I could explain such a new and challenging theory in ten minutes. Perhaps we should revert back to our original idea of your reading my article in your own time."

"That might be better," said Clare soothingly. "I myself often find it easier to understand something on the printed page."

Tyler leaned back in his chair and stared at the ceiling. He could see a spider running along one of the struts. "I understand quite well what Dr. Beck has said. That does not mean

I agree with him. However, you are quite right, Doctor, it might be better if I take your article with me and read it when I have a chance." He brought his chair back to the upright position with a thump. "To tell the truth, I was actually hoping that you could share with me any more mundane observations you might have had about the dead girl, Elsie Bates. She was well known at the camp. In your professional view, were any of the men here besotted with her? She was a flirt, a very attractive girl. Did any of them become jealous, do you think? Who knows what sexual frustration will do to a man."

Dr. Beck sighed. He knew a lost cause when he met one. "I did see the young woman on a few occasions and my fellow internees welcomed her. But even with the few young men here, I don't believe any of them would allow themselves to be involved emotionally with a girl like that . . . after all, she is on the other side of the wire, is she not? For most of us, she is *goyim*. The unattainable." His lips curled slightly at the corners. "But then the forbidden does have its own particular attraction, does it not? The serpent did not perhaps have such a difficult task to persuade Eve to eat the apple."

Clare laughed. "Thank goodness you didn't add, 'and brought all our woe into the world.'"

My God, they are actually flirting with each other, thought Tyler. He picked up his watch and strapped it on.

"I really must be off. Thank you for your time, Doctor. I will let you know how my investigation develops. Now, we should probably have you escorted back to the camp."

Beck slumped in his chair. "I must admit I find it disconcerting to have an armed soldier at my side as if I am a dangerous offender. I am, and have been for many years, a sedentary man with not the slightest proclivity toward violence, which in fact I abhor. How could I possibly be considered a threat to this nation? My career is in tatters thanks to the Nazis; many of my friends and relatives are trapped inside a country that persecutes them because they are Jewish. Is it likely I would be a fifth columnist and support the very regime that would destroy me?"

Tyler saw for the first time the pain beneath the doctor's calm professional façade.

"I'm sure your tribunal will take all of that into account, Dr. Beck."

"Why don't you and I stay here a little longer?" said Clare to the doctor. "I wanted to talk to you about preparing some of your lectures for publication."

"Ah. That is the apple indeed," said Beck.

Tyler got up to leave when Clare called out.

"Tom! Don't forget the article."

"Right! Thanks," said Tyler, picking up the slim volume from the table, and, with a nod, he left the tent.

He heard Clare say something in German to the doctor and he wondered if she was apologizing for Tyler's behaviour.

Well done, lad. You sure made an eejit of yourself in front of Clare.

The Humber refused to start and he had to get out and crank it. He did not do it smoothly or gently.

29.

The fox had lost most of his hair and his skin was raw and infected. The mange which had invaded his mouth made it difficult for him to eat. He was slowly starving. He crept through the underbrush of the woods, drawn by the noise of the rooks. They were collected around the base of an uprooted tree. As he darted toward them, they flew away in a black, clamouring cloud and landed on the tree branches, squawking angrily. The fox crept forward, his nostrils quivering at the smell. He pushed through the branches into the dark interior, where he sniffed at the ravaged body.

On the way back to Whitchurch, Tyler kept rerunning the conversation over and over in his mind. He had to admit that the doctor had a point. He and other officers tended to think of criminals as making silly mistakes which led to their capture, but if there was anything to that psycho stuff, it could explain some of the more ridiculous clues the criminals left behind. One silly sod who had tried to rob a Birmingham bank had handed in a note written on the back of an envelope that was addressed to him.

However, what had struck Tyler the most was the doctor's use of the word "reverence." The way Elsie Bates had been moved and straightened, her arms neatly at her side, the poppies on her chest, did suggest something like that. Beck said the killer felt remorse. Tyler wondered if that was true, and if it was, whether it could be of help in solving the case.

By the time he arrived in Whitchurch he was thoroughly

riled up and in no mood to take any shite from his father-in-law regarding Janet's situation. Walter Lambeth was always going on about "our Vera" and what a good lass she was, but in Tyler's opinion, he used her to fetch and carry whenever he could, and he wasn't above belittling her in front of people. Could be anything, but mostly he made fun of her intelligence. "Not her strong suit," was his often-repeated remark, and Tyler knew Vera was hurt by this. He'd tried to get her to stand up to the old man and take a strip off him but she wouldn't.

Tyler parked the Humber in front of the shop, where Lambeth was standing puffing on a long pipe. He liked to cultivate a John Bull persona, which meant in his case a striped butcher's apron, bushy sideburns, and a walrus moustache. His clay pipe was all part of the image. Never mind the Mr. England act; in Tyler's view, Walter was ignorant, bigoted and as narrow-minded as any county matron. If, to boot, he was also into profiteering, Tyler wouldn't be surprised.

"Morning, Tom. What brings you to these parts?"

The butcher shop was only a ten-minute walk from Tyler's house, but Lambeth made it sound as if they were in different counties.

"Just going by. Thought I'd say hello."

Lambeth eyed Tyler curiously. "What's up? Troubled hearth, is it?" He glanced down the street, then beckoned to Tyler to move closer. "Can I give you a word of advice, son?"

Tyler didn't move. "I think I'm all right for advice at the moment, Dad."

Lambeth stepped forward, waving his pipe in front of him. "My Vera isn't as happy as she should be and I'm concerned about that. What goes on between you and her in the bedroom isn't my business . . ."

Damn right about that, thought Tyler.

"Vera's getting on now, and man to man I can understand

why that might make a chap's eyes stray. She does take care of herself, mind, and she's a good lass for all her being a bit slow. But she's on the high-strung side, and she'd be better if you paid her a bit more attention, like. Take her to the pictures once in a while or out for a drink. She's always afraid of what people think. 'We never go out together, Dad,' she said to me just last week. 'What'll people think?' Let 'em think what they like, says I, but she worries about it." He paused and sucked on his pipe, which seemed to have gone out. "Women like a bit of show. Flowers now and again, sweets in a fancy box, the occasional compliment."

In all the years he'd been in the presence of his in-laws, Tyler had not once seen Walter compliment his wife or hand her a bouquet of flowers. Once he'd given her a bag of sweets to share, but that was all. The same held true for his daughter.

"Thanks for the advice, Dad. I'll think about it."

"Suit yourself. By the way, how's our Janet? Is she feeling better?"

"I didn't know she was poorly."

"Oh yes, she left early. She said she had a tummy ache." He winked. "Her monthlies, I suppose, but she's too shy to tell me."

Tyler knew it wasn't that. You can't live in a small house with two women and not be aware when they're having their monthly. Janet had hers last week.

"What time did she leave?"

"Oh, hardly more than twenty minutes ago. She was all doubled over, said she had to lie down. She's asked for the morning off tomorrow. Mind you, it's inconvenient. Saturday's our busiest day."

He was eyeing Tyler, looking for him to dispute Janet's story; to confirm she was a malingerer.

"I'll look in on her. Well, I'd better be off . . ."

"Any development on the Land Army girl case?" Lambeth asked. He had an expression of prurient curiosity on his face. "I'd see her in town. Nice bit of crumpet. Too bad. I hear another one's missing?"

"Who told you that?"

"Our Vera. It put the wind up her. She thinks there's a Jerry on the loose."

"There isn't."

"Who's done them in then?"

"First of all there is no confirmation that the second girl is dead. She was good pals with the one who died and she's probably gone somewhere to be quiet for a while."

If he said that often enough, he might start believing it, thought Tyler. But it irked him that rumours about Rose had rushed through the town. It seemed a bad omen.

"I hope you never let our Janet join the Land Army," continued Lambeth. "Some of those gals are no better than they should be . . . Speaking of the devil." Two girls in Land Army uniform, riding bicycles, were heading toward them.

"Oi, hello! Inspector!" It was Molly and Freckles.

They pulled up in front of the shop.

"What good luck we ran into you," said Molly. "We need to talk to you."

"I'll leave to your business then," said Lambeth. A woman had just rounded the corner with her shopping basket dangling from her arm. A customer.

"Good day to you, Mrs. Walker," said Lambeth. "I've got in a nice bit of pork, not too dear all things considering."

Tyler tipped his hat. "Hello, Barbara. How's Bobby?"

"Hello, Tom. No change."

She looked as if she wanted to stay and talk, but the two girls were waiting for him. She followed Walter into the shop. Tyler felt a pang of sadness. She was the same age as he was, but she seemed stooped and careworn. He'd known Barbara since they were children and he'd always liked her. A quiet, rather shy girl; as a woman, she was the kind who could easily vanish into the woodwork. Decent, hardworking, uncomplaining, he'd been sweet on her once. The situation with Bobby had to be very hard for her.

He turned his attention back to Molly and Freckles.

"What's up, ladies?"

"It's nothing we can talk about on the street," said Molly. "Can we meet at De Berg's?"

"Fine with me. Go ahead and get a table. Order some cakes as well."

They remounted and biked off. He followed, walking briskly. These young women tended to make him feel as if he had to suck in his stomach, stick out his chest, and move with vigour.

The girls had nabbed a quiet spot at the back and he joined them.

"We ordered a pot of tea," said Molly. "Neither one of us is hungry."

"I am," he said and when the waitress arrived, he ordered a plate of cakes. Both girls were decidedly subdued but they were young and worked hard. He had a feeling the cakes would be welcome.

"No word on Rose yet, is there?" Molly asked.

"I'm afraid not."

The waitress returned with their order. He was right. The girls were happy with the cream buns.

He gave them a chance to tuck in. "So what is this important information that you've got for me?"

Molly as always spoke first. "We talked a long time among ourselves – Freckles, Titch, Sylvia, and me. We don't want to snitch on anybody, but we're honestly dead scared. You said

that we should report anything at all that might be relevant –"
She stopped. "Oh you tell him, Freck. I feel like a rat."

Freckles swallowed down a piece of bun. "It's to do with Florence Hancocks. We don't think she was telling the exact truth yesterday. We don't think she was at home looking after her mum. She was having a, er, what do you call it, Moll?"

"A liaison. She was having a secret liaison."

Freckles continued. "She told Miss Stillwell her mother was ill, but just before she was getting ready to leave, I happened to be in her room. Muriel was lending me some socks and I had come to get them. Florence was packing her suitcase and she held up a pair of cami-knickers, lovely item in pink silk with black lace trim. 'My, you're dressing very swank for your mother, aren't you?' I said. She got all flustered. 'They belong to my sister. I'm returning them to her.' I just couldn't believe her. They were really nobby camis. The kind of thing Collette's sells."

Freckles paused and fidgeted with her teaspoon.

"That's it?" Tyler asked.

"We thought you should check on her . . . er, on her alibi."

"I am in the process of doing just that," he answered.

Freckles pointed her finger at the other girl. "That's only half of it. You tell him the rest, Moll."

Molly bit her lip. "We told you that little things appeared to be going missing. Well, last week Florence and Elsie had a big barney. Flo accused Elsie of stealing. She said she had some silk stockings in her chest of drawers and they had disappeared. She said Elsie had taken them. Elsie denied it and they started to call each other all sorts of bad names. It was very nasty . . ."

"We were afraid they would attack each other," interrupted Freckles. "I've never seen Florence like that. Nor Elsie either for that matter. She could be shirty sometimes, but not like this, not all-out screaming. Florence seemed to have got her goat good and proper."

"What were the bad names?"

"Florence said that Elsie was a cockney guttersnipe and that she was a hoor and everybody knew it."

Tyler whistled through his teeth.

"I left out all the *bleedings* and *soddings*," said Freckles.

Molly picked up the narrative. "It was being called a whore that seemed to send Elsie off the deep end. She said, 'That's a case of the pot calling the kettle black as you know only too well.'" Molly put her head in her hands. "It was horrible to hear two of our girls screaming at each other like that. I remember thinking, 'This will never be fixed. This is irrevocable.'"

"We didn't know what to do," added Freckles. "Then Florence just turned and ran out of the room. Elsie was livid. She said, 'Bloody cow' – excuse the language, but those are her words, 'I'm going to my digs.' And she left too."

Molly reached into her handbag and took out a packet of cigarettes. "Wouldn't happen to have a light, would you?" she asked Tyler. She put a cigarette in her mouth and waited for him to snap his lighter. As he did so, she held his hand lightly and looked into his eyes. She took a draw, then grinned at him. "Elsie, God rest her soul, she taught me that."

"How to smoke you mean?"

"No, how to flirt," interjected Freckles. "She gave us all a lesson one day. Molly did it just right. You lean forward, put your delicate little paw on his hand, and look into his eyes like he's the best thing you've seen since last night's dinner."

They both laughed, then Molly abruptly looked at her watch and pushed back her chair.

"We've got to go. We decided to work today. Couldn't stay in, to tell the truth. Too fidgety. We hope we haven't been out of line, telling you all this, Inspector. Florrie is a good sort really. It's just that given the circumstances we thought you should know what happened."

"You haven't been out of line at all. I'm sure it will all be sorted out. Is she out working today?"

"No, she wasn't feeling well, so she stayed at the hostel."

Tyler waved the waitress over. "This is my treat, ladies. And why don't you take those last couple of cakes."

"Thanks. Thanks for everything." Molly took out her handkerchief and wrapped the cakes carefully. "I do hope Rose is all right. You will let us know when you hear anything won't you?"

They left, and to his eyes, in spite of the sheen of youth, they both looked vulnerable.

Given the brutality of the attack on Elsie, he doubted a young girl had committed the crime, but Florence Hancocks did own a car, not to mention a Luger. Now, according to the girls, she may have hated Elsie Bates.

30.

TYLER LEFT THE TEA SHOP AND WALKED ALONG MAIN Street. Near the corner was a ladies' wear shop called Madame Collette's. About three years ago, a London woman had bought out old Mrs. Kilpatrick, who had been there ever since he could remember. The new owner had introduced fancy, high-priced frocks and imported lingerie. Today, the window displayed a single mannequin in a long nightgown of shimmering scarlet with thin straps; not particularly practical for the English unheated bedroom, but definitely provocative. All the other shops crammed as much of their merchandise as they could into their windows, but Madame Collette's message was clear: "We don't need to do anything as vulgar as display everything we have. We cater to the discriminating customer of taste, not to mention money."

As he entered the shop, the bell on the door tinkled softly. The place was empty of customers and looked more like somebody's front room than a shop. The carpet was light blue and thick, the walls papered in a delicate green and fuchsia. By the window was a grouping of chintz-covered chairs around a low table. Shelves stacked behind a counter at the far end of the room were the only concession to commerce that he could see.

A woman stepped out from the back room. She was wearing an elegant, simple black frock. She might have been forty, she might have been sixty; it was hard to tell with her immaculately made-up face and stiffly coiffed hair. She gave him a smile, perfectly balanced between warm (must look welcoming) and cool (mustn't look too eager).

"May I help you?" She had a French accent but he couldn't tell if it was real or fake.

"Good day, ma'am. I'm Inspector Tyler. I'm conducting a police investigation right now and I wonder if I might ask you a couple of questions."

"But of course. I have heard of the tragedy that has occurred."

"Did you know the young woman in question? Her name was Elsie Bates."

Madame Collette, if that was indeed who she was, thought for a moment. "No, that name is not familiar to me."

"As part of my investigation I'm interested in tracking down, er, a pair of pink silk cami-knickers with a black lace trim that you may have sold recently."

One pencilled eyebrow rose slightly. "Yes, I remember very well the article you describe. They were an original design from Paris. Quite lovely appliqué in lace. Most feminine."

"Do you recall who bought the, er, article?"

"Certainly. It was a young man. He said he was purchasing them for his fiancée."

So much for Florence's story about the cami-knickers being on loan from her sister.

Madame eyed Tyler shrewdly. "A most generous present I would say. They were not cheap."

"Will you describe this young man to me?"

She pursed her lips. "I regret to say I am not good at paying attention to such detail. He seemed quite an ordinary young man, a soldier."

"You mean he was in uniform?"

"Yes. But then they all are these days, aren't they?"

"How tall was he? Fair or dark?"

"As I said I don't particularly pay attention to such things. He was quite undistinguished. Darkish hair, about your height. I'm afraid that is all I can say."

She was acting like the madam of a brothel and Tyler wondered where the hell she came from. This was only a bloody lingerie store surely.

"Did this young man buy anything else?"

"A pair of silk stockings. He did consider my best imported scarves but he did not buy one. Allow me, monsieur." She went to the counter and took out a long, narrow scarf that was the colour of a robin's egg. She draped it across his hands.

"Feel how soft and silky it is. It would make a wonderful gift for a special woman." She waited while he let the fringes run through his fingers like water. "I can see there is indeed such a woman in your life, Inspector. These scarves are made in France and it will be impossible to get any more. Why don't you surprise her with this gift?"

"How much?"

She shrugged delicately. "They are quite dear normally but I am a patriotic woman. For you I will charge three guineas."

"For a scarf!"

She wasn't in the least perturbed by his reaction. "It is unique. In these days of such pervasive uniformity, that makes it special, don't you think?"

It was extortion. He put it back on the counter. "I'm afraid I'm not a customer today, ma'am."

She refolded the scarf. "I quite understand."

"Do you know a young woman by the name of Florence Hancocks?"

"No. But not everybody gives their name when they purchase lingerie here."

"Tall, pretty, with light brown hair. She is with the Land Army."

"I have no such recollection. My prices are generally beyond the means of those particular young women." She smiled a rather tight smile. "I wish I could be more helpful, Inspector."

"Thank you, madam, you have been helpful."

As he turned to go, she held up the silk scarf. "For you, I can offer a special price. And this is my last. Two guineas."

She slipped the scarf around her neck, the gesture elegant and so French. The blue looked beautiful against her black dress.

He was mad, he knew he was, but he succumbed. "All right, I'll take it."

She whisked the scarf off and started to wrap it in tissue paper.

"Can I interest you in anything else? A nightdress for instance? I have a rather exquisite one in black taffeta. Also from Paris."

"No, thank you. The scarf is quite enough."

"I do have a small box with my monogram on it, but whereas ladies like to display the place of purchase, I find many gentlemen prefer anonymity." She gave him a sly look. "All the better to surprise the lady who is the lucky recipient."

He handed over the money, stuffed the tissue parcel in his jacket pocket, and practically ran from the shop. Mad. He was quite, quite mad.

31.

IT WAS RIDICULOUS TO THINK THAT A FLIMSY PIECE of silk could generate heat, but Tyler's pocket felt hot. He walked quickly through the station to his office and stashed the package in the top drawer of his desk with the two paintings. He was getting a nice little guilt collection. He was tempted to take out the paintings and have a look at them, but managed to resist. Instead, he called Gough in.

"I've got some news about Rose Watkins." He filled the sergeant in on his conversation with Father Glatz. "If we don't hear anything by tomorrow, I'm going to designate her a missing person."

"How was your chat with the esteemed head scratcher?"

Tyler laughed. "Not bad considering. He presented me with this article." He tossed it to Gough. "You can read it if you like, then give me the gist."

The sergeant looked dubious. "I've got rather a lot to deal with at the moment, sir. I don't know when I'll be able to get to it."

"Coward. Never mind. I'll look at it later. I don't suppose we've heard from Eager or Collis, have we?"

"No, sir. They've got quite a wide area to cover. But I did get hold of most of the reservists. They'll be reporting in later this afternoon."

Tyler gave Gough the piece of paper from his notebook. "Good. Will you type this up? It's a description of Rose and what she was wearing. We can circulate it if she doesn't turn up soon." He sighed. "But let's hope it doesn't come to that."

The telephone rang in the front hall and Gough went to answer it. Tyler got up and stared at the blackboard he'd left up. He supposed he should write: "Florence Hancocks not telling the truth." At least it would give him more in the "certain" column.

The intercom sounded. "A call from London, sir."

"Put it through."

Tyler picked up his receiver. The connection was full of static and he could hardly hear the voice on the other end.

"Sergeant Donaldson 'ere, sir. I'm calling further to my visit to the Bates family. Like I reported, sir –" Crackling intervened, then Donaldson's voice was back. "I was able to speak to Mr. Bates. He says they can't come up to Whitchurch at the present time unless their transportation is paid for. Can't say he seemed very sorry about his daughter. No love lost there." More static.

"Thanks, Sergeant. We'll just have to keep her here until they're ready. Now while I'm talking to you, there is another job I need you to do. Elsie Bates's friend, a girl named Rose Watkins, has vanished. It is possible she has got herself down to London to be with her family."

Tyler could hear the exhalation on the other end of the line. "When I went to the Bates residence, the local fire warden did say that one of the other houses belonged to a family named Watkins. The daughter was good chums with Elsie Bates and had joined the Land Army. It has to be the same girl you're asking about."

"That's the one. I'm not banking on her having got to London but we need to check it out."

"She'd get a shock if she did get here. There's hardly anything left standing on the street. But I'll see who I can track down." He coughed. "And what shall I tell them, sir? How shall I explain why I'm asking?"

"Shite. They're going to have to be told sooner or later. Just see if you can find out if anybody has heard from the girl. If they haven't, just waffle until I can get back to you with more news."

"Do you think she's dead, sir?"

Tyler's anxiety made him irritable and he snapped out. "I have no idea. Let's hope not. Sorry, Sergeant, I didn't mean to take your head off."

"That's all right, sir. We're all on edge these days."

"Aren't we though. But get on to that for me as soon as you can."

"Yes, sir."

They hung up and Tyler snapped the intercom on.

"Sergeant, get hold of Dr. Murnaghan for me. Tell him that we can't get any of Elsie Bates's family to claim the body just now. He's going to have to keep it for the time being. Did those casings and bullets get sent over to the Brummagen lab?"

"Yes, sir. They went on the ten o'clock train. They promised to get back to us in a couple of days."

"Any word from Bath yet?"

"No, sir. The police there claim they're short-handed."

"Who isn't? Ring them again, will you, Guff. Put a cracker up their arse. I'd like to confirm Miss Hancocks's story as soon as possible. Apparently, she and Elsie had a nasty fight recently." He paused. "Do you remember that speech Superintendent Davies made when he was retiring last year? We had it typed up and framed."

"Yes, sir, I do remember. Very moving it was. Sorry the super didn't last long after that, he was always something of a poet."

"He said the qualifications of a good policeman were the strength of a lion, eyesight of an eagle, tact of an ambassador, worldly knowledge of an undergrad, patience of a husband, and memory of a wronged wife."

Gough chuckled. "My wife took a bit of exception to that last bit, sir. It got quite a laugh as I recall, but Julie said it was wives who had to have the patience, and men were more likely to remember wrongs than women."

"She's probably right about that. The super certainly had very high standards for coppers. I wouldn't mind having the eyesight of an eagle right now, never mind the other things. Anyway, keep going. Is there anything else I should be looking in to?"

"We've had the usual complaints about black marketeers and fifth columnists. Mrs. Marshall called again to report on Mrs. Thorne. She claims she was flashing a light intermittently, and according to Mrs. Marshall that's a sure sign Mrs. Thorne was signalling to the Luftwaffe."

"There was no warning of enemy aircraft in the area as far as I know, was there Gough?"

"No, sir. None."

"All right. I was going to talk to Mrs. Thorne anyway. I'll ask her about it. What else?"

"A new one this time. Came in on the telephone call but the caller refused to identify himself. He says that Fred Walker is using his pigeons to send messages to the Jerry. He saw him removing a piece of paper from the bird's leg."

"Idiot. He's right about one thing. Fred *was* removing a piece of paper. It was a record of the time when the pigeon was released. He flies his birds competitively."

"I know, sir. The complaints get more ridiculous every day. Somebody said Ewen Morgan has ploughed his field in the shape of an arrow to direct the Luftwaffe."

"Direct them to what?"

"I don't know, Liverpool I suppose, or Birmingham."

"My God, it won't be hard to defeat an enemy that has to rely on ploughed fields for directions. Any more?"

"Mrs. Newey on Green Lane wants to know why we are allowing evacuated children to come here when they are obviously of enemy origin. Why aren't we giving the space to our own English children?"

"What the hell is she talking about?"

"Apparently there are three kiddies in town who have been evacuated from Birmingham. They're dark skinned. I heard they're French, but some people are saying they're Italian. You know how people are. Mrs. Newey isn't the only one giving them the cold shoulder by all accounts."

Tyler sighed. "Makes you wonder sometimes what we're fighting for. Is that it?"

"One more. Cecil Russell says the internees are getting out of the camp at night and poaching his rabbit traps."

"Why the internees? Surely it's village boys?"

"He says he saw one of them. Claims he was muttering to himself in a foreign tongue."

"Where was this?"

"In the Acton Wood, not far from the Heath."

"All right. See if one of the lads can go and chat with Mr. Russell."

"You don't believe it was an internee, do you, sir?"

"No. It was probably Alice Thorne springing the traps. She hates them with a passion."

Tyler replaced the receiver in the cradle. He knew people were nervous and jumpy but sometimes he lost his patience with the nonsense that got phoned in. Pretty well everybody had known each other and their families all of their lives. Couldn't they use some common sense?

The intercom buzzed again.

"Bath just got back, sir. The young lady was definitely fibbing. She wasn't in Bath at all. She hasn't been there since June."

"Oh, great! Did they talk to her brother about the Luger?"

"That part is true. He did lend it to her when she joined the Land girls."

"This calls for another drive out to the hostel. You'd better requisition some more petrol before we run out."

"Will do. Why do you think she lied, sir?"

Tyler sighed. "Because the silly girl was shagging some fellow. She's engaged but I'll bet it wasn't him. Anyway, let's see what she has to say for herself."

32.

Tyler had Gough ring the hostel and Florence Hancocks was waiting for him in the library when he arrived. She was seated in the same chair that Rose had been in before. Unlike tiny Rose, her feet touched the floor. She clasped her hands together in her lap.

"Miss Hancocks, we are all under strain here and I don't want to keep you longer than necessary, or to waste my own time while you run me around the Wrekin." He didn't mean to make his voice harsh, but her flinch revealed he had. "I will come straight to the point. I happen to know that your mother is in excellent health, and that you did not go to visit her as you claimed. She has not seen you since early June."

"I . . . I . . ."

"Let me help you out here and save us time. Rather than going home, you had an assignation with a lover. A man who gave you a lovely gift of a pair of silk cami-knickers for this self-same assignation. You spent the time with him, not beside your mother's bed of pain. Am I right so far?"

Florence's knuckles were white. She gave the slightest of nods.

"I take it that was a yes. Were you with your fiancé?"

Florence shook her head.

"I take it that was a no. Given the circumstances, I will have to ask for the name of the man you were with to confirm your story."

That got her head up in a hurry. "Oh, no, I can't."

"Is he a married man?"

"No. Not at all. I'd never . . ."

"Screw a married man?"

She turned red but didn't reply.

Tyler bared his teeth. "Oh, I get it. How could I be so crude? I do apologize, Miss Hancocks. This was a romantic interlude, not a sordid secret romp in the hay. You are in love with this man and he loves you, and as soon as you can extricate yourself from your engagement you will be married. Is that closer to the mark?"

She was focused somewhere over his shoulder. "No. I have no intention of marrying . . . this man. I have a fiancé already. He is overseas."

"Is he now? You're just sort of keeping in shape, are you, until he returns?"

She was biting her lip to keep from crying.

"So, this man that you're *not* going to marry – does he know that, by the way, or is he under the illusion that all will be bliss eventually? Did you leave your ring behind?"

"He's quite aware we are not . . . we are not serious."

"That's a relief. I don't want another heartbroken man wandering around Shropshire."

Her eyes flicked. "What are you referring to?"

"The Bible tells us to beware the woman scorned, but I think the male scorned is even more dangerous. I suppose I am in the way of warning you, Miss Hancocks. We men can carry strong feelings in our manly breasts that might not be apparent to the inexperienced eye."

"I assure you, Inspector, the man I was with knows how I feel. He prefers it that way."

Does he? thought Tyler. *Or is it convenient for you to believe that?*

"Miss Hancocks, given the seriousness of this investigation, I will need to determine your whereabouts on Thursday morning. Were you with your boyfriend at this time?"

To his surprise, Florence looked absolutely stricken, as if she was struggling with what was to her a calamity of huge proportions. She had difficulty speaking.

"No, I was not with him. He . . . he left the previous night, Wednesday. I was alone."

"Did you have a quarrel?"

"No, nothing like that. He had to get back. I didn't; I thought I'd take advantage of the hotel and just sort of lounge around."

"Where were you?"

"Market Drayton."

"That will be easy for me to check. But Market Drayton isn't far at all if you have a car, which you do, do you not?"

"Yes."

"Even if the hotel staff can vouch for the fact that you didn't check out, who's to say that you didn't slip out without being seen? You could have been on the Heath Road in no time at all. Elsie was struck by a car before she was shot. I didn't mention that, did I?"

"Oh my God." She shrank back in her chair. "Inspector Tyler, I swear to you, I had nothing to do with Elsie's death. It's unthinkable."

"Good. Then there won't be any problem with you providing me with an alibi, will there? Shall I ring the hotel now? What was the name of it?"

"The Royal."

"Oh yes, rather a tacky place as I recall. But nobody cares who comes or goes or who is wearing a wedding ring, so that more than compensates for rather dodgy sheets, doesn't it? The staff makes a point of minding their own business. So if I were to ring they may not be able to tell me if you stayed there or when you left."

"No, they may not." Her voice had dropped back to a whisper.

"All right then, let's go over this again. Your friend left you on Wednesday evening and you stayed on in the room until late on Thursday, just lounging around and buffing your nails, darning your stockings, that sort of thing. Sometime on Thursday evening, you left the hotel and came directly here to Beeton Manor, is that correct? Arriving about nine o'clock, which was when the rest of the girls returned."

"That's right."

He got to his feet and walked over to her. "Miss Hancocks, may I remind you of one other little piece of this difficult puzzle. There is no doubt that the gun that killed Miss Bates was the same Luger that you had in your possession. The one your brother gave you when you joined the Land Army in case you were attacked by a squirrel or a Jerry parachutist. You said that gun disappeared from your room, but of course we only have your word for it."

She was holding on for dear life. "It was stolen. I was telling you the truth."

"Perhaps you were, but you're hiding something. Are you protecting somebody?"

"No."

"What is it then?" He spoke gently to her and she looked up at him, her eyes so full of misery, it was all he could do not to reach over and comfort her.

"Oh Inspector, I have done one of the worst things of my entire life." She buried her head in her hands and began to sob, cries that seemed as if they would tear her apart.

He put his hand on her shoulder. "Lass, come on now. I'm for believing that you didn't harm Elsie, but what is troubling you?"

She still couldn't speak, and he crouched down in front of

her and offered his handkerchief. "Here, wipe your nose. That's my girl."

She held the handkerchief to her face. "I wasn't in the hotel on Thursday. I was in a hospital, I went in on Wednesday night. I was released the next evening." She stopped trying to gain control over her sobs and he had to wait until she had quieted down.

"And you are going to tell me why you were in hospital, aren't you, Miss Hancocks?"

"I have . . . er . . . have contracted a disease. I had to get some treatment."

"Is this disease a venereal one?"

She nodded and whispered. "Gonorrhea."

That was a thump in the stomach. Tyler sat back.

"From this young man, I assume?"

"Yes."

"Did he know what you were doing?"

"No. I didn't want to tell him. I was too ashamed."

She was wiping at her eyes, but hardly stemming the tears that were rolling down her cheeks.

"They said I should be all right, but I have to continue with the treatments. It's not something that will be easy to explain to my fiancé, is it? He's due home on leave in a couple of weeks."

Tyler returned to his crouched position in front of her.

"Bear up, lass."

"David is a man of rather strict morals, Inspector. He has made it quite clear he wants me to be pure when we marry. He as well. He's fair about that. We have been engaged for over a year and we've never . . . well, you know what I am referring to." She scrubbed at her eyes. "That's why I was so foolish. I was lonely. Oh Inspector, am I so very wicked?"

Tyler removed the punishing handkerchief. "No, lass, of

course you're not wicked. You're not the first gal to fall for some smooth-talking rascal and you won't be the last."

"You see, if David finds out, he won't forgive me, I know he won't. He comes from a good family. One with a long and, as they say, storied history."

"If it's that long and that storied, it'll have lots more skeletons in the closet, you can count on that."

She managed a smile. "But you have to admit, my particular skeleton is a rather spectacular one."

"Aye lass, it is." He straightened up. "I will have to check up on what you've said. It's my job. What hospital did you go to?"

"Market Drayton General."

"And what is the name of the young man who has carelessly got you into this mess?"

Panic shot into her eyes again. "Do you need to know that?"

"Surely he's aware he has VD?"

She sighed miserably. "I don't know."

"Give me his name, lass. Infecting a nice young lady is not a criminal offence, but I'd like to make sure he is more careful in the future."

"His name is Dennis McEvoy."

Mrs. McEvoy opened the door.

"Tom. How nice. Come in."

"No, I won't stop, Lily. I just wondered if your Dennis was at home. I'd like a word with him."

"He's not here. He's on the night shift at the camp." She regarded him anxiously. "You're looking a bit grim, Tom. Is Dennis in trouble?"

"This isn't an official call, Lily, but I'd like to have a bit of a chin wag. Tell him to drop in at the station when he's off."

"I will. Sure you won't come in for a cuppa? I don't see much of you these days."

"Soon as I can, I'll take you up on that. I'm really busy at the moment."

Before she could ask him more questions, he stepped down from the porch.

"Ta ta, Lily."

Lily had been widowed several years ago, and Tyler thought not having a father had had an effect on her son and only child. Of the four musketeers, Dennis was the one who seemed to get into hot water first and most often. Tyler had done his best over the years to step in, but most of the time Dennis hadn't taken it kindly.

Not that you're a model of paternal effectiveness, thought Tyler to himself. *Your own son is hardly talking to you and you don't have a clue how to reach him.*

33.

CLARE PUT THE FIVE POUND NOTE INTO THE STRONG box, recorded the amount, and wrote a receipt for the money. Howard Silber received a regular allowance from an uncle, but none of the internees were allowed to use money. Instead they were issued disks with a monetary value written on them. The Ministry thought this would bypass problems of different currency and ensure nobody could accumulate a stash. Not that there was anything to spend money on in the camp. Barter flourished.

The hut where she worked, outside the wire fence, had been initially erected for Major Fordham. He found it too small, preferring the more military, field-operations appearance of his tent, and he'd turned the hut over to the mail sorter and censor.

Clare had tried to make the place as comfortable as possible, but it remained crude and workmanlike. There were unpainted shelves built along one wall, with pigeon holes labelled alphabetically and according to sections, where she could put the sorted letters. There was a scarred desk, two chairs, and a rickety table she'd found somewhere for the tea things. She'd also brought in a wool rug and some colourful pillows to make the place a bit more homey and less institutional.

Mail was handed out at the camp and collected twice a week, Mondays and Thursdays, and it was Clare's job to examine all of the correspondence, both coming in and going out. The majority of the examinations were straightforward. The internees had learned the drill by now. They were permitted to write only two letters a week and only twenty-four lines per letter.

The correspondence of certain people and organizations that might be problems for the government or were already considered subversive went into the middle tray. These ranged from left-wing anti-war groups, such as the Peace Pledge Movement, to the far-right, the British People's Party and Oswald Moseley's fascists, the BUF. Letters to and from all these groups would all be photographed and checked before being passed along.

There were fewer outgoing letters today, and she reached into that tray first. Occasionally one of the correspondents forgot and made a forbidden reference to the weather or to morale: "Continuing to be hot and sunny"; "The English are so jittery, many of us despair of getting a fair hearing." These sentences she blacked out. All approved letters were stamped and sealed.

She picked out a letter that reeked of tobacco, stuffed it into another envelope, and dropped it into the middle tray. She had no doubt the sender was a heavy smoker, but she had to send it to be examined further. As far as she was aware no secret messages had been detected, no microdots under the stamps, no ciphers. But if, by some remote chance, the letter had so-called invisible writing in the margins, the smell would be citrus-like. Tobacco could mask that.

She stretched, rubbing her neck to ease the stiffness. She could hear the internees on the other side of the barbed wire as they set up their stalls for the weekly market. It was a popular event, although everything was bartered and exchanged.

These familiar sounds were suddenly drowned out by a strange wail, rather like a lusty tom cat. This was immediately followed by an angry shout. The second voice was powerful and penetrating, professionally trained; the language English.

"Put a sock in it, Schmidt. I'm getting ready for my performance. Others have a right to the stage as well, you know."

Clare walked over to the window to have a look at what was going on. Oscar Schmidt, the sound poet, his back to her, was standing in the open square. It was he who had been giving forth with the cat noise. He was holding a megaphone constructed from cardboard. In front of him was Howard Silber in a black tunic and tights.

Schmidt brandished his megaphone in the air.

"You went before me last week. I'm going first today," bellowed Silber, and he made shooing motions with his arms as though Schmidt were a kind of large, recalcitrant bird.

Clare saw Dr. Beck emerge from between the tents. He went over to the two combatants and said something quietly to Silber, who shrugged him off angrily.

"Speak to Schmidt, why don't you? You know what happens when he gets going. Everybody disappears into their tents. I'm planning to deliver my St. Crispin's speech and I'd like an audience, if you don't mind."

Beck spoke to Schmidt, and the poet gave Silber a sweeping, ironic bow, tucked his megaphone under his arm, and stalked off.

"Good night, sweet prince!" Silber shouted after him. "May choirs of angels sing thee to thy rest."

The few men nearby who could understand him laughed. Around the edges of the grass square, the other internees went back to setting up their tables.

"My performance will start right after the concert," pronounced Silber.

Clare was about to return to her own tasks, then decided, the heck with it, she needed a break. Anyway, this could give her a chance to get to know the internees better.

She left the hut and went to the gate where a young guard, full of flustered admiration, let her into the compound.

Dr. Beck came over immediately.

"Greetings once again, Frau Devereau."

Clare was uncomfortably aware of the softness of his brown eyes.

"What was all the fuss about?" she asked.

"It was nothing. When egotistical men are cooped up together for a long period of time, there are bound to be squabbles. Both Herr Silber and Herr Schmidt wish to claim the position of resident artist. They are both used to flatterers and admirers. Unfortunately for the camp, Herr Silber is not fluent in German and performs entirely in English, and Herr Schmidt is, shall we say, a little too avant-garde for this particular collection of people. But he is really an affable fellow. Come, let's smooth his ruffled feathers."

He took her by the elbow and led the way to one of the stalls on the opposite side of the square. Schmidt had gone to stand behind his table and he beamed at both of them as they approached. He had broken, uneven teeth and a flattened nose which indicated a less than affable previous existence, but he certainly seemed like a friendly giant. He clicked his heels together and bowed to Clare.

"Frau Devereau, I hope the puffed-up ranting of the imbecile with no talent did not bother you."

He spoke in German. He had a strong Bavarian accent and Clare found him a little hard to understand. The Shropshire native versus the cockney.

"Not at all. I'm glad you settled the matter."

Schmidt uttered an obscenity but saw Beck's frown of disapproval. "Ah, hah, I beg your pardon. Here, allow me to present you with one of my latest pieces to make up for my appalling bad manners." He took a small figurine off the table and held it out to her. "I'm afraid it is ultimately perishable because I was forced to make it from dough, which is all that is available to me."

The sculpture was of a nude man, standing with legs apart, arms held up in boxing position.

"You are not offended by the naked human body, I hope, Frau Devereau?"

Clare shook her head. She had actually stifled a moment of slightly shocked amusement. The boxer's male member was rather extraordinarily long.

"It looks a little disproportioned to me." Hans Hoeniger had come up behind Clare and was studying the sculpture. "What other phallic monstrosity have you got today?"

Unfazed, the poet showed his yellow teeth in a big grin. "My masterpiece, if I say so myself."

He reached into a box behind him, took out a large square canvas, and laid it on the table. He had made a collage from pieces of wood and scraps of newspaper. Here and there were glued plump tubes of stocking material that he had stuffed and dyed red. The dye dribbled down onto the newspaper so that the entire canvas looked as if it were weeping tears of blood.

Mockingly, Hoeniger put his finger to his chin and made a show of studying it.

"Most interesting, Herr Schmidt. Does it have a title? The phallus as weapon perhaps?"

"Not at all. I'm thinking of calling it *White Poppies* or *The Follies of War.*" He beckoned to Clare to look more closely. "See the blue patch here in the centre? I made the dye from borage flowers. In the Middle Ages, the borage plant was used solely to paint the Virgin Mary's robes. It was considered as close to the colour of heaven as could be found on earth."

"It's very beautiful," said Clare. The colour was indeed an astonishingly vivid blue.

"I didn't know you were a pacifist," said Beck. He pointed to the white poppies that were glued onto the blue square.

"Can a thinking person be anything else?" retorted the poet.

"Can any thinking person be a pacifist at this time?" asked Hoeniger. His teasing tone had vanished.

Dr. Beck jumped in to change the subject. "Let's keep that until Monday for our discussion hour. The concert should be starting momentarily." He turned to Clare. "The quartet is performing a Beethoven piece, opus 131. It is quite exquisite, full of pain, but always reaching for the divine aspect of mankind wherein lies hope."

Schmidt grinned wolfishly. "Some people feel that way about the American singer, Frank Sinatra."

Dr. Beck refused to be baited and steered Clare in the direction of the small dais that was set up at the far side of the square.

Silber called, "Take your seats, gentlemen. *Henry V* is the flower of English literature. I will be performing selected readings directly following the musical interlude. World premiere."

"Forgive me," said Schmidt, and he spat on the floor. Real spit, not just a show.

"Schmidt, you give Bavarians a bad name," said Hoeniger in disgust, and he followed Beck and Clare toward the row of chairs in front of the dais.

One of the internees smiled at her as they went by. "Mrs. Devereau, what an honour. Can I be interesting you in a tattoo today?"

He indicated where he'd set up two chairs and a small table. A cardboard sign read: TATTOOS. PERSONAL DESIGN. GOOD RATES.

He was a scruffy man, dressed in mismatched, shabby

clothes. His dark hair and blue eyes indicated his Celtic origins. Not to mention his thick Irish brogue.

"You need have no worries about the tattoo being permanent. I use an indelible pencil, which eventually fades. If you do change your mind after a week, poof, I will remove it."

Clare shook her head.

"Not for me, thank you, Mr. O'Connor."

"Sure now, 'tis great fun. A flower on the shoulder perhaps? Or the wrist? I could do a dainty English rose for you." He beamed, more of a leer really. "I can put it in an intimate place that is quite hidden from view . . . under usual circumstances. Very arousing."

Beck jumped in. "For goodness sake, O'Connor. The lady said no. Don't pester her."

"That was not my intention, Doctor. And Mrs. Devereau is quite capable of telling me herself if I bother her."

Clare smiled at him. "Thank you, Mr. O'Connor. Perhaps another day."

She was aware he was watching her as she took her seat in between Hoeniger and Beck.

Three men approached the dais, each carrying their instrument cases. One was elderly, rather stooped, the others younger, sombre as befitted performing the great master. She had met the older man recently. His name was Hartmann. He had a fragile, other-worldly appearance that touched her.

The musicians took their seats, and each began to take out their instruments from their cases. Clare saw Herr Hartmann open the case and reach into it. Then he let out a strangled cry and collapsed backward off the chair onto the ground, where he lay, his entire body twitching. Dr. Beck was on the dais in a second, and he dropped beside the fallen man. Another couple of internees, including the performers, gathered around. The seminarian also leaped up.

"Stand clear, gentlemen. Stand clear. Dr. Beck is in command of the situation."

The Irishman had come up behind Clare. "What the feck happened? Has he had a fit?"

"I don't know."

Beck was kneeling beside the stricken man, rubbing his hands. Hartmann was still twitching, a gush of blood coming from his mouth.

"What do you want us to do, Doctor?" asked Hoeniger.

"Let's get him back to his tent," said Beck. "Make a chair for him."

Willing hands helped to lift the violinist, and Hoeniger and O'Connor carried him away, Dr. Beck with them. All around Clare, the men were agitated, throwing questions at her, as an authority figure. She had no idea what had happened.

Silber climbed on the dais, reached into the open case, and lifted out the violin. Those who could see the instrument gasped in horror. The gleaming wood of the body had been deeply gouged and splintered, the strings wrenched out of their pegs.

Somebody had totally destroyed Herr Hartmann's beloved violin.

34.

"Oh, Tom. It was dreadful. The violin is ruined."

Tyler and Clare were seated at a corner table of the Acton Lodge restaurant, close to the kitchen, where a large, if bedraggled, potted palm tree offered some privacy.

"We all thought he'd had a heart attack at first. He'd bitten his tongue and the blood was pouring out. Major Fordham insisted on having him taken to hospital. Dr. Beck was allowed to accompany him, thank goodness. He rang me just before I left. He said it wasn't a heart attack. The poor man had collapsed from the shock of seeing the destruction of his violin. Dr. Beck says he has gone into what he calls a fugue. Herr Hartmann cannot or will not communicate with anybody. Who knows how long that will last. Bruno wanted to stay at the hospital with him, but they wouldn't let him. He is most upset about it."

The waiter came over with two menus, each in a heavy cloth cover with a gold tassel. He was wearing a shabby black suit that gave off a whiff of old sweat as he stooped over them to drape napkins on their knees. He drifted off.

"Herr Hartmann is not an emotionally strong man at the best of times. Too much tragedy in his life. He's elderly and not in good health," continued Clare. "Why would anyone be so cruel as to commit such an act of vandalism?"

"That's more the head doctor's province than mine, Clare. Was there anything else vandalized?"

"Not that I know of. Is there nothing you can do?"

"Technically, no. The camp is under military control. The major will have to pursue an investigation himself."

"But do you have an idea what it is all about, Tom?"

"If nobody else was targeted, I'd say it has to do with the professor himself. Professional jealousy perhaps? An old grudge? Could be anything. Men who are behind barbed wire become stir-crazy."

"I suppose so." She sighed. "One dreadful thing seems to follow right after another. I know this incident wouldn't be considered a major crime, but the violence that had been vented on that lovely musical instrument was shocking. It was more than two hundred years old and worth a lot of money. It's all he had."

The waiter reappeared and gave a soft cough to remind them to get on with placing their order.

Tyler opened his menu. There was a splotch of grease in the corner. Not too much on offer, but that wasn't surprising these days. A potato and onion soup which sounded good, a turnip pie which didn't, and grilled plaice which he thought he'd have.

"Me too," said Clare. "And a bottle of your best wine, please."

"Very good, madam."

"It's my treat, don't forget, Tom." She glanced around the room. There were only two other couples in the restaurant, both middle aged, and both not talking. They had been served and were eating their meals in silence. Tyler was relieved not to recognize either pair.

He and Clare had liked the hotel restaurant twenty years earlier. Being in love made everything exciting, even this fusty place, which then had seemed the height of luxury, at least for him. On their last night together, she'd been the one to rent a room for them. The hotel staff would never have said anything, even if they suspected. She was too posh for that, with her accent and county clothes. As always he'd given her half an hour, then slipped in by way of the back stairs.

She was sitting on the bed, waiting. She looked unexpectedly shy and his heart melted at the sight. Her hair was long and wavy and she had let it fall to her shoulders. She had good legs, one of her best features; her breasts were small but they cupped perfectly into his hands. Her privates had golden hair and there was golden down on her arms and legs. He remembered the feeling that he was drowning in her. That night they made love passionately, tenderly, slowly, fast.

Clare tapped his arm. "Tom? Hello, Tom. A penny for them. Where did you just go?"

"Nowhere. I was wool gathering. What were you saying?"

"This place hasn't changed a jot. I remember the awful carpet and the curtains that look like they belong in a funeral parlour. Not to mention the waiter who hasn't changed his shirt in twenty years. I do believe his name was Jonas. My God, Tommy, why on earth did we like this place?"

Tyler had vowed to himself that he wouldn't bring up the past unless she did, but now he didn't really like the way she was speaking. He could be any old school chum she'd gone out for a meal with. Where was the magic stardust of love remembered? The waiter returned with the bottle of wine and two glasses.

Clare smiled up at him. "I was here many years ago and I think you were the waiter then. Is your name Jonas?"

"No, madam. It's Charles, and I have only been working here for the past two years. However, I do believe my predecessor was named Jonah." Not the slightest whit succumbing to Clare's charm, he turned to Tyler. "Will you taste the wine, sir?"

"Not me. The lady will."

Unperturbed, Charles poured out a taste into the glass, Clare pronounced it acceptable, and he filled the two glasses.

"Your meal will be here momentarily, sir."

He glided away. Clare raised her eyebrows. "I got well and truly snubbed, didn't I? Well, he does look like the other chap. It was probably his father. Where were we? Oh yes, you were about to share your thoughts with me."

"Was I?"

Her eyes met his. She was wearing a silky blue frock that brought out the colour of her eyes. The ridiculous scarf would go well with it. She smiled wistfully.

"This place does bring back memories. We spent our first night here, didn't we?"

"And our last. We had a flaming row."

"I know. I'm sorry."

That night she said she had to tell him something. She was leaving in a week's time to go to some swanky school in Switzerland to study languages. "For how long?" he asked, but she said she didn't know. He'd yelled then. "What do you mean you don't know? What am I? The peasant stud you can rut with to keep him quiet but drop when it suits you?" "No," she'd shouted back. "What do you take me for?" "I thought we loved each other," he said, "that we'd get married and be together 'til death us do part." Too caught up in his hurt feelings, he'd got all melodramatic. "Go then. Get the hell away from me. Amputations should be done quickly."

And that was essentially that. She'd written later, but he didn't answer. Time had numbed his anguish; at least that's what he'd thought until he'd seen her in the market.

Clare looked away. "We were too young, Tom. I hadn't done anything with my life and neither had you."

"So you said." He raised his glass. "Hey, come on, that was a long time ago. There's been a lot of water under the bridge since then. Let's drink to the present."

She clicked her glass with his. "To the present."

The waiter came out of the kitchen, wheeling a trolley. The platters had silver lids which he removed.

The fish looked as if it had been around for as long as Charles himself, but the chef had endeavoured to hide it in a thick buttery sauce.

After a few minutes, Clare dabbed at her lips with the napkin. "I think the accoutrements are rather outclassing the food. We'd better polish off the wine."

By now they were the only two people left in the dining room. Charles came in and drew the blackout curtains.

"Speaking of the present, do you have any leads in your case?" Clare asked.

"Not really. I'm hoping something will come from the car registrations, but it's a long shot."

She looked puzzled. "I don't understand."

"Oops! It's some information I haven't released. Keep it under your hat."

"Of course."

"According to the coroner, shortly before she was shot Elsie Bates was hit by a car. She was seriously injured."

"Good Lord!"

"You weren't driving on the Heath Road between five-thirty and six o'clock yesterday morning, were you by any chance?"

"What? At that hour, I was still tucked up in bed, trying to decide whether or not to throw the alarm clock out of the window. I'm still not used to country hours. Why are you asking?"

"That's where Elsie was knocked off her bike. On the Heath Road, not too far out of Whitchurch."

Again Clare wiped at her mouth. "I had no idea that's where

she was. You never specified. You just said she was found on a country road."

"Police tactics. Keep that quiet too, please." He had the odd feeling that she was relieved.

He placed his hand lightly over hers. "Don't worry. We'll catch the culprit."

"I have no doubt of that, Tom Tyler. Unlike me, you found your calling." She held his hand in both of hers. "I tell you what. This has been a lovely evening except for the food. Why don't I cook you a proper meal? I'm quite a good cook. Can you come for luncheon at my place tomorrow?"

"I'll have to ask my wife."

He'd meant it as a joke. At least, he thought he had.

Abruptly, Clare removed her hands. "My apologies. Forgive me if I don't invite her as well." She picked up her handbag. "I should get going while there's even a trace of daylight."

"Clare wait! I was trying to be funny. You don't have to invite Vera. Of course you don't. You and I are childhood friends. Strictly platonic." He was digging the hole deeper. "I'd love to come for dinner. What time?"

She studied his face for a moment. "Oh, Tom."

"What? What, 'oh Tom'?"

"Never mind. Come early. How about one?"

"Perfect."

She stood up. "Why don't you stay a bit longer and finish the bottle. It's a shame to waste it. I'll pay on the way out."

She blew him a breezy kiss and headed for the door.

Tyler swished the wine around in the glass. He stared gloomily at the ruby-red liquid.

35.

ALICE THORNE HAD DRAWN THE CURTAINS AND LIT the oil lamps. The dogs, well fed, were lying at her feet. Jimmy was sitting at the kitchen table watching her skin the rabbit she had just killed.

"How can you bring yourself to kill rabbits when you are so anti-war?"

"Because I'm not a sentimental idiot. My dogs are carnivores and so are humans. These creatures die immediately, I make sure of that. And I don't seek them out to kill them just because I don't like the colour of their fur."

"I realize that, but it still seems pretty callous to me."

"You might make completely different decisions about the animal world, Jimmy, but that's mine and I don't come by it casually."

She was about to remind him how much he'd enjoyed the rabbit stew she'd cooked yesterday, but he was so edgy and restless, she bit her tongue.

Suddenly, he jumped to his feet and walked over to the window. "Why is it that nothing seems simple anymore?"

She concentrated on dismembering the carcass, then dropped each piece into a pot of brine beside her. The rabbits tended to be a bit tough as she didn't like to kill the younger ones if she could help it. Soaking for an hour in salt water made them more palatable. She rolled up the rabbit pelt and put it into another bucket to be cleaned more thoroughly later. When she had accumulated a sufficient number of them, she'd make the skins into a hat, or stole, or even a jacket to sell at the market. In the past, they were very popular.

Jimmy came back to the table.

Finally he said, "Can I tell you what happened, Mrs. Thorne? I need to tell somebody . . . No, I'm sorry that sounds as if it doesn't matter who, but that's not true. It's you who I want to talk to."

"All right."

She didn't mean to stiffen her shoulders but she couldn't help it.

"It's about what happened at Dunkirk."

Much later, this is the story that Alice related to Tyler.

The four of them, the musketeers, Jimmy, Bobby, Wilf and Dennis, had got separated from their unit. Their captain had said, "Every man for himself," but with them, it was one for all and all for one, so they never even considered breaking up. They had walked all day pushing through the stream of refugees who were all heading in the other direction, trying to get away from the coast. A military policeman they'd encountered on the road had told them to head for Dunkirk, "where the smoke was," but they didn't get that far before it got dark. They spent a night in a farmhouse listening to the sound of the German mortars getting nearer and nearer. They could even see the Jerry soldiers coming along the road less than half a mile away. Finally Jimmy, who always took the lead, had said they had to make a run for it.

To his mind, the boots the army had issued to Bobby were the cause of the trouble that followed.

They were one size too big, heavy and stiff, and he kept tripping over his own feet. They were all running, Wilf first, then Bobby, behind him, Dennis. Jimmy had twisted his ankle leaping into a ditch when the Stukka dive-bombers attacked the column, so he was bringing up the rear. There was a particularly loud bang from one side and a plume of dirt and rocks showered down on them. Too close for comfort. Jimmy was covered with dirt, choking on it, hardly able to see. Bobby stumbled and fell to the ground. He should have put the safety catch on his rifle, but in the rush and panic to get out of the farmhouse, he'd forgotten to.

Bam. The gun discharged.

Wilf was actually lifted in the air and flung on his face. At first Jimmy thought Wilf had been hit by the shell. He caught up with Bobby and tugged at his shoulder.

"Keep moving," he said.

Wilf was writhing on the ground, his right thigh and buttock were crimson with blood, a chunk of flesh was shot away. They heard voices from the farmhouse. Some Jerries were running out, one of them setting up a machine gun.

"Come on," said Jimmy.

They scrambled up the slope to where Wilf lay. He was going into a seizure and it looked as if he were trying to bite into the ground.

"Grab him," said Jimmy, and he took Wilf under his armpits.

Wilf groaned; saliva and blood were running down his chin.

"Don't leave me," he gasped. A little pink bubble popped out of his mouth.

Jimmy didn't reply but said again to Bobby, "Let's get him off this fucking hill."

Dennis was still lying flat on his stomach just behind them, and for a minute they thought he'd bought it too, but he staggered to his feet and half ran, half crawled up to them.

"Christ, Bobby. You shot him. You fucking well shot him."

"Shut up," said Jimmy. "Let's get him out of here."

Bobby seemed unable to act so Dennis took Wilf's other arm and he and Jimmy dragged him up the hill as if he were a bag of potatoes. Once over the crest, they slid and rolled down to a ditch half-filled with stagnant water. Wilf had left a trail of blood behind them. Jimmy could see the white tendons and glistening *exposed bone in his thigh. Bright red blood was pulsing out of the wound.*

There was a road running alongside the ditch and, on the other side, a thick stand of trees.

"Come on," said Jimmy. "We can't stay here. Let's get under cover."

He and Dennis picked up Wilf, who was trying to help by using his good leg, the shattered right leg dragging uselessly. They managed to climb out of the ditch and scramble across the road to the safety of the trees. They pushed in as far as they could but the underbrush was dense, clawing at them, holding them. It was obvious they weren't going to get far with the injured man and they were forced to halt. They lowered Wilf down to the ground.

Bobby looked at Jimmy, who shook his head. Wilf saw the look. "Don't leave me lads. Jerry'll shoot me. I can manage, you go ahead and break the trail. I'll keep up with you."

"You can't," hissed Dennis. "They'll get all of us."

"No, they won't. I can do it, I swear."

They heard shouts and a spray of bullets ripped through the trees overhead. The Germans hadn't found them yet, but they would at any minute.

"Come on," said Jimmy again and he tried to hoist Wilf to his feet. Wilf let out a half-choked yelp, more like a bark than a human sound.

"I'll carry him," said Bobby. "Get him on my back." The other two didn't argue, just hoisted the injured man up and across Bobby's shoulders. The blood from Wilf's wound immediately soaked through his collar. Dennis went first, then Jimmy, trying to break the trail. There were loud explosions from behind them but they kept going.

"Here," cried out Dennis. There was a narrow animal track leading through the trees, which made them able to move faster. They must have gone like that for ten, fifteen minutes until finally Bobby had to stop.

"Just a minute," he gasped. He fell to his knees and let Wilf slide as gently as he could off his shoulders onto the ground.

Jimmy scrambled over. "I'll take him," he said.

Wilf's eyes were turning up in their sockets and he was chalk white. However, he suddenly took in a shuddering breath and his eyes focused.

"I'm done for," he whispered. "Leave me. Get out of here."

A trickle of dark blood was running from the corner of his mouth.

Hardly able to breathe, Bobby leaned over him. "I'm sorry, Wilf. I'm so sorry."

Wilf lifted his hand, made a fist and bumped Bobby on the cheek. "You stupid bugger. I warned you about that fucking safety catch. Now get the fuck out of here. No sense in all of us dying."

He closed his eyes.

Dennis had joined them. "I think he's dead," he said from over Bobby's shoulder.

"No, he's still breathing," cried Bobby.

"He's a goner, mate," said Dennis and he grabbed Bobby by the arm. "We've got to leave him or it's all of us gone. Jimmy tell him."

Bobby shook him off. "No. We can't let him die alone."

Jimmy stared down at Wilf. "Dennis is right. We can't help him."

They heard another shout. Jerry was following the trail and closing in fast.

"Come on," said Jimmy, tugging at Bobby's sleeve.

"He'll be all right," said Dennis, almost dancing with agitation. "The Jerry will take him prisoner. He'll be living the life of Riley in no time."

Wilf managed to wave his hand at them.

"Go, you silly sods," he whispered. "Just leave me my gun."

"I'm going if you're not," said Dennis and he started off along the trail.

"*Come on, Bobby,*" said Jimmy. *He stood straight and gave a formal salute in Wilf's direction.* "*Best of luck, mate.*" *He handed Wilf the gun, then grabbing Bobby's arm, he shoved him ahead and they ran.*

Moments later that they heard a burst of machine-gun fire.
Somebody howled.
There was more gunfire, then silence.
They ran on.

Alice covered Jimmy's hand with hers for a long time.

36.

PRIVATE DENNIS MCEVOY WAS COMING TO THE rendezvous directly from his shift at the camp. He was still wearing his uniform even though it was itchy and hot. Girls liked to see a lad in uniform. He'd taken the precaution of reporting in sick, pleading a bad stomach. Not that this was entirely untrue. He hadn't been feeling that grand for the last couple of weeks. Cleverly, Janet had also pleaded a bad tummy to get off work. She couldn't get away in the evenings, just the early mornings, which suited Dennis just fine. He could see another girl in the evening.

He'd got there first and he stood in the clearing smoking a cigarette. It was barely light, and the grass was damp from yesterday's thunderstorm. Good thing they had somewhere dry and comfy to go. The place known as the Fort had been a favourite spot for couples for decades.

"A woman will always remember her first time, Denny," one of the chaps had told him while they were sitting around the barracks, waiting for something to happen. The talk fell, as it usually did, to girls and sex and whether, or how much, of both you'd had. Dennis hadn't forgotten the man's words and he wanted to make sure Janet's memories were going to be fond ones. He'd been warned that most virgins didn't always enjoy themselves, but he was experienced. He knew a thing or two and he was sure he could satisfy her. He couldn't help but preen himself a little, giving his pencil-thin moustache a stroke. He'd had no complaints from the other girls. They couldn't get enough of him. Practically had to fight them off.

He felt a strong urge to urinate and relieved himself at a tree.

Phew, what a pong. Smelled like a dead animal. Maybe a fox had got himself caught in a trap. Well, he wasn't about to go and find out. Young girls were sensitive and if Janet knew there was a creature dead nearby, she'd probably want to bury it. They'd practically grown up together, and he knew she was that kind of girl. Dead, maggoty animals, however, were not conducive to romance.

He heard twigs snapping and she appeared at the edge of the clearing. She was wearing a yellow raincoat, and the damp air had made her dark hair stand away from her head in an explosion of curls. His heart wasn't the only thing that leaped up when he saw her. He didn't immediately go over to her and give her a whopping kiss. He let her come to him, which she did. She was smiling.

"Fancy meeting you here."

"Likewise. Here." He offered her his cigarette. "Have a drag."

"I don't mind if I do. Might wake me up."

They passed the cigarette back and forth until it was finished, Janet handling the fag with the clumsiness of the novice. They still hadn't touched, Dennis allowing the anticipation to build up. Finally, he took one last drag and stubbed out the butt under his boot. Then he took her in his arms and tongue-kissed her deep and passionately, until both of them had to break off to get breath.

"Ready?" he asked.

"As much as I will ever be," she said. He wasn't sure if he liked that answer and gave her breast a soft caress.

"Do you need a little more preparation?" he whispered against her ear.

She stepped away from him, giving him a little push. "No.

Let's do it before I come to my senses."

He put his arm around her.

"Ugh. What's that rotten smell?" she asked.

"Nothing we can't forget about."

He moved aside a couple of the branches that were block-ing the entrance to the lean-to, and then stood aside and gave a little bow.

"After you, madam."

Janet didn't move and made a mock pout.

"Aren't you going to carry me across the threshold?"

"I would if I could but there isn't room."

"You can crouch."

"Spoiled rotten, aren't you," said McEvoy. "Come on then."

With a grunt he lifted her into his arms, ducked his head and stepped into the gloom of the Fort.

37.

TYLER WOKE EARLY. AS SEEMED TO BE BECOMING THE norm, his night had been restless and troubled. Vera was still asleep beside him and he slipped out of bed as quietly as he could. For once he hadn't been late getting home, but she was at one of her wvs meetings so he hadn't had to answer any questions. There was a note on the kitchen table from Janet saying she'd gone out early to run the dogs with Jillian. Her friend's father kept whippets and the girls often exercised them in the mornings.

Jimmy was still asleep and he didn't disturb him. To tell the truth, he didn't know how to approach him. "Come on, lad, open up to your old dad, there's a good chap. Tell him what's bothering you." Tyler, himself, could not remember a single instance when he had confided in his own father about anything. The unaccustomed intimacy that confidences might bring was embarrassing.

He washed his face and had a quick shave, then left for the station. The sky was overcast, the air damp. It was just past seven o'clock.

He unlocked the front door and went straight to the duty room to make his tea. He wasn't sure that the dinner with Clare had been a success. What had he expected? That a fairy would touch them both with her magic wand and change them back into the people they had once been? The only fairy was the waiter, and he hadn't brought much magic with him. Clare hadn't wanted to linger, although Tyler would have been happy to. At least she'd wanted to meet again soon. And at her flat. Tyler had to smile at himself. *Down boy, down. As the good doctor might put it, sometimes a flat is only a flat.*

He took the paintings out of the drawer and put them on his desk. The more he looked at them, the more beautiful they seemed.

He heard the sound of his sergeant arriving, and he returned them to the drawer with the silk scarf.

"Morning, Guff. I'm in here," he called out.

Gough popped his head around the door. "Morning, sir."

"Kettle's just boiled. I'm about to ring the hostel. Nobody's called. I'm afraid the lass is now a missing person. Have one of the lads pick up the hand-outs, will you. We're going to have to organize a search and a door-to-door."

While Gough went to make his tea, Tyler rang the hostel. Miss Stillwell answered, and he could tell she had been awake for some hours.

"No, nothing, Inspector."

"I'll give the police station in London another call, just in case. If there's no news, we'll start a search."

He had just hung up the telephone when his door banged open and Janet burst in.

"Daddy, Daddy. We found the girl. She was in the woods. She's dead."

Tyler pulled her close to him.

"There, there, pet. Take your time. Tell me what happened."

Gough came to see what the matter was, and Tyler signalled over Janet's head for him to take a seat. She was shaking violently and could only talk in between bouts of weeping.

"It was t-terrible what has h-happened to her . . ."

Tyler rocked her. "Hush, sweetheart . . . It's all right now.

I'm here. Come and sit down." He guided her to his chair and squeezed in beside her as if she were a child. She smelled of cigarettes. "Start at the beginning."

"It must be the missing Land Army girl . . . she was in the Fort." She buried her face against his chest. "Oh, Daddy. It was horrible. Animals must have got to her. Her face . . ." Janet's voice was lost in a fresh burst of weeping.

Tyler waited a few moments. "Now, Jan, I need to know what happened. Look, your favourite sergeant is here. You don't want him to think you're a big cry baby, do you?"

She shook her head like a child. Finally she was able to sit up, and she wiped her eyes with the handkerchief he handed to her.

"That's my girl. Now start at the beginning. What were you doing in the woods?"

"Sometimes the smell of the meat in the shop makes me feel sick, so I thought I'd take the morning off. I know I shouldn't have told a fib but I didn't feel like explaining everything. I told Granddad I had an upset tummy. I knew he would tell me off if I didn't give him a good excuse. I got on my bike and went to Acton Woods. I decided to have a look at the Fort. You know where I mean?"

Tyler nodded.

"There was a bad smell in the air but I didn't think too much of it. I thought a badger or a fox had been around. I poked my head inside the Fort." Janet stopped at the memory.

"Keep going, Jan, you're doing grand." Sergeant Gough pulled the other chair closer.

"I didn't realize at first that there was a . . . body. A girl's body. The flies were so thick I couldn't even see her face . . ."

Tyler lifted his daughter's chin and wiped away her tears.

"Do you want to have a glass of water, pet?"

She shook her head again. Her eyes were dilated with fear.

"I ran back to my bike and got here as fast as I could. My legs were so wobbly I could hardly ride."

Tyler gave her a hug. "Good girl. How's Jillian?"

She looked at him, bewildered.

"You left a note saying you were meeting Jillian this morning. Wasn't she with you?"

"No, no. That fell through. I was by myself."

"All right, pet. Now I'm going to have to get over there. Can you stay with Sergeant Gough? You can sit in my office if you like."

Janet looked frightened. "No, I don't want to be by myself. Is Mummy at home?"

"She was when I left. Do you want me to come with you and tell her what has happened?"

Janet sniffed. "Yes, please."

Outside in the hall, they heard the sound of the constables arriving.

"Send them over to the area," said Tyler to the sergeant. "They know where it is. They should take the police van. Get hold of Dr. Murnaghan right away. Ask him to meet me here. I'll go in his car."

"Right. Shall I notify Miss Stillwell?"

"Wait until I come back. Let's make absolutely sure it's Rose Watkins." Tyler straightened up. "Come on, Jan. Let's get you home."

Her face crumpled into tears again. "Do you have to go?"

"I must, sweetheart."

"What happened to that poor girl, Daddy?"

"I don't know yet, pet." Again he lifted her chin so he could look into her eyes. "Was anybody else with you?"

She shifted her glance immediately. "No, Daddy. I told you, it was just me."

—

Vera was up and making breakfast in the kitchen when Tyler and Janet came in. Janet started to cry again, and Tyler explained succinctly what had happened. He'd been afraid Vera would choose to scold Janet for even being in the woods, but she didn't. He waited until his daughter had calmed down.

"I'm going to have to get back in a minute, Jan, but I wonder if you and I could have a bit of a chin wag before I go."

"What for?" Vera demanded. "Can't you see she's had a dreadful shock? Can't it wait?"

"I wouldn't ask if it wasn't important." He turned to his daughter. "Maybe we could go to your room?"

Vera was about to protest but Tyler forestalled her. "Sorry, but I need to talk to her in private. It's a police matter."

"What do you mean? Talk to her in private? There you go again. She's my daughter too, don't forget. I don't want her having a nervous breakdown. One child with bad nerves is enough, thank you."

Janet cried out. "Mum. Dad. Please, not now."

Vera put her hand to her throat. "Go ahead. Do what you have to do. I can't bear this anymore. It's too much. You two stay here. I'll go upstairs."

"Vee . . ." but she had already left the room.

Tyler pulled out a chair at the table. "Sit down, Janet."

She was tear-stained and white as a sheet but his own fear made him angry.

"I want you to listen to me and listen good. I'm not going to mess around here. I don't know why you're lying to me but you have been."

She started to cry in good earnest. "Daddy, don't. Please don't be so angry with me."

"Have you taken up smoking?"

"No, I . . . er."

"You stank of cigarettes when you came to the station. And

you said *we. We* found the girl."

She buried her face in her hands. "It was just a manner of speaking."

"I don't think so. You were with somebody. I'm guessing it was a lad."

The uncontrollable blush of an adolescent flooded her face, but she still held out.

"I told you, Daddy, I don't want to talk about it. It was too horrible. What matters is that we found her body. It doesn't matter whether or not I was with somebody."

He caught hold of her hand and held it tightly. "You are both material witnesses. I'll need to get his statement."

"Why? I've told you all you need to know. There's nothing more to say."

"Janet, there are people in this world who don't think like you and me. They kill for pleasure. It gives them a thrill, a sexual thrill. Then these same men go back to where they have left their victim and pretend to be innocent passersby. This is another secret thrill for them. Sometimes, they take another girl with them because an even bigger thrill is to kill again, before, during, or after sexual intercourse."

Never in their life together so far had he spoken this way or even mentioned the word sex. Janet looked at him in horror.

He let go of her hand. "So who did you go to the Fort with? Was it a boy from school?"

"No."

"Who then? Who were you with?"

She whispered. "Dennis McEvoy."

Tyler felt as if he'd been kicked in the stomach. "Why didn't you want to tell me?"

"He asked me not to. He said he'd booked off sick from guard duty and he'd get into bad trouble if it came out what he was really doing. He said he could be court-martialled, and he said these days they'll hang you for nothing . . . Oh Daddy, I didn't think it would matter if I told a white lie. Dennis isn't like what you said. He grew up here, he's our Jimmy's friend. How can you suggest such things?"

"Every murderer known grew up somewhere, and some of them had friends."

He desperately wanted to ask if she'd had intercourse, but he supposed that would soon become evident.

"I'll talk to him, and it probably won't be as serious as he led you to believe. At the most, maybe a few days on KP duty. I'm sorry I had to put you through the ringer, pet. Chalk it up to worry. I don't know what I'd do if anything happened to you and I could have done something to prevent it."

"I know, Daddy. I know." She hesitated. "We didn't, you know, go all the way, so you don't have to worry."

He could have burst out crying. "Thanks for telling me."

And thank God for that.

Tyler hurried back to the station, leaving Vera to take care of their daughter.

"Sergeant, I want you to send somebody around to the McEvoy house, 22 Green Lane. Have them bring Dennis back here immediately."

"Is there a charge, sir?"

"Call it obstructing justice."

"Very well, sir."

"You don't have kids, Guff, and sometimes I think you're lucky. Janet has informed me that she was with Dennis McEvoy when they found Rose's body. He asked her to keep quiet about the fact they were together. He told her he'd get into hot water and the silly girl agreed to lie for him. But it's not only that. The bloody little sod has the clap."

"Good Lord."

"He was having it off with one of the Land girls and she fessed up that he gave her a dose. And he was about to have it off with our Janet. She says they didn't, thank God, or you'd have to lock me in the cell before I killed the bugger."

"Is there any chance he didn't know about his, er, condition?"

"Not a snowball's chance in hell. Having the clap is something you know about. It hurts like hell to piss and when you do, the stuff that comes out looks like thick yellow snot. Your goolies swell to the size of tennis balls and feel like a mouthful of teeth, all with abscesses. McEvoy didn't give a damn whether he passed it on or not as long as he got his tool in."

Gough's face was grim. "I'll keep him in the cell until you get back, sir. Can do wonders, a little quiet reflection in that place."

"Thank you, Sergeant. Oh, and Guffie? If he happens to trip over a bucket and bang his head, I won't protest."

"Yes, sir. Funny how clumsy people get when they're in that cell."

Tyler heard the sound of a car drawing into the driveway. He involuntarily took a deep breath. It was Dr. Murnaghan, ready to go view the body of Rose Watkins.

38

THERE WAS ROOM FOR ONLY THE CORONER TO STAND inside the Fort. Tyler peered over his shoulder. The blue-bottles were thick on the body, which was lying on its side, facing away from the entrance. The stench was overpowering. One foot and part of the lower leg was severed where an animal had gnawed at it and dragged it to the edge of the blanket. There was something incongruous about the neat shoe still on the intact foot. Spiders were crawling over it. The skirt of a flowered summer frock was pulled up high on the white thighs. Murnaghan crouched down and shooed the flies away. They didn't move far and were back feeding almost immediately.

"Bloody things. Can you get in here, Tyler, and keep them off so at least I can get a look at the face?"

Tyler squeezed inside, trying to breath as shallowly as possible. He waved his hand over what was left of the face. Birds had taken her eyes and picked at the soft flesh of the cheeks, but she was still recognizable.

"It's Rose Watkins all right."

"Poor sod. Remind me that dead bodies have no sensation, will you?"

He didn't really need a reply and Tyler just nodded.

"Look at that, Inspector." Murnaghan was pointing at a length of thin rope that was wrapped tightly around Rose's neck. "She's been strangled and God knows what else. Well, I can't do anything until I get her into the morgue." He started to back out of the opening and Tyler followed suit.

Eagleton and Collis were waiting outside the Fort. They both looked nervous. Country policing wasn't usually like this.

Both Tyler and Murnaghan took in deep breaths of air as they emerged.

"You'll probably want to supervise the removal," said Murnaghan. "I'll meet you at the hospital." He tugged his hat down tighter and strode off across the clearing. He showed none of the excitement at being back at work that there had been with Elsie. Tyler thought that the coroner at this instant would have preferred to be cleaning out his mother's attic.

He turned to Eagleton and Collis. "We've got to bring out the body. I don't really want to drag her out, but I don't think we can remove her otherwise."

"Is it Rose Watkins, sir?" asked Eagleton.

"Yes."

The constable bit his lip. "I met her at a dance a couple of weeks ago. Tiny little thing. She was shy. I wanted to accompany her back to the hostel but she said she was with her friends."

He looked upset but Tyler knew he had to be tough. "Let's save the reminiscences until we've got the job done, shall we? Right now, I think the best thing we can do for Rose Watkins is get her out of here and into a proper grave. We're going to have to break away some of these branches. I don't suppose either of you thought to bring an axe, did you? No? I thought not. Next time be prepared for all eventualities." He was taking out some of his upset on the two young men and he immediately regretted it. "Never mind, do the best you can. Eagleton, you take the upper part, Collis the lower. Get her onto the stretcher. It's not a pretty sight, so be prepared. If you concentrate on the task, which is to disturb as little as possible, you might find it a titch easier. But there's nothing to ashamed of if you feel queasy. If you've got to upchuck, get yourself outside quick. Ready?"

Tyler went back to the station, where Sergeant Gough greeted him immediately, coming round from the desk. Tyler thought for a minute the sergeant might even embrace him, he looked so concerned.

"I've got a pot of tea freshening, sir. I thought you'd need it."

"I need a bloody stiff drink, that's what I need."

"I took the liberty of purchasing a medicinal bottle of whisky. You can add it your tea."

In spite of the situation, Tyler almost laughed. How a big, tough-looking man like Gough managed to come across as the perfect valet, he didn't know, but right now he appreciated it.

"Thanks, Guffie. Give the lads the same treatment, will you, when they come in. I think Eager is all right, but young Collis was looking green at the gills. They've taken the body to Dr. Murnaghan."

"Was the lassie murdered, sir?"

"No doubt about it. She was strangled. Murnaghan is getting to the post-mortem immediately so we may have more information later today. The rooks had got to her and some animal had chewed off her foot."

Gough cleared his throat with a polite cough. "Saw a lot of that on the Transvaal, sir. Over there it was jackals and hyenas, nasty brutes."

Tyler gaped at him. "I didn't know you fought in the Boer War."

"Two years of it. I was a mere lad when I signed up. Needed my head examined I would say, gave me a broken nose and a leaky gut and I don't know that it did anybody else any good. When you come to think of it, the Boers were only defending their own land, weren't they? Same as we are doing now. Three bloody wars in my lifetime. Will we never learn? Animals behave better. They only kill for food."

"But you go to church on a regular basis, Sergeant. Doesn't that . . ." he waved his hand, not finishing his sentence. Gough understood him.

"I sing in the choir, sir. I like music. It calms the savage breast."

Tyler made a mental note to take his officer out for a beer soon. He had no idea Gough was capable of such depth. That'd teach him to take people for granted. Next thing young Eagleton would be telling him he was writing poetry.

"Are you going to enlist help from A and B divisions, sir?" Gough asked.

"Probably . . . oh shite, I don't know. You get too many men on the case and they trip all over themselves and they're more of a right hindrance than a help."

Even to himself, the excuse sounded thin. Of course, more manpower could be an asset if they were organized properly. The problem was, he wanted to hog the case to himself. He didn't want anybody else interfering.

"I'll decide tonight when we see if the reservists come up with anything. Bring in the medicine, will you, Sergeant?"

He walked back to his office, picked up the phone, hesitated, and replaced the receiver as Gough came in carrying a tray. Without being asked, he poured out a cup of dark strong tea. There was a whisky bottle standing beside the cup.

"I'll let you add to it, sir."

Tyler felt like dumping the tea and filling the cup with whisky but he restrained himself and poured in two large shots.

He sipped. "Ah. Heaven. And that's where you'll go, Guff. I personally will recommend to God that you get a place of honour in Heaven for such thoughtfulness."

"Thank you, sir. I wasn't aware you had the ear of the Almighty but I appreciate the offer."

Tyler took another swallow. "I'm going over to the hostel to talk to the warden. Ring me there if there are any new developments. I'm not sure how long I'll be."

"When will we notify the girl's next of kin, sir?"

Tyler sighed. "Now, I suppose. There's no point in putting it off. We'll have to get one of the London bobbies to do the dirty."

"I'll put you through right away, sir."

"All right, just give me two minutes to finish my tea."

"Yes, sir."

Gough's talents were wasted in this backwater, thought Tyler. He drank down more of the hot whisky-laced tea and felt the warmth flood his belly. It was almost unbearable to imagine how Rose's parents would take the news. First they were rendered homeless, now this. And Mrs. Watkins was injured. The intercom beeped and he pressed the *on* switch.

"I have Scotland Yard on the line, sir," said Gough.

39.

CLARE'S CAR SKIDDED A LITTLE AS SHE NEGOTIATED a sharp turn, and she realized she was driving too fast. The tall hedgerows made it impossible to see if any other vehicle was on the road. She checked her speed. It was as if she were trying to outrun her own thoughts.

"Damn you, Tommy Tyler," she said out loud. "Stop comparing me with that young girl I once was. She's gone a long time ago and will never return. We can't go back, Tommy. We simply can't."

She raced the MG over a rut in the road with such a thump she was afraid for her axle. She slowed down, not having noticed that her speedometer had crept up again.

She reached Whitchurch and turned on to the long, secluded driveway that led to the Old Rectory. The sentry was new, and he examined her identification carefully before opening the gate. She parked at the rear of the building and let herself in through the heavy wooden door. The office was on the top floor, and she climbed the stairs, panting a little as she reached the top.

The secretary, Miss Nicholls, was at her desk in the anteroom typing with great speed. She looked at Clare over the top of her spectacles and reluctantly stopped what she was doing. She reminded Clare of the headmistress of the school where she'd boarded as an adolescent. She had been the bane of Clare's life, always critical, rigid about the rules to the point of mummification. Clare's hand went automatically to her hair to smooth it down into an acceptable tidiness.

"I wasn't aware you had an appointment today, Mrs. Devereau."

"I don't. It is quite important."

"He has a rather severe toothache and I'm trying to keep his appointments to a minimum. But if as you say it's important –"

"Yes, it is."

The secretary frowned suspiciously. "Please have a seat. I will tell him you are here."

She flipped the switch on her intercom and, leaning close to it, whispered her message. Clare couldn't hear the reply but Miss Nicholls nodded at her.

"He says you can go right in. Try not to tire him out."

Clare went over to the connecting door and did as ordered. The director was behind his desk, which was the only place she had ever seen him. He was smoking his smelly pipe and his desk was strewn with papers.

"I didn't expect you today, Mrs. Devereau." He didn't add, "This had better be as important as you say," but he might as well have.

He reached inside his mouth and touched his gum tentatively, then withdrew it quickly. In spite of herself, Clare felt sympathy. He looked wretched; his usual pasty complexion was worse than ever.

"Your secretary says you have a toothache. I'm sure it would be worthwhile to visit a dentist, sir."

"It's not serious. I'm attempting to wait it out. I suppose I'm a coward where dentists are concerned."

Clare was rather taken aback. Perhaps he was human after all.

She instinctively clasped her hands in her lap. "There is something I thought you should know, sir. It has to do with Thursday morning."

—

Herbert Grey had walked over to his window, and he watched as Clare backed up the MG and drove away. In public, he never swore or took the Lord's name in vain; in private, he often vented his feelings with a string of choice words.

"Stupid, bloody woman. Sometimes I think women are more sodding trouble than they're worth. Christ, what was she thinking of?"

He snapped his teeth around his pipe stem and winced.

40.

TYLER HAD CONSTABLE EAGLETON COME WITH HIM to the hostel.

"I hope you never get used to delivering bad news, lad, but it is part of the job and you might as well have the experience. You don't have to say much, let them talk if they want to. Oh, you'd better put your bike in the back of the car. I'm not sure how long I'll have to stay at the manor."

Violet answered the door, took one look at Tyler's face, and whimpered, her eyes filling with tears.

"'Ee've found 'er, haven't 'ee? And she be dead."

"I'm afraid so, Violet. Her body was discovered this morning."

Violet wiped her eyes on the edge of her apron. Her head bent, she said, "Did she have a peaceful death, Mr. Tyler? She was a sweet gal and I hate to think of 'er end being anything but peaceful."

God, what the hell could he say to that? Rose had been strangled. Rarely a fast death. He squeezed Violet's arm.

"She died instantly."

"But somebody killed 'er, like Miss Elsie?"

"Yes, it appears so."

The maid crossed herself. "May the Lord have mercy on 'er soul."

"Keep her room locked for now, will you Violet? I'll take the key."

"Yes, sir."

"I've come to tell Miss Stillwell. Is she in?"

"Aye. She be in a meeting with Mr. Trimble. Shall I fetch her or do 'ee want to go into the common room where they is?"

"Are any of the girls at home?"

"Just Miss Florence, who is poorly. The others decided to go to the fields. It be harvest time and a lot to be done."

"I'm sure. Violet, this is Constable Eagleton. Just announce us to Miss Stillwell, there's a good lass."

"Come this way, sir."

Miss Stillwell and Trimble were seated at the table, papers spread in front of them. Like Violet, she realized at once why Tyler was there.

"Inspector? You have bad news?"

Tyler wasn't sure if he wanted to deliver this in front of Trimble, but he supposed in the long run, it didn't matter. He'd find out soon enough.

"We've found the body of Rose Watkins. I regret to say that she appears to have been strangled."

The warden turned white. "Poor, poor Rose. Where was she?"

"In the Acton Woods."

Miss Stillwell was struggling to control her tears. Tyler was aware of his young constable shifting uneasily behind him.

"Do you have the culprit?" Trimble asked. He too looked stunned.

"Not yet."

"First Elsie, now Rose. What is going on, Inspector?" Miss Stillwell asked him, her voice shaky.

"I don't know at the moment, ma'am, I wish I did."

She stood up slowly. "I suppose the best thing to do would be to get the girls. I don't think we can wait until they return. They are all upset already."

"I can fetch them, ma'am, if you like," said Trimble. "I know where they are."

He hurried off.

The warden addressed Tyler. "They aren't far away today. We can have them here within half an hour. Does Rose's father know?"

"Yes."

"I should talk to him at once. Excuse me, Inspector."

Miss Stillwell went off to make the telephone call. Tyler beckoned to Eagleton to come outside with him. They walked a little way down the gravel driveway. The hostel was surrounded by flower beds. Bright flowers and shrubs, birds chirruping and pecking for worms in the lawn belied the darkness that had descended on this old house.

Tyler offered the constable a cigarette, which he declined.

"Doing all right, are you, lad?"

"Yes, sir. As you say, I hope I never get used to this."

Tyler shrugged. "There's a war on. You might have to. Anyway, you did the right thing, which was to keep your mouth shut."

He puffed on his cigarette for a moment. "The sooner we find out where Rose's body was in the hours before she was found, the better chance we have of getting some clear evidence. Her body must have been hidden somewhere because she wasn't in the Fort on Friday. At least not during the day."

"Shall I attempt to retrace her footsteps, sir? The maid last saw her walking out of the gate up the road."

"Good idea, Eager. Let's take a guess here. She was intending to go to Mass at the camp but she was already late. What if she took a shortcut through the woods? That would save her ten to fifteen minutes. There's probably some kind of path. See what you can find. Walk like a Red Indian. I'll stay here until the girls return, then I'll go back to the station."

The constable set off and Tyler went back into the house.

There was nobody around and he decided to have another look in Rose's room.

It was exactly as it had looked before, but this time with a terrible emptiness. It seemed to Tyler that a layer of dust had already settled over everything.

He descended, and went out to the stable yard. Clare's MG was not there.

41.

THE AIR WAS HEAVY. ANOTHER STORM WAS THREAT-
ening and the V-shaped black clouds were like eyebrows
scowling down on the camp. At least that's how Dr. Beck
rather saw them. The camp was quiet. Out of deference to
the observant Jews, all activity was curtailed on the Sabbath.
No football, no chess, no poetry being bellowed through the
tents. He was sitting on a canvas chair in the "reading room,"
where he had more space than beside his tent, which was
cheek by jowl with the others. Beck often yearned for the privacy of the bed-sitting room that he'd rented from Mrs. Swann
in the centre of Birmingham. He'd even started up his therapy
practice again, and had three patients undergoing analysis
when he'd been arrested. He hoped they were all right. He'd
barely had time to relocate them with his colleague, Dr.
Binswager, a fellow German who had been in England for
some time and whose papers were quite in order.

Beck sighed. He should write to his wife but he'd already
sent one of his two allowed letters to her. She had remained
behind in Dover while he was establishing himself in
Birmingham, and she too had been swept up in the surge
of fear about aliens. Margareta wasn't a strong woman and
she was finding the quarters where the women were interned
very uncomfortable. Understandably, as they were incarcerated in the old Holloway prison for women, a relic of the
Victorian era. He was looking forward to seeing her when
they were all sent to the Isle of Man. Surely, they'd be
released soon.

He took his notebook from his box, wrote the date in one corner of the page, then chewed on the pencil. A shadow fell across his paper. He hadn't seen Hoeniger approaching.

"Good afternoon, Doctor Beck. You are looking far too serious. Shall I disturb you or go away and leave you in peace?"

The seminarian was smiling at him mischievously.

"By all means disturb me. I am completely unproductive today."

"I see you have your writing box with you. What are you working on today?"

"A paper for the *London Journal of Psychoanalysis*. It may or may not see the light of day but it keeps me occupied."

"And the topic?"

"Do you really want to know? It's quite esoteric."

"I have already benefited from being in this camp with so many brilliant men, a little psychoanalysis would be a nice addition."

Hoeniger plopped himself down on the grass, tucking his long soutáne under his knees as a woman would. His gold cross glinted in the sun. Beck often thought the religious restrictions Father Glatz placed on the young seminarian might be oppressive, but Hoeniger always seemed agreeably compliant.

"All right. You asked for it. Perhaps explaining it to you will help me clarify my thoughts." He pressed the tips of his fingers together. "I am exploring the role of the analyst when presented with what appear to be paranoid delusions on the part of the patient."

"Ah . . . will you explain that?"

"Certainly. Some more orthodox practitioners believe the analyst must under no circumstances break the bubble of delusion. That the patient will eventually come to see the reality if one simply continues with the psychoanalytic process . . . Others think that the patient must be presented with evidence that his beliefs are delusional, rather like metaphorically dousing them with cold water to bring them to their senses."

"What view do you side with?" asked the seminarian.

Beck chewed more on the pencil. "It requires a lot of patience to wait out the paranoia, and sometimes, especially if an underlying psychosis is present, the delusions are never relinquished. What I have always taught my students is that trying to force the patient to face their own paranoia is a mistake. They will often end the analysis in a state of what we call negative transference, and the delusions will continue and proliferate."

"This is all going over my head I'm afraid, Doctor. Can you give me an example? I do better with examples."

"Certainly. Look at Professor Hartmann. It was imperative that he felt his, shall we call them, delusions were not being dismissed."

"You mean when he was convinced that Herr Silber is a German spy?"

"Exactly."

"Maybe he is a spy? If not Silber, perhaps somebody else in the camp was coming and going. Maybe the professor wasn't delusional."

"Believe me, the poor man is in a severe fugue at the moment. I'm very concerned that he might not come out of it. On the other hand, you're quite right. There can be a grain of truth in even the most outlandish belief."

Hoeniger looked alarmed. "Oh dear, I was just playing the devil's advocate. That's a rather frightening thought."

"Paranoia grows like a disease in times of war. But we cannot abandon trust and common sense. You should know that as a good Catholic."

"I stand corrected."

Both men were momentarily distracted. Alice Thorne was fastening her cart to one of the fence posts.

Hoeniger nodded in her direction. "In my opinion, there is a woman of courage. She is always trying to persuade us to take the peace pledge. Many people see that as supporting our enemies. I've seen men here get really angry with her, calling her traitor and so on."

"What about you, as a man devoting his life to the Christian God of peace, have you taken the pledge?"

The seminarian grinned. "Of course. Does Mrs. Thorne live in town, by the way? I'd think she runs the risk of having people burning crosses on her lawn if she does."

"Oh, no, she told me she has her own cottage in the woods. Perhaps for exactly that reason. She raises rabbits and fresh vegetables. She rescues unwanted dogs."

"She is indeed saintly."

Alice had put a wooden yoke around her neck from which dangled two baskets of apples. It was an old-fashioned but effective way to transport them. She disappeared into the mess tent.

Hoeniger lay back on the grass, his hands underneath his head. "Pretend I am one of your patients. Let's say one of the three *H*'s."

"Who?"

"Herr Hitler, Herr Heydrich, and Herr Himmler."

Beck chuckled. "I have to say that one man I would truly have liked to have on my couch would be Herr Himmler."

"Good heavens why? The man is a devil incarnate."

"I don't believe in devils, my dear Hans, just troubled men."

"But why Herr Himmler? Why not Heydrich? Or the Fuhrer himself?"

"I have heard on the absolutely best authority that Herr Himmler suffers dreadfully from his stomach. I have no doubt that it is his guilt that is eating at him."

Hoeniger squinted up at him. "Guilt about what?"

"He has acquired much power, but temperamentally I believe he is a timid man whose more natural inclination would be to follow a leader. However, he is also extremely ambitious, and the two opposing drives are creating an internal conflict which is causing his stomach distress."

"Bah. And not that he eats too much sauerkraut and sausage for instance?"

"That too," said Beck with a laugh. "So there you have it. Are you more enlightened now?"

"It's been most edifying. Do you miss being in Berlin?"

"Very much. I joined the Berlin Psychoanalytic Institute in 1920, and was most content until the Nazi menace began to make itself felt. I had no choice but to leave."

"When did you get out?"

"Right before the declaration of war in '39. I was lucky."

They heard a familiar clanging of the warning bell. A voice came over the loudspeaker.

"All internees to gather immediately in the mess tent. The major has an important message. All internees to gather immediately."

"What's that all about?" asked Hoeniger. "I must say, I always get the shivers, thinking that they're going to announce England has been invaded."

"Let's hope not. We're all sitting ducks in here. Come on, we'd better go."

Beck closed up his file box and tucked it under his arm, and the two of them joined the flow of men walking to the tent.

The doctor felt chilled to the bone. He'd been quite sanguine when he was talking to Hoeniger, but there was a terrifying tide of evil that had been unleashed upon the world, and he had a sinking feeling that this little backwater was far from exempt.

42.

TELLING THE LAND GIRLS THAT ANOTHER OF THEIR friends had been murdered was one of the hardest things Tyler had ever done.

Nobody had much to say, but Miss Stillwell assured them that anybody who wished to apply for leave could do so. Likewise, anyone who did not want to work for the rest of the day was excused. Tyler left as they were discussing this, but all seemed in favour of continuing work. He promised he would return as soon as he had any developments in the case. As he was leaving the room, Molly Cooper impulsively ran over and hugged him. Freckles and Sylvia followed suit.

"We know you'll find out who the culprit is, Inspector."

From the hostel, Tyler drove straight to the hospital. To his relief, Miss Parsons was not at the desk and he went straight down to the morgue, where he found Dr. Murnaghan busy weighing out some rather slimy looking pieces of liver.

"I'll just be a minute. I'm portioning out some rations for the cats. It's not human liver; don't worry. I just keep the meat down here where it's cool. If you go over to my desk, you'll find my report on the Watkins girl. I put the cord that was around her neck in a separate envelope. It looks like your common garden variety of rope to me, but the lab might find something more. You can deal with that. I had to cut off her clothes and they'll need to be burnt. They stink to high heaven. She had a rosary in her pocket and I've salvaged that. It's in that other envelope. Her family will probably want it. There was nothing else."

The coroner began to wrap up each piece of liver in brown paper.

Tyler went over to the desk and opened up the report.

"I see she was *virgo intacto*. No sign of rape?"

"Nope. There was no semen anywhere on her body so she wasn't assaulted in that way. She had a nasty wound on the back of her head which wouldn't have killed her, but would most likely have rendered her unconscious. There were bits of bark in the wound, so I'd say she was hit with a piece of wood."

Tyler turned the page. "Cause of death definitely asphyxiation?"

"Yes. It was sudden, violent, and quick. Tiny little thing she was, wouldn't have put up much of a fight, but I didn't find any defensive bruising on her arms, nothing under her fingernails." He went over to the sink and began to wash the blood from his hands. "Her assailant came from behind. She probably didn't know what hit her. Literally."

"Before she was moved to the Fort, do you think she was first buried somewhere in the woods?"

"I'd say not. There weren't a significant number of leaves or dirt in her clothing."

Tyler was skimming through the report as the doctor was talking. The last things Rose had eaten were biscuits and a savoury pie of some kind. He had a sudden vivid picture of the two of them in the library at the hostel and how Rose had tucked into the biscuits with such pleasure.

Dr. Murnaghan dried off his hands. "You'd better have a look at the body. I haven't tried to tidy her up. The family will have to have a closed coffin."

When Tyler returned to the police station, Sergeant Gough was at the desk, and he read the signs immediately.

"Tough go, sir?"

"I'll say."

"I'm afraid I have some troubling news, sir. Dennis McEvoy has scarpered."

"What?"

"I sent Aston round to his house and his mother said that Dennis has been called back to his regiment in Liverpool. He packed a suitcase and left."

"Is that true? Has he been recalled?"

"No, it's not. I rang Major Fordham at the camp and as far as he is concerned, McEvoy is under no orders other than his. He is now considered to be AWOL."

"Put out an all-station alert. We've got to find him."

"He has a motorcycle, but according to Aston it's up on blocks, so he's not using that."

"Shite. He must have taken off as soon as Janet came here."

"Is she all right?"

"Considering the circumstances, not bad, I suppose."

"I brought the major up to date concerning Rose Watkins. He was going to make an announcement to the camp. Are you going to go over there, sir?"

"I don't see anything to be gained at the moment. But ring Fordham again, will you, Guff. Tell him I'd like to consult with that psychiatrist bloke. Say I'll come to the camp tomorrow morning."

"Becoming a convert are you, sir?"

"No, I wouldn't say that. But I'm damned if I'm going to be accused of having a closed mind. If he helps me one iota, I'll take it."

He was heading for his office when the front door swung open with a bang and Constable Eagleton burst in. He was holding his gas mask box in front of him as if it were a bird's nest full of eggs.

"Sir. I found Rose's hat and handbag."

Carefully, Eagleton removed a straw hat and white handbag from the box. He put a handkerchief on the counter and unwrapped it. There were half a dozen cigarette butts inside.

"I found these a few feet away from where the hat was. And there's this."

He was holding a chunk of wood. The smear of blood at one end was clear.

"Dr. Murnaghan found some bark in the wound on the back of her head," said Tyler. "That must have been what the killer used. Guff, will you tag it. Well done, Eager."

"The hat was just lying on the ground, and the handbag was close by."

Tyler examined one of the butts. "Good old Woodbines. Where were they?"

"Quite a long way from the Fort, sir. When I was retracing her footsteps through the woods, I'd only walked six minutes. The path runs almost at right angles from the road. Fairly easy to walk."

"Does this mean she was meeting somebody?" Gough asked. "He was waiting and, for whatever reason, let loose and clobbered her."

"I don't know. If that is what happened, he was there for a while. Even a chain smoker would take a couple of hours at least to go through that many cigarettes."

"Is it the same person who was at the Fort?"

"I don't think so. These fags have been smoked to the bitter end. The others weren't that way at all." He studied the butts more closely. "You know what, lads. These were not discarded all at the same time. Have a good look. See, those two are thoroughly soaked and soggy. Those three less so, and this one's dry. Eager, were they close together or scattered?"

"I'd say scattered around, sir."

"So the smoker goes back to this spot on a regular basis,

smokes a fag or two and does what? Studies mushrooms?"

"None there, sir."

"Figure of speech, Eager. All right. I want you to head up the search. Guff, let's get as many men on to it as we can."

"Yes, sir."

"Eager, you said you walked for six minutes. How far is that?"

"About a quarter of a mile, sir. I picked up a path about half a mile along the road from the hostel. I'd say I was walking west toward the camp. The land slopes downward and the trees are thick so the spot is well hidden."

"All right. Let's keep an open mind, as the man says, but I'm betting Rose wasn't meeting anybody. She was hurrying to get to Mass but she disturbed somebody. Somebody who didn't want to be discovered. She was attacked from the rear and she didn't defend herself."

"As if she was running away," said the constable.

"Exactly. Let's get everybody out there. Go over every inch of ground. I want to know what our fag-loving chappie was doing."

"Could it be a Jerry parachutist?" asked Eagleton.

"So many people keep suggesting this, I'm going to start believing it myself," said Tyler in exasperation. "But this killer hid Rose's body from Thursday night to Saturday. Where? Dr. Murnaghan is sure she wasn't buried before she was moved to the Fort."

"He had a vehicle of some kind," said Gough.

"That's my guess. Eager, scour the side of the road where the path into the woods starts. The rain might have created a little mud and, God help us, some tire tracks. Measure and photograph whatever you find. Guff, how long before you can muster a posse?"

"An hour."

Tyler gave Eagleton a swipe on the arm. "Get going. Leave a marker at the road and the others will join you there. Don't give up until it's dark."

The constable, trying unsuccessfully to hide his pride in the assignment, hurried off.

Tyler lifted the piece of wood and slipped it gingerly into a large cotton evidence bag. "We'll send this to the lab for confirmation but I'd say that's what she was hit with. Poor lassie. And then whoever it was made sure she was dead. Thoroughly and totally dead."

He pinched the bridge of his nose. "She was eighteen, Guff. Eighteen!"

43.

CLARE'S FLAT WAS ABOVE THE FORMER STABLES, NOW being used for storage of furniture taken from the dowager house. She was waiting for Tyler at the top of the covered stairs that ran outside the building.

"Welcome to my humble abode," she said, smiling. "I'm in here."

She turned and led the way into the flat. She was wearing a pair of green silk trousers that flowed from her hips, and a halter top, which showed off the vertebrae of her neck and back. Her hair was piled on top of her head, and as she walked in front of him, she left a slight waft of a flowery scent on the air. He knew his pulse rate increased – from walking up the stairs, probably.

The flat reminded Tyler of a converted railway carriage. It was one long narrow space, no walls demarcating the different rooms except for one at the far end, behind which he guessed was the bathroom. A wicker screen partitioned off a space to the right, near the door, and through the slats, he could see a double bed.

"Dinner is almost ready."

"Smells delicious."

"Does it? Good. I'm afraid the place does still get a bit pungent on damp days even though the horses have long gone. There's a fly swatter on that chair. If you can dispatch a few, I'd be most grateful."

She continued on to a tiny galley kitchen. He dispatched several flies buzzing around the window.

"What do you want me to do with the corpses?"

"Knock them into the corner. I'll sweep them up later. Sit down at the table. I'm almost ready."

Even though she might be living above a converted stable, Clare's cutlery and dishes would have been quite suitable for a posh stately home. The plates had gold rims; the knives and forks looked like silver, not plate. Flowers were arranged in a cut glass vase on the table. It was a far cry from the shabby restaurant.

She was stirring the gravy on the stove and she called to him over her shoulder. "Pour us some wine, will you? It's not quite as good as we had last night, but it's palatable."

He did as she asked, pouring the red wine into crystal glasses as Clare came over to the table with a platter of meat. A roast of beef was surrounded with potatoes swimming in the juice from the meat. He was practically salivating from the mere sight.

"Help yourself. I'll get the vegetables."

She returned to the kitchen, spooned the carrots and peas into their respective covered vegetable dishes, and brought them to the table with the gravy boat.

He raised his glass. "Cheerio and pip, pip, dahling."

She threw him a surprised glance and he chuckled.

"Sorry, can't help it. It's the furnishings. My diction is improving in sheer self-defence."

"Everything belongs to Aunt Gwen. My things are all in Switzerland."

"Does your husband mind that you are here and he's over there?"

Clunk. *What had made him ask that?*

"Not really." She looked discomfited.

The next several minutes were spent with the typical dining rituals. She dished out the vegetables, asked how the meal was;

he exclaimed at the tenderness of the meat. But he cursed himself for the remark about her husband. *Couldn't resist, could you, Tyler?*

"Major Fordham made an announcement at the camp about Rose," said Clare. "It really is quite dreadful. What is going on, Tom?"

"I wish I knew. It's pretty certain she was killed in the woods, not too far from here. She was hidden somewhere and then moved back to the Fort. Much closer to town and not too far from where Elsie was found."

Clare was toying with her food. "Funny how this sort of topic takes one's appetite away."

Tyler sliced through the beef and forked up some potatoes.

"I'm not so delicate. I'm not going to let this go to waste. But let's change the subject. How did you get to be such a good cook?"

"Cooking classes in France. I actually don't get much opportunity to practice."

"Why is that? Do you only eat once a month?"

"Tom!"

"You don't cook at home in Switzerland?"

"No, we have domestic help. Valentin has to entertain a lot and I certainly am not the kind of woman who can whip up a gourmet meal for ten or more, then dash upstairs and change into evening dress and deal with pompous boring men for hours. I would get the screaming meemies."

"So you sacrificed the cooking part?"

"That's right."

"Perhaps it should be the other way around. You do the cooking you like so much and hire somebody to be the hostess."

He'd tried to make his tone jocular, but she sighed. "We came back to that familiar place pretty quickly, didn't we Tom?"

"What do you mean?"

"Don't play coy. You know exactly what I'm talking about. I didn't choose to be born into gentry, albeit impoverished gentry."

"You might not have chosen that at birth but you can choose what you do now. You could give it all up if you wanted to and live like a dairy maid in a cottage. A dairy maid, on the other hand, has not the choice to go and live in Switzerland where she could entertain guests with silver cutlery and fine china dishes."

"Please don't let's quarrel, Tom. I was looking forward to making you a nice meal and the two of us having a pleasant time together catching up like old friends."

"Sorry. It is a wonderful meal. Better than I've had in ages. I promise I won't make any more cracks about your life of privilege."

"Tom!"

"Joke. That was a joke." He fished in his jacket pocket, took out the little tissue package, and put it on the table. "A gift for the hostess."

"How did you know you'd be needing a peace offering?"

He didn't answer, eager as a boy to see if she liked the present. She opened it with maddening slowness and revealed the scarf.

"Tom, it's beautiful. Thank you so much."

She draped the strip of silk around her neck. He'd been right about the colour. The blue-green of her eyes was intensified.

"Looks good on you." He took her hand and brought her fingers to his lips. "Clare, I will never be just an old friend. If that's what you want and expect, I'd better go home now."

She tapped his nose. "You got too much sun, you're peeling."

"Sod that, woman. Are you going to kiss me or not?"

She blinked, jokingly. "Don't you want your sweet? I made apple pie."

"You're all the sweet I need."

She leaned toward him and her lips were everything he remembered.

44.

THEY STAYED ON THE BED FOR A WHILE IN A POST-coital languor. Finally, Clare propped herself on her elbow and regarded him. He was lying on his back.

"I told myself we wouldn't do that. It probably wasn't such a good idea."

He pulled her head down to his and kissed her.

"Are you sorry?"

She broke away and rolled away from him.

"Tom, please, I'm serious. I can't afford complications in my life right now. You're married, I'm married."

"Clare, I'm planning to leave Vera. We've been miserable for years. When I saw you again, I knew what a farce my marriage has been . . . and I can't believe you love your husband. You don't. I can tell."

She got out of bed and picked up her robe. "I tell you what, Tom Tyler. I am going to use the loo and I want you to make us a pot of coffee while I do so. Then you can sit down on the couch, and keep your mouth shut, if that's possible, and I will tell you all you want to know and have been fishing for ever since we ran into each other in the market. Is that a deal?"

"Sounds good to me. Don't you want to know my story as well?"

"No. Not yet. Later maybe."

He liked the "later" and grinned at her. "Go on then. Take your time. I'll have my apple pie now."

He went into the galley to make the coffee and cut up the pie. She didn't take long and returned dressed, this time in a pair of casual khaki shorts and an open-necked white shirt. She had tucked the silk scarf into the shirt.

"You've changed your clothes. Does that mean mission accomplished?" he asked her.

"No, Tom. It wasn't like that. I, well, I just wanted to dress up for you."

He wagged his finger at her, mockingly. "Come on, Clare. I've been seduced before. I can tell when a woman's laying a trail."

"I think that's your conceit talking. What time should you be getting back, by the way?"

"Soon, but not until I've heard at least Part One. See I am going directly to the couch, and I will sit here and listen without a word."

"I think I'd feel more comfortable if you got dressed."

"I can listen even better if I'm naked."

She picked up a pillow and threw it at him. "At least do me the courtesy of covering up your John Henry. It's too distracting."

"That's what I like to hear."

But he plonked the cushion in his lap.

"I'm going to sit over here. I don't trust you. Or myself." She sat down in the chair opposite him. "All right, here goes. Once upon a time there was a little poor princess. In spite of a long, long pedigree, her family was very poor although they went to great pains to hide it. See, even you didn't know that, did you?"

"I knew you weren't rolling in money like your cousin Percy, but I was used to being with a crowd that didn't have much either. I never noticed."

"Hmm. Well, the princess had two very different parents who didn't much like each other. Her father was kind but distant and took longer and longer absences from home until he disappeared completely. Nobody explained this until she was older when she discovered he had, as the saying was ,'taken up with another woman.' The princess's mother had never been very loving and this separation made her even more bitter. The princess was very fond of her father, although he was a scoundrel in the eyes of the world. She simply couldn't switch her feelings. Every night, when she went to bed, her mother would say, 'Make sure you ask God's forgiveness for all your sins. Ask Him to melt your heart of ice.' Eventually the poor little girl believed what her mother told her. She did have a heart of ice. She was like Miss Havisham's Estelle."

"And I suppose that makes me Pip with the thick boots."

To his surprise, her eyes suddenly filled with tears. "Forgive me, Tom. Please don't be angry. I didn't mean that."

He felt like a right piece of shite. He saw what he had truly never seen before, what that cool, collected demeanour was hiding.

"I apologize. Please go on."

"All right." She wasn't looking at him now, running the fringe of the silk scarf through her fingers, the way he had done in the shop. Her voice was low. "The princess grew up, and one day she met a very wealthy man and she married him. Unfortunately, as it turned out, the man was wealthy because from an early age he had devoted himself to making money. He and the princess had nothing in common and within the year they were living virtually separate lives." Clare dropped her shoulders. "I am of course talking about me and Valentin. After the first few months we had no intimate life. So . . . I took lovers –"

"Of course, why not," said Tom, stung.

"Hush. Not many lovers, four to be exact. They were nice young men who were fun to be with and didn't want anything more from me than a boisterous roll in the hay . . . and a little money." She stood up abruptly. "I need a proper drink. Do you want one?"

"I won't say no to that. I need a little fortification."

She went into the kitchen and returned with two crystal glasses. She splashed generous shots of brandy into each and handed one to Tom. She sat down again, holding the other glass in both of her hands. He took a gulp of the drink, watching her.

"We are now getting to the climax of the story," she said with a wan smile. "You'd better take another drink of your brandy."

Suddenly, they were both startled by the shrill ringing of the telephone.

"I'd better answer it," said Clare.

She went into the living room and picked up the receiver.

"Clare Devereau here . . . Yes . . . yes, he's here." She held out the receiver to Tyler.

"It's for you. It's the station with an urgent call."

45.

GOUGH WAS THE ONE WHO HAD CALLED. HE SAID HE couldn't talk over the phone but there had been an unexpected development in the Rose Watkins case and Tyler's presence was urgently needed. Tyler had dressed, kissed Clare, and, declaring he would return that evening to hear the rest of her story, hurried to the car and drove off as fast the ancient vehicle could manage.

The sergeant was in the front office, and he greeted Tyler with great relief.

"I took the liberty of putting everything in your office, sir. I'll get the constables concerned."

He was so obviously het up that Tyler was afraid he'd find another corpse on his desk, but there was nothing except a shabby, black leather suitcase.

Gough came in, trailing behind him Constables Eagleton and Collis and one of the reservists, Stan Richards, a straight-backed former sergeant, now retired.

"Eagleton, tell the inspector exactly what you found."

"This was in the woods, sir. It was buried not too far from where I found the hat and handbag."

Tyler stared at the suitcase, which was covered with dirt and bits of leaves.

"How did you find it?"

"It was sheer chance, sir," sputtered Collis. "I had to take a leak – I mean urinate, sir."

"I know what take a leak means, Constable. Go on."

"Well, I had rather a lot to, er, discharge, sir and I noticed that I was making a hole in the dead leaves. I thought I could see something underneath. I called to Eager and Mr. Richards to come over and take a look."

"I hope you'd finished pissing by then."

"Yes, sir. Anyway we soon saw that something was buried there. Not too deep though. We pulled it out and found it was this suitcase. It's locked but it's quite heavy. I thought we'd better bring it straight back to the station."

"You don't think it's a bomb, do you sir?" asked Richards.

"Good Lord, I hope you had a listen before you brought it to my office. Your ears are as good as mine." He put his ear to the side of the case but couldn't hear any ominous ticking, nor did he expect to. He had a good idea what the suitcase contained. He had a try at snapping open the locks. They didn't budge. "I don't suppose you found the key handy, did you?"

"No, sir. Sorry."

"All right, we'll have to pry it open. Give me your trusty Swiss army knife, sergeant."

Gough took the knife out of his pocket and handed it to Tyler.

The locks yielded easily.

"Let's see what Father Christmas sent us," said Tyler.

He lifted the lid.

Inside the suitcase was a radio transmitter, clean and gleaming.

The chief constable of the Shropshire constabulary, Lieutenant Colonel Horace Golding, was not happy. He was snuffling and puffing at the end of the line like an asthmatic piggy.

"I don't understand why I wasn't informed earlier, Tyler."

"We only found the transmitter a couple of hours ago, sir. I rang your office right away but you hadn't come in yet so I left a message for you to call me as soon as possible. I did say it was urgent, sir."

"Yes, well, not all calls that are said to be urgent actually are."

"That explains it, sir. I did wonder why it took you so long. You were considering the merit of the case."

Golding sniffed. "When I say I didn't understand why I wasn't informed earlier, I'm not simply referring to that. I mean the fact that you have two murders on your hands. Two young girls. Land Army gals, I understand."

"That's right, sir."

"Lady Somerville herself rang me earlier today. She is most alarmed. Not only is she concerned for the safety of the rest of the girls under her care, she is most anxious that nothing besmirch the reputation of the Land Army. There are some well-brought-up young women in the ranks. We don't want to scare them away, do we?"

"No, sir. But so far there is no clear evidence to suggest that any other Land Army girl will be targeted. I'm pursuing the possibility of a lover's quarrel."

Tyler wished he was really as confident as he was sounding. For all he knew the killer was a barmy farmer out to eliminate this scourge of buxom young women who wore trousers. In a world gone mad, anything was possible. Besides, the discovery of the radio transmitter might put a different complexion on the matter.

Golding was continuing to natter at him. "We must get all divisions involved."

"I believe the situation is in hand, sir. I'm sure manpower is short everywhere."

"That is the case. I have had a request from Chief Constable Davis at the Shrewsbury constabulary for extra help to deal with the visit of one of the royal family. We don't know which one yet, but it will be an important occasion for the town and a great boost to morale, so naturally he wants everything to proceed smoothly."

"Naturally, sir." A visit from some no-chinned cousin twice removed was more important than bringing justice to two young women from the east end of London, thought Tyler, but knew he was being contrary. He hadn't yet asked for help and didn't intend to unless he had no choice. He also thought Golding was taking the matter of the radio rather casually. Whatever happened to national security? However, the chief constable returned to the subject.

"Now then. As soon as I heard that you had discovered a buried transmitter, I telephoned the secret service branch of the war office. They said they will have one of their men come over right away. Do you have the damn thing secure?"

Tyler wanted to say, "Well no actually. I thought I'd put it out in the town centre so somebody could pick it up and have fun."

"Yes, sir. Quite secure."

"Good. An agent will be with you in about half an hour, I understand."

"Half an hour?"

"Yes. They're virtually up the road. MI5 has been operating a base in Whitchurch since May."

Tyler exhaled noisily. "Perhaps as police inspector for the town, I might have been informed, sir."

"It's all highly hush-hush. The fewer people who know the better."

"What exactly are they doing here?"

"I'm not going to answer that right now, Tyler. You can speak to the director himself. What he tells you is at his discretion."

If he could have reached through the wire and wrapped it

around the chief constable's scrawny neck, Tyler would have. There had been a mutual antipathy between him and Golding from the beginning. The chief constable was known as a "by the book" man. An army man who didn't have a clue about policing, but did have a lot of highly placed friends in Whitehall that he could enjoy chewing the fat with. Tyler had actually heard him say, "Can't get good recruits these days." As if he was oblivious to the fact that the young men who might have joined the police force were being conscripted into His Majesty's army.

Golding snuffled again. "I have to go now. Please keep me informed as to the progress of the case on a daily basis."

"Certainly, sir."

After they hung up, Tyler remained at his desk. It was all very well to prance and stick out his chest, but he felt no further forward with his case. Whether or not the transmitter had anything to do with the murder of Elsie and Rose he had no idea. And what the hell it was doing in the Acton Woods he couldn't imagine, except clearly it was serious if MI5 was paying him a visit. He felt like a useless prat.

There was a tap on the door and Gough popped his head in.

"A Mr. Grey to see you, sir."

"Who's he when he's at home?"

"I don't know, sir, but he said you were expecting him."

"What the f– Oh shite." It had to be the MI5 man. "Show him in. And make us some tea or coffee, will you."

"I'm not sure we have coffee, sir."

"See what you can find. He's probably the kind of bloke that will only drink coffee. And some biscuits."

"I'll do my best, sir. I didn't expect we'd be entertaining the gentry today."

He withdrew, and Tyler shut his own dirty tea cup into the drawer.

The door opened and Gough ushered in a tall, bespectacled man in a grey trilby and baggy tweed suit. He looked like a schoolmaster. Tyler came from behind his desk and they shook hands. Grey's hand was dry and bony.

"Please sit down, Mr. Grey. Can I offer you something, a cup of tea? Coffee?"

"Good heavens, if you have coffee I'd love that. I haven't had any in ages."

He had a slight accent that Tyler couldn't quite place but might have been Dorset. He went to the door and called through to Gough to bring them some coffee. The sergeant held up a bottle of Camp Coffee and pointed at it, silently questioning.

"That'll do nicely, Sergeant, thank you. We'll both partake."

The last time he'd drunk Camp Coffee Essence, Tyler had loathed it, but he wanted to go step for step with the new man. He returned to his desk. He'd half expected the agent to be having a look at the suitcase, but he wasn't. He was studying one of Tyler's photographs. The winning football team from C district. They'd triumphed over their archrivals from the Bridgenorth E division at last year's championships.

"You play football I see. What position?"

"Centre half."

Grey turned around and smiled. "Football is a game I enjoy to watch but alas was never good enough to play. Not well co-ordinated."

Another tap and Gough entered with a tray. He'd found some biscuits somewhere and decent china cups and saucers. Tyler wondered how he'd managed that in so short a time. He moved a file folder off the desk to make room for the tray.

Grey took one of the cups and sipped at the turgid-looking coffee. He beamed. "Wonderful. It makes a change from the ubiquitous tea, doesn't it?"

Tyler was certain now the man had been a schoolmaster. Who the hell would use a word like ubiquitous in ordinary conversation? He drank some of the coffee, which he found as unpalatable as ever, and waited. There was something rather peculiar about the way his visitor was behaving. He'd expected a secret service man to be quite excited about what they'd found, but in fact, he appeared almost uninterested.

Finally, he said, "Am I to assume from your presence here, Mr. Grey, that we have a spy in our midst?"

Grey put down his cup and dabbed at the corners of his mouth with the tip of his fingers. "Yes, as a matter of fact that is the case."

"And you obviously knew about it?"

"Yes, we do. To tell you the truth, Inspector, it is most unfortunate that you have unearthed the transmitter. And even more unfortunate that you moved it from its location."

Tyler forced himself to swallow more of the soupy coffee. "I think I deserve an explanation for that remark, Mr. Grey."

"Indeed you do, but I must warn you that what I am about to tell you comes under the Official Secrets Act and you must not under any circumstances disclose the information I will impart." He tentatively touched his jaw and winced. "I beg your pardon, a little tooth problem that I must have tended to. Now, where was I? Ah yes. Explaining to you what MI5 is doing in Whitchurch and so on." He pointed at the coffee. "Do you know, I have found this quite soothing to my aching tooth."

No wonder, thought Tyler. It tastes like mouthwash.

"Please continue, sir." Strictly speaking, Tyler didn't have to address the agent as sir, as he didn't know his rank or if he even had one. But there was something about the man that made him address him that way. Grey seemed distracted, but whether it was the pain in his jaw or something else, he didn't know.

"Sometime in early June, MI5 set up an intercepting station in the Old Rectory. You know the place, I see?"

"I thought it had been turned into an army laundry for the duration."

Grey gave something like a chuckle. "We bruited about that's what it was, but the washing that is done there is of quite a different sort. We're one of several such stations and we intercept and monitor any wireless transmissions going between Europe and England. These are decoded and then sent down to our headquarters in Bletchley. Since the end of July, we have been picking up regular transmissions from the Acton Woods. They have been most interesting." He held up his hand although Tyler had made no move to interrupt him. "You are probably wondering why we have not arrested our fifth columnist. We have two reasons. First, quite simply, we don't know who it is. He – let us say for the sake of conven- ience, it is a man we are dealing with – he has to be a local resident who knows the area well. He changes location regu- larly. What he transmits is mostly low-importance news such as weather conditions, local morale, any signs of troop move- ments. Up here, in our quiet county, as you can imagine, that is not of significance since there are none. What is more important is that he is working for a German agent."

Again he sipped on the coffee, swished it around in his mouth, and swallowed. He glanced at Tyler to determine his reaction to this information. "There is an internee in the Prees Heath camp who answers to ss commandant Reinhold Heydrich himself."

Tyler was impressed.

"We intercepted some transmissions from German Intelligence, the Abwehr, themselves. I'm sure we were intended to pick up these messages. There is no love lost between the Abwehr and Herr Hitler's men. They would each be more than happy to discredit the other. Heydrich versus Himmler, Himmler against Goering, and so on. The Abwehr against all of them. Apparently the Fuhrer believes that if you keep your underlings in a state of constant rivalry and also in the dark, you can hang onto your own power longer."

He paused again to make sure he had Tyler's undivided attention.

"When we discovered this, we wondered what was so important about the Prees Heath internees that Heydrich would plant one of his own men as a mole." He sighed. "So far, I regret to say we don't know. And we also don't know who Heydrich's man is. What we do know is that the man they are interested in left Berlin in August of 1939."

He began to pat his pockets and fished out a pipe.

"You don't mind if I smoke, do you, Inspector?"

"Not at all. I'll light up myself."

Grey tamped down his pipe fussily. "So our second reason for not capturing our very own British traitor, which would probably be easy to do as he is not very adept, is because the devil one knows is far better than the devil one doesn't. We have been allowing him to continue passing along what is essentially unimportant information in the hope that soon he will reveal the reason for Herr Heydrich's interest in the camp residents. They won't be here much longer. A couple of weeks at the most. That should get the hares on the run." He concentrated on getting the pipe to light. "So you see now why I said it was unfortunate that you discovered the transmitter. To mix metaphors, we are not yet ready to flush out the fox."

Tyler sat back in his chair. "Do you want us to put it back?" He'd intended it as a sarcastic question, but Grey nodded.

"Actually, yes, we do. The last transmission we intercepted was Thursday night. He usually transmits in the early evening every few days so I'm hoping he hasn't gone back to the spot yet. It's a risk we'll have to take."

"How would this person have made contact with the German agent? If you have no idea who he is, how would our collaborator know?"

"Our mole would have recruited him. To recruit somebody to work for their country's enemy requires great perspicacity, patience, and, believe it or not, money. It's rather like trout fishing. You send out the bait on the water, light and delicate, and it must be the right bait. Is your target mercenary? Ready to sell out for forty pieces of silver? Or are they full of hot air and principle? And strange as it may seem to us, some people do believe that Hitler is right. That the Jews are responsible for all that ails us and that the Aryan race is superior." He puffed out a dense cloud of smoke. "And there are those who are susceptible to coercion of the emotional kind. If you don't do this for me, your family and loved ones will suffer. From our point of view, they are the most dangerous because they are the most desperate."

Tyler frowned. "If they are going to receive instructions, the collaborator must be somebody who comes and goes in the camp without question. There must be at least a good dozen or more people who fall into that category, including the guards."

Grey chuckled with pleasure as if Tyler was a particularly bright pupil. "Quite right."

Tyler swilled the coffee around in his cup but didn't drink it. "You also said that his last transmission was on Thursday evening. What time?"

"Six minutes before seven."

"It is quite possible then that Rose Watkins disturbed him. You do know what I am referring to, I presume?"

"Yes, most unfortunate."

"We found evidence not far from where the transmitter was buried that indicates it was where she was killed. Maybe the collaborator was the one who murdered her."

"Yes, that is, as you say, quite possible."

"But I am not allowed to find or arrest the bastard?"

"Not just yet, Inspector. I promise you as soon as our own case is wrapped up, we will know who this person is and you will be informed at once. At the moment, there is a much greater good that can be achieved by letting him continue unsuspecting."

"And what do you want my role to be, Mr. Grey?"

"Shall we say, the collie, or perhaps the shepherd? We want the sheep to believe the heat is off. Perhaps you would be so good as to contact the local newspaper and say that you are stumped. Repeat your request for witnesses. Say you suspect the two dead girls were involved in a love triangle."

"Do you think the two deaths are connected?"

"I really can't say. My concern is solely to do with the collaborator and the mole. Perhaps it is a coincidence that the young women were killed in the same general vicinity." Grey turned his head toward the door. "Would it be possible to get another cup of that excellent coffee? It really does seem to alleviate the pain in my jaw."

"Of course." Tyler went out and forwarded the request to Gough who looked surprised. When he went back to his desk, Grey was sitting back in his chair with his eyes closed.

He sat up quickly. "I beg pardon, too many late nights. Now where were we?"

"You were trying to persuade me in the interests of national security to slow down my investigation."

"Ah yes, quite so." Grey laced his long slender fingers. "Inspector, I was hoping I wouldn't have to tell you what I am now going to tell you, but I see it is necessary. There is even more at stake than our transmitter chappie."

Tyler bit back his own retort. *For God's sake get on with it mate.*

"In our work, we have to use all kinds of information-gathering. It doesn't matter how small the information is, little pieces can add up to a big and important picture . . . one of the reasons I would like you to lie low with your investigation is not only what I have already told you, although that is all true. There is another factor that frankly I was hoping not to reveal."

My God, the man's constipated. Tyler was saved from snapping at him by a tap on the door, and Gough entered with another jug of coffee.

"Ah, thank you, Sergeant. I do so appreciate this. And a chocolate biscuit, how super."

"You're welcome, sir," said Gough, and where Grey couldn't see him, he raised his eyebrows in an amused lift to Tyler.

When Grey had sipped at his coffee and dipped his biscuit 'til it was a soggy mess that he caught just in time, Tyler went back to the conversation.

"You were saying there is another reason you don't want me to pursue the investigations of the murders of Elsie Bates and Rose Watkins. I'd be more than happy to know what it is and I promise you I won't have hysterics."

Grey grinned at him. "Don't speak too soon, my dear chap. You might not like what I am going to tell you."

Tyler felt his stomach clench.

"I understand that Mrs. Clare Devereau is an old friend of yours?"

"We knew each other many years ago, if that's what you mean."

"Mrs. Devereau is employed by MI5."

46

Tyler stared at Grey. "What! You're telling me Clare Devereau is a spy?"

"My God, I deplore that word. It sounds as if we're in a penny dreadful. Let's say she feeds us any information she considers relevant that she gleans from the correspondence and interactions of the internees at Prees Heath. We are at war, after all, and they can hardly be surprised at that." He paused. "Now, you must keep this totally under your hat. Any leak would jeopardize her safety. The camp will be breaking up soon and Mrs. Devereau will be reassigned. She hasn't lived here for many years, but she considers herself a patriot and, in her own words, 'the Germany that she once loved has become a frightening place.' She has been invaluable. So you can see it is most important that she remain completely in the background. No scandal, no unwanted attention. Part of her usefulness to us depends to some extent on the fact that the people she interacts with trust her. In their eyes, she is an interpreter, pure and simple. They know she acts as an official censor but they expect that. For us, she, er . . . makes reports."

"I see."

"Surely as a policeman you have used informers. It is no different."

"But the men in the camp are not criminals."

"At least one of them is what you would call a spy, and dangerous to our country's welfare. That is why we must proceed as we have been doing until the time is ripe. No further stirring of the hornet's nest. All I am asking for is two weeks at the most, then you can proceed as you would normally."

He hadn't caught his next biscuit dip in time and he was forced to fish out the soggy mess with his spoon. He swallowed it with obvious enjoyment, then put his cup and saucer on the floor beside him.

"Thank you so much. That was most appreciated. I'd better get back."

"One moment, sir. I am surprised that Mrs. Devereau works for MI5, but she isn't involved in the case I am currently investigating. I fail to see why her name would even come up."

Grey touched his jaw gingerly. "I had a word with Dr. Murnaghan . . . got to keep our fingers in any problematic pies, don't you know. He said that the Bates girl had been struck by a vehicle before she was shot."

"That's right. That's his assessment."

"I know you will be checking all car registrations and Mrs. Devereau drives a car. A nice little MG."

"I know that."

"You can cross her off your list."

"Why?"

"Because I am happy to say I can provide her with an alibi for the time in question. Some time between six and seven o'clock on Thursday morning, as I understand?"

Tyler nodded.

"I myself was with Clare Devereau at that time. We had spent the night together."

Grey looked up at Tyler.

"Good heavens, Inspector, I didn't mean to imply anything scandalous. We had work to catch up on. I took papers to her flat. It got so late, she suggested I stay for the night, which I did. I left about seven thirty the next day. Is that cast iron enough for you? I thought I'd save you the trouble of interviewing her."

"Very thoughtful, sir. And where does Rose Watkins fit into this picture? Shortly before she died, Rose left a message at my home that she had important information for me. I did not get that message so I don't know what she was referring to. Do you?"

"No, I don't. With these young girls anything can assume the level of importance when to us it is quite trivial. And in case you are wondering, I do happen to know that Mrs. Devereau was working at the camp until quite late on Thursday. There would be many people who could testify to that." He pulled back his coat sleeve, revealing his bony white wrist, and checked his watch. "My goodness gracious, I really must be going. I shall leave you to return the transmitter, Inspector. Thank you for your co-operation. I promise I shall keep you informed of any developments at our end."

He left, and Tyler put his elbows on the desk and rested his head in his hands.

Grey had made such a point of giving Clare an alibi. Until now, as far as Tyler was concerned, she was just one more person on a list of car owners. But he couldn't quite shrug off his earlier feeling that she was being evasive. Was that just secret service stuff or did Clare *need* an alibi? And if she did, what the hell did she have to do with Elsie Bates?

Another niggling thought was at the back of his mind. Was the reunion between him and Clare as spontaneous and joyful as he had thought? Or did Grey have something to do with orchestrating it? And why was she so interested in his investigation?

47.

Tyler rang Clare's number but there was no answer. He presumed she was at the camp, where he had already arranged to meet Dr. Beck. Leaving Gough to explain what he could to the constables and get the transmitter back where they'd found it, he set out once more for the Heath Road.

He drove by the spot where Elsie's body had been found. The police tape had been removed and soon there would be no indication that a young girl had met her death on this pass-by.

As he pulled up at the camp, he could see no sign of Clare's MG. But Arthur Trimble was unloading a box from the back of his lorry.

"I presume you have permission from her ladyship to sell those eggs?"

Trimble scowled at him. "Of course I do. I didn't know these petty matters were of importance to you, Inspector. I was under the impression you had a murderer to bring in."

Shite. Tyler hated how Trimble seemed to best him. He moved on without saying anything more.

Dr. Beck was waiting for him on the other side of the gate. This time he was dressed more informally in khaki shorts and a short-sleeved white shirt. All he needed was a pith helmet. He greeted Tyler warmly as the sentry let him through.

"In spite of the circumstances, it is a pleasure to see you, Inspector. I always welcome the opportunity to talk to a colleague."

Tyler didn't think he would have put himself into that category, but Beck seemed sincere.

The guard saluted. "Major Fordham sends apologies for not being here, but he has offered his tent for your use."

"Thank you, Corporal."

"Shall I bring you some refreshments?"

"Dr. Beck?"

"I never refuse refreshment."

The guard left them at the tent.

"Have you read my article yet?" Beck asked.

"No, sorry, I haven't had the chance. But you do have some very interesting theories, Doctor, and I am in fact keeping an open mind. Frankly, I'm stumped, and anything you can say, theory or not, might be helpful."

"My theory, as you call it, I would prefer to call observation. It is impossible for us not to reveal our individuality in virtually every aspect of our corporeal life. We walk a certain way, talk with our own speech rhythms, which is why mimics are so popular."

Tyler was waiting for him to make a tent with his fingers, and he did.

"In the same way, killers have their own distinctive methods. One may use a knife, one may always strangle, another beat the victim, and so on. I don't need to elaborate, I'm sure. You have two murders on your hands. I would ask, is there any similarity to the method of death? To the scene of the crime itself?"

Before Tyler could comment, they heard the sound of a trumpeter playing the reveille.

Beck jumped to his feet. "My goodness, I almost forgot. I hope it's not unconscious resistance. I have agreed to be the master of ceremonies for the entertainment which is to take place tonight. I have to prepare people. Mr. Silber is going to recite from *Henry V* and Mr. Schmidt will be presenting a new sound poem. Both need a bit of explaining. I'm sorry not to be able to finish our conversation. There was something I wanted to get your opinion about."

As they stepped out of the tent, Tyler saw a familiar car turning onto the dirt road. At last. It was Clare's green MG.

"Good. The lovely Mrs. Devereau is arriving," said Beck. He pointed to the road again. "And there is Mrs. Thorne, I see." Alice, in her goat cart, was entering the road to the camp. "I'm so glad. She brings fresh herbs to our wonderful cooks. Alas, I must admit to the power of the lower appetites. There are even some men in the camp who have admitted to some degree of lust."

"For Alice?" Tyler asked, startled.

"Not Mrs. Thorne. Her little goat. In some cultures, roast goat is a great delicacy."

Alice was hobbling Nellie on a patch of grass.

"She is also quite a healer," continued Beck. "We only get a visit from the army Medical Officer once a month and frankly, he isn't very good. He was a dentist previously and he's always focused on our teeth. Mrs. Thorne dispenses all sorts of remedies, for headaches, sprains and bruises, insomnia. She has treated them all. She is highly thought of in the camp. Well, I should return to my side of the wire and leave you to greet Mrs. Devereau."

The corporal opened the gate and Beck went inside.

Tyler walked over to Clare's car.

"Tommy, how nice. I didn't expect to see you here."

"I was having a chin wag with Dr. Beck, unfortunately cut short."

He held the door open and she climbed out of the car.

"Did you sort out the emergency?" she asked as they walked to the gate.

"Yes, I would say so."

Clare looked over at him. "Perhaps we could continue with the thousand-and-one-nights theme. Seems as if there's a lot more to say."

"I can't tonight. I have to work. How's tomorrow – as long as the beef dripping will still be good."

"I promise. Shall we say six?"

"Did you say 'sex'?"

She laughed. "No, I did not."

"I'll be there."

"Why don't you come and have a glass of our excellent lemonade before you leave?"

"Sounds good."

As they moved toward the mess tent, Clare received and replied to many greetings. All the men eyed Tyler curiously. One shabby-looking individual fell in beside them as they walked along the barbed wire–lined alley.

"Good afternoon, Mrs. Devereau. Always brightens up the day to see you here. Did you decide to get a tattoo?" He touched her wrist with the tip of his finger. "Right there. It'd look lovely, like yourself. An English rose."

Clare smiled at him. "Not today, thank you, Mr. O'Connor."

Tyler noticed that the man had a tattoo himself at the junction of his thumb and forefinger. A green and red snake crawled up from his wrist.

He tapped him on the arm. "I'd like a word with you, Mr. O'Connor."

O'Connor frowned. "Beg pardon, sir. But we didn't have the opportunity to get introduced."

"Sorry," said Clare. "Michael O'Connor, this is Inspector Tom Tyler."

The Irishman showed his tobacco-stained teeth, presumably smiling. "I'd have put you down for a nark any day. What's your business here? There ain't no Irish for you to hassle. They're all Germans."

O'Connor's manner sent a jolt of anger flooding through Tyler. *Little Paddy prick.*

"We'll catch up with you," he said to Clare. "Come, Mr. O'Connor. Police business." He took the Irishman by the arm so he had no choice but to accompany him. "Is there anywhere we can have a little privacy?"

The Irishman showed his yellow teeth again. "'Tis joking you are, Inspector. Unless you want to sit in the latrines, there isn't anywhere. Anyway, the lav's not even that private at this time of day."

Tyler looked around. "We'll use the major's tent. Come on."

He led the way back to the gate and the sentry opened it for them.

"Don't get any ideas of running away, O'Connor."

"Now Inspector, I'll bet you didn't say that to the doctor. Why would you think I'd be more likely to try something than anybody else?"

"Because you're a Paddy prick, that's why. You're probably plotting every minute of the day to get out of here and blow up a railway station in the name of independence. As far as I'm concerned you can have your independence up the fanny. Who'd want to hold on to such pieces of bog shite anyway?"

O'Connor stopped dead and stared at Tyler. Then he laughed. "Very funny. I almost believed you for a second there."

Tyler shrugged. "Isn't that what you expected me to say? Or if not say, at least be thinking?"

"I did that, Inspector. I'll confess I thought that, like all other fecking English coppers, you'd automatically take me for an enemy."

"Aren't you?"

"Depends on how you want to look at it. I was interned with all these fecking foreigners because I said I was a con-chie and a card-carrying communist to boot. Jesus love me, that got their knickers in a knot. I think they'd rather I was an Irish Nationalist committed to overthrowing the imperial-ist English oppressors. That they can understand."

They were at the tent.

O'Connor hesitated. "Do you mind if we bring the chairs out here? I haven't been outside of the barbed wire since I arrived in May. It feels good to be out here. Reminds me that there is such a thing as freedom."

"If the Nazis invade us, you'll be in worse trouble," said Tyler. "They hate Bolsheviks."

"I know it." He gave Tyler a playful punch on the arm. "Even though I'm an Irish Paddy prick, I hope in this case England is victorious."

Tyler brought out the canvas chairs. He took out his case and offered a cigarette, which O'Connor accepted greedily. They each drew in a few drags, then O'Connor said, "What's this police business you were so keen to talk to me about?"

"It concerns your tattoos."

The Irishman burst out laughing. "Don't say you want one. I could do a nice heart with the initials of your lady love entwined."

"This is serious, O'Connor. Elsie Bates used to come here to help people with their English. I'm trying to find out every-thing I can about her life."

O'Connor blew out smoke. "Tragic that was. A smasher of a girl." He swivelled around to look at Tyler. "Is that what you mean by me and me tattoos? She was keen as mustard to have one herself."

"Did she?"

"Not exactly. She said she had something special and private she wanted, so she was going to get her boyfriend to do it. She bought an indelible pencil from me. The only tattoos I can do here are with an indelible pencil."

That fitted.

"Has anybody asked you for any . . . well, unusual, tattoos?"

The Irishman smirked at him. "One man's unusual is another man's usual. Do you mean pussy and pricks or what? Not too many of them, to tell you the truth. Not in this place. In fact, to be truthful, nobody has asked for anything like that."

Tyler took out his notebook and made a quick sketch of the tattoo that had been on Elsie's buttock. O'Connor looked at it.

"Nope. Not mine. Nothing I've done. I'm more original than that. Must have been the boyfriend."

"Any idea who that might be?"

"Nope. Nobody in this place, I'll tell you. They're either too old to remember what it's for or too young to know."

"Did you ever meet a young woman named Rose Watkins?"

"Ain't that the one the major said was offed as well? Shite, what the hell's going on?"

"She used to come here for Mass sometimes. Did you see her?"

"No. I gave up religion for Lent years ago. I stay as far away from all that mumbo jumbo as I can."

"Do you know who Dennis McEvoy is?"

"Nope. Never heard of him."

"Okay. Thanks for your help. We'd better get back."

"T'weren't much. But you wouldn't be able to spare some fags, would you?"

Tyler snapped open his cigarette case. "Here. Take some." He held out his hand. "Are you above shaking hands with a Limey?"

O'Connor grasped his hand. "Nope. As long as you don't mind pressing the flesh with a Paddy Bolshie prick."

Tyler decided to forgo the lemonade. He'd met up with Clare, and even if it was brief, his conversation with Bruno Beck had given him something to think about. The two murders were very different in style. Was the doctor right? Did this indicate two different murderers? The killer had placed a gun beside Elsie and she had been left in the open where she could be discovered. There was something respectful about the way she'd been laid out. And then there were the bloody flowers.

Rose's killer had taken pains to hide her body. Who knows when she would have been found if it weren't for Janet and Dennis. There certainly wasn't anything reverential about the way *she* had been treated.

48.

TYLER SPENT THE EVENING WITH JANET, COMFORTING her when she broke into tears, talking about anything and everything when she was calmer. He spent the night on the couch, claiming he was too het up to sleep in the bed. This turned out to be true and he tossed and turned until he finally fell asleep in the early hours, only to be catapulted into wakefulness by the ringing of the telephone. Groggily, he squinted at the clock on the mantelpiece. Seven o'clock.

He hurried to answer, not wanting to wake everybody up on Sunday morning. It was Sergeant Gough.

"Crikey, Guff, don't you have a home to live in?"

"I thought you'd want to know right away, sir. Dennis McEvoy has been caught."

Tyler gave a soft cheer. "Where was he?"

"He got as far as the Welsh border when he was picked up. He claims he was just out for a drive but he had a haversack stuffed with enough rations for a week."

"You said, 'out for a drive'?"

"He was on a motorcycle." There was a pause and Gough cleared his throat. "It's registered to your son Jimmy. McEvoy says he borrowed it because his is out of commission."

"I see."

"The Welsh plods are bringing him directly to the station," said Gough. "They should be here shortly."

"I'll be right over."

—

Tyler got dressed and shaved, made a fast breakfast. and headed across to the station. He looked in on Janet, who was fast asleep, and Jimmy for once was at home, also asleep. He debated waking him up, but decided to see what Dennis had to say for himself first.

When Tyler walked into the station, two Welsh police officers were waiting for him. They were having a good natter with Sergeant Gough while a subdued Dennis McEvoy languished on the bench. He got to his feet when Tyler entered, and one of the officers caught his arm and shoved him back down.

"Steady, mate. I'd prefer it if you had your arse on the bench if you don't mind."

"That's all right, sergeant," said Tyler. "I'll take care of Mr. McEvoy. Sergeant Gough, would you take him into my office."

He didn't say hello to the frightened young man; he was too angry with him.

Gough did as requested and Tyler turned to the two other officers. "Thanks, lads. How are you, Bryn?"

Tyler had played against Bryn Jones in several police league football matches over the years. In fact, Jones had given him a solid "accidental" kick on the shins in their last game, which he intended to repay when he could. They shook hands and Jones introduced his constable, Evan Llewellyn.

"How did you catch McEvoy?" he asked Jones.

"A bit of luck really, good for us, bad for him. He ran out of petrol just outside of Presteigne. He tried to buy some at the local petrol station, but the owner wondered what a Brit was doing on our side of the border with a heavy rucksack on his back and a nervous manner. He thought he might be a Jerry spy so he rang us up while the lad was waiting for his fill up. We'd had his description come over the wire, so one of our constables hopped over there right away. First off, he said his name was Bobby Walker. I happened to know that wasn't true as I've met that particular lad before at one of our away games. We did a recce of this one's identification papers, which confirmed his name was, as suspected, Dennis McEvoy, private in His Majesty's army. His rucksack was stuffed with rations, tins of meat, powdered milk, you name it. He said his mother had given them to him for a picnic. Not too imaginative that one." He looked at Tyler curiously. "What's McEvoy wanted for, Tom?"

"He's a witness in a murder case I'm investigating. He took off before I could talk to him."

"The bike's registered in your lad's name. Did McEvoy steal it?"

"That's what I've got to find out. Let me go and have a word or two with our boy here. Help yourself to some tea before you start back." He winked. "Sergeant Gough has got something he can add for the journey. A nice little pick-me-up. That is unless you've become teetotallers?"

"Not this side of the border. Thanks, Tom. Much appreciated. If there's anything else you need just let us know."

Tyler turned to go to his office, and Jones said, "Our team's in good fettle now. The next match is as good as won. Start shaking in your boots."

"Don't count your chickens, Jones."

He went into his office. Dennis was now slumped in the chair, with Gough standing beside him.

"Thanks, Sergeant, I'll take over now. Look after the Taffies, will you?"

Gough left and Tyler took his seat behind the desk. He did some unnecessary shuffling of his papers, not looking at Dennis. Finally he sat back and laced his hands behind his head.

"You've got yourself in a shit load of trouble, Den."

"Yes, sir." He looked so miserable, Tyler almost felt sorry for him. Almost; not quite.

"Where did you think you were going?"

"I didn't have a very clear idea, sir. I thought I'd head for Ireland."

"Fat lot of good that would have done you. They're a neutral territory. They're interning our own pilots who are shot down. You'd have been stuck there for the duration. You were supposed to report for duty on Saturday night. You didn't do so, and that makes you absent without leave. A serious crime. You could go to prison."

"I know, sir. I wasn't thinking. I . . . I just had to get away."

"From what?"

"Just things. The war—"

"Did you steal our Jimmy's motorcycle?"

Dennis stared at him, round-eyed. "Oh no, sir. He said I could borrow it."

"Didn't he know you were supposed to report for duty?"

"Er, no. I didn't tell him. I just said I wanted to go for a ride. Clear my head." Dennis wriggled uncomfortably on the chair. "I need to use the lavatory, if you don't mind, sir."

Tyler pointed to the toilet. "It's over there. Leave the door open."

The lad scuttled off. Tyler could see his back. It seemed to take him a long time to start urinating but finally he did, finished up, and returned to his seat.

"Hurt, did it?"

"Pardon, sir?"

"I said, did it hurt to piss?"

"Er, yes, it did rather."

From outside the room they heard a burst of laughter. Sergeant Gough was no doubt plying the Welshmen with whisky and football stories.

Tyler got to his feet, came around the desk, and sat on the edge so he was only a foot away from Dennis.

"Now then lad, there are a few things we need to clear up. First off, I had a chat with a young Land Army girl, name of Florence Hancocks, nice girl. You know her, don't you?"

"I, er . . ." He saw Tyler's expression and the denial froze on his lips. "Yes, sir."

"You were aware that she was off at the hospital on Thursday? She had to get some treatment – for a venereal disease she'd picked up from her boyfriend. Any idea who that might be?"

"I think that was me, sir."

"Are you saying you've got the clap, Den?"

"It seems that way, sir."

Tyler leaned to within a few inches from the soldier. "It might have been a nice gesture of support to accompany her at least to the hospital. She was all by herself."

"I didn't know. Honest I didn't. I just thought she had something female happening. She said she wanted to stay on at the hotel. I had to get back for sentry duty on Wednesday night."

"What time did your shift end?"

"Seven o'clock the next morning . . . at least it was supposed to end then, but I had to stay on because of Bobby and the corporal finding the girl's body."

Tyler pursed his lips. "Do you have a good memory, Dennis?"

"Er, yes, I think so, sir."

"On Wednesday, Florence Hancocks tells you she's not well. I wonder why, then, that only two days later, you were prepared to take another young woman, this time a girl who is barely sixteen years old, to a liaison in the woods in order to have a sexual encounter with her. You must have forgotten that you could infect her with a most unpleasant disease."

He had raised his voice and McEvoy looked frightened.

"No, sir."

"No, sir, what? You didn't meet up with this girl, my daughter

Janet, to be precise? And the sister of your best mate. Or, no, you didn't forget?"

"I'm sorry, Mr. Tyler. I wasn't sure what was wrong with me. I wasn't thinking."

"That, Dennis, is an understatement. Unfortunately, instead of your little lover's tryst, you discovered the decomposing body of Rose Watkins. Why did you make Janet promise not to say you were together?"

Again Dennis wriggled on the seat. "I'd said I was ill and couldn't come on duty on Saturday. I'd be in hot water if the commandant found out I was lying. We had nothing to do with her death. Nothing."

"Did you ever go to that particular place before?"

"Yes, sir. I went with Florence a few times."

"What about Elsie Bates? Did you go there with her?"

Dennis shook his head vigorously. "No, sir. Never."

"Why not? She was a pretty girl. Quite accommodating to young soldiers as I understand."

"She wasn't my girlfriend."

"She was somebody's girl though. We know that much. Who was it?"

"I, er, I don't know, sir."

Tyler moved even closer, his breath on Dennis's face.

"I'll ask you again, son. Who was Elsie Bates's sweetheart?"

This time, Dennis met Tyler's eyes.

"Jimmy. Elsie was your Jimmy's girlfriend, sir."

49

Tyler had to spend time booking Dennis. He made him go over all the sexual contacts he'd had recently. There were four including Florence Hancocks. The station would have to get in touch with each girl, order medical checkups, and follow up on any other men they might have infected. Dennis himself would be handed over to Major Fordham.

Tyler left him with Sergeant Gough and walked across the road to his house. The skies had cleared and it was a beautiful sunny morning; the sky a brilliant blue, small puffs of clouds dotted here and there. Usually his spirits lifted in weather like this, but nothing could do that at the moment. The patch of lawn at the front of his house was looking as wilted as he felt. All of his fears about his son had come flooding back. A voice kept going round and round in head. Surely not. Not Jimmy. Not his gentle son.

He went in.

Vera was in her dressing gown, hair still in curlers, sitting in the kitchen with her father. She looked as if she had been crying. From the cool way Lambeth greeted him, Tyler guessed they had been talking about him.

"Where's Jimmy?" he asked.

"Don't we even warrant a 'Hello' or 'Good morning, Dad'?" said Lambeth.

"Good morning, Walter. Sorry I can't stop to chat. I need to talk to our Jimmy. Is he upstairs, Vera?"

"I don't know if he's up yet. Do you have to disturb him, Tom? He looks exhausted."

Lambeth wiped his moustache. "I'm off then, Vera, just dropped in for a minute. Tell Janet I expect to see her tomorrow. I can't get in help at short notice."

Tyler turned around. "I'd rather she had the next few days off. She's had a shock."

"It might do her good to work," interjected Vera. "Take her mind off her troubles. Besides, you heard Dad. He needs her in the shop."

Tyler looked at his wife. "I said no. She's not going in."

Lambeth patted his daughter's shoulder. "Don't worry, Vera. I'll manage. I'm not going to cause trouble between a man and his wife. I'll give you a bell later on today."

Vera's lips were tight. "I'll see you out, Dad."

"That's all right – I need a quick word with Tom."

At the door, Lambeth paused. "I've got some information about that case you're on. It concerns the lady of the manor. Not the old Lady Somerville. The one who just came back. Her's got a fancy French name, and her's stuck up, if you ask me. Even worse than she was twenty years ago. You know who I mean, don't you?"

Tyler nodded, not trusting himself to say anything.

"Drop by the shop, and I'll tell you," said Lambeth.

He winked and nodded his head in the direction of the kitchen. "Better keep it between you and me." He left, and Tyler returned to Vera.

"Is Janet home?"

"No, she's not. All of a sudden, she's up with the larks. She's gone over to Jillian's. I can't fathom that girl. First of all she's crying for her mummy, then she starts to act as if she can't get away from me fast enough."

Probably because reality set in, thought Tyler.

"She's not poorly, is she?" he asked.

"Not that I know of. I think that was just a cock and bull

story she told Dad. Wanting to go for a walk in the woods. Bloody nonsense. It's my guess she was meeting a boy from school." She halted. "Why did you ask if she was poorly?"

"I just wanted to make sure she was all right."

His wife put her hands to her face. "My God, Tom, she hasn't got herself in the family way, has she?"

"No, no, nothing like that," answered Tyler. He turned. "I've got to see Jimmy."

Vera caught his sleeve. "What's wrong? Please don't shut me out, Tom. I have a right to know, I'm his mother."

Tyler tried to extricate himself. "I can't tell you at the moment, Vera, it's police business."

Fear made Vera's voice shoot up an octave, and she managed to block his way. "Police business? With your own flesh and blood. What are you talking about?"

Before Tyler could answer, the door at the top of landing opened and Jimmy came out.

"What's all the commotion?"

Tyler was shocked at how his son looked. In less than twenty-four hours, Jimmy seemed to have lost weight and was even more haggard and drawn. His fair skin was pasty white and his eyes puffy and red-rimmed; from crying or sleeplessness or both, Tom didn't know.

"I need to have a word with you, son," he said over Vera's shoulder.

She turned and addressed Jimmy. "You don't have to if you don't want," she said.

"That's all right, Mum. Dad has his job to do. . . But I'm not going to be questioned on the landing. Shall we go back downstairs? Or do you want me to come to the station, Dad?"

"Kitchen'll do fine."

"I'm going to be in on this," said Vera.

"That's up to Jim," said Tyler.

Jimmy shook his head. "Don't worry, Mum. If it's police business, it'll probably be better if it were just Dad and me."

Vera started to protest, but seemed to see something in Tyler's face that stopped her. Her eyes filled with tears.

"I don't know what's come over everybody. You look like a ghost, your sister is lying to us, your dad's biting my head off all the time. Aren't I entitled to know what's going on?"

It was Jimmy who answered. "Of course you are. Dad and I just have to sort something out."

Vera wouldn't look at Tyler. "I'll be in the bedroom then. Shout up if you need me."

Tyler headed back downstairs, Jimmy behind him. Vera hovered on the landing then went into their bedroom.

When they were in the kitchen, Tyler went to the sink to fill up the kettle.

"I don't know about you but I'm parched. I'll make a cuppa."

"I'd rather have a fag. Have you got one? I'm all out."

"Here, help yourself." Tyler tossed him the cigarette case. He continued with the tea making and Jimmy lit up, inhaling gratefully. He was about to slide the case back across the kitchen table when he paused.

"*Love forever, C.* Who gave you this? I don't remember seeing it before."

"That? I found it in an antique shop in Church Stretton. I needed one so I bought it."

"Nice. Somebody appreciated somebody."

Tyler got the tea caddy down from the cupboard and spooned some tea into the pot.

"I think rationing tea is going to be one of the hardest things for people to tolerate."

There was an awkward silence. Finally, he was ready and he sat down opposite Jimmy, poured himself a cup, and stirred sugar into it.

"We've caught Dennis McEvoy. He'd got as far as Wales." He'd made his voice as casual as he could, but he noticed Jimmy made no pretence of surprise. "He says you lent him your motorcycle. Is that true?"

Jimmy answered through a cloud of smoke. "Yes, it's true. His was out of commission."

"Didn't you know he was planning to go AWOL? The army doesn't look kindly on deserters. He's in big trouble. I'm surprised you didn't try to talk him out of it."

"Why should I? He's old enough to make his own decisions."

"But you knew the consequences. Weren't you lot the four musketeers? One for all and all for one."

Jimmy flinched as if he'd slapped him. His hand was shaking. Tyler felt like a rat pushing him like this but he had to. There might be worse to come.

"Dennis had had it. He said he needed to go for a ride out in the country. I dunno, I thought maybe that'd be enough and he'd be back in time to report in."

Tyler wasn't sure he believed him but he let it go. He got to the point.

"Dennis said that you were Elsie Bates's boyfriend. Is that true?"

Tension was like a blanket in the room. Jimmy was concentrating on flicking ash from his cigarette.

"Jimmy, I asked you a question. Were you and Elsie Bates going out together?"

"Yes."

"Why didn't you tell me?"

"I'm twenty years old. I don't have to tell my father every facet of my life."

Tyler put down his cup so hard, some of it slopped over onto the table.

"Cut it out, Jimmy. You know bloody well what I mean. After she was killed, you didn't utter a peep about knowing her."

They heard the door upstairs open and Vera called down.

"Is everything all right down there?"

"Yes, Mum. We're fine." They heard her go back into the bedroom. "She's really worried, Dad." The reproach in his voice stung Tyler.

"So are we all, Jimmy, so are we all. My guts are in a knot because I'm investigating a brutal murder and my own son is giving me the runaround, What am I supposed to think?"

"You seem to be implying I'm a murderer."

"Do me a favour, will you, Jimmy? Answer my questions."

More ash flicking. Jimmy's face was white, except for two red spots on his cheeks, as if he had a fever.

"When did you last see Elsie?"

"We were together on Wednesday night."

"In the old Fort?"

"Yes, as a matter of fact."

"What time?"

"Night. It's quite cosy in there if you don't mind a few spiders. Then she left because she had to get to work."

"And you stayed on in your comfy bed with the wildlife?"

Jimmy's jaw was pulsing. He touched the spot to try to stop it. "For a while. Then I got up and went to visit Mrs. Thorne."

"What time was all this coming and going?"

"I'm not sure. It wasn't light, I know that. Maybe five-thirty, a quarter to six."

"And you didn't see anybody else on the road? Or hear a gunshot or voices?"

Jimmy stubbed out his half-finished cigarette. "No."

"You must have been shocked when you heard your girl-friend had been shot?"

"Yes, I was."

"I understand Elsie wasn't averse to accepting little presents from her admirers. Did you give her anything?"

"Nothing special. Just some cream and lotions that Mrs. Thorne made."

"She had two pound notes sewn into her dungarees. I wonder where they came from and why she was hiding them."

Tyler could see that was news to his son, but Jimmy didn't answer, preoccupying himself with shaking out another cigarette and lighting it.

"Am I to understand from your lack of response you don't know where that money came from?"

"No, I don't. But Elsie had had a hard life. She didn't trust many people. The money was probably what she saved up and she wanted to keep it safe."

"There's another matter I have to ask you about. As Elsie's boyfriend. She bought an indelible pencil from one of the men in the internment camp. She said she wanted her boyfriend to draw a tattoo for her. There was one on her buttock. Did you do that?"

"Yes."

"What was it? The tattoo, I mean."

"A heart around the word 'love.'" Jimmy pretended to smile. "Nothing you would understand, Dad."

Tyler ignored that. "Did Elsie's mate, Rose Watkins, have a boy?"

"Not that I know of."

Tyler got up and brought the teapot over to the table with a second cup. Without asking, he poured some for his son.

"Here. You look like you need it."

Reluctantly, Jimmy took a sip of the tea. Tyler went to the cupboard again, reached way into the back, and brought out a bottle of brandy.

"We keep this for emergencies." He added a stiff shot to

Jimmy's tea and a smaller one to his own. "Now then, there are a couple of more things that I've got to ask you. All right?"

"Go ahead."

Tyler ignored his tone and fished in his jacket pocket. He took out the card he'd got from Alice's stall.

"Have you signed this?"

"No, not yet. I'm thinking of it."

"White poppies are a symbol of the peace movement, and I found a bunch of white poppies on Elsie Bates's body. Any idea who would put them there?"

Jimmy averted his eyes. "I saw some of the Jerry up close. They were the same age as we are and they looked just as scared. They didn't want to fight any more than we did."

"At some point we're going to have a good old chin about the philosophy of defence and unprovoked aggression, but I'm not in the mood right now. Answer my question, please. Do you know who put the poppies on Elsie's body?"

"It could have been anybody. They grow near the Fort and it's a popular spot for couples. You know that. You told me you went there yourself when you were younger." He tapped the cigarette case. "The anonymous *C*, perhaps?"

Touché and gotcha.

Jimmy drained his cup.

"Is that everything? I'm bushed. I'm not sure I can take much more."

"Elsie was shot with a German Luger. It's most likely that she stole it from one of the girls at the hostel. Do you know anything about that?"

Jimmy shook his head.

"Are you sure? By all accounts, Elsie Bates was on the light-fingered side."

"Dad, give her some respect, will you? She's dead."

Tyler gripped his son's hand. It was icy cold.

"Jimbo. I'm sorry. I know you've had a rotten time, and if I could have done anything in the world to make that easier for you, I would have but –"

"But it's something a man has to do, go to war for his country. Isn't that what you were going to say? Makes us grow up. Of course, those that don't – grow up I mean – are another matter all together. They're usually dead or insane." Jimmy shoved his chair back. "Is that all you want to ask me?"

Defeated, Tyler nodded. "For now." He tried a feeble joke. "Don't leave the country without telling me."

"I'll be at Mrs. Thorne's. I told her I'd help her out in the garden."

"Go ahead. I'll see you later."

"Tell Mum I won't be home for dinner."

He left, and Tyler got up and went upstairs. Vera stuck her head out of the bedroom.

"Where's Jimmy?"

Tyler didn't answer but went into the bathroom and opened the medicine cabinet. There wasn't much in there, some plasters, some iodine, a bottle of aspirin. He opened it, but there were only three pills remaining so he left them. On the bottom shelf was a bottle of prescription pills made out for Jimmy Tyler. *Take two nightly for sleep. Do not exceed the dosage.*

He opened the bottle and poured the contents into the lavatory bowl, jerked hard on the chain, and flushed them away.

"What did you do that for?"

He turned and saw Vera was standing in the doorway. But she knew the answer, and her face crumpled into tears.

She ran over to Tyler and pressed herself against him. He held her close, rocking her soothingly. "He'll be all right, Vee. He's just going through a bad patch. He'll come out of it."

He was saying it as much for himself as for her, and he didn't know if even he entirely believed his own words.

50.

Gough's voice came over the intercom. "Your daughter is here, sir. She'd like to speak to you."

Tyler got up at once and went to the door. Janet was sitting on the bench outside. She was pale, dark circles under her eyes, the lids reddened.

"Come in, pet."

She followed him into his office and took the chair across from his. "I'm sorry, Daddy. I know you're busy but I had to talk to you."

"What's up, chick?"

Tears welled up in her eyes and she pulled out a handkerchief and rubbed at them, making the redness worse. "I can't go back to work for Granddad. Every time I think of the meat hanging up, the smell . . . I can't get the sight of that girl's body out of my mind . . ." She sobbed. "It was the foot, just sitting there in her shoe but all gnawed at. I could see the bone."

He went over to her and stroked her hair. "I know, my pet. It was horrible. And you don't have to go back to the shop."

"Mum says I must. She says it's not good to run away. Besides, I'll be letting Granddad down." She started to cry in good earnest, her body shaking. Tyler drew her close against his chest.

"I'll speak to your mother. We'll work something out."

Slowly, she calmed down, and finally he got her to blow her nose and wipe her eyes.

"Would you rather be staying at Jillian's for now?"

She nodded. "Her mum's nice. She doesn't poke at me to

talk unless I want to. I don't want Mum to be upset or anything but I'd like to be at the Vanns' for now." She looked into his face. "Have you found anybody yet?"

"Not yet. But we're getting there." He wasn't sure that was strictly speaking the truth, but he desperately wanted to reassure her.

"What's going to happen to Dennis?"

"I've had to turn him over to the military police. He went AWOL and they're the ones to deal with him." He paused.

Janet said in a low voice, "We didn't go all the way, Dad. I know that's what you were worried about, it was written all over you. But we didn't." She dropped her head. "To tell the truth we might have if we hadn't found the body. . . . Are you angry with me?"

He hugged her again. "No, of course not, but I'm like any old dad. I don't want you to get into . . . anything serious . . . too soon. You're only sixteen. There's lots of time."

"Is there? I hope so. Anyway, I was being silly, I know that. I mean, I do like Dennis, but he's a bit conceited really. I think I was just one more in a long line of conquests. I can wait for somebody who's more sincere."

"Good girl. Sincere sounds good." He let her go. "Now why don't you go off to the Vanns' and I'll come by later."

She gave him a kiss on the cheek. "Thanks, Daddy."

After she had left, Tyler sat for a few minutes at his desk. His gut was churning. What a bollocks he'd made of his marriage, and how hard this had been on his children. He actually wondered it that had anything to do with Janet wanting to grow up so quickly. If he got the chance, he'd have a chat with Dr. Beck. Maybe he should find a couch and lie on it. He was beginning to think he needed it.

Instead, he took his hat off the peg and went in search of his father-in-law.

—

Walter Lambeth was outside his shop, sweeping the doorstep.

"Hello, son, just doing a bit of tidying. I was hoping you'd drop by."

"Let's go inside, shall we, Dad."

Just at that moment, a woman walked up. She had a basket over her arm, and Tyler recognized her as the wife of the Anglican vicar.

"Good afternoon, Mr. Lambeth. I've come for my rations. Sorry I couldn't be here yesterday, I had to go to Wem."

"Don't worry, Mrs. Pound. I saved yours for you. Come in. How's your husband today?"

"Still poorly. The war is weighing on his spirits dreadfully."

"Some fresh kidneys should cheer him up." He nodded at Tyler. "I'll be with you in a jiffy, son."

The three of them went into the shop.

"I'll wait in the back," said Tyler.

Lambeth's living quarters were directly behind the shop on the ground floor. The main living room smelled of tobacco and meat. It was messy and looked as if it hadn't had a good dusting for some time. Vera was always offering to clean for her father, but he refused. "Had enough of women sticking their noses into my affairs," he'd muttered to Tyler one day. There were newspapers and plates with congealing food on them, several cups with the dregs of his tea ringing the bottom. Tyler thought if any of Lambeth's customers saw how he lived, they might think twice about buying here.

He looked around. He suspected his father-in-law wouldn't be that imaginative in terms of hiding places, and he was right. There was a rolltop desk in the corner of the room. He pulled open the top drawer. Underneath a magazine with a nude girl on the front cuddling up to a tractor was a school notebook.

He took it out and leafed through it. Lambeth had a list of about thirty private customers. What they received and what they paid for was meticulously recorded. All of them were getting meat way beyond what they were entitled to, and each paid handsomely. *Bloody old hypocrite.*

He heard the bell on the outside door tinkle, and Mrs. Pound called out a goodbye. He closed the drawer but kept hold of the notebook. Lambeth pushed through the curtain that separated the store from the sitting room. He saw immediately what the situation was and, rather to Tyler's surprise, didn't bluster or try to get out of it.

"I see you found what you were looking for, son. I hope you ain't going to get all righteous with me. The way I see it, I ain't doing anybody harm. I get a bit of extra money for the family and folks get a bit of extra meat. All's fair in love and war, as they say."

"Do they? They also say you could be charged with profiteering and dealing with the black market."

Lambeth shrugged. "It don't really be worth it. Them folks are all going to deny paying me. They'll just say I gave them a gift of a leg of mutton, or a pork chop, out of the goodness of my heart. And I'll say the same. I received more meat than I could sell and passed it on. As long as money doesn't change hands, what we're doing ain't illegal."

Tyler practically shouted at him. "Yes, it is! Everybody in the bloody country is supposed to be on rations. Rich or poor. They have to show you their ration book and you have to take out the coupons. Not to do that is against the law. There isn't a judge in the country who would buy that crock of shit you just handed me."

Lambeth fished in his pocket and took out his pipe. He proceeded to light it, and it irritated Tyler even more to see his hands were quite steady. "What are you going to do, then, son? We don't want a scandal, do we? Won't do any-body any good if word gets out that my own son-in-law is prosecuting me."

Tyler slapped the book into his hand. "First off, we're going to lose this little list, Walter. No more favours. These people will get their regular rations and no more. Secondly, I want to know who's been supplying you with extra goods."

"Lots of folks. If you think people are going to live by the rules when they can get a bit of extra for their family, you're dreaming."

"Let's put it this way. If you don't give me their names, I'll go straight to Percy Somerville, give him this notebook, and explain what you've been up to."

Lambeth laughed. "He won't like that. He enjoys the occa-sional extra roast, does the magistrate. He just thinks his dear old mum goes without, I suppose. Don't ask questions if you don't want the real answers."

Tyler took a step closer. "I'll say it one more time, Walter. Give me the names of your suppliers. I'm going to have a word with them and you will close up your operation. Do I make myself understood?"

Lambeth glared at him. "Don't be such a wanker, Tom. You'll feel it if I close down."

"What do you mean?"

"I mean Vera has been keeping you comfortable for a while now. Didn't you notice?"

Tyler hadn't noticed, and he felt angry with himself. Vera ran the house and he had chosen to think she was a good manager. He advanced so his father-in-law's face was only a few inches from his own.

"Suppliers, Walter. Now!"

Lambeth shrugged. "I've got four steady and a few others occasional. Ewen Morgan is a regular, mostly for beef; Bill

Wardell the same; Arthur Trimble and me exchange eggs and chicken; Syd Newstead brings me pork. Satisfied? You'll not be able to suppress, it you know. They'll find other ways and means."

"Not if I have anything to do with it. When do you work this little operation?"

Lambeth shrugged. "Whenever's practical."

All of the men he mentioned had registered their vehicles, but according to Constables Eagleton and Collis, only two of them could account for their whereabouts on Thursday morning. Ewen Morgan and Bill Wardell. Tyler knew Syd Newstead, who was another old farmer like Morgan. He'd already spoken to Trimble.

Tyler contemplated his father-in-law. "Tell me, Walter, was anybody bringing you a delivery on Thursday morning, early? Say before six?"

"I'll have to think. One day's much like another."

"Let me make this a bit more distinctive for you, Walter. Thursday was the day when a young girl in the prime of her life was brutally murdered on the Heath Road. Somebody driving a car, or a vehicle of some kind, knocked her off her bike."

Lambeth drew on his pipe. "I know what you're getting at, but these are all respectable men. They wouldn't have anything to do with that tart. If you ask me, you need to be looking into that sports car—"

"Let me decide that, will you, Walter? Who came by here on Thursday?"

"No one that I recall."

Tyler crammed the notebook into his pocket. "I'll call on these folks. Don't worry, I'll be tactful, just scare the shite out of them ... By the way, Walter, our Janet doesn't want to come back and work for you. She's had a terrible shock and I don't think she can handle it. Vera says she must come back, but I know she'll listen to you. You agree with me, don't you, that Janet's nerves are too bad for her to continue here?"

"And if I do agree with you, what then?" Lambeth's expression was sullen.

"I want you to persuade Vera that under no circumstances do you want Janet back here. Let's all start fresh, shall we."

"No charges?"

"Not just now. I'll see this as a first offence born of ignorance. And it won't happen again, will it?"

Lambeth knocked out his pipe on his boot. "Thursday morning I'd got up to take a leak, when I heard this car came roaring down the road. I looked out of the window and saw the MG."

"It was dark at that hour; how did you know it was an MG?"

"Because the lights were low slung. There ain't any other sports cars in the area."

"Did you see if Mrs. Devereau herself was driving?"

"Didn't need to. It were her all right. Who else'd it be?"

"Was the top up or down?"

"Up. But it was her, I tell you. She was heading for the Heath Road."

"How do you know that? The car must have been past in a second. It could have been going anywhere."

"Don't be stupid, Tom. There's only two turnoffs from Main Street. Alkington and Heath Road, otherwise you're on your way out of town. She's staying at Beeton Manor by all accounts. That's where she'd be going." He glanced slyly at Tyler. "Don't know where she was coming from, mind."

"Why didn't you tell me this before?"

Lambeth growled. "It slipped my mind."

Tyler knew that wasn't true. Lambeth hadn't told him because he'd have to explain why he was up so early. He was probably waiting outside by the laneway for his next delivery. He could have seen the car from there. So which was it? Clare snug in bed with the alarm clock at that hour, or Clare in her flat after a hard night of work with Grey, or Clare driving her car in the early morning hours heading for the Heath Road . . . and Elsie Bates?

"Is there anybody else who could verify your statement, Walter?"

"Just me. And her of course. If you ask her, she'll tell you. At least I assume she will."

Tyler got the innuendo. "I'll follow up on what you've told me."

"Enjoy yourself," said Lambeth ambiguously.

51.

TYLER WENT STRAIGHT BACK TO THE STATION. WHAT now? According to Mr. Grey of MI5, it was against the interests of national security to pursue the killers of the two girls. The country would collapse and be overrun by Nazis who would destroy English culture for the next five hundred years. Bollocks. Wasn't this war about defending the rule of law against the rule of anarchy? He lit a cigarette. Reluctantly, he decided he did have to go along with Grey's request for now. In spite of his tendency to be rebellious against stiff-necked authority, Tyler was no fool. Perhaps the fellow did have a bigger picture in mind that he himself was ignorant of. However, that shouldn't stop him from pursuing his own very discreet enquiries.

He went into the front hall.

"Where's young Eager?" he asked Gough.

"He's in the back, sir, having a cuppa."

"Bloody hell. Are we running a rest home?" He bellowed in the general direction of the duty room. "Eager, get your arse out here." He didn't wait but turned on his heel. "Tell him I'm in the car park."

The first crank was useless and Tyler kicked the tire in exasperation. Eagleton came over to him, buttoning his jacket.

"Sorry, sir, I heard you wanted me."

Tyler stepped back. "Can you make this bloody machine turn over? It's got a mind of its own where I'm concerned. It hates me and delights in making my life miserable."

"You have to be a bit more gentle, sir. Steady, not too hard and fast, just brisk and masterful. It'll surrender and be purring away in no time."

Tyler grinned at him. "Sounds like you're talking about a woman, Eager. Is that the voice of experience I hear?"

The constable blushed. "No, sir. Just with cars." He got to his task right away. He only had to crank a couple of times before the engine coughed into life. Tyler got in. "Go and get your bike."

Eagleton ran over to the shed, retrieved his bicycle, and fastened it to the rack on the boot. Tyler barely waited until he was inside before accelerating out of the car park. He turned onto Main Street, going as fast as he dared and the Humber could manage. Fortunately, there were only one or two people out. All the shops were closed on Sunday, and with nothing to draw them, the residents of the town were at home with their roast dinner, if they had one, listening to the latest bad news on the wireless.

Tyler got the car out of the town before he spoke. "There are two people I want you to talk to. Syd Newstead and Arthur Trimble. One of them, or both, may have been delivering black market goods to Lambeth's butcher shop on Thursday morning. Trimble says he was in the barn at that time. See if he can produce any witnesses. Same with Newstead. He lives in Ash Magna, so if he was coming from Main Street, he would probably turn off at the Heath Road."

"He's an old fellow, isn't he, sir? I can't see him killing a young girl in cold blood."

"Frankly, neither can I, but we have to rule him out."

"Beg pardon, sir, but I thought we were supposed to lie low with this investigation, sir. In the interests of national security?"

"We are. We're simply going on a scouting mission." He patted the constable's arm. "I know how clever you are, Eager, but they don't. Arrogant sods like Arthur Trimble can be lulled into dropping their guard if they think you're a fool. See if you can get him to say where he was on Thursday evening about seven."

"Yes, sir." Eagleton looked pleased at being given so important a task. "Excuse me, sir, but Mr. Lambeth is your father-in-law, isn't he?"

"Yes, but that doesn't mean my exemplary character has rubbed off on him. He's been trading in the black market."

"Sorry to hear that, sir."

"Not half as sorry as I am, Eager." Tyler stuck to the middle of the narrow road, trusting he'd have time to pull over if another vehicle came along. "I've closed him down for now, but we're going to keep a closer eye on him than a dog watching a rabbit."

"Yes, sir."

"While you chase up the yokels, I'm going to talk to Mrs. Devereau."

Startled, Eagleton looked over at him. "Is she a suspect, sir?"

"No, of course not, but she might have witnessed something that could help us. Her flat is above the former stables and who knows, she may have heard or seen something. Trimble for instance."

"I saw her in town last Wednesday. She's quite a swell, isn't she?"

"She is that."

Tyler wondered if he was fooling his shrewd young constable for one minute. "While you're talking to Trimble, keep your eyes open for any twine on the premises. It's common as muck but if he has some lying around, I'm going to sit on that slimy sod until he howls, national security or not."

They drove on for a while in silence until they reached the lane that led to Beeton Manor. Tyler pulled up in front of the house.

"Trimble has a cottage just down the path. He might be there; he might be working on the estate. I'll meet you back at the station."

"When would that be, sir?"

"God help me, I don't know, Eager. Whenever I've done what I've got to do."

"Yes, sir." He got out of the car and collected his bicycle.

The windows of the flat were all open and he could hear the sound of a wireless. It sounded like George Formby was plucking his ukulele. Tyler liked George and felt absurdly glad that Clare might like him too. He was the working bloke's entertainer. Tyler climbed the stairs and knocked on the door. His heart was beating faster but he couldn't do anything about it. She opened right away and gave him a warm smile that melted the tension building in his stomach.

"Tom, I thought we were getting together tonight? Come in."

She stepped forward, put her arms around his neck, and kissed him. Then she leaned away and scrutinized his face. "What's wrong? Don't tell me you're regretting already?"

"No, of course not. Nothing like that, but I need to talk to you."

"Oh dear. Let's go to the living room. I've just made some lemonade. Not as good as we got at the camp, but decent enough. Would you like some?"

"Love it."

He followed her down the long passageway. The screen to the bedroom was moved aside and he could see her unmade bed. She was wearing the white cotton top and khaki shorts. Once again, he was aware that the clothes fit loosely on her frame. She was too thin.

She poured his glass of lemonade, took it to the couch, and sat beside him. "I was afraid you'd regret everything and wouldn't want to see me again."

It had never occurred to him that Clare might be insecure after their coming together, but he saw that she was.

"I think I've fallen in love with you all over again," she whispered.

At another time, those words would have filled him with ecstasy.

He put down his glass on the table. "Clare, I have to talk to you regarding Elsie Bates."

He saw her unguarded expression of fear.

"I gather this is as Inspector Tyler, policeman?"

"I suppose you could put it that way. I'm sorry but it's something I couldn't ignore."

She shifted slightly away from him on the couch.

"I had a visit from Mr. Grey, the big hugga mugga from the security service," continued Tyler. "He told me something rather, shall we say, unexpected. He said you were working for MI5."

"Oh God, Tom. That's all supposed to be completely hush-hush. Why on earth did he tell you that?"

"He was very anxious to provide you with an alibi for the time when we know that Elsie was killed."

She frowned. "I don't know what you mean by 'anxious to provide me with an alibi.'"

"He says you were working overtime. That you were here in your flat and he fell asleep. You both had breakfast at seven and he left to go back to Whitchurch. You told me you were in bed contemplating throwing the alarm clock at the wall at six o'clock. Which is it?"

Clare shrugged. "Both things. Grey was here. We had a lot of translating and transcribing to do. He fell asleep on my couch so I let him stay. He always looks exhausted. My alarm did go off at a quarter to six and I did think of throwing it out of the window."

"Right. So you told me half of the facts?"

"Yes. Clearly, I couldn't tell what I was doing with Grey."

Tyler couldn't resist going one step further. Although even as he did, he knew it was ridiculous. "He also insinuated you were together all night having it off in rhapsody until dawn tiptoed over the misty mountain tops."

She stared at him incredulously. "He told you we were having a sexual relationship?"

"He *implied* you were."

She banged her hand on her forehead. "Men! You let your imagination run away with you, Tom. Did you honestly think I would sleep with somebody like Grey?"

"Frankly, no. But that could just have been my own basic conceit. He didn't get his leg over?"

"Please! Grey and I have a purely business relationship."

"He didn't even try?"

"No. He did not."

Tyler took out his cigarette case. "He certainly considers you a valuable agent. One who must be protected at all costs, even if it means feeding the police false information . . . because he was lying, wasn't he, Clare? I happen to know that you weren't here tucked up in your bed until morning. Your car was seen much earlier in Whitchurch, driving along Main Street at about a quarter to six."

"That's ridiculous, Tom. It must have been somebody else."

"Did you lend out your MG?"

She shook her head.

"Given that he was baring his bosom, it would have been easy for Grey to say you were both working at the Old Rectory. From there it was quite plausible that you'd be driving home. But he didn't say that. He wanted me to know that you were in your flat, a long way from the Heath Road. Why was that, Clare? Why was Mr. Grey so intent on giving you an alibi?"

He saw her shoulders slump.

"Can I have a cig?"

He gave her one but she didn't light it.

"So why was Mr. Grey making up a story, Clare? Or is it too secret for even my ears?"

"No, it's not exactly that . . . Grey told you he was with me because there was nobody to confirm that I was in my flat." She gave a wry smile. "We should have got our stories straight."

"Why? Why was it important to convince me you were snug in your flat?"

"Because I wasn't. It was me driving along Main Street at that time."

"Fair enough. What were you doing in Whitchurch at such an early hour?"

Rather awkwardly, she started to light a cigarette. He did it for her, waiting.

"I was visiting my daughter."

It was Tyler's turn to struggle to light up another cigarette. "I take it you're going to give me an explanation."

"The whole kit and kaboodle, Tom. I would have told you before but we were interrupted." She smiled at him rather impishly. "Shall I fetch the scarf and wave it around, à la Arabian nights?"

"That's all right. I don't need stage effects."

"Well, I need some brandy. Do you want some?"

"Just lemonade."

She went into the kitchen. He watched her while she poured the brandy, took a big gulp, then returned to the chair across from him. She was carrying the bottle and an extra glass which she put on the coffee table.

"In case you change your mind."

Tyler finished off his lemonade, then added a splash of brandy to his glass.

"Go. I'm all ears."

Clare took a deep breath. "There's a preamble. Be patient."

"My strongest suit."

"After I married, life went on, busy, empty, demanding and boring at the same time. Then when I was thirty-six and staring down a bleak future, I went to Paris for a holiday. Valentin was busy as usual so I was alone. One evening I went to an after-hours jazz bar, the new music from America. I met Paxton, a saxophone player. He wasn't like my other young men; he was a brilliant musician, passionate about his music, rather aloof. I went back several times. We started to talk between sets; he asked me to come back to his digs." She drank some of the brandy. "I accepted his offer and that was the beginning of a short but intense love affair." She paused. "Don't look like that, Tom. I'm telling you the truth, which you say you want."

"Don't worry about me. I'm a big boy. I can take it."

"What about you?" she fired back. "You were probably tom-catting around the countryside not thinking of me for a minute."

"I've never stopped thinking about you, Clare. I wish I could have."

She was silent for a moment, looking at him. "Do you want me to go on or not?"

"Of course." He reached for the brandy and poured a slug into his glass.

"All right then. As I was saying, Pax and I had a brief but good time. We shared cannabis, even cocaine, and an awful gritty bed. I was infatuated with him, although I knew the affair would never go anywhere."

"Why not?"

"He wasn't interested in any permanent commitment and I . . . well frankly, I had got used to a certain way of life.

I couldn't bear the thought of being poor again. So we kissed goodbye, cried a few tears, and I returned to Switzerland. I never saw him again." She sighed. "After he had gone I discovered I was pregnant."

"Oh."

"Yes, oh. I couldn't imagine getting rid of the child but, given our situation, there was no chance I could fob it off as my husband's. As I told you, we hadn't been intimate for years. Besides, Valentin is a highly conventional man and most unforgiving to those he feels have betrayed him. He would have cut me off without a penny if I had left him. I was, as they say, in a quandary."

Her face was filled with pain as she remembered. He wanted to comfort her; he wanted to punish her.

"What did you do?"

"I told Valentin I needed to improve my German. I said I could study in Berlin. He liked the idea and didn't demur. I went to Berlin, found a private hostel, and carried the child to term."

"Your husband never guessed the truth?"

"There had already been long stretches of time when I didn't see him from one month to the next. It wasn't hard to remain out of sight in those last few months. There were always things about my life that Valentin didn't want to know and vice versa. He preferred if I didn't enquire too closely as to what he was up to."

"He was screwing other women, you mean?"

"Not that. He's not really a very sexual being. It is more to do with some rather secretive negotiations with various important figures in Nazi Germany concerning his manufacturing plant."

"Great, so you married a Nazi collaborator?" Tyler knew his voice was harsh.

"Please, Tom. I'm sorry, but as you can imagine, this is a

painful subject for me. Here, give me your glass, I'll freshen up your drink."

He sat motionless on the couch, trying to absorb what she had told him. When she'd gone through the ritual of pouring out the brandy, she was more in control; the moment of anguish she had revealed was covered up again.

"This child is the one you just referred to, I presume? The daughter you were with in Whitchurch?"

"Yes. I arranged to have her adopted by a local family who were living in Berlin but are actually French. They have two other children like her, and she fitted in perfectly. She knows them as *mama* and *papa*, and I am nice *tante*, the auntie, who visits regularly and brings presents."

Clare was running her finger around the rim of her glass.

"I stayed on in Berlin applying myself to my studies." She shivered. "Germany, a place I have always loved, was becoming more and more frightening. Rumours were rampant about what the Nazis were doing but people didn't want to hear them. Many were only too glad that the country was prosperous again, that German pride was restored. I feared that my little family was in danger, so I got them out of the country and into England. I came as well. I went immediately to London and volunteered to work for the Security Service. My fluency in German is an asset. I was sent to Birmingham, dealing with refugees."

"And now here?"

"That's right. I was able to have my daughter and the other children evacuated here. They are billeted with Mrs. Pettie on Orchard Road. I actually spent the evening and the night at Mrs. Pettie's. I wanted to help them settle in. Amelie is a sensitive child and she easily feels like an outsider. I left early in the morning. I had to come back here, then go over to the camp."

Something was coming back to him. Gough reporting a complaint from Mrs. Newey. Foreign children. Dark skinned.

"You said, children like her. Was your lover Italian?"

"No. Paxton is from New York. He is a negro."

"Oh!"

"Yes, oh again . . . My daughter and the other two children in the family are of mixed race. Mama is a negress, Papa is a white man. In addition, Amelie has mild cerebral palsy. As you can see, she is amongst the most vulnerable to the Nazi philosophy. She is one of the 'useless' people." Clare put her glass down on the table and came over to him, kneeling in front of him and taking his hands. "I told you I grew up believing I had a heart of ice. Even with you, my dear Tom, that feeling didn't totally go away. Not until I gave birth to Amelie. When she was put into my arms, I felt as if my heart was being ripped out of my chest. It was almost physically painful, I loved her so much. I mean it when I say I would give my life for her."

He leaned his forehead against hers. "It must be very hard for you not to have her with you all the time."

"Sometimes it's sheer agony."

They sat like that for a while, then she shifted and sat in his lap, putting her head on his chest as if she were a child. "Thank you, dear Tom. Thank you for understanding." She kissed him. "You looked like such a boy just now when you felt I was leaving you out of the story. Well, this is your part. When the princess was still quite a young girl, she met a handsome young man, not a prince exactly, but of noble birth."

"Hah."

"She fell in love with this young man, but she was too frightened to give herself to him completely. She had to leave before her heart melted and she lost her own soul."

"That's not what you said."

"I didn't know it myself at the time. I made up excuses. Now I understand. When I saw you again in the market I was gobsmacked, as the East Enders say. There you were, with your beautiful blue eyes, your copper hair glinting in the sun, your sunburned nose . . . I knew I still loved you and that I had made a terrible mistake."

He took her hand and kissed her palm. "Mistakes can always be rectified."

She spoke into his neck. "Can they? Can they really? I wish I could be so sure." She pressed herself against him. "Oh Tom, my dear. Can we make love again?"

"Right now?"

"Yes, right now."

On impulse, he said, "Why do I keep getting the feeling there's more to this than meets the eye? You said you didn't know Elsie Bates. Is that true?"

Clare didn't flinch. "No, it's not."

"Ah. And I presume there is another explanation forthcoming?"

"I promised the whole kit and kaboodle, and that's what you'll get. I was, shall we say, acquainted with Miss Bates."

"You don't seem shocked by what happened to her."

"Shocked? Of course. Sorry? I wish I could say I was sorry. I am not."

"And the reason for that is?"

"Do you want me to tell you now, or can you wait until afterward?"

He pulled her into his arms. "Afterward."

They made love and it was more tender and close than anything he had yet experienced.

After a while, Clare got off the bed and put on her dressing gown.

"Final story."

"I'll sit up."

He reached for his cigarette case.

Clare began. "Keeping the nature of the real relationship between Amelie and me a secret is vital for a continuing good life for her and her adoptive family. By the worst bad luck, Elsie Bates saw me in Birmingham. I'd brought the family up there and I was coming out of the house with Amelie. Elsie happened to be going by, God knows why. She had the acuity of a rat, and suspected this was no ordinary relationship. Then lo and behold, she saw me again when I was here in Whitchurch. She deliberately followed the three children to the park. She wheedled out of them a few facts. Amelie is a trusting child. She speaks English well. It didn't take much for her to spill out her life story and how much she loved her auntie Clare who she has known since she was a baby, when they were all in Germany . . . how easy for that guttersnipe to put two and two together. She knew it was the last thing I would want revealed. You have to admit, it's one thing if I have had a child outside of my marriage with a white man, another if the father was a negro. I saw the shock in your face Tom, when I told you."

He couldn't deny it.

"Go on. So Elsie put the squeeze on you?"

"I was foolish. I panicked. I might have been able to bluff my way out, but I couldn't bear for my daughter to be the subject of gossip and whispers. I immediately offered Elsie money. I was only too happy to pay if it bought her silence." She exhaled as if she had been holding her breath the entire time. "That's it. That's the whole story."

She stood up, but he pulled her back. "One more piece, Clare. There's something I must know. As you were leaving Whitchurch, which road did you take to get back here?"

"I came by way of the Alkington Road, it's faster. And if that's a pointed question, I swear I had nothing to do with the murder."

"But you've just told me Elsie was threatening to reveal your secret life, and that you would give your life for your daughter. Elsie's death would relieve you. Why should I believe you?"

Clare regarded him steadily. "Because it's true, Tom. If you know me at all, you know it's true."

52

When Tyler came down to the courtyard, he found Eagleton already sitting in the Humber waiting for him.

Tyler slid into the driver's seat. "Any luck?"

"I think we can eliminate Mr. Newstead. He's got bad lumbago and has been in bed for four days. He said he was being treated by Dr. McHamer from Wem."

"Let's confirm that. I don't want to take anything for granted. Maybe Newstead is the fifth columnist. He could be feigning lumbago."

"Really, sir?" said Eagleton doubtfully. "He's a good actor if that's the case."

"Precisely. Always temper your investigations with common sense. What about Trimble?"

"He wasn't in his cottage nor on the estate. I took the liberty of seeking out Lady Somerville in case she had any information."

Tyler whistled through his teeth. "Did you indeed? What did she say?"

"She was very accommodating, actually, sir. She said that Mr. Trimble had told her he was going in search of pullets so they could build up the hen flock." He looked sideways at Tyler. "She's very knowledgeable about breeds of poultry, leghorns and such."

"I'm sure she is, Eager, and I'm sure she thought you were a very nice lad. Did she say when Trimble was expected back?"

"No, sir. She didn't know."

Tyler sighed. "I hope the bastard hasn't done a runner."

"Is he our prime suspect, sir?"

"Let's just say he is a person of interest. Great interest. We've got motivation and opportunity for Elsie's murder. As for Rose Watkins, if the bugger turns out to be fifth columnist, it would put him sending out his messages right where and when Rose was cutting through the woods to go to Mass at the camp."

"You don't think the two of them had an assignation, do you, sir?"

"No, I don't, but as the head doctor said, we've got to keep an open mind at all times."

"Yes, sir."

"You know what the problem with that is, Eager?"

"No, sir."

"The bad guys can slip through the net, easy as pie."

"We need to find Trimble soon, don't we?"

"On the nail, lad. I want you to go back to his cottage. Leave a note where he can't miss it. Tell him he must report to the station immediately. Now that you've got cosy with her ladyship, go back to her and tell her we want to talk to Trimble at once." He opened the car door. "While you're doing that, I'm going to see how the girls are. I won't be long."

"Sir!" Eagleton was regarding him anxiously.

"Yes?"

"Sir, your fly button is undone."

As it turned out, Tyler didn't spend much time at the hostel house. He didn't have any more information to impart, and the girls seemed as good as could be expected. Including the warden, they were all in the common room listening to the gramophone. The sun was streaming through the windows and at first glance, the scene was happy and normal. However, he was immediately aware of how subdued the girls were. Not even Molly and Freckles waved at him as he came in. Nobody was chatting, the music was a piece of classical piano, mournful and sombre. Miss Stillwell hurried over to greet him.

"We've been talking a great deal about what to do and so forth, but so far all of the girls have decided to stay on here and keep working. I have to say, Inspector, I am most impressed with them. Harvest time is so demanding and important I hate to think what would happen if they deserted now. Would you like to address them yourself?"

Tyler spoke briefly, commending the young women for their decision to stay on. He emphasized the importance of being on the alert and reporting to him anything at all that they thought was amiss. He scanned the young faces, the eyes that were fixed on him. Florence Hancocks looked a little better, less pale and ravaged. She was seated in between Molly and Freckles on the couch, and Tyler had the sense that Florence had unloaded her secret. Sylvia was on the floor leaning back against Muriel's knees; Lanky was next to her, hugging a cushion to her chest. All of the girls had clearly drawn closer to each other through this ordeal.

There was a bit of chat back and forth, but Tyler didn't stay long. He promised to return soon with a progress report.

Miss Stillwell escorted him to the door. "The vicar from St. Alkmund's has offered to come over this evening and conduct a service. He is a good man, surprisingly eloquent for a vicar, and I think it will be of comfort to the girls." She held out her hand. "Thank you, Inspector. You have been most considerate."

Tyler drove back to Whitchurch with his constable.

"Go around town. See if anybody has seen or heard of our

man. I'm going to have Collis get over to the estate and watch in case he returns. I'll send out the alert to all stations in the area. If you have anything new to tell me, doesn't matter what, come to the house. I might as well be there as anywhere."

53

At the appointed time, Arthur Trimble made his way into the woods, trying to move quietly. Every sound, the crack of a twig underfoot, the sloshing of the petrol in the cans, made him jump and curse to himself. He was desperately in need of a fag but couldn't risk lighting up. He stopped and popped a boiled sweet into his mouth instead. His hand was trembling and the sound of his heart thumping in his chest was deafening.

They'd established early on that in a matter of extreme emergency, he would receive a note in a packet of cigarettes, to be destroyed immediately, and that the rendezvous would happen that night. He'd stayed out of sight until darkness fell, going back to the estate only to do the job. There was a constable leaning against his own door but he was fast asleep. At first, Trimble considered just getting the hell out, but he needed the other man's help.

When he reached the small clearing with the dead tree in the middle, he stopped, straining his ears to listen. He didn't hear the man move but a shadow separated itself from the tree. It was him.

"Good evening, Arthur." His voice was muffled and he didn't speak above a whisper, but for Trimble the words seemed dangerously loud.

The man took another step toward him. "Did you do what I asked?"

"I did and bleeding difficult it was. I had to siphon some from the old lady's Rolls and God knows how I'm going to explain that to her. But I could only get two gallons all together." He put the cans down. "I don't suppose you're going to tell me what's this all about, are you?" His voice was truculent, going as far as he dared

to the edge of defiance. As usual the man was wearing a black balaclava. Trimble had never really seen his face.

Trimble stepped closer. "I think the police might have found the transmitter."

"How did that happen?"

"When I went by this afternoon just to check, I thought the leaves were disturbed. The coppers have been combing the woods looking for clues to the Watkins girl's death."

"That was unfortunate," said the man ambiguously.

"It wasn't my bloody fault. She saw what I was doing. She'd have reported me immediately. I had to do it."

"Is the transmitter still there?"

"It is. But I'm not taking any chances. I'm getting out. You said you could give me the name of a contact in Ireland and that's where I'm going. First thing in the morning. I'm not going to stick around and get my neck stretched."

The other man sighed ostentatiously, making his impatience obvious. "Well, there's no good crying over spilt milk. The problem is that everything could completely unravel at a moment's notice. Maybe the Secret Service do know about you and are playing you like a fish."

Trimble had been wondering the same thing and he could feel his bowels loosen at the thought.

"My job here is over," said the other man. "The camp is breaking up soon. I'm getting out too."

"Don't tell me you're going to Ireland?"

"Like I said before, what you don't know won't hurt you."

"You're not planning to renege on our agreement, I hope. I'm going to need a lot of dosh."

"Of course."

They were standing close together so they could speak quietly, and the other man reached into his pocket. When his hand came out, he was holding a switchblade. He flicked it open. Trimble didn't see it, didn't have a chance to move or defend himself. One swift stroke and the blade penetrated his heart with complete efficiency, right under the ribs. He dropped with hardly a sound, just one gasp as if he'd been punched and the wind knocked out of him.

The man poked at him with his foot, then checked Trimble's pockets to make sure he had nothing incriminating on him. There was nothing except the keys to the lorry, some loose change, and a couple of pound notes. He took everything. Then he rolled the body underneath the tree and pushed dead leaves over it until it was completely hidden. He did the same with the two containers of petrol. He'd brought a torch with him and, keeping it pointed low to the ground, he made his way to the road. He was taking a risk being away from the camp for long, but he'd noticed that since the announcement that the camp was being disbanded, the soldiers on guard duty had become even more lax.

Trimble had parked the lorry in a pass-by a hundred yards up from the entry to the woods. The man started the engine and slowly drove further away, pulling the lorry off the road at a break in the trees. He drove it into the woods as far as he could go, the branches making hideously loud cracking noises. Finally, he reached a place where the ground sloped sharply downward. He inched the lorry as close to the edge as he could, then, slipping the gear into neutral, he got out and pushed. The lorry obeyed easily and rolled down the slope until it crashed into a rock and tilted on its side. It wouldn't be a good hiding place in an extensive search, but it was far from the road and he didn't think it would be detected immediately. All he wanted was to buy some time for his escape.

He tossed the keys into the trees as far as he could and headed back to camp, regaining his tent without incident. Once on his cot, he lay on his back for a while, thinking.

54.

On Monday morning, Clare Devereau found what they had been waiting for.

There was only a light post delivery, and the thick, brown envelope addressed to Dr. Beck stood out. It was stamped with the letterhead of the London Psychoanalytic Institute and, according to the postmark, had been mailed on Thursday, arriving with a speed unusual these days with the demands of war slowing the post.

Carefully she slit it open. Inside was a short note from the director of the LPI. He simply said he was forwarding the papers Dr. Beck had requested from his desk at the Institute. He had been forced of necessity to reassign the doctor's office given the uncertainty of the date of his return, but he wished him luck and he was sure he would soon be released from the camp. He also enclosed a sealed letter which was addressed to Dr. Beck in care of the Institute. This letter had been franked four months earlier from Berlin. It had gone via Switzerland.

Clare opened that envelope next. The letter was written in German, the handwriting scrawling and hurried.

Berlin. May 1940.
Dear Dr. Beck,
I do hope this letter reaches you. I'm sending it to the London Psychoanalytic Institute in the hopes they will forward it. We have heard that many Germans residing in England are being interned as enemy aliens. If that has happened to you, I do hope

you will be released soon. If you do get this and can write back to me, I would most appreciate it as I am at a loss as to what to do and as always would welcome your wise guidance. First, let me bring you up to date about matters here.

We are all struggling. Although patients are now plentiful because of the government subsidies, we are scrutinized in a way we have not been before. We are only allowed to take so-called deserving patients, and we have to make a decision as to whether they can be so considered. Whereas previously this was a matter strictly of diagnosis – no latent psychosis, no narcissism, no mental retardation; those whom it was obvious cannot benefit from psychotherapeutic analysis – now we are forced to take on patients because of our financial circumstances, accepting even doubtful cases. However, even more important, rumour has it that anyone who is turned down as not treatable stands a very good chance of disappearing for good. It is the most dreadful dilemma and I have already taken on two young men who are quite unsuitable. One is a soldier who was injured during the invasion of Poland. I suspect he is suffering from brain damage, although it might be a matter of shell shock. He cannot concentrate at all and his thought process is most strange and incoherent. I believe he is a hopeless case but dare not turn him away. The Hitler regime doesn't like soldiers who might throw a negative light on the military. So I lie and say he is making steady progress.

The other client is also a young man, the son of a wealthy manufacturer here in Berlin, but he is clearly a borderline mental defective and psychoanalysis is incomprehensible to him. His father begged the director to take him on. At least it gives him somewhere to go four times a week and they pay handsomely, but it is a travesty to think I am helping him. However, I am also afraid that even his wealthy father cannot protect him from being considered a "useless life." And then what? I shudder to think.

However, enough of my woes; I have sufficient interesting cases

*to keep me going, and really it is about one of them that I am
writing to you.*

*Do you remember that when I was under your supervision
(how I wish I still had that privilege), I was assigned a Frau
Mueller? It was over a year ago now, so may I refresh your memory.
She came to the Institute in May of 1939, complaining of severe
headaches and suffering from a general malaise and anxiety. A
not untypical story of a middle-aged, middle-class housewife with
no work to occupy her mind. Very quickly, she began to complain
about her husband, his neglect and indifference. I considered she
was making some progress in the analysis when she finally revealed
her suspicions that her husband was a homosexual. She also let slip
that he was a high-ranking member of Herr Hitler's inner circle,
but she never said his name. Hers was undoubtedly false. She
became more and more insistent that I believe her story. I followed
your advice and constantly emphasized that this need was coming
from her transference toward me as her indifferent father. I insisted
it didn't matter what my views were; it was more important that
we examine this transference. She fought me tooth and nail and
said she would prove what she was saying was true. I didn't think
we were making much headway. Then, alas, you had to leave the
country and I was on my own. Shortly afterward, she came to her
session with an envelope which she said contained photographs of
her husband that were of a decidedly incriminating nature. Not
only that, he was cavorting with young men who hardly seemed
to be at the age of consent. I have no idea how she came by these
pictures and I didn't ask. Following orthodox practice, I refused to
look at them. I again tried to get her to understand why it was of
such paramount importance that I believe her. (Perhaps, dear Dr.
Beck, I was also somewhat afraid. I had no idea what I would do
with evidence of that nature in this climate of suspicion and fear.)*

*She was utterly furious, cut the session short, and left in a huff.
She cancelled her next appointment and I have not seen her since.*

However, a few days ago, I received a letter which I have copied out as follows.

Herr Schreyer. I left some photographs with you at our last meeting. It is imperative that I have them back. My husband has discovered I have these pictures and frankly I don't know what will happen to me if I do not return them to him at once. You can send them to the above address.

My dear Dr. Beck, you can imagine my chagrin when I realized I could not lay my hands on the package she had given me! Then I remembered that in all the confusion of your departure, I had gathered together all my case notes from my patients so that you might be able to peruse them at a later date. I dropped Frau Mueller's photographs into the envelope with the other papers. Do you still have that package? Even as I write this I realize the absurdity of the question. Even if you do have it, I don't know how you can get it to me. However, I can but try. I understand some post is going via Switzerland where the Red Cross may distribute it. Perhaps the best thing, given current censorship rules, would be to hold back the photographs and simply advise me as to the best course of action to take with my patient. If these pictures are indeed "proof" that her husband is a homosexual, what approach shall I take? The same question applies, of course, in reverse. If there is no "proof," how shall I proceed? And if, as she says, he is a high-ranking member of our illustrious government, is there anything I should do about that? I shall write to her at once with some excuse and perhaps she will come in. If she does, I shall have you in my mind and I know that the kind guidance I have received from you in the past will stand me in good stead.

I hope this letter finds you in good health. I am your ever faithful servant,

Otto Schreyer.

—

Clare put his letter aside and removed the papers from the brown envelope. There were four bunches each clipped separately. One was in the same handwriting as Otto Schreyer's. And there under the paper clip was a smaller envelope, sealed, addressed FOR DR. SCHREYER.

She removed it and opened it carefully.

Inside were three photographs. All of them compromising indeed. In two, in spite of a certain haziness as if the picture had been taken through a fine screen, the face of the main participant was clearly visible. And identifiable. Frau Mueller was quite right. If these photographs were genuine, her husband was indeed engaging in homosexual acts with very young men. He was indeed a high-ranking Nazi and his name wasn't Mueller.

She was admitted to Grey's office immediately, and found the director seated at his desk, holding a cloth to his jaw.

"I've an appointment later this afternoon with my dentist," he explained. "In the meantime, he suggested I apply a hot compress to the sore place and that is what I am doing. So, Mrs. Devereau, what do you have for me today? Better news than last time, I hope."

"Much, much better. This will clear up your toothache."

Clare handed him the envelope containing the photographs. Grey dropped his hot cloth and gave an uncharacteristic whoop of delight.

"So that's it. That's what Herr Heydrich was fishing for. Splendid. Well, well. I admit I'm surprised. It's not what I expected. So much for purity of mind and body. I thought he was after some egghead in the camp who had developed a new super bomb or some such thing. Far from it."

"Do you think the pictures are genuine?" asked Clare. "It

would be quite easy for somebody to impersonate the man in question. Just stick on a wispy moustache, give your hair a monk's cut, add wire rimmed glasses and there you are."

"It doesn't really matter if they are fake or not. If you pit two male wolves against each other in a struggle to be alpha male wolf, one or the other will be injured, even killed, and that is precisely what we want. It is up to Herr Heydrich how he deals with this material. An ambitious man is Reinhard Heydrich, with his oh-so-Aryan features. We know that he keeps secret files on everyone in Herr Hitler's high command." Grey rubbed his hands together in glee. "There will be squabbling in the den. Let us hope for very fierce squabbling."

"What is our next step?"

"We will make photographs of all of this correspondence and our little Happy Family snaps and then hand them over to their intended recipient, Dr. Beck. I shall set our own chappie to keep a very close eye on the good man. He is bound to take some action when he receives this material. That in turn should provoke a reaction in the mole. It would be very valuable for us to take the spy into our tender custody."

"What if Dr. Beck decides to keep this to himself?"

"I am gambling on my judge of human character, my dear Mrs. Devereau. The doctor is no fool. He knows that these pictures could be very valuable to the Allied cause. He will be compelled to do something with them. I want you to make it obvious that he is receiving this package."

He placed the compress against his jaw again, which muffled his voice.

"We heard that Dr. Beck's student, Otto Schreyer, is dead. He had a most unexpected heart attack. Very unexpected. No medical history, not quite forty. Quite tragic. The authorities are saying that he must have surprised a thief who was looking for money or drugs or some such. His office was ransacked.

I want you to make sure Dr. Beck knows about it."

"He will be upset. I had the impression he and Schreyer were good friends."

"That was unfortunate for the young man."

"Why would Heydrich have him killed?"

"I don't think it was him. I'd say Herr Himmler must have sniffed out where the photographs were. He must be in a panic to recover them before they are, shall we say, shared. I'd bet my boots it was he who had Schreyer eliminated."

"According to his letter, he didn't see those photographs."

"Quite true but a mere technicality to our suspicious Gestapo friends." Grey drummed his fingers on his desk. "Good, good. This is working out very nicely. Good work, Mrs. Devereau."

"I can't claim to have done very much, really sir."

"Quite so. But it does go on the credit side, not the debit, doesn't it? We can let our own man at the camp know that we're on the move. He must be on his toes." He pulled open the top drawer of his desk and took out a piece of paper and an envelope. He scrawled out a note, put it in the envelope, licked it sealed, and addressed the front.

"Please deliver this as if it were part of the regular mail."

Clare took the envelope, saw the name, and looked up at Grey in surprise. He smiled.

"Good. If you didn't suspect that he was our chappie, probably nobody else in the camp would guess either."

He turned his attention back to the photographs. "My goodness, some of these positions look remarkably athletic, don't they?"

Clare went straight back to the camp. When she got there, Major Fordham was addressing the general assembly. He had just finished telling them they would be transferred to the Isle of Man by the first week in September. Even though they already knew what was in store, most of the internees became very agitated at the news. They knew change wasn't always for the better. However, some of them who had wives already on the island were able to reassure the rest that it was a much better situation than the one they were currently in. Clare had waited outside the gate with her sack of letters. When he had finished, the major greeted her with relief.

"Poor fellows. How can they trust us? We could be sending them to a forced labour camp for all they know. Reassure them, will you, Mrs. Devereau?"

Private Nash opened the gate, calling out, "Post delivery. Post delivery. Come and get it."

Momentarily distracted, the men buzzed around her.

Dr. Beck was among them and he gave Clare his usual warm greeting.

"Anything for me?"

"Yes, Doctor. If you will wait just a minute, I need to speak to you."

She finished handing out the post, then drew the doctor to the side. She was holding the package underneath her arm.

"I'm afraid I have some bad news for you, but I thought you would want to know. One of your students from the Berlin Institute has died. A Dr. Otto Schreyer."

Beck gasped. "Otto? Surely not. He is a young man. What happened?"

"An apparent heart attack. But he was also the victim of a break-in at his office. He may have surprised the thief." She looked at Beck. "I wonder what a thief would think to find in an analyst's office? Surely not drugs."

Beck shook his head. "We kept no such things. Poor Otto. He showed so much promise. I had no idea he had such a weakness."

Clare murmured sympathetically. She glanced around. Most

of the others had drifted off to read their mail or to share with each other.

Clare handed Beck the package, making sure it could be seen. "This is for you."

"Thank you."

Still shocked by what she'd told him, Beck showed little interest in the package.

"I believe it's from the London Institute," said Clare, feeling like a hypocrite as she tried to tempt him. "Perhaps it's the papers you've been hoping for."

Beck opened the package and started to read Schreyer's letter. Clare pretended to be paying attention to the other internees, some of whom wanted to share parts of their letters with her. She saw Beck open the envelope containing the incriminating photographs. He didn't reveal much reaction but she supposed that was his training. A psychoanalyst can't indulge in his own personal feelings. She called out to him in German.

"Is everything all right, Doctor?"

Quickly, he stuffed the photographs back into the envelope. "Not exactly."

Hoeniger was on the fringes of the group, and Beck beckoned to him.

"Hans, where is Father Glatz?"

"In his tent."

Beck nodded at Clare. "Thank you, Mrs. Devereau," he said politely, and clutching the package as if it were on fire, he hurried off to the priest's tent.

"Did he receive bad news?" the seminarian asked Clare. "He seems upset."

"One of his former students has died suddenly."

"What a shame. I shall go and see if I can be of help."

He too went off to the tent. The internee whom Grey

referred to as "our chappie" hadn't yet shown up to receive his mail. Clare dropped it off at his tent, then returned to the hut. She sat down at the rickety table. The game was afoot. Except it wasn't a game. It was in deadly earnest and the stakes were very high indeed.

Beck patted the seminarian on the shoulder. "I'd like a private talk with Father Glatz if you don't mind, Hans."

"Not at all. I believe Kurt is expecting me to show up for a game of chess. He thinks he can trounce me."

"No chance of that," said Beck.

Hoeniger bowed himself away and left the two of them together. Beck sat on one of the cots and Glatz pulled up a canvas chair.

Beck took out the letter from Schreyer and handed it to the priest to read.

Glatz grimaced. "Are there photographs?"

"Indeed there are." He handed over that envelope as well. "And worse, my dear Philipp, I heard just now from Mrs. Devereau that Otto has died. A completely unexpected heart attack." Beck's professional calm demeanour was disappearing. He was becoming very agitated. "Am I to accept his death as a coincidence, or is it related to the situation he describes? The woman says her husband discovered she has the photographs, so I presume she has also revealed what she did with them."

"Is she alive?"

"I have not heard otherwise." He looked at the priest. "I am quite at a loss as to what to do. I consider all case notes, whether mine or those of a student of mine, to be completely confidential. I have always considered the nature of the analysis to be as sacrosanct as the confessional. However, this material is another matter. It is quite subversive and concerns men with whom we are now at war. Does that release me from all obligations? The woman in question, the analysand, is not a soldier. Should I respect her privacy regardless? I was Otto's supervisor and therefore she is nominally under my protection. I have never had a situation quite like this before. I would most value your advice."

The priest studied his hands. "With all due respect, Bruno, our situations are not exactly the same. I am bound by canon law and I am exempt from criminal law. I have priest-penitent privilege. In equivocal cases I would consult with the Holy See. Each situation would be judged on its own merit. You are not so exempt. Your decision to keep your own counsel is a professional one, not a religious one." He indicated the package sitting between them on the side table. "If the subject of these photographs was anonymous, would you be so eager to hand them over to the authorities?"

Beck shrugged impatiently. "But he is not anonymous."

"He is breaking the law; surely you cannot countenance that?"

"I realize sodomy is on the criminal code in both Germany and England but frankly, if the act is between consenting adults, I am not inclined to interfere."

"Come, Bruno. It is you who are being a generalist. The participants shown in the photographs, except for the main actor, appear to be quite young, barely pubescent. Even more serious an offence."

"But they are beyond the reach of British justice. Are you suggesting I should send all of this to Herr Hitler? They might be executed. In Nazi Germany, capital punishment is on the statutes for such men, whatever age. We know that homosexuals are being imprisoned under the most brutal of conditions."

"If that man were to be executed, or disgraced even, it might be of benefit to the Allies, don't you think?" Father Glatz pulled at his lip. "You know what I would advise, Bruno? I would advise you to sleep on it . . . No, I am quite serious. Nothing will be altered by one more day, and in the morning you may be clearer in your mind as to what you want to do."

Beck had been about to protest, but he nodded. "You know, I do believe you are right. What I need to do is to turn the problem over to my unconscious mind. Perhaps I shall have a dream that will give me some direction." He pointed at the package. "I wonder if you would mind if I left the thing with you. I'm sure I would be tempted to examine the notes in the middle of the night if it sits beside me and—" Just as he said that, the flap of the tent was lifted and Hoeniger came in.

"Oh sorry, Father, I didn't know you were still here."

"That's all right, Doctor Beck and I are finished, are we not?"

"Yes." Beck turned to the young man who was hovering on the threshold. "I think a game of chess will clear my mind. It helps me to focus on something other than the current problem. Did you defeat young Bader?"

"I did. He was reckless."

Beck chuckled. "I would have bet on it. Come then, Hans. I am cautious to a fault. Let's see what you do with that."

The priest took the package and stashed it in the little cupboard beside his bed.

"Wait one minute and I will come with you."

He put his arm over Beck's shoulders and guided him out of the tent.

55.

THE DAY SEEMED TO BE TAKEN UP WITH ENDLESS RED tape, reports being the bane of a police inspector's existence. Tyler couldn't even claim greater priority as there were no new developments in the murder cases. Arthur Trimble was nowhere to be found. The lorry was missing as well. Tyler repeated the "hold if seen" warning to other stations and set the available constables to renew their follow up in Whitchurch. He kept another man on watch at Trimble's cottage. He was afraid he may have acted too soon and frightened the man off.

He'd gone back to confront Lambeth, but his father-in-law was adamant he had nothing to do with Trimble on Thursday morning. He also said that Trimble occasionally drove down to London to see a friend. No, he didn't know what her name was. Maybe it was more than one friend. Tyler could do nothing else at the moment but fume.

When he finally finished what he had to do, it was late. Sergeant Gough had waited for him and on him, bringing him fish and chips for his tea. At ten o'clock, he sent Gough off home, and he walked slowly across the dark street to his own house. He let himself in, relieved that Vera had already gone to bed. Janet was at her friend's house and Jimmy's room was empty. God knows where he was. Tyler wished Alice Thorne was on the telephone but of course she wasn't. As always, his anxieties about his son hovered in his head like so many midges. He was going to have a talk with him tomorrow if it was the last thing he did. He contemplated calling

Clare, but it was late and it seemed too furtive to phone from his own house. For a moment, the yearning to be with her was almost overwhelming.

He didn't want to lie beside Vera in the marital bed, so he made up the couch for the night. Eventually he fell into a restless sleep.

He was at the station and the intercom telephone was ringing but when he lifted the receiver it was dead. He jiggled the hook, trying to summon Gough, but there were all sorts of complicated buttons that he had to press and nothing was working. The bloody thing kept on ringing.

He opened his eyes, disorientated. Finally he realized it was his own telephone that was clammering relentlessly. The clock showed five o'clock. It was pitch dark. He swung his legs off the couch and hurried into the hall.

Major Fordham's voice came through immediately. "Inspector Tyler. Can you get over to the camp right away? We've had a serious fire. We've got it under control but there have been casualties. At least five men dead as far as we can determine." Fordham made a sort of throat-clearing noise. "I thought I had better contact you right away because I suspect arson is involved."

Tyler scrubbed at his face to make himself wake up. "Why is that, sir?"

"I didn't think so at first. We've warned the internees to be careful when they smoke in their tents – their palliasses are filled with straw, and with this dry weather everything is such a fire hazard. But there's no doubt. You can smell the petrol. And we've since found two empty petrol cans over by the latrine."

"I'll be right over. I'll just pick up one of my constables."

They hung up, and Tyler hurried back to the living room for his clothes. He heard a door open upstairs. Vera appeared on the landing, tousled and fearful.

"What's happening? It's not Jimmy, is it?"

"No, don't worry. A fire broke out in the camp and the major wants me to come over and represent calm and order."

"Was anybody hurt?"

"Yes, I'm afraid so."

She started down the stairs. "Do you want me to make you a cup of tea to take with you?"

"I don't have time, Vee. I can get one at the camp. Thanks."

"Tom . . ." Her voice trailed off. "Never mind."

She turned around and went back upstairs.

Tyler hurried across the street to the police station. What had he been thinking? That he could just pack a suitcase and move away? Too many people would be hurt if he did that. He stopped, fished out his cigarettes, and lit one, shielding the match with his hand. He looked up at the sky, overcast, with just the hint of silver where the moon was. No stars.

Tom Tyler had never considered himself to be a religious man since he had grown to adulthood. More agnostic than anything was how he described himself, but in the cool earth-scented night, he was moved to utter a kind of prayer. *Please help me, Lord. I need some guidance here. I'm bloody lost, if you must know and will excuse the profanity. I am, my family is, the entire bloody world is, if it comes to that. I'm not going to say that you're on our side because the Germans probably think the same thing, but I know there are forces at work here that I've never seen before. Not even in the previous war, and I was witness to lots of bad things. We are in the grip of a terrible darkness. I'm not going to promise to be a good man from now on, I'd probably renege at the first opportunity, but I also want to do the right things by the people I love. However small, if there is anything I can do to pro-tect this country of mine, I will do it. As Winnie keeps nattering at us, we must overcome. And we must.*

He continued on to the car, slightly embarrassed with himself, although he hadn't spoken out loud. No thunderclap, no burning bush presented itself, just the far-off barking of a dog, telling somebody or something that he was the boss.

56

TYLER COLLECTED EAGLETON WHO, WITH THE resilience of youth, was immediately alert and ready to accompany him. They drove as fast as they could to the camp, and as they approached along the north road, they could smell the acrid smoke on the air. The generator lights were on and the entire camp was bathed in light. Tyler parked the Humber, and a sentry let him and Eagleton through the gate.

They headed in the direction of the thin wisps of smoke. It looked as if all of the internees were awake and standing in small groups outside of their tents. Nobody was moving, and they watched him silently as he went by. The fear was as palpable as the lingering stench from the fire. Some of them had cloths over their mouths and nostrils and as he got closer, Tyler could understand why. There was a sickening smell of roasted flesh in the air. What was left of the tent was a blackened mess, and on the grass there were mounds, covered with tarpaulins, that he assumed had once been the occupants.

Here he found Major Fordham and a couple of soldiers. A few feet away, Dr. Beck was sitting on a camp stool.

The commandant greeted Tyler immediately. "Inspector. Thank goodness. What a terrible thing this is."

"Do you know what happened?"

The major waved his arms vaguely. "I was called about an hour ago, but by the time I got here the sentries and internees had managed to extinguish the fire. Although, according to my corporal, the bloody tent had burned itself out. Nothing left of it." He coughed. "The bodies were still burning but the men succeeded in smothering the flames."

Tyler glanced around. The tents were packed close together, and he could see the ones in the immediate area were blackened but otherwise untouched. They were lucky. The fire had been so fierce that it actually hadn't spread once it consumed the tent.

Fordham indicated Dr. Beck. "Fortunately, the doctor detected the fire before it got completely out of hand. He attempted to pull out the men from the tent that was on fire, but the flames were too fierce. He's still rather shaken."

Beck saw them and got to his feet uncertainly. Tyler could see the burn marks on the doctor's hands, and his beard and hair were singed. He smelled of smoke. He was wearing an elegant dressing gown which was darkened with smoke residue.

"Doctor, will you tell the inspector what happened?" asked the major.

Beck nodded. "I couldn't sleep and I had just stepped out of my tent to get some fresh air. I heard a sort of swoosh, and suddenly there were flames leaping up from this direction. I yelled 'fire' and ran over as fast as I could. By the time I got here, the tent was completely ablaze, although it was a matter of seconds only." He paused. "I did try to get through to the occupants but I was unable to do so." He swallowed hard. "Father Glatz was my good friend. I'm afraid he has perished."

Fordham took up the narrative as Beck was clearly struggling with his emotions.

"We have always made sure there are sand and water buckets at every entrance After Dr. Beck's call, many of the men were awakened. The sentries came running. We've had fire drills so everyone knew what to do, but all they could do was extinguish sparks landing on nearby tents. It's a miracle more people weren't seriously hurt."

"What time did this happen?"

Beck shook his head. "Frankly, time has stood still, but I would say it was around half past three."

"Did you hear anything other than the swoosh?"

"No . . ." he hesitated. "I heard no screaming from inside the tent when I got close enough. Nothing at all."

Meaning the men were all dead before the fire started.

"Do we know who was in the tent?"

Fordham turned to the guard, who pulled out a piece of paper from his pocket.

"This was tent number thirty-three. Here are the names of the occupants, sir."

There were seven names on the list. Five mounds.

"We seem to be missing two men," said Tyler.

Another clearing of the throat by the major. "In a camp this size not everybody is inclined to stay where they are assigned. I don't mind if they go visiting, as it were, as long as they answer to the morning roll call."

It dawned on Tyler what the commander was referring to and why he seemed so uncomfortable. He meant assignations.

"I'd appreciate it if you would start a roll call now, Major. And I'd like to clear the immediate area of all internees."

"Of course. Er, I am wondering whether or not I should ring Mrs. Devereau. I will need to address the camp and you may have questions yourself. It makes it so much easier to have an official interpreter. Besides, having a woman present at a time like this can be so comforting, can it not?"

"I think that's an excellent idea. Eager, come here for a minute."

A rather white-faced Eagleton stepped over to him.

"Go to the commandant's tent. He has a field telephone

and the corporal will show you how to use it. Get hold of Mrs. Devereau. Don't alarm her any more than you have to, but tell her to get here as soon as she can. If she doesn't answer, she may be in Whitchurch. In which case, you'll have to rouse Sergeant Gough and have him fetch her. She'll be at Mrs. Pettie's house in Orchard Lane."

"Yes, sir."

Obviously only too glad to get away from the horrors, Eagleton scooted off. Fordham clapped his hands as if he were in the playground and was summoning the children back to classes.

"To the mess tent, gentlemen, if you please. We have to take roll call. We will give you information as soon as we can. Move along now, there's good chaps. Tea will be served. Come along."

Tyler waited until the area was completely cleared. Beck had returned to his camp stool, waiting for his directions. Fordham came back from his shepherding task.

"All right then, Inspector. Ready when you are."

"Let's have a look shall we, Doctor? Can you handle this?"

Beck nodded.

Tyler walked over and lifted one of the tarpaulins.

The head was burnt beyond any recognition, all of the flesh charred to the bones. The exposed teeth grinned at him. He uncovered more of the body, aware of the strong odour of petrol as he did so. The upper chest and arms were likewise severely burned, but from the waist down, although the clothes had gone, the skin was less destroyed.

Tyler straightened up. "Do you know who he is?" he asked Beck.

"The bodies are more or less lying where they were found. Although the attempts to put out the flames meant they were rolled further away from the tent. The entrance to the tent was about where we are standing and I believe Howard Silber slept closest to it as he was rather claustrophobic. The fire has shrunk the body but I would guess it was that of a tall man in life." Dr. Beck's voice was measured and dispassionate but Tyler thought it cost him a lot to be so controlled.

"I'm going to have to take a look at each body," said Tyler. "If you can make an identification, Doctor, it will help us."

One by one, Tyler moved to the covered mounds and laid them bare. Like the first body, the remaining four were black and bloody. Unrecognizable. And like the first body, the worse burning had been to the upper chest and head.

Beck could not remember exactly what order they had slept in but thought that the second body might be that of Herr Gold, who he recalled had the bed next to Silber.

"Tragic loss. He got this far to safety and died in this way. Terrible. And Silber was a quite splendid actor. Completely British through and through, except for having German parents. Another great loss."

When they came to the third body, he stopped and, for the first time, looked as if he was going to lose control. Lying on the burned chest was a gold crucifix, blackened and misshapen but recognizable.

"This would be Father Glatz," said Beck. "The position is right, he was farthest from the opening. That would be his cross. If you rub at his front teeth, Inspector, you might find he had a gold tooth. Forgive me but I cannot quite bring myself to do it."

Tyler rubbed off some of the soot with his finger and there was indeed a tooth with a gold filling.

"He was a splendid man, good thinker," said Beck. "We had some wonderful talks. I myself am not of the Christian faith but I would describe the father as a profoundly good man . . . and he was a good friend."

Tyler checked off the name on his list and they moved to the next body.

This one was still wearing the remnants of leather shoes, the uppers burned away but the lace holes and part of the sole remained.

"It's Herr Stanislas for sure," said Beck. "He never took his shoes off even when he went to bed. He said he'd gone through one pogrom when he lived in Poland. He'd been caught with bare feet and he wasn't going to go through that a second time." Beck wiped at his eyes. "He was an elderly man and deserved better than to end his days in this fashion."

He could not positively identify the fifth body at all.

Tyler consulted his list. "In other words, there are three men unaccounted for. We've got positive identifications of Father Glatz; Howard Silber; Manfred Stanislas, and Herr Gold. The remaining body could be that of Kurt Bader, Hans Hoeniger or Professor Hartmann."

"It isn't Professor Hartmann," said Beck. "He has had a complete collapse and he is in the infirmary in Shrewsbury."

"That leaves Kurt Bader and Hans Hoeniger. It has to be one or the other."

"They are about the same size. As I remember, Hoeniger slept next to Father Glatz and Bader was beside Professor Hartmann." He stared at Tyler. "Do you believe it is this missing man who has killed these others and set them afire?"

Fordham shuddered. "I still don't understand this. I can see no rhyme or reason why these particular men were targeted or by whom."

Dr. Beck was looking very grim. He walked over the still-smouldering ashes. Tyler could see the remains of a small cupboard near where Father Glatz had slept. Beck bent over, disregarding the heat, and poked at the charred wood. He pulled out something that Tyler could see had once been a chess piece.

"Philipp was very proud of his chess set," said Beck sadly. "It is quite destroyed." Gingerly, he stirred the inside of what remained of the cupboard. There was nothing visible except ash and curled bits of burned paper.

He turned around.

"I must have a word with you in private, Major. And you, Inspector Tyler. There is something you should know. I believe I know who is responsible for killing these men. No, I beg your pardon, I don't know *who*, but I believe I do know *why*."

57.

He had put his gun in his pocket. The knife was inside his jacket. The last killing had stimulated him and he didn't feel the least tired even though he'd had no sleep since the previous night. He was lucky to have got away. He'd thought the latrine was deserted until the man had called out to him. He'd tried to stop him, the fool. Too bad for him. The killing was easy.

He walked quietly and steadily along the path that Trimble had told him about. It wasn't well trodden and the tree branches slapped him in the face, stinging him. He bit back exclamations and kept walking. It wasn't long before he came to the clearing. He stood sniffing at the air like a dog. The smell of wood smoke told him this was where the cottage was, although he could see nothing as yet. Cautiously, he took a step forward. Immediately, a dog barked a warning. He took another step. The dog barked more loudly, his voice proclaiming an enemy. Another dog joined in and he could sense rather than see that they were heading straight for him.

He removed the Luger and snapped off the safety catch.

58.

THE THREE OF THEM WERE GATHERED IN THE MAJOR'S tent. Fordham had ordered some first aid for Beck, and while Tyler bandaged the doctor's injured hands, Beck poured out his story of the letters he'd received from Otto Schreyer and the incriminating photographs.

"Are you telling us, Doctor, that five men have been slaughtered in cold blood so that somebody could destroy photographs that are of an allegedly incriminating nature regarding a highly placed Nazi?"

"I can think of no other explanation, Inspector," said Beck. "I've been thinking about it as objectively as I could." The oil lamp was casting shadows on his face, making him appear old. "I heard nothing. There were no cries for help or such. I think he killed everybody before they could even wake up. Probably to ensure they couldn't give the alarm. That would have occurred before the fire. He deliberately obliterated their faces which suggests to me he wanted to delay identification as long as possible. He wanted to buy time to escape." He lowered his head. "I feel most acutely responsible. I should have immediately brought the photographs to you for safekeeping, Major. I believed I was protecting patient confidentiality."

Fordham sighed. "Never mind that now. You should have but you didn't. You had no way of knowing there was an enemy agent in our midst."

Tyler could see that the doctor's sense of guilt was not going to be easily assuaged, and he felt sorry for him.

"And it must have been pure chance that he saw you hand over the envelope to Father Glatz," added Tyler.

"But he also knew the significance of the self-same envelope," said Beck. "That is most puzzling."

Fordham continued. "If the killer has escaped, and it seems that is the case, where has he gone? A German-speaking man on the loose is going to alarm every man and woman in the countryside. He doesn't stand a chance."

"Perhaps he speaks perfectly good English," said Tyler. "What about the two men who are so far unaccounted for? Did they speak English?"

"Bader did a little, but badly," replied Beck. "Hoeniger had none. At least not that I know of. He said he couldn't."

Tyler heard the doubt in his voice. "It's easy to pretend you can't speak the language when you can."

"Yes, sir, that is true. I mean, generally I have found Bader to be a well-mannered young man with no indication that he is a cold-blooded killer. Hans Hoeniger was studying to be a priest and he appeared to be a good soul."

"We'd better get on to MI5 at once," said Fordham. "This is out of my province. We need the experts. You say they're hunkering down in the Old Rectory, Tyler?"

"Yes, sir. I would ask for a Mr. Grey."

"Confounded silly if you ask me. I know it's national security and all that but surely they could have let me know what they were up to."

"I wasn't informed either. I suppose they operate on the principle of what the right hand doesn't know, the left hand won't punch, or whatever that bloody expression is."

Beck looked over Tyler's shoulder. "Ah, here comes Frau Devereau's car. She seems to have brought somebody with her."

Tyler turned. Grey was seated beside Clare.

"The very man you wanted to see, Major."

One of the guards came trotting fast along the path.

"Have you got a complete roll call yet?" the major asked him.

"I have, sir. I had the tent captains do it. We do seem to have one more man unaccounted for. He was in tent twenty-six, which is two rows down from here. His name is O'Connor. Michael O'Connor. According to the tent captain, sir, he was present when they all retired for the night but he's not there now."

Tyler experienced a wrench of disappointment. Was O'Connor indeed an Irish terrorist?

He got his answer. A second soldier was running toward the major's tent. He skidded to a stop, saluted, and said breathlessly.

"We've found O'Connor, sir. I'm afraid he's dead. His throat's been cut."

59.

JIMMY WAS AWAKENED BY THE NOISE OF THE DOGS
barking. He could tell by the sound that they were both in a
warning mode, and he raised his head, wondering if a fox
was on the prowl. Then he heard two bangs in quick succes-
sion. One of the dogs started to yelp, there was another bang,
and silence.

He got out of bed at once. Alice had provided him with a
cot tucked underneath the window in the living room. The
curtains were drawn, and he lifted the edge cautiously. It was
still pitch black outside and he couldn't see anything. Alice
came out of her bedroom, Skip close behind her.

"Jimmy, I think somebody just shot my dogs." she whispered.

The collie hopped past her to the door and put his nose to
the bottom, tail alert, nostrils quivering as he tried to pick up
a scent. Alice and Jimmy stood motionless, ears straining to
hear. Nothing.

"I've got to go and check," she said.

"No, you won't. There's somebody out there with a gun."

Alice reached for a mackintosh that was hanging on the
door. "I can't imagine whoever it is would want to shoot me.
I've got to see if the dogs are alive or wounded."

"I'll go. Where's your shotgun?"

"In the case. But Jimmy, for God's sake be careful."

He bolted the front door. "I'll go out the back way; lock it
behind me."

Skip was dancing around, eager to get outside. Alice spoke
to him sharply: "Lie down. We're not going anywhere."

Alice followed Jimmy to the back door. He removed the shotgun and checked that the safety catch was on. Alice extinguished the oil lamp she had been carrying. She wasn't showing any fear, and Jimmy drew strength from that. They stood quietly while he got used to the darkness.

"All right, now. Stay inside."

He opened the door quietly and stepped out. Only the rustle of the wind in the trees; no murmur from either dog. He could hear agitated chirping from the birds in the nearby bushes.

He became a soldier again.

Moving away from the door, he crouched, ready to run along the side of the cottage to the tool shed, which would give him some protection. He assumed the shooter, if he was still there, was in front of the cottage, which was where the gunshots had come from.

He was using his senses, sharpened by those weeks of warfare, as if he were a dog, smelling the air, listening, trying to sense if there was somebody hiding in the trees across the clearing. They had the advantage of being prepared. They knew where he was; he didn't know where they were.

He scrambled toward the shed, which was a slightly darker shape just discernible in the faint light of the moon. Just as he reached the corner of the cottage, he stumbled over a soft heap on the ground. He reached out, his fingers touching something wet and soft. It was one of the dogs. Lightly, he put his hand on the dog's side, but there was no indication of breath. It was too dark to completely make out which dog it was but he felt for a tail. There was the long plume of the mongrel, Scruffy. Jimmy could make out another shape close by. Lucy. He inched over to determine if she was alive. She wasn't.

He backed away from the two dogs. His throat was tight, not with fear so much as sorrow. Alice had said more than once how unpopular she was with people since the war had heated up. She was stubborn about declaring for the peace movement. Was this an act of revenge on her? He listened again but could hear nothing above the chatter of the birds. Whoever had shot the dogs seemed to have gone.

Still cautious, but moving more slowly, he retraced his steps to the cottage. Now that his eyes had adapted to the dark, the two dogs were more visible. Both had been shot through the head. He went to the front door and tapped lightly.

"Mrs. Thorne, it's me," he whispered.

He heard the bolt and she opened the door, Skip pressing at her legs.

Everything that came next happened with bewildering speed.

The man was hiding in the cover of the shed, and when Alice opened the door, he ran toward them. Skip saw him first and let out a peal of barks. Jimmy turned as the man fired his gun.

The bullet went straight through his neck, and he died instantly, dropping in a heap at Alice's feet.

The man halted and trained his gun on her. "Control your dog, Mrs. Thorne, or I shall be forced to shoot him as well. Step back please."

She grabbed Skip's collar as he tried frantically to get at the man. He stepped over Jimmy's body and closed the door behind him.

60

GREY, FORDHAM, AND TYLER STOOD TOGETHER looking down at O'Connor's body. The Irishman had been stuffed into one of the latrine stalls. His throat had been cut so deeply his head was almost severed at the spine. He was fully dressed in dark trousers and black jersey.

"He was one of ours," said Grey. "We thought it important to have somebody inside the camp since we knew that Jerry had a mole in here as well."

"Is that why O'Connor was murdered?" Fordham asked. "Do you think he caught the German in the act of escaping?"

"Could be. I asked him to be on high alert. Poor fellow. He never was a very effective spy." Grey's voice was even softer than usual.

"He must have been killed here right beside the stall and then shoved inside," said Tyler. "There's no blood anywhere else."

"Inspector Tyler, gentlemen, please take a look at this," said Beck.

He was pointing to a gap in the barbed wire between the latrine wall and the final fence post. The screws holding the wire had been loosened and it was bent back, leaving just enough room for a man to squeeze through.

Grey turned to the major. "We must get up a search party at once. Our chappie has got about two hours' lead. That could put him across the border if he's going straight to Ireland. On the other hand, he could be going south, east, or north. There might be a U-boat waiting for him for all we know. Mission accomplished, get back to home sweet home."

"Come on, Doctor," said Tyler to Beck. "You believe that every criminal will leave a clue because in the bottom of his heart he feels guilty. All right then. Where's the clue here for this sod?"

"I'd like to go back to the tent and have another look."

Tyler, Fordham, Grey, and Beck all returned to the burned-out tent. In the mess tent, the internees huddled together, watching. Clare was with them, and Tyler saw her place her hand on the shoulder of an elderly rabbi.

"What do you want to see exactly, Doctor?" Tyler asked.

"The body I couldn't identify," answered Beck.

Tyler pulled back the tarpaulin and the doctor stared down at the burned corpse. Then he walked over to the body they had identified as Father Glatz and uncovered it as well. He straightened up.

"Of course. I have been blind. I can tell you exactly who we're looking for. He did leave us a clue. Or, more accurately, a telltale sign. Look at Father Glatz. He always wore his gold crucifix. It was the symbol of his vocation, his identity. It was always with him even when he went to bed. Hans Hoeniger, as a seminarian, would have done the same."

Tyler cautiously rolled over the fifth corpse. Some of the flesh came away from the bone and stuck to his fingers. He wiped them on the grass.

"There is no cross."

"Then this body is that of Kurt Bader," said Beck. "And we are looking for the soft-spoken devout Christian who is supposedly studying to be a priest. Herr Hans Hoeniger. He must still be wearing his cross. He didn't think about it. He's probably going to be in his dog collar and soutane as well. All utterly above suspicion."

61

ALICE HAD TIED UP SKIP BY THE HEARTH AND, following orders, was sitting at the table across from the man. His face was scorched and his eyebrows and much of his hair was singed. His hands had been burned as well and looked swollen. He was holding his gun in front of him on the table. He'd placed a briefcase beside him.

"Madam, I would appreciate it if you would find me some cream or salve. I am a little fried, as you can see. I know that you must have some around. That's what you do, isn't it? You're a healer. Your fame was widespread throughout the camp." His English was perfect, with a slight Irish lilt. Ireland was where he'd learned to speak it.

"I'll get some," she said.

"Move slowly, if you please madam, and keep your hands where I can see them at all times."

She did as he said and walked into her scullery, where she kept the creams and salves.

She recognized him now, although at the time he'd seemed not to understand English. The internees had been kinder to her peace pledge proclamation notice than the people in Whitchurch. Quite a few had joined, including this man.

She remembered now, his name was Hoeniger. He was still wearing his black seminarian's garb and a large gold cross hung around his neck.

Her mind was racing, trying to assess the situation the way she might have if she'd been called out to deal with a danger-ous dog or wild animal. She made herself speak calmly and not show any fear. Inside she was screaming, every fibre of her being protesting at what he'd done to Jimmy, to her dogs. Surprisingly, what was uppermost in her mind was not the need for survival but the desire not to be defeated by this killer. That desire was a core of steel in her spine.

"You will leave the door open, won't you, Mrs. Thorne? If you don't, I shall immediately shoot your dog. It would be a pity. And he's such a handsome fellow. Aren't you boy?" He clicked his tongue at Skip, who, accustomed to friendly visitors, wagged his tail.

Hoeniger watched her as she reached for the ointment. She brought it back to the table and set it down.

"Take the lid off if you please. Good, thank you."

"How did you get burned?"

"That isn't important." He grinned; for a moment she saw how attractive he might have been. He tapped the briefcase. "What is important is that finally, finally, I have completed my task. It was, frankly, a long wait, but I presume the result will be very satisfactory."

He stuck his fingers in the ointment and daubed it over his right hand, and then switched the gun and did the same for his left and his face.

"Ah. That is nice. Much better."

"May I ask what you are planning to do?" said Alice, matching her tone of voice to his. They could have been talking about taking a walk into town.

"I'm going to wait an hour or so until it is completely light, then we are going to go on a journey. You will drive. Not the goat cart, if you don't mind. We'll take your car. We will bring the dog. We will look so wholesome and innocent nobody will question us. The sweet old woman, the clergyman, the pet dog. You will do exactly what I say or I shall kill Skip. Well, you know that already, I don't have to repeat it. I have a contact across the border whom I will seek out. He will help me to get to Ireland and Bob's your uncle. I shall be free and clear."

The car hadn't been functional for several weeks but Alice didn't think it was prudent to mention that right now.

"There will be a search party out for you when they find you are missing."

"I hope not yet. I have covered my tracks quite well, I believe. They don't know who they are looking for." He shrugged. "Even if they do, they don't know in what direction I have gone. I'd say I have several hours' start and that is plenty of time. The border is less than two hours away."

"But we all have to show our identity cards these days."

"I have a passport. I will be travelling as Father Conal Malone. With you at my side, nobody will be suspicious, especially if you vouch for me, which you will. For Skip's sake."

She wanted to shout at him, as if she were a child confronting a bully. *You think you're so tough. Well you're not. You're a coward threatening those who are weaker than you, shooting dogs who would have licked your hand if you'd given them a chance.* But she didn't say any of these things. There was something about this man that was beyond anything she had experienced before. He had a plan but she knew that he could easily abandon it if he needed to, if she proved difficult. There was no softness anywhere in his being that she could sense. He would as easily kill her as he would wipe out a fly that had irritated him. He would let her live as long as she was useful to him.

Suddenly, he yawned. "I could do with some brandy or something like that. What have you got?"

"Nothing like that."

"Are you sure? I thought I saw some bottles in your little pantry there."

"That's wine. Homemade raspberry wine."

"That'll do. Bring me the bottle."

"You probably won't like it. I didn't have quite enough sugar. It's a little on the bitter side."

He waved his hand dismissively. "I don't care about that. Does it have alcohol in it?"

"Yes. Quite a lot."

"Bring it then."

She returned to the pantry and opened the lower cupboard where she kept the medicines she used on the dogs and animals. She took out a bottle. She'd labelled it but she'd been in a hurry or perhaps the Goddess was looking out for her because the label wasn't secure on the bottle. It was hanging half off. As she reached for it, she turned her body so that for one brief, all-important moment, she obscured what she was doing from Hoeniger and was able to rip off the label. Casually, she closed the pantry door behind her.

She put the bottle in front of him.

"Mrs. Thorne, you aren't being a very good hostess. Pour me a glass if you please. No, wait. I don't want to drink alone, make that two glasses."

She fetched two glasses from the cabinet and poured out the wine. Her hand was shaking slightly but she was unconcerned. He would expect that.

He reached for his, then paused. "Here am I speaking of manners. You should drink first." A smile was on his lips. "You are a witch after all. I don't want any shenanigans at this stage." He raised his glass and waited until she had picked up hers.

"Prosit."

Alice took a sip of the wine. She made a face. She couldn't help it. It was all she could do not to spit it out. "It certainly needs more sugar," she said.

She took another sip, making it seem more than it was.

"Good," he said, and with one quick gulp, he downed his drink.

She knew she had seconds in which to act and she did.

As the antimony hit his throat, he retched involuntarily, spewing out the liquid across the table. But the corrosive impact was so severe that he clutched at his neck, letting go of the gun. Alice snatched it up and with two rapid shots, fired at first his right knee, then the left, shattering the bones to fragments. He fell off the chair and onto the floor, screaming. She ran to the kitchen, stuck her fingers down her own throat, and vomited, gasping in pain as the poison scalded her. Skip barked frantically.

Hoeniger writhed on the ground, struggling to get away from his own agony. The gold cross that was around his neck bounced on his chest.

Later, recounting what had happened, Alice found it almost hard to remember. Time seemed both interminable and moving with enormous rapidity. She offered the German sweetened tepid water to purge the poison. At first he had refused, too suspicious of her. She had drunk a large glass herself to show him and he finally took what she offered. He also accepted a cloth she'd brought him that she'd soaked with chloroform. He'd wanted to fight that too, but the pain in his shattered legs was too severe, and when she slid it across the floor toward him, he placed it across his face and forced himself to breath deeply. Only when she could see he had slipped into unconsciousness did she dare to come close to him so she could tend to his injuries as best she could. She knew he must have medical attention soon but she couldn't move him herself.

She went outside to where Jimmy had fallen. Her hands were shaking violently and there was a fierce pain in her stomach both from the poison she had swallowed and her own grief. On impulse she went to the garden and picked some white poppies.

"May you rest in peace, dear tormented soul."

She placed the flowers on Jimmy's chest the way he'd placed white poppies on Elsie Bates's body.

The two dogs were lying close to each other near the edge of the clearing. She touched them gently and closed their eyes. She didn't have the energy to bury them now but she would later. She felt as if she were on the verge of collapse.

There was a spot, a hollow in the ground with bricks around it where she often lit fires. She piled up the dry wood and lit it, then gathered some grass, wet it down, and piled it on top of the flames, producing a dense smoke.

She sat down, leaning against the wire rabbit fence. She prayed to the Goddess of the Earth that somebody would see it.

Tyler dropped the tarpaulin back over Bader's body. Dawn was creeping in over the heath.

"I shall always remember the pleasure we both took in our chess," said Beck sadly. Suddenly he pointed to the northern strip of wood where a thick column of smoke was curling above the trees. "What's that?"

"Alice Thorne's cottage is over in that direction." Even as Tyler spoke, he was running toward the gate.

62

HOENIGER WAS IN VERY BAD SHAPE, AND FOR A FEW days it seemed possible he might die. With Grey's help, Tyler pieced together his story. Given the chaos of the times, it had been easy for him to impersonate a seminarian and get himself interned. Relying on the thorough training in theology that he'd received in a Jesuit school in Cologne, Hoeniger had attached himself to Father Glatz, who hadn't questioned where he'd come from.

Murnaghan saw the scars underneath his arms where he'd burned off the tattoos which identified him as an SS officer. Grey said he had been recruited by Heydrich, away from Himmler's army. He had the scar from an earlier bullet wound in his calf, which might explain his availability. The complete story had yet to come out. The antimony had burned him so badly he couldn't speak at all; maybe wouldn't be able to again above a whisper.

The entire investigation into the deaths of Elsie and Rose was taken over by Don Kinsey of B division. Tyler knew Grey had talked to him and revealed MI5's knowledge of a person spying and transmitting to the Germans. When Arthur Trimble's body was discovered in the woods, Kinsey was sure he was the traitor. He had been working for the German, Hoeniger, who had killed him when he had outlived his usefulness. The murders of the two young women were two more crimes to be laid at his doorstop. Trimble's Ford and the lorry were taken off to Birmingham to be examined. They found blood spots in the Ford's boot and stains in the back of the lorry where he'd transported Rose's body to the barn. The technician even found a trace of fibre on the fender of the lorry that matched Elsie's dungarees. The question of how Trimble got the Luger was puzzling, but Kinsey was happy to leave that as a minor quibble. The white poppies, he made no attempt to explain. Criminals acted outside the pale, as far as he was concerned. With the entire Shropshire constabulary breathing down his neck, Lambeth finally admitted that Trimble was at his shop on Thursday morning. Kinsey concluded Trimble was travelling down the Heath Road and had knocked Elsie off her bike. Whether on purpose or accidentally, they would never know. Regardless, according to the Inspector, Trimble had then shot Elsie to silence her. He had strangled Rose when she accidentally discovered him using the transmitter.

Tyler accepted that Trimble had killed Rose, but he had serious doubts about Elsie.

He both wanted and feared to know the truth.

Shortly before Jimmy's funeral, Grey requested a consultation with Tyler. He told him that the incriminating photographs had been retrieved from Hoeniger's briefcase. They had not been destroyed. He had taken them from Father Glatz's cupboard and replaced them with something else, which had burned. Ironically, the laboratory determined the replacement was most likely a bible. Grey said the photographs were on their way to Heydrich, who, he said with a chuckle, would undoubtedly enjoy them.

When he spoke of Clare, Grey was surprisingly sympathetic. He informed Tyler that Mrs. Devereau would be returning to Switzerland immediately. She was still in the employ of MI5 and would be keeping an eye on her husband and his dealings with the Nazis. Amelie and the Lalonde family were going with her, where they would be safe, for the duration of the war.

"I'm glad we got the matter of the dead girls all sorted. Mrs. Devereau continues to be very valuable to us," said Grey. There was no mistaking his meaning. The case was closed.

63.

JIMMY TYLER WAS BURIED IN THE GRAVEYARD OF THE ancient church that had served the town for centuries. Most of Whitchurch turned out for the service. Major Fordham came with Dr. Beck. The murdered men at the camp had been given their own memorial, but Tyler asked the minister to include a special prayer for them, Jewish and Catholic. Miss Stillwell sat next to Lady Somerville, both dressed in black crepe. By contrast, the remaining Land Army girls were young and fresh in their best uniforms, green skirts and matching felt hats. Tyler would have given anything to have seen Elsie and Rose with them.

At Grey's instigation, the local paper had published a general account of what had happened, emphasizing that Jimmy Tyler, while defending Alice Thorne, had been shot by a German spy. Her own act of bravery was related in detail. Tyler was glad to see how this immediately changed her status in the community. At Vera's request, she joined them in the pew.

Percy Somerville, on his return, had asked if he could read the lesson and say a few words, and Tom agreed.

"James Tyler was a soldier who gave his life to save Mrs. Thorne, as many of our young men have already given their lives to save their country and the people they love. I'm sure you will understand, therefore, if I give him a soldier's send off." Percy placed a piece of paper on the podium. His hand was trembling but his voice was steady. "This is a poem you are all familiar with. It was written during the war to end all wars, but it speaks to all soldiers everywhere. I shall read the second verse."

They shall not grow old as we that are left grow old;
Age shall not wither them, nor the years condemn.
At the going down of the sun and in the morning,
We will remember them.

Vera was on one side of Tyler and Janet on the other, both clinging to his hands. He held on tightly.

At the conclusion of the service, they filed out after the coffin. Grey and Clare were seated at the back of the church. Tyler kept his eyes straight ahead as he went past.

64.

Tyler took a leave of absence from the station and spent the dwindling days of summer with both Vera and his daughter. They needed him.

Finally, he went to see Alice Thorne. She had been persuaded to stay in town for the next month or two and she had taken a room with the rector and his wife, a pleasant old couple who tried to live like Christians in deed as well as word. Alice said they were all surprisingly compatible considering she called herself a pagan.

She and Tyler were sitting in the rectory garden in the cool afternoon of the dying summer, drinking a sweet fruit wine that the rector's wife made. Skip lay beside them, bored, watching the birds, hoping for a rabbit or two to hop by to liven things up.

Tyler fidgeted with the unpalatable drink. "Alice, the investigation is all wrapped up as far as the police are concerned, but the story has one hell of a big hole in it. I don't believe that Arthur Trimble killed Elsie Bates." He put the wine down. "I accept that he was driving his lorry and knocked her over, but she was not dead then, she was paralyzed. Somebody else shot her. That wasn't Trimble, was it, Alice?"

She looked at him and almost imperceptibly shook her head.

"It was Jimmy, wasn't it? My son was the one who shot Elsie Bates."

Alice didn't answer immediately. She looked dreadfully frail; the events of the summer had added years to her age.

"Please answer me. I can't live with this doubt for the rest of my life."

She hesitated. "If I tell you what happened, I will do so only to give you some peace, Tom. I see absolutely no reason for anybody else to know."

"They won't, believe me."

"Very well. This is what Jimmy confided in me that night." She stroked the dog's head for comfort. "Jimmy and Elsie had had a liaison in the old Fort. He had hardly known her more than two weeks but he was quite besotted, and for a brief period of time she made him very happy." She glanced at Tyler, who wasn't looking at her. He understood that kind of feeling for a woman. "They were together that night, but in the early morning she left before he did. She was driving the Land Army lorry and had intended to go straight to the hostel to pick up the other girls. They'd a bit of a tiff earlier and Jimmy decided to pick some white poppies, intending to give them to her as a peace offering. He was on foot. He came across her broken body lying at the side of the road. Her bicycle was nearby and he assumed she had fallen off. There are big pot holes on that road. It was dark . . . she was alive and conscious but severely injured. She was paralyzed. However, she was still able to speak. When she saw Jimmy she begged him to, as she put it, finish her off." Alice paused to get her breath. "She had stolen a German Luger, you see, from one of the girls at the hostel and given it to him that night as a gift, a souvenir. He was carrying it with him." Again Alice stopped, her hands tightly clasped in her lap. "He repeated her words to me several times. 'What future is there for me, Jimmy? I know what's happened to me. I can't move my arms or my legs. I know what this is. I'll never be able to dance again even if I do survive. I don't want that kind of life. I want you to shoot me. Quickly. Like you would a horse with a broken leg or a dog.

Don't let me stay like this. Please Jimmy, if you ever loved me, do it. Give us a kiss and do it.'

"So he did. Jimmy shot her, then he moved her to the pass-by and laid her out, 'like a soldier,' against the hedge. And placed the gun beside her and then put the poppies on her chest."

"Why didn't he wait and let nature decide?" Tyler interrupted, his voice harsh with grief. "He could have fetched a doctor."

"He was convinced he was doing the right thing . . . I'll have to tell you about that another time. It is not a decision that everybody would make, but Jimmy had already seen too much suffering, too many mortal injuries. He knew that Elsie was dying. That there was no hope. I can understand him. I have put animals out of their misery on several occasions."

"With all due respect, Alice, this was a human being."

"Jimmy came back from Dunkirk a tormented young man. At a later time I can tell you what happened. We will see more such young men before this war is over. You must not judge him too harshly, Tom." She shivered and pulled her shawl about her shoulders. "I hated that German, Hoeniger. For a few terrible moments, I lost my own humanity and I wanted revenge." She paused, her face full of sorrow. "For a woman of peace, it is a vile memory."

"But you actually saved his life," said Tyler.

"How could I not? After I shot him, after I saw his agony. He was a fellow creature, after all."

"You're a better person than I am, Alice. I'd have killed the bastard," said Tyler.

"And then what, Tom? Then what? His death would restore nothing."

He had no answer and allowed the silence to fall between them again. He was grateful for what she had told him about

Jimmy. Afraid he was going to cry, he swallowed hard and looked intently at the flowers neatly lining the edges of the lawn.

Finally, he checked his watch. "I'd better get going. Janet doesn't like me to be out of sight for long."

Alice held out her hand for him to help her to her feet. "I'll walk out with you. Skip, you stay there."

At the gate, she halted. "Tom, forgive me for asking, I don't mean to pry, but what are you intending to do about . . . about you and Clare?"

He didn't question how she knew. "She's moving back to Switzerland so I don't expect to see her again until the war is over. Jimmy's death has changed everything with Vera and me. I can't leave her and Janet now. Not for a long time. But I'm thinking of signing up. They'll soon be needing old men like me. I can still do something useful."

She gave him a wry smile. "What a pity, I had rather hoped you would join the Peace Pledge Union."

" 'Fraid not, Alice. Not right now."

They went through the gate into the quiet street. A few women were out with their baskets over their arm. It was only if you looked closely that you would notice the absence of men and that the women were anxiously on the lookout for something to buy for their dinners.

Tyler planted a kiss on Alice's cheek. "Thank you. I badly needed to understand what had happened."

At that moment, the doors of the pub across the street burst open and a group of Land girls spilled out. One of them recognized Tyler and waved at him. It was Molly Cooper. She didn't come over, but linked her arm with one of her companions and together they walked off. He heard Molly's laughter.

—

Tyler saw Clare once more, the day before she was to leave. They met in her flat, and she held him while he wept in her arms. "I will stay in touch as much as I can," she said, "but it might not be until the war is over that we see each other again. Keep me in your heart, Tom."

He'd promised to be home before dark, so he left. Hurrying down the stairs so fast, he almost fell headlong.

He hoped he would be happy again, some day.

Author's Note

This is a work of fiction, although I have tried to stay as true as I could to the larger canvas, to the events of the time.

On September 3, 1939, Britain declared war on Germany. For months, the English people were lulled into a false sense of security, referring to the "phony war." Then on May 10, 1940, Hitler's army invaded Belgium, France, Luxembourg, and the Netherlands. The British Expeditionary Force had to retreat to the beaches of Dunkirk. On May 26, a massive evacuation of troops from the beaches began. Finally, as the German panzers were moving in, the evacuation ended on June 3, having accomplished the impossible by rescuing more than 250,000 Allied troops. The incidents I ascribe to my characters are an amalgam of true incidents at Dunkirk.

For the next three months, England teetered on the edge of the abyss. She stood alone, facing the ever-present threat of a Nazi invasion. As a consequence, the government decided to intern all German nationals and any other people who might be considered a risk to national security. These "enemy aliens" were sent to internment camps throughout the country, although most eventually ended up on the Isle of Man. One such camp was at Prees Heath in rural Shropshire, where during the summer of 1940 about 1,200 men lived in tents pitched on the ancient free land. The majority were Jewish intellectuals from the professional classes who had fled Nazi Germany. Unfortunately, many had not had time to get their British naturalization papers, and as fear washed throughout the country, they were looked upon as German first, Jewish second. The camps were top-heavy with highly educated men: philosophers, musicians, scientists, psychologists. To escape the boredom of camp life, the internees quickly set up a "university," and it was possible to take classes all day long from men who in civilian life were masters in their field.

The nation had to rally, and it did. A call for help on the land brought responses from hundreds of young women, many of them city dwellers. The Land Army girls, in many ways the unsung heroines of the home front, helped keep England fed. They helped to save the country from starvation and deserve much more recognition that they received.

The British Intelligence service, now known as MI5, struggled desperately to get vital information concerning the enemy, often only one short step ahead of Germany. MI5 did operate a base for intercepting transmissions at the Old Rectory in Whitchurch.

Dr. Bruno Beck is based on a real person, Dr. Theodore Reik. He was not interned, having managed to escape to the United States, where he became an important pioneer in the psychoanalytic movement. I have used his books *Fragments of a Great Confession* (1949) and *The Compulsion to Confess* (1925) and given his theories to Dr. Beck.

The artist whose work Tom Tyler buys was also a real person named Pamina Liebert-Mahrenholz (1904–2004). She was the great-aunt of my friend Ian Markham, who let me read the letters she wrote when she was interned, initially in Holloway prison. A very successful artist in Germany, she saw most of her work appropriated by the Nazis, and she fled to England where, after the war, she was able to resume her artistic career. She never received compensation for the artwork that was stolen and recovered only some pieces after the war with great difficulty. The Boundary Gallery (www.boundary-gallery.com) mounted a show of her work after her death.

Throughout that summer of 1940, people went about their lives; some fell in love, some succumbed to despair. The land had to be cultivated, pleasure found wherever it could be; the police, of necessity, went about the business of enforcing the law.

Acknowledgements

I owe a huge debt of gratitude to my friends in the UK. Jessie Bailey, Enid (Molly) Harley, and Pam Rowan cheerfully allowed me to interrupt their lives and drove me hither and yon while we were in Shropshire so I could go to the actual places where the events of this novel take place. Pam found me the most helpful material, and she, Enid, my husband Iden, and I spent a magical afternoon on the Prees Heath – Pam and Enid in search of wild flowers and the rare silver-studded blue butterfly, while Iden took photographs and I communed with the spirits of those men who, as enemy aliens, were forced to spend the summer of 1940 behind barbed wire.

John Harley kindly set up a meeting for me with Joan Phillotts of Ludlow, who shared with me her experiences as a Land Army girl.

I am also grateful to Eric Koch, who told me his story of being interned as a young man in Canada.

The Imperial War Museum in London is one of the most marvellous museums I have ever been in. No sabre rattling; just a meticulous, dispassionate collection of war material and archives. The resources there were invaluable.

The BBC gathered together a collection of personal stories from World War Two, which they called *The People's War*. It was absolutely fascinating to read and immensely helpful.

Cheryl Freedman read an early draft and gave me great feedback.

Finally, this book would not have come to life without the ideas and suggestions of Helen Heller. Much thanks. And thanks also to M&S and Dinah Forbes for supporting this endeavour. As well, I owe a debt of appreciation to my initial editor, Lara Hinchberger, who, together with Jennifer Glossop, showed superhuman patience and helped me slim down the book and write a more effective story.

If you enjoyed **Season of Darkness**,
treat yourself to the new
Detective Inspector Tom Tyler mystery,
Beware this Boy,
coming in November 2012.

Read an excerpt here . . .

Sunday November 24, 1940

HE'D WAITED PATIENTLY, KNOWING EVERYTHING HAD been set in motion. There was nothing more for him to do. At six o'clock, he switched on the wireless. A slight crackle, then the announcer's voice came on. *"This is the BBC Home Service. Here is the six o'clock news and this is Alvar Liddell reading it. There was an explosion in a Midlands factory this afternoon. Three fatalities have been reported. Four other workers, two men and two women, were also injured, one of them seriously. However, work is expected to resume within a few days."*

That was enough. The rest of the news didn't interest him. He turned it off and sat back. "Work is going to resume, is it indeed? We'll see about that."

. . .

The meagre fire in Detective Inspector Tom Tyler's office seemed to be in its death throes, smoking continuously. The old police station, with its ill-fitting window frames and doors, couldn't cope. Tyler knew he shouldn't use up his coal ration all at one go, but he was very tempted. He was dressed warmly enough, but he craved brightness and warmth.

He got up from his desk, where he'd been trying to justify being at the station on a Sunday afternoon by filling out the endless forms that the Ministry of War required these days. They were mostly requests to replace missing ration books or identity cards. Each had to be considered carefully. Not exactly an exciting task, but being at home with Vera was so painful, he avoided it as often as possible. It's not that they squabbled anymore; they didn't. It was just that there was a silence between them that he found impossible to bridge. Had he even tried? Perhaps at first after the tragedy, but Vera had made it clear she didn't want to. So he'd stopped and they remained locked each in their own loneliness and sorrow.

He went over to the window. Outside, a fine drizzle was falling on the empty streets. Even before the war, the shops and pubs in the little country town were always closed on the Sabbath, but today everything looked bleak and uncared for. Flowers gone from the front gardens, few displays in the shop windows. The weak afternoon light was fading fast but there were no lights showing in the houses. It was the hour for blackout. Whitchurch had not so far experienced the bombing that the big Midlands cities of nearby Birmingham and Liverpool had, but the townsfolk were conscientious. For a brief moment, Tyler leaned his forehead against the cold windowpane. Then he swivelled around and stepped away.

"For Heaven's sake, Tyler," he said to himself. "Moping isn't going to make any difference to what happened."

He was about to go into the front hall to see if he could get Sergeant Gough to stir up a cup of tea when the intercom buzzed. He answered it.

"Call for you, sir. From Mr. Grey at Special Branch."

Tyler felt a pang of alarm. "Grey? What's he want?" He hoped the man wasn't calling with bad news about Clare. He'd had only one letter from her in three months. He assumed she was still in Switzerland.

"He didn't say. Just that it was important."

"It always is with that bloke. He probably reports his daily bowel movements to Winnie himself."

Gough chuckled. "Shall I tell him you're not in?"

"Good God, no, Guffie. What are you thinking? If the local

boffin needs to talk to me urgently, I'd better answer. Could change the course of the war."

He didn't add, "and give me something to do," but he had the feeling that Sergeant Gough understood that.

"I'll put him through. And I was just about to make a pot of tea. The wife sent over some fresh baked tarts for us."

"Now, that is important. You should have said so earlier."

"I was saving the surprise, sir."

Tyler picked up the telephone receiver.

"Evening, Tyler. Beastly weather, isn't it."

"Certainly is, sir." He felt like saying, *It's November. This weather comes about regularly every year*, but he waited for Grey to get to the point. He could hear him sucking on his pipe.

"I'm calling because I have a job for you. There's been an explosion in one of the Brum munitions factories. Rather a nasty affair, truth be told. Some fatalities. Happened earlier today. I had a ring from the inspector at Steelhouse Lane. Name of Mason. He's an old chum of yours, I understand. He said you were stationed in Birmingham at one time."

"I was. Several years ago now."

"He said his officers are stretched thin what with dealing with raids and so forth. He asked if we could spare you to handle the investigation."

"Investigation, sir? I don't consider myself an expert in explosives."

"Don't need to be. It's no different from any other kind of police work. All a matter of common sense, really. You'll no doubt find the blow-up was caused by carelessness, but we want to make sure there was no sabotage involved."

Grey had a way of tailing off the ends of his sentences as if his energy was expiring, like the air from a pricked balloon. With that and the ubiquitous pipe in his mouth, his listener was constantly forced to ask him to repeat himself.

"Did you say sabotage, sir?"

There was a light tap at the door and Sergeant Gough entered, balancing a tray on one hand. Tyler waved to him to put it on the desk.

"... always a possibility," murmured Grey. "The commies have quite a following in the industrial towns. Not to mention all the nationalists, who are as active as fleas on a dog in these places. If it's not the Welsh, it's the Irish or the Scots. Next thing every piddling county in England will be demanding to have its own government."

Tyler nodded to Gough, who poured out a cup of tea and mutely pointed at the jam tarts.

"You are up for this, aren't you, Tyler?" said Grey. "Change of scene is as good as a rest, as they say." Tyler had been about to bite into one of the tarts, but he stopped. He wasn't in the slightest bit tired; he wasn't suffering from any bodily fatigue. But Grey said something else, which got lost.

"Beg pardon, sir."

"According to my secretary, there's a train leaving at nine tonight. As this is a special operation, you can put in a requisition for expenses. Keep them reasonable, there's a good chap. We don't have a lot of dosh to fling around. Mason said you can bunk in at the station. They've got spare rooms." He paused and Tyler heard him strike a match. "All right, then? Ring me in a couple of days and let me know how you are getting on. The explosion was probably just what it seems to be – human error. But keep your eyes open. If any of those fanatics have been monkeying around we'll string them up."

Before Grey could disconnect, Tyler said, "Have you had any word from Mrs. Devereau, sir? I mean, is she all right?'

Grey muttered something that Tyler managed to catch this time. "She is well. We are thinking of having her return to

London while she can, but that is up to the ministry. Good luck, Tyler."

The telephone clicked off, leaving Tyler to hang on to that morsel of news like a starving man.

Iden Ford

Born in England, MAUREEN JENNINGS taught English before becoming a psychotherapist. The first Detective Murdoch mystery was published in 1997. Six more followed, all to enthusiastic reviews. In 2003, Shaftesbury Films adapted three of the novels into movies of the week, and four years later Shaftesbury (with CityTV, Rogers, UKTV, and Granada International) created the Murdoch Mysteries TV series which is now shown around the world, including in the UK, the United States, and much of Europe. In Canada, CBC television will begin airing season 6 in Fall 2012. Her new trilogy, set in World War II-era England, got off to a spectacular start with 2011's *Season of Darkness*. Maureen lives in Toronto with her husband and their two dogs. Visit www.maureenjennings.com.